Praise for the *New York Times* bestselling novels of

Jayne Castle . . .

"DAZZLING . . . [a] scintillating foray into love in another place and time . . . An oasis of delight for readers who appreciate nuance and wit, as well as the heady charm of a great romance." —*Romantic Times*

"Writing under Jayne Castle, Jayne Ann Krentz takes her trademark combination of witty, upbeat action, lively sensuality, and appealing characters to [a] unique, synergistic world." —*Library Journal*

"Jayne Castle, one of the pioneers of the futuristic sub-genre, continues to set the standard against which all other such books are judged." —*Affaire de Coeur*

"A fun read, as are all Castle/Krentz's books." —*The Southern Pines Pilot* (NC)

. . . and Jayne Ann Krentz

"GOOD FUN." —*Cosmopolitan*

"A delight." —*Publishers Weekly*

"ENTERTAINING." —*People*

"Lively . . . filled with strong protagonists and witty dialog." —*Library Journal*

"FAST-PACED . . . interesting characters . . . a good time is had by the reader." —*Chicago Tribune*

"Along with Nora Roberts, Krentz is one of the most reliably satisfying romance writers publishing." —*Sunday Times* (CA)

"AN ABSOLUTELY, POSITIVELY FUN READ . . . Krentz's characters are always people you'd like to meet for yourself and know more about." —*Southern Pines Pilot* (NC)

NO GOING BACK

Jayne Ann Krentz

and

Jayne Castle

BERKLEY BOOKS, NEW YORK

A Berkley Book
Published by The Berkley Publishing Group
A division of Penguin Group (USA) Inc.
375 Hudson Street
New York, New York 10014

This is a work of fiction. Names, characters, places, and incidents either are the product of the author's imagination or are used fictitiously, and any resemblance to actual persons living or dead, business establishments, events, or locales is entirely coincidental.

PRINTING HISTORY
Berkley trade paperback one-volume edition / July 2004

Library of Congress Cataloging-in-Publication Data

Krentz, Jayne Ann.
   [Soft focus]
   No going back / by Jayne Ann Krentz, Jayne Castle.—Berkley trade pbk. one-volume ed.
      p. cm.
   Contents: Soft focus / Jayne Ann Krentz—After dark / Jayne Ann Krentz writing as
Jayne Castle.
   ISBN 0-425-19930-4 (pbk.)
   1. Businesswoman—Fiction. 2. Parapsychologists—Fiction. I. Krentz, Jayne Ann. Soft focus.
II. Castle, Jayne. After dark. III. Title.

PS3561.R44S6 2004
813'.54—dc22

2004043411

CONTENTS

Soft Focus   1

After Dark   253

Soft Focus

Prologue

Six months earlier . . .

He saw her coming toward him, an avenging warrior princess in a crisp black business suit and high heels. Her dark hair was swept up into a stern knot at the back of her head. The little scarf at her throat matched the diamond-bright fire in her blue-green eyes. One look at her and the white-jacketed waiters leaped out of her path. She strode through the maze of linen-and-crystal-set tables, her gaze never wavering from her target.

The movers and shakers of Seattle's business community sensed disaster, or, at the very least, excellent gossip, in the making. A hush fell across the club's formal dining room.

Seated in the leather-cushioned booth, Jack watched her approach.

"Oh, shit." He spoke very, very softly. It was obviously too late to pray.

One look at the fury that etched Elizabeth Cabot's intelligent face told him that he had lost his gamble. She knew everything this morning. What had happened between them last night clearly made no difference to her now.

A heavy cloud of stoicism settled on him. He waited for her with the patience of a man who knows he is facing an inescapable fate.

She was almost upon him now, and he knew that he was doomed. It was not his whole life that flashed before his eyes in those final moments, however. It was the memory of last night. He recalled the sweet, hot anticipation and the hungry rush of desire that had flashed between them. Unfortunately, that was all they had shared. The concentrated excitement had taken him by surprise, probably because he had worked so hard to contain it for the past month. In the end it had swept away his self-control and the lessons of experience that any man his age was expected to know. He was well aware of his mistakes. Elizabeth did not believe in faking her orgasms.

She had been very nice about it last night. Polite as hell. As if her fail-ure to climax was her fault and hers alone. Actually, she had seemed quite unsurprised, as far as he could tell. It was as if she had not expected any-thing more from the encounter and had, therefore, not been disappointed. He had apologized and vowed to make amends just as soon as physically possible. But she had explained that she had to go home. Something about an early-morning meeting for which she had to prepare.

Reluctantly, he had driven her back to the gothic monstrosity she called home on Queen Anne Hill. When he had kissed her goodnight at the door of the mansion he had assured himself that he would get a second chance. Next time he would get it right.

But now he knew there wasn't going to be a next time.

Elizabeth arrived at the booth, vibrating with a degree of passion that had been noticeably missing in the final scenes last night.

"You conniving, two-faced, egg-sucking son of a bitch," she said between her teeth. "What made you think you'd get away with it, Jack Fairfax?"

"Don't be shy, Elizabeth. Tell me what you really think of me."

"Did you actually believe that I wouldn't find out who you are? Did you think that you could treat me like a mushroom? Keep me in the dark and feed me manure?"

There was no hope of defending himself. He could see that. But he had to try. "I never lied to you."

"The hell you didn't. You never told me the truth. Not once during the past month did you give me any hint that you were the bastard who engi-neered the Galloway takeover."

"That was a two-year-old business deal. It had nothing to do with us."

"It had *everything* to do with us, and you knew it. That's why you lied to me."

In spite of the hopelessness of the situation, or perhaps because of it, he started to get mad. "It's not my fault the Galloway deal never came up between us. You never asked me about it."

"Why would I do that?" Her voice rose. "How was I supposed to guess that you were involved in it?"

"You didn't work at Galloway. How was I supposed to guess that you had a connection to the company?" he countered.

"It doesn't matter. Don't you understand? That takeover was as ruthless, as cold-blooded, as anything I've ever seen in business. The fact that you were the hired gun who tore that company apart tells me exactly what kind of scum you really are."

"Elizabeth—"

"People got hurt in that takeover." Her hand clenched very tightly around the strap of her elegant shoulder bag. "Badly hurt. I don't do business with men like you."

Jack saw Hugo, the maître d', hovering uneasily at a nearby table, obviously at a loss to decide how to quell the escalating scene. The waiter who had been on the way to the booth with ice water and bread halted, unmoving, a short distance away. Everyone in the dining room was listening now, but Elizabeth was oblivious to her audience.

Jack was morbidly fascinated himself, even though he was at ground zero. He would never have guessed that Elizabeth was capable of such drama. For the past month she had seemed so calm, so composed, so controlled.

"I think you'd better cool down," he said quietly.

"Give me one good reason."

"I'll give you two. Number one, we've got an audience. Number two, when you finally do cool off you are going to regret this scene a lot more than I will."

She smiled at him with such freezing disdain that he was amazed there were no icicles in her hair. She waved one hand in a wide arc that encompassed the entire dining room. He took that as a very bad sign.

"I don't give a damn about our audience," she said in ringing accents that no doubt carried all the way into the kitchen. "The way I look at it, I'm doing everyone here a public service by telling them that you are a lying SOB. I won't regret a single thing about this scene."

"You will when you finally remember that we've got a signed, sealed contract for the Excalibur deal. Like it or not, we're stuck with each other."

She blinked once. He saw the jolt of shock in her eyes. In the heat of her outrage, she had apparently forgotten the contract they had both signed yesterday morning.

She rallied swiftly. "I'll call the Fund's lawyers as soon as I get back to the office. Consider our contract null and void as of today."

"Don't bother trying to bluff. You can't get out of our deal just because you've decided I'm an SOB. You signed that damned contract, and I'm going to hold you to it."

"We'll see about that."

He shrugged. "If you want to tie both of us up in court for the next ten or twelve months, be my guest. But I'll fight you all the way, and I'll win in the end. We both know it."

She was trapped, and he was pretty sure that she was too smart not to recognize that simple fact.

There was a tense moment while he watched her come to terms with the realization that he had won.

Frustrated rage flared once more in her face.

"You will pay for this, Jack Fairfax." She reached out and swept the pitcher of ice water off the tray held by the motionless waiter. "Sooner or later, I swear you will pay for what you did."

She dashed the contents of the water pitcher straight at him. He did not even try to duck. The only escape route was under the table, and somehow that option seemed more ignominious than staying in his seat.

The icy water splashing in his face ignited the temper that he had been struggling to control. He looked at Elizabeth. She was staring at him, the first signs of shock and horror lighting her eyes. He knew that it was just beginning to dawn on her that she had made an almighty fool of herself.

"This isn't about the Galloway deal, is it?" he said softly. "This is about last night."

Clutching her purse, she took a step back as if he had struck her. "Don't you dare bring up last night. This is not about last night, damn you."

"Sure it is." He swiped a chunk of ice off the shoulder of his jacket. "I take full responsibility, of course. It's the gentlemanly thing to do, isn't it?"

She sucked in her breath in a stunned gasp. "Don't try to reduce this to sex. What happened last night is the least important aspect of this entire affair. In fact, what happened last night was so unimportant and so unmemorable that it doesn't even register on the scale."

Last night had meant nothing to her. He lost what little remained of the control he had been exerting over his anger. His hands closed around the edge of the table. He rose deliberately to his feet, heedless of the fact that he was still dripping ice water. He smiled slowly at Elizabeth.

"On my own behalf," he said with grave politeness, "I would like to say that I didn't know going in that I was dealing with the original Ice Princess. You should have warned me that you've got a little problem in that department. Who knows? With some extra time and effort, I might have been able to thaw you out."

As soon as the words were uttered, he regretted them. But they hung there in the air above the table, frozen, glittering shards of ice. He knew they would never melt.

Elizabeth fell back another step. Her face was flushed. Her eyes narrowed. "You really are a bastard, aren't you?" Her voice was low and much too even now. "You don't care a damn about what happened in the aftermath of the Galloway deal, do you?"

He ran a hand through his hair to get rid of some of the cold water. "No, I don't. Business is business, as far as I'm concerned. I don't believe in getting emotionally involved."

"I understand," she said. "That's precisely how I feel about last night."

She turned on one needle-sharp heel and walked out of the restaurant without a backward glance.

Jack watched her leave. He did not take his eyes off her until she disappeared through the door.

The twinges of impending fate that he had experienced when she had entered the dining room grew stronger. He knew that she must be feeling them, too.

They both knew the truth.

She could walk away from what had happened between them last night, but she could not walk away from the business contract they had signed. For better for worse, for richer for poorer, it bound them together more securely than any wedding license could have done.

Chapter One

He waited for her at the rear of the parking lot, huddled against the brick wall, shivering in the light windbreaker. The streetlamp wasn't working right. It cast a faltering, sickly glow that did little to dispel the shadows. There were only a handful of cars left in the lot. Pioneer Square was quiet at this hour. The nightclubs and the taverns were closed. Other than the drunk he'd tripped over in the alley, he'd seen no one else. That was a good thing, because the kind of folks who did show up in this part of town at this time of night were usually quite scary.

It was raining, a relentless mist that drove the predawn chill deeper into his bones. But he knew it wasn't just the night air that made him feel so cold. It was the fact that he hadn't kept his twice-daily date with Madam Lola this evening. He hadn't been able to afford her tonight, and now he was paying the price.

He'd first met Madam L. back in grad school. He had been a good student in those days. Everyone had said he had a bright future in chemical engineering. Probably would have held a few patents by now if he hadn't met Madam Lola. It was a woman, a student in one of his classes, who'd introduced him to Lola. She'd assured him that sex was great after just one dose. She'd been right. But Lola soon became more interesting than sex. More interesting than getting a Ph.D. in chemical engineering. More interesting than the successful future he'd once planned for himself.

Lola had taken over his life, and the lady was a harsh mistress. She demanded his obedient attendance twice a day. If he missed even one dose, he felt like that stuff on the parking lot pavement that he'd stepped in a few minutes ago. And he also felt cold. Very, very cold.

But *she* would be here soon, and she would bring the money she had promised to pay him and he would buy some more time with Madam L. and everything would be okay again. He could maintain pretty good when he kept up with his twice-daily appointments. Good enough to hold a job. For a while, at any rate. Balancing work and Lola was never easy. He could usually get by for a few months, and then something always went wrong. Either he failed a drug test or he started taking too many sick days. Or something.

He hoped he could last a while longer in his present job. He sort of liked it. Sometimes when he was working at Excalibur he pretended that he really had finished that doctorate; that he was a respected member of the research team like Dr. Page, maybe, not just a lowly lab tech. He felt bad about what he'd done tonight. But he hadn't had a choice. His salary at Excalibur was good, but it wasn't good enough to pay for the amount of time he had to spend with Lola these days. His other employer was very generous, though.

And *she* would be here soon. With lots of cash for Lola.

He heard her footsteps first, high heels echoing lightly on the wet pavement. He straightened away from the damp bricks, anticipation driving out some of the chill. Not long now and he would have what he needed to warm him once more.

"Hello, Ryan."

"About time you got here," he muttered.

She walked toward him through the thick shadows. The hood of a long, black raincoat concealed her face. "Everything went well tonight, I assume?"

"No problem. Lab's a mess. It'll take 'em days to clean up."

"Excellent. It was probably unnecessary. Just a precaution in the unlikely event that Fairfax or Excalibur security calls in the police. It will send them off in the wrong direction."

"Companies never call in the cops on this kind of thing if they can help it. Bad public relations. Freaks out the investors and clients."

"Yes. And that is the one thing that Excalibur can't afford to do right now." She moved her hand, reaching into her purse. "Well, I think that takes care of everything. You've been a fine employee, Ryan. I shall be sorry to let you go."

"Huh?"

"I'm afraid I don't need you anymore. In fact, you've become a liability." She removed her hand from her purse. There was just enough light from the dying streetlamp to reveal the glint of dark metal.

A gun.

He struggled to come to grips with the reality of what was happening. But by the time he understood, it was too late. She was like one of those women in the old black-and-white films that Dr. Page loved, he thought. A femme fatale.

She pulled the trigger twice. The second shot was unnecessary, but she wanted to be quite certain. There was a line in the script that summed up her philosophy on details.

A lady with a past has nothing to lose. But a woman with a future can't be too careful.

Chapter Two

Some CEOs had bad days.

Some got stuck with entire weeks that went so far south a map and compass were required to avoid the dreaded Sea of Red Ink.

He was now officially in that unfortunate latter group of corporate mariners, Jack concluded. He could even read the small printed warning at the edge of the map. *Beyond these shores there be dragons.*

It was enough to make a man superstitious. Apparently disasters really did occur in threes.

"We'll need damage control," Jack said. "Lots of it."

He surveyed the chaotic wreckage of what was left of Lab Two B. Broken glass and smashed equipment littered the workbenches. Sensitive instruments lay in pieces on the floor. One of the vandals had used a can of bloodred spray paint to scrawl the words "Vanguard of Tomorrow" on the east wall.

"This is too much," Milo moaned. "It's just too much on top of everything else. Excalibur will be ruined."

The monotonous litany was starting to get on Jack's nerves. But then, his store of patience had already been badly frayed.

The vandalism of Lab Two B was only the latest in a series of ominous incidents that had struck tiny Excalibur Advanced Materials Research in the past few hours. In the grand scheme of things, it was not even the worst incident that had occurred. The murdered lab tech topped the list.

"We'll deal with it, Milo," Jack said. He was paid to say things like that, he reminded himself. Today he was going to earn every cent of his salary.

"Deal with it?" Milo snapped around to face Jack, his thin face working furiously. There was a feverish light in his eyes. "How do you deal with the end of everything we've worked for for so long? How do you deal with a disaster? We're not going to get a second chance. The Veltran presentation can't be canceled. You know that."

"I said we can handle it."

"How are we supposed to do that?" Milo bounced wildly. "Getting Grady Veltran's attention in the first place was an incredible stroke of luck. You know his reputation. If we start making excuses and try to postpone the presentation even a day, he'll cross us off his list."

Jack suppressed a groan. He did not need this. He had enough problems on his hands. But Milo Ingersoll was his client. Clients needed to be handled with kid gloves at times like this. It was part of the job.

Milo was barely twenty-five, but as the only member of the eccentric Ingersoll clan who displayed any potential for leadership and management, he had assumed a heavy burden. Following the death of his great-aunt, Patricia Ingersoll, the founder of Excalibur, he had left engineering graduate school and taken the helm of the small, family-held company. Within days he had realized that he was in over his head. Patricia had been bedridden during the last year of her life. Without her guidance, the company had floundered. When Milo took charge he realized at once that the firm was on the brink of bankruptcy. He also understood that he lacked the management skills and experience to pull it back from the brink.

He'd known that he needed help, and he'd known that he needed it fast.

Displaying the foresight, determination, and raw passion that Jack figured would one day make Milo a formidable executive, he had sought out a turnaround specialist, a consultant who might be able to save the faltering little high-tech company.

Jack would never forget the day the intense young man had burst into his office and alternately demanded and pleaded for assistance. Milo had been passionate, frenzied, willing to do anything, promise anything, sign anything, to save the family firm.

The Excalibur situation presented just the kind of problem that intrigued Jack. Saving small, closely held companies in dire straits was his specialty. Training his replacement, in this case Milo, was part of the package deal. He had long ago understood that teaching and mentoring the next generation of leadership was crucial to real long-term success. There wasn't much point salvaging a small company if it went under the day after the turnaround specialist walked out the door because no one left behind could manage it.

Milo had all the qualities needed for his future job. He was enthusiastic, intelligent, hardworking, and, most important, wholly devoted to Excalibur. During the past six months he had begun to imitate Jack in a variety of ways, not the least of which was his choice of attire. He now routinely eschewed the casual look that was endemic throughout the high-tech industry in favor of a classic suit and tie. Unfortunately, his taste still tended toward green and brown. Jack had made a mental note to take Milo to a good tailor before he finished the Excalibur project.

But this morning Milo was not a model of the conservative business style. He had still been in bed when Jack had phoned him to tell him about the vandalism. Milo had apparently been so shaken by the news that he had not bothered to finish dressing before he left the house. He had managed to pull on a pair of jeans, but he was still wearing the top half of what looked like very old, very faded, striped pajamas. His bony bare feet were encased in worn, scuffed slippers. His red hair stood up in jagged little tufts. Behind the thick lenses of his heavy, black-framed glasses, his sharp hazel eyes glittered with a combination of outrage and frantic despair.

Jack took pity on him.

"This isn't a disaster, Milo," he said quietly. "It's a setback, but it's not a disaster."

"I don't see how you can tell the difference."

"Trust me, I can tell." Jack glanced at the thick-bellied man hovering uneasily in the doorway. "All right, Ron, let's get this lab cleaned up."

"Yes, sir." Ron Attwell, the head of what passed for Excalibur's small security department, was sweating. There were dark stains under the arms of his khaki uniform shirt. Perspiration beaded his forehead.

Jack didn't blame him. He wasn't feeling real cool himself, in spite of the fact that, like everything else in Lab Two B, the HVAC system was state-of-the-art. The air-conditioning was the only thing that was still working in the trashed research wing.

Milo was right, the ruined lab definitely qualified as a disaster, but damned if he was going to admit it out loud, Jack thought. He was the guy in charge. It was his job to pretend that there were no problems that could not be dealt with here at Excalibur.

"I want full security maintained," Jack continued quietly. "Use only janitorial staff who have been authorized to work in this building and make certain no one throws anything away, not even a broken bottle, until someone on the Soft Focus team has looked at it first. Got that?"

"Yes, sir."

Milo twisted his long-fingered hands in a gesture that would have done credit to a character in the last act of *Carmen*. "What's the point of employing full security measures now? Talk about closing the barn door after the horse has gone."

"Milo," Jack said very softly.

Milo jerked at the tone of voice. He blinked quickly and broke off abruptly.

Jack held Ron's gaze. "Box up all the debris and leave it here in the lab. Make sure nothing gets hauled away."

"Yes, sir." Ron wiped his forehead on the back of his khaki sleeve. "I'll get right on it, Mr. Fairfax."

"Make sure everyone involved in the cleanup keeps his or her mouth shut. Understood?"

"Yes, sir."

"Anyone who discusses the situation outside the company will receive an automatic pink slip."

"Yes, sir." Ron dug a notepad out of his left pocket and fumbled for a pen. "I'll do my best, sir, but you know what rumors are like in this business."

"I know," Jack said. "But our official stance is that no serious damage was done."

Milo scowled. "Is that why we're not calling the cops?"

"Yes."

"But why bother trying to keep this a secret? We're not the only place that's been hit by those damned Vanguard of Tomorrow crazies. They ransacked one of the labs at the UW last month. It was in the papers."

"And there was that software-design firm they tore up a few weeks ago," Ron volunteered. "Tried to torch the place."

Jack gave each man a level look. "We don't need this kind of publicity. The last thing we want to do is call attention to Excalibur's security problems."

Ron blanched. "Yes, sir."

Milo scowled. "It's not as if—"

Jack quirked a brow in Ron's direction. Preoccupied with making notes on his pad, Attwell did not notice the small gesture. Milo, however, finally seemed to get the point. He shut his mouth, tightened his lips into a thin, disgruntled line, and reluctantly subsided.

"Any kind of publicity which implies a weakness in our internal security measures is bad for the company," Jack said with a patience he was far from feeling. "That type of news tends to make potential clients and customers very, very nervous. I doubt if we'll be able to keep a complete lid on this, because the Vanguard of Tomorrow crowd will probably go straight to the media to take the credit. But we're going to try to minimize the story on our end. Understood?"

"Yes, sir." Ron snapped his notepad closed.

"It's your job to limit the in-house leaks, Ron," Jack said. "Langley in PR will handle the press."

"Right." Attwell shoved his fingers through his thinning gray hair. He drew himself up with a visible effort and straightened his slumped shoulders. "I'm sorry, sir. This shouldn't have happened. Those thugs never should have gotten in like that." He made a disgusted sound. "We've never had any kind of trouble like this before. Who'd have figured?"

"Yes," Jack said. "Who'd have figured?" Obviously no one in Excalibur's creaky, painfully old-fashioned security department, he thought. But he refrained from pointing that out.

Updating security at Excalibur had been on the list of priorities he had made six months ago when he had agreed to take the CEO position. But retooling a low-tech group of night watchmen, most of whom were nearing retirement, into a modern, streamlined, security team required time and money. There had been so many other priorities, he reflected, none of them cheap. Excalibur's financial resources were limited. It had been his decision to pour everything into the Soft Focus project.

But sometime during the past twenty-four hours, Tyler Page, the research scientist who had finally made Soft Focus work, had disappeared together with the only existing specimen of the newly developed, high-tech crystal. It was enough to give even a sane, logical, reasonable executive a case of paranoia.

He turned on his heel and walked toward the swinging doors. "I'm going back to my office. Keep the area clear of unauthorized personnel during cleanup, Ron. Report to me when you're finished."

"Yes, sir." Ron cleared his throat. "Sir, I'd like to tell you again how damned sorry I am about all this."

"If you apologize one more time," Jack warned, "I'll fire you."

Ron flinched. "Yes, sir."

Jack planted a hand against one of the heavy doors, shoved it open, and went out into the hall.

"Wait," Milo called. "Hold up there a minute, Jack. I want to talk to you."

"Later, Milo. Right now I've got to get hold of Langley. I want to brief him before the press starts calling."

"I know, I know." Milo trotted into the hall behind Jack. "But we've got to talk about the other situation."

"Later." Jack kept moving toward the elevators.

"No. Now." Milo bustled along beside him. "What if this business with the murder and the trashed lab brings that . . . that *woman* here? She'll start asking questions."

"Don't worry, if Elizabeth Cabot shows up, I'll handle her." Talk about wild, outrageous promises. If his recent track record was any indicator, he'd be lucky not to get impaled on the heel of one of her expensive, made-in-Italy, leather pumps.

Milo snorted. "But you know what she's like at the monthly board meetings. Always wanting details and demanding information. If she gets wind of the fact that Page and the specimen are missing, there's no telling what will happen."

"You're wrong."

Hope flared in Milo's eyes. "I am?"

"Sure." Jack smiled grimly. "I know exactly what she'll do. She'll cut off our funding before we can finish sweeping up Lab Two B."

He was pretty sure Elizabeth had been looking for an excuse to rip up their contract for the past six months. The destruction of the lab and the disappearance of Soft Focus would give the Aurora Fund lawyers grounds to claim that the company was no longer financially viable. As the major creditor, the Fund could force Excalibur into bankruptcy.

"I knew it," Milo whispered. "We haven't got a prayer."

"Get a grip. If Elizabeth Cabot calls about the vandalism, I'll deal with her. There's no reason for her to suspect that we've got a problem with the Soft Focus project."

"But what if she does suspect something?" Milo quivered in agitation. "What if she starts nosing around? Asking questions? You know how pushy she can get."

"If she asks any questions, I'll answer them."

"But *how?*"

"Dunno. Maybe I'll try a nice, bald-faced lie."

Milo stared at him. "How can you make jokes at a time like this?"

"I wasn't joking. Like I said, I'll deal with Elizabeth Cabot. You concentrate on handling your family. We don't want any of them to get word of this, either."

Milo blinked several times and then grunted. "Aunt Dolores would have hysterics. Uncle Ivo would probably collapse. God only knows what my cousins would do. Especially Angela."

"You know damn well what Angela would do. She'd start demanding that Excalibur be sold or merged. She's been pushing for that since your aunt died."

Milo's hand closed into a fist. His head came up. "Never. This is my company. Aunt Patricia left it to me because she knew I would take care of it for the family."

Jack smiled slightly in spite of his foul mood. "That's the spirit, Milo. Don't worry, we'll recover Soft Focus."

"But how are we going to do that?"

"Leave it to me." Jack stopped in front of the elevators and punched the call button. "I'll get it back. But it will take some time. I'm going to have to turn everything else over to you for the next ten days or so."

"Ten days? But the Veltran demonstration is scheduled for two weeks from today. We have to have the crystal back in the lab by then or everything goes right down the toilet."

"As you just pointed out, we've got two weeks," Jack said quietly. "You haven't had as much experience as I'd like yet, but we don't have any choice. You're going to have to handle your family and the press and day-to-day operations here at Excalibur all by yourself while I'm gone. Think you can do it?"

"Of course I can do it. That's not the issue. The issue is the crystal."

"I'm aware of that."

The elevator doors finally opened. Mercifully, something was working right today. Jack got into the car and stabbed the button that would take him to the third floor. He looked out at Milo's haunted face and dredged up another dose of reassurance. "I'll find it, Milo."

"How the hell are you going to do that?" Milo wailed.

Jack smiled humorlessly. "Thought I'd start by taking a vacation."

The elevator doors finally closed, cutting off Milo's keening cry in mid-shriek.

Alone in the cab, Jack propped one shoulder against the paneled wall and gazed unseeingly at the lights on the control panel. The bottom line was that Milo was right. The loss of Soft Focus was a major catastrophe for Excalibur.

With its unique optical properties the hybrid colloidal crystal had the potential to play a critical role in the development of the next wave of computer development, a generation of systems founded on light-based technology. Optical computers worked by encoding information into light pulses. Soft Focus was designed to control and transmit light in highly specific ways on a microscopic level.

Patricia Ingersoll, a brilliant researcher with a host of patents, had developed the concept, but she had become ill and died before she could make it a reality in her labs. Tyler Page, an equally brilliant, but extremely eccentric member of Excalibur's R & D team, had worked closely with her for years. Page had been certain that he could complete the work on the crystal.

When Jack had taken on the task of saving Excalibur, he had made the decision to base the entire future of the company on the development of Soft Focus. In retrospect, it was possible that he had made a monumental mistake, he thought as he got off the elevator. But it was not as if there had been anything else to go with. Without the crystal, there was no way to salvage Excalibur.

He had sought funding from all the usual sources and had been rejected by all of them, in spite of his personal track record. The bottom line was that no one was willing to back Excalibur now that Patricia Ingersoll was gone.

Late one night, while going through a pile of the company's old financial records with the assistance of a medicinal glass of scotch, Jack had made the discovery that once, several years ago, the Aurora Fund had backed an Excalibur project. From what he could discern, it looked as if the deal had been some kind of personal arrangement between Patricia Ingersoll and the

Fund's previous manager, Sybil Cabot. The contract had been nothing more than a paragraph-long agreement. It would have meant little in court.

He had soon learned that Sybil had died two years before. She had left the Fund in the hands of her niece.

Without a lot of hope but seriously short of alternatives, he had contacted the Fund's new manager, Elizabeth Cabot, and proposed a renewed financial commitment. To his amazement, she had agreed to discuss it.

The morning he walked into her office, located on the first floor of the old mansion, he had known he was in very serious trouble. After an hour in Elizabeth's company, he had finally acknowledged to himself that he was going to consign all his ironclad rules against mixing business and pleasure to hell.

She had gone for the Excalibur pitch. She had also accepted his invitation to dinner.

Two weeks later, he had discovered her connection to the Galloway deal and he had known that he was walking a tightrope.

He forced aside thoughts of the past as the elevator doors opened. He went down the carpeted hall to the executive suite. It was early, not yet eight o'clock. This floor was still quiet.

In his mind, he quickly made his list of priorities. The first item on the agenda was to ask his secretary to check with HR to get a phone number for Ryan Kendle's next of kin. Durand, the detective in charge of the murder investigation, had said he would take care of notifying the man's relatives. But as the CEO of Excalibur and Ryan Kendle's employer, Jack knew he had a responsibility in the matter. He did not look forward to the task.

According to Kendle's personnel file he had no family here in the Seattle area. He had been hired a few months ago to work as a lab technician. He had been a loner with no close friends at Excalibur. And now the man was dead.

Durand's working theory was that Kendle had been into the drug scene. He'd explained that the lab tech had been shot when a drug transaction apparently went sour sometime between midnight and dawn in a deserted parking lot in Pioneer Square.

Jack walked into the outer room of the executive suite. A wave of relief went through him when he saw that his secretary had come in early. Marion was on her feet behind her desk, making coffee.

She turned quickly, a strained expression on her round face. Behind the lenses of her oversize glasses, her eyes were wide with anxiety. The coffee scoop clattered on the table.

"Mr. Fairfax."

"I can't tell you how glad I am to see you, Marion. We've got a hell of a day ahead of us. Remind me of this when we do your next performance review."

"Mr. Fairfax, there's something you should—"

"Later. The only way we're going to get through this morning is one step at a time."

Jack slung his black windbreaker over a hook on the aging brass coat-rack in the corner. When he had assumed the CEO position at Excalibur six months ago he had discovered that the company had taken the concept of dress-down Fridays to the outer limits. All the way to Thursday, in fact. Flannel shirts, jeans, and running shoes were the norm for most of the staff.

From the start, however, he had routinely come to work in a suit and tie, even on Fridays. He was an old-fashioned kind of guy in some ways. This morning, however, when the three A.M. phone call informing him of Excalibur's newest disaster had come, he had yanked on the first items of clothing he had found in his closet, a long-sleeved black pullover and a pair of jeans.

The call had not awakened him. At three this morning he had been sitting in the darkness in his living room, staring at the lights on Queen Anne Hill, a glass of scotch in his hand, contemplating the loss of Soft Focus. He had discovered only hours earlier that it had vanished from the lab vault.

He glanced at Marion as he went past her desk toward the door of his office. "I take it you've heard what happened in Lab Two B, Marion?"

"Yes, sir. The security guard told me when I arrived."

"The media will be on the phone soon. The Vanguard of Tomorrow bunch won't waste any time crowing about their latest strike against the evils of technology." Jack paused, his hand on the doorknob. "Call Langley. I want to see him immediately."

"Yes, sir."

"No one except Langley or me talks to the press. Got that?"

"I understand, sir." Marion gazed at him with an odd expression. She lowered her voice. "But that's not what I wanted to tell you, sir. When I got here a few minutes ago, I found someone waiting in your office."

"That homicide detective? Durand? Is he back?" Jack looked at Marion over his shoulder as he pushed open the door. "What's he want now? I've already instructed HR to give him a copy of everything we've got in Kendle's files."

"No, sir." Marion cleared her throat in a very pointed manner. "Not the detective."

"Who the hell would have the nerve to go into my office without—" He stopped when he saw the woman who stood in front of the floor-to-ceiling window.

Damn. He had been wrong earlier when he had concluded that disasters came in threes. Today his came in fours.

Chapter Three

She had sweated out this confrontation for most of the night. Now that the inevitable was upon her, she was surprised by her own reaction. She was cool.

True, she could feel the telltale tingling on the nape of her neck, but she always got that disturbing sensation when Jack was in the vicinity. And she was definitely a little tense. No, make that very tense. But she could handle some tension. She was accustomed to it after having attended six monthly meetings of the Excalibur board of directors.

The important thing was that she was in total command of herself. Her hands were not waving in the air. She was not shivering with anger. She had her back to him as she studied the view of the Excalibur parking lot and the broad expanse of Lake Washington in the distance.

Definitely cool.

She'd dressed for battle this morning. Her hair was pulled into a severe, sleek twist. She wore a silver-gray suit with a very fine stripe woven into the expensive fabric. The fitted jacket was padded a bit to give her shoulders a strong line. The cuffs of the trousers broke across the instep of a pair of high-heeled leather pumps. Gold gleamed discreetly in her ears.

All she lacked was a riding crop to complete the image. It was a depressing thought.

"Good morning, Elizabeth. Always nice to have you drop in for a visit."

Whatever happened, she would not lose her temper and start yelling at him.

She was cool.

That was good to know, because she was furious with him. And ever since the disaster in the Pacific Rim Club dining room, she had harbored the deep, abiding fear that one day she would again lose her self-control with Jack and make a fool of herself a second time.

She turned slowly away from the view of the mist-shrouded lake and the ghostly monoliths of the Seattle office towers that lay beyond.

She made certain that her coolest, coldest smile was firmly fixed in place. It was not easy. She wondered how long it would take before she could look at him without feeling that little rush of excitement that made her insides tighten and her breath catch in her throat. It had been six months now. The situation was not improving.

She sought refuge in the business that had brought her here today.

"Good morning," she said crisply. "I understand you've got a problem here at Excalibur."

"Nothing we can't handle." He closed the door and motioned her to a chair. "Have a seat. I'll ask Marion to bring in some coffee."

"Thank you." She walked to the nearest padded leather chair and sat down. Very deliberately she twitched the fine wool fabric of her hand-tailored trousers and crossed her legs.

She was cool and she was in control, all right, but she was breathing a little too fast and she could feel her own pulse. All she had done was walk across the office, but her body was reacting as though she were thirty-five minutes into her forty-five-minute daily workout routine.

She watched Jack go to his desk and sink down into the black leather chair. He leaned forward, punched a button, and spoke briefly to his secretary.

With a small sense of shock, Elizabeth noticed that his thick, dark hair was a little tousled looking, as if he had combed it with his fingers. Either that or someone else's fingers had recently been running through it. Very firmly she suppressed the twinge of dismay that thought induced.

Still, it was odd to see him looking so casual, she thought. On the handful of occasions they had been in each other's presence during the past few months, Jack had always been dressed in full executive battle dress: expensively cut suit, a crisp shirt, and a conservative tie.

This morning his black pullover and jeans made him look even more dangerous than usual, she thought. Probably because the snug-fitting clothes made it obvious that the power in his shoulders and the lean, graceful strength of his body were for real, not a product of good tailoring.

At some point during the course of those first, heady few weeks together, she had discovered that he worked out regularly, too. But instead of pursuing a standard physical fitness program at his athletic club, he studied one of the more obscure martial arts.

At the time she had taken his interest in the exotic exercise and philosophy as an indication of a deeply buried romantic streak. Which only went to show what lust had done to the analytical side of her brain, she decided. It was perfectly clear now that Jack studied the ancient theories of strategy and defense because he was endowed with a ruthless, not a romantic, streak. The bastard was a born predator.

The door opened. Marion appeared with two cups of coffee. She glanced uneasily at Jack, as though seeking guidance. Then she plastered a smile on her face and handed one of the cups to Elizabeth.

"Thank you," Elizabeth said.

"You're welcome, Miss Cabot." Marion put the second cup on Jack's desk and fled.

Elizabeth pretended not to notice. She was well aware that here at Excalibur she was viewed with great wariness. Everyone knew that she held the reins of the Aurora Fund and that the Fund controlled the fate of Excalibur.

She wouldn't be surprised if all of the employees had heard the tale of the disastrous scene in the Pacific Rim Club dining room, too. Gossip like that had a way of getting around town.

Jack took a deep swallow from his cup, lounged back in his chair, and looked at Elizabeth. "So you heard about our little problems already? I'm surprised the news reached you so quickly."

She raised her brows. "Yes, I'm sure you are. How long did you intend to keep it quiet?"

He shrugged. "Just found out about it, myself, a few hours ago. Haven't even heard from the press yet."

She frowned. "You're going to talk to the media about this?"

"Probably won't be able to avoid it."

"I see. And just what, exactly, do you plan to tell the reporters when they do get here?"

"Not much to tell, is there?" Jack took another swallow of coffee and set down his cup. "We got hit by the same crowd that trashed the university and the Ecto-Design labs. The cleanup will take a few days, but Two B should be functioning at full capacity again by the middle of next week. In the meantime, we're strengthening our security measures."

She stared at him, momentarily thrown off stride. "What in the world are you talking about?"

He gave her a politely inquiring look. "I beg your pardon, Miss Cabot. I assumed we were discussing the incident we had here at Excalibur early this morning."

"What incident?"

"Last night one of our labs was hit by the Vanguard of Tomorrow group. You've heard of them?"

"Yes, of course." His air of excessively civil patience made her want to toss her coffee cup at his head. She reminded herself of what had happened the last time she had given in to the temptation to throw stuff at Jack Fairfax. "A bunch of antitechnology nuts. How much damage was done?"

He shrugged. "The lab is a mess. We lost some expensive electronic equipment. Insurance should take care of most of it. Like I said, we'll have things back in operation in a few days."

"I see." She drummed her fingers on the arm of her chair. "Excalibur seems to have hit a run of bad luck lately."

Jack's brow climbed. "You know about Kendle, too?"

"Kendle?"

"The lab tech who got killed in Pioneer Square sometime early this morning. The cops say he was into the drug scene. Someone pulled a gun on him in a parking lot."

"No, I hadn't heard about Mr. Kendle's death. I'm sorry."

"So are we all, Miss Cabot." Jack sat forward and clasped his hands on his desk. "But rest assured neither Kendle's death nor the VT break-in will have any impact on the Soft Focus project. The Veltran presentation will take place on schedule. There was no need for you to come running all the way over here from Seattle to check on the status of your investment."

He had gall, she thought, trying to make her sound like a coldhearted Scrooge. As if she were mean-spirited to worry about the sizable amount of cash he had tricked the Aurora Fund into pouring into Excalibur.

She met his eyes. "I appreciate your assurances, Jack. And I believe you when you say that your employee's death and the trashing of the lab will not affect the Soft Focus project."

"Good. Now, then, if you're satisfied with the situation, I've got a full calendar today. I'm going to have to ask you to leave so that I can do my job."

"But I'm not satisfied," she said smoothly. "I merely said I understood that the murder and the break-in had no impact on the project. How could they?" She paused for a beat. "According to my information, Soft Focus has disappeared."

She had to give him credit, she thought. He did not even flinch.

"Where the hell did you get that idea?" he asked.

She took her time recrossing her legs. "I had dinner with Hayden Shaw last night."

"How nice for you." Jack gave her a politely inquiring look. "His divorce is final, then?"

She stiffened. "I didn't ask. It was a business dinner."

"Right. A business dinner. So Shaw is courting investors to help him get his new generation of fiber-optic networking devices off the ground, huh? I wondered when he'd finally get that project moving. It's been stalled for nearly a year."

Hayden would have been stunned to know that word of his top-secret development plans had already reached his archrival, Elizabeth thought. She reminded herself to proceed with caution. Jack and Hayden had a history. She knew nothing about the origins of the feud between the two men, but she was well aware that it went far beyond the scope of any reasonable business competition.

"You're aware of the Frontrunner project?" she asked.

"Sure. Shaw's going to throw a lot of money down that rat hole before he's finished, but that's his problem, not mine."

She ignored the amused disdain in his voice. "Hayden said he'd heard rumors that the only existing specimen of a newly developed material had been stolen from an Excalibur lab."

Jack steepled his fingers. "I've got some free advice for you, Miss Cabot."

"That's a very kind offer, especially in view of the fact that nothing else in our association has been even remotely inexpensive, let alone free," she murmured. "However, I'm not in the market for advice."

"That doesn't surprise me. But out of the goodness of my heart, I'm going to give it to you anyway." Jack met her eyes. "Don't trust Hayden Shaw any farther than you can throw him."

"Funny, he gave me some very similar advice concerning you."

"I'll bet he did."

She picked up her coffee again. "I suggest we get back to the subject of the rumors."

"You know as well as I do that in this business rumors are as common as stock options in new start-up companies, and even less likely to pay off."

"Are you telling me that the rumor Hayden heard has no basis in fact? Soft Focus is not in trouble?"

"I'm telling you that everything is under control here at Excalibur."

In spite of all the promises that she had made to herself on the way here this morning, she lost her temper. "Damn it, Jack, don't lie to me. I've sunk several hundred thousand dollars of Aurora Fund cash into this venture. I've got a seat on your board."

He winced. "You don't have to remind me about your position on my board."

"I've got a right to know what's going on."

He said nothing for a moment, just studied her intently, as if she were an interesting lab specimen. Then he shrugged. "What, exactly, did Shaw say?"

With an effort of will she regained her self-control. "I just told you, he said he'd heard that a new R & D specimen was stolen from your labs. We both know that the only secret Excalibur has is Soft Focus. Has the crystal disappeared, Jack? I want the truth. Yes or no?"

He gazed at her for a very long time, a dark, brooding expression in his honey and gold eyes. Her heart sank. He was going to lie to her, after all, she thought. What had ever made her think that he would tell her the truth? He had his list of priorities. If she was on it at all, her position was no doubt very near the bottom with a little notation next to her name: Ignore whenever possible; stonewall when cornered.

"True," Jack said. "The crystal is gone, and so is Tyler Page."

She stared at him, more stunned by the unexpected honesty than by the news that Soft Focus really had disappeared. She got her mouth closed and regrouped quickly.

"You weren't going to tell me, were you?" she asked.

"Not if I could avoid it." He unclasped his hands and spread them slightly. "I had a plan, you see."

"Yes, I'm sure you did. You always seem to have a plan, Jack. But it's a bit late to come up with one now, isn't it? Speaking as a member of the board, I think it would have been smarter to tighten your security *before* Soft Focus disappeared."

"The plan, Miss Cabot, was to find Tyler Page and the crystal before you or anyone else learned that they were missing."

"When, exactly, did they disappear?"

"I'm not sure. I worked late last night. On a whim, I performed an unscheduled security check at about nine o'clock. That's when I found out that the crystal was gone. An empty, duplicate container had been left in its place. If I hadn't checked the contents, I still wouldn't know that Soft Focus was gone."

She frowned. "A duplicate container was left behind?"

"Yes. It's still there in the vault. I've told no one else except Milo. As far as everyone else is concerned, the crystal is still safe in the lab. The research team has been instructed not to touch it until Dr. Page returns."

"You must have some idea of when it disappeared?"

His mouth twisted slightly. "Tyler Page went home sick yesterday afternoon. I think he took the specimen with him when he left Excalibur."

"Are you telling me that he just walked out of here with Soft Focus?"

"Tyler Page is the most respected member of the research team. Security had no reason to search him."

A fresh wave of outrage shot through her. "Why wasn't I told immediately?"

"Primarily because I knew you'd go ballistic and start threatening to yank our funding."

She smiled coldly. "You were wrong."

"Was I?"

"On one count, at least." She shot to her feet. "I'm not going to go ballistic. But I certainly intend to speak with my lawyers as soon as I get back to the office. Without the crystal, Excalibur is dead in the water, and we both know it. The Fund has a right to terminate the contract."

"That's a little shortsighted, don't you think? You and your precious Fund stand to lose a fortune in future profits. Soft Focus will be worth millions in the long term."

"You'll have to find it first, won't you?"

"I'll find it, Miss Cabot." His eyes were brilliant, unwavering. "Don't doubt that for even a second."

The relentless certainty in his voice sent an electric chill across her nerve endings. He meant every word he said. He would do whatever it took to recover the crystal.

Slowly she sank back down into the chair. "So, what's this plan of yours?"

He studied her thoughtfully for a long time. Then he got to his feet and dug a set of car keys out of the pocket of his jeans. "Come with me. I want to show you something."

She hesitated.

He glanced back at her over his shoulder as he went toward the door. "Don't worry. I'm not planning to invite you to view my etchings again. I learned my lesson six months ago."

Chapter Four

She was still seething with resentment fifteen minutes later when Jack brought the car to a halt in front of the nondescript little house. She hated the fact that he could put her on the defensive so easily. Just a single, pointed reminder of their one-night stand, that's all it had taken. How was it possible that he could still have this effect on her? He was the one who should have been mortified by the reference to the short-lived affair, not her.

She studied the dirty windows, the unkempt, overgrown front yard, and the chipped and flaking paint on the porch.

"This is Dr. Page's home?"

"Yes. As you can see, he's not big on the details of household maintenance." Jack shut off the engine, removed the keys from the ignition, and climbed out. He leaned down to speak to her through the opening. "I came here looking for him last night as soon as I realized that Soft Focus was missing. He was already long gone."

She slowly got out of the car. Jack walked around the hood to join her. Together they went up the cracked sidewalk. She watched him remove a key from his wallet.

"Where did you get that?" she demanded.

"You are a suspicious woman, Miss Cabot."

"Some things I learn the hard way, but I do, eventually, learn them. I've come to understand, for instance, that it pays to ask questions first where you're concerned."

He acknowledged the unsubtle accusation with a slight inclination of his head. "I know what you mean about learning things the hard way. Take me, for instance. I haven't ordered ice water in a restaurant in six months."

She eyed him sharply. This was the second nasty crack he had made concerning lessons learned. Surely he was not hinting that he considered himself the injured party in that debacle six months ago? Talk about raw nerve.

"It sounds as if you may have developed some type of phobia," she said with saccharine-sweet concern. "Perhaps you should see a therapist."

"Haven't got the time." He inserted the key into the lock and twisted the doorknob. "Besides, bottled water is cheaper than therapy."

"Are you going to tell me how you came by Page's house key?" She cringed inwardly when she heard the prim edge in her own voice. It was Jack's fault, she thought. He had a way of bringing out her least endearing qualities.

He shrugged and opened the door. "Page keeps a second set of keys in his office desk. He's the classic absentminded scientist. Always locking himself out of his own house and car."

"So you just helped yourself?"

"Yes, ma'am. In the same spirit in which he helped himself to my Soft Focus specimen."

"*Our* Soft Focus specimen," she corrected automatically. "You're going on the assumption that Page stole it?"

"That's my current working hypothesis, yeah." Jack stood aside to allow her to enter the heavily shadowed living room. "Given the fact that he's missing and that he's the only one who had motive, opportunity, and the technological know-how it would take to remove it from the lab, I'm going with it for now. Unless, of course, you've got a better one."

"No, I don't." She came to an abrupt halt as her eyes adjusted to the gloom. "Good grief. You're right. Page isn't much of a housekeeper, is he?"

The room had a shabby, neglected air. Faded cushions adorned a sagging sofa covered in cheap orange fabric. There was a film of dust on virtually every surface. The threadbare carpet looked as if it hadn't been vacuumed in at least a decade. There were crumbs on a plate that had been left balanced precariously on the arm of the plump, overstuffed sofa. A cup with dried brown residue in the bottom sat on the coffee table. Something green was growing in it.

The room didn't just feel cluttered, Elizabeth thought. It felt old. As if it were in a time warp. There was an oddly familiar look about it, she realized. Something about the way light slanted through the blinds creating bars on the floor reminded her of a scene from an old film. The sleazy detective's office, she thought. Just before the mysterious lady client walks through the glass-paned door.

And then she noticed the movie posters on the walls. Cold-eyed men with guns, sultry, dangerous femme fatales, lots of screaming yellow and red ink. Lots of shadows.

She glanced at some of the titles. *The Blue Dahlia. Mildred Pierce. Stranger on the Third Floor.*

"Page is into film noir," she said.

Jack closed the door. "You don't know the half of it."

She walked slowly through the room. "On the face of it, it looks like he just walked out the door and might be back any minute."

"Don't think so," Jack said. "His closet is empty and his personal stuff has been cleaned out of the bathroom. He's gone, and I'm damn sure he took the crystal with him."

"But why would he steal it? What can he hope to do with it on his own?"

"Sell it," Jack said succinctly.

"But Excalibur holds several patents on the crystal. No competitor would touch it, because you could tie him up in court for years."

Jack's mouth twisted in a humorless smile. "That leaves a whole lot of other potential buyers, including several foreign business interests and the governments of a half-dozen countries, who don't give a damn about patent rights."

She sighed. "Yes, it does."

"It also leaves us," Jack said quietly.

"What?" She spun around to look at him. "You think Tyler Page might try to sell it back to Excalibur?"

"Why not? Page knows exactly how important that crystal is to the company. He also knows that we're under a tight time crunch. If we don't have Soft Focus available for the Veltran presentation, we're dead. It will take months to produce another sample of the crystal large enough to use for a demonstration."

"But that's equivalent to taking it hostage and holding us up for ransom."

"Yeah."

"Why, that little—" She broke off as a depressing thought struck her. "I don't think he'll try to sell it back to us. Excalibur doesn't have any extra cash. And even if I dig into the Aurora Fund reserves, we couldn't possibly compete with bids from foreign business consortiums or governments. Tyler Page must know that."

"Sure." Jack paused. "But there are two reasons why I think we might be in the running."

"Go on."

"First, Page is brilliant in his field, but he's a man of limited horizons in other respects. He's spent most of his life in a lab. I doubt that he knows how to go about contacting foreign business interests, let alone foreign governments. That kind of thing takes a certain amount of sophistication and experience."

"Maybe some foreign interest contacted him first and offered to buy it from him."

"It's possible, but if he'd sold us out already, I think he would have been smart enough to leave the country. He's got to know that I'll be looking for him and I won't stop until I find him."

She frowned at the cold determination in his voice. "You'd use your own time and money to look for Page, even if it was too late to save Excalibur?"

"I wouldn't have any other choice," he said simply.

"What do you mean, you wouldn't have any other choice? Of course you'd have another choice. You can cut your losses at Excalibur and find a new client."

"I don't do business that way." He looked around the room, as though the conversation had begun to bore him.

"Wait a second," she said. "Are you saying this is about your reputation?"

"I'm a consultant, Elizabeth. My reputation is all I have to sell. I always fulfill my contracts. No client of mine has ever been burned this badly on my watch. I sure as hell don't intend to set any new precedents with Excalibur."

"For heaven's sake, you sound like a hired gun who makes his living shooting down your clients' enemies for them."

He shrugged. "Whatever."

"You're talking revenge here, not your professional reputation."

He managed to appear even less interested in the direction the conversation had taken than he had a moment ago. "Call it what you want. The bottom line is that I'll do whatever it takes to find Page, and I have a hunch he knows that."

She eyed him warily. "All right, I get the point. You said the first reason you think Page is still in the country is because he lacks the know-how to sell Soft Focus abroad. What's the second reason you think he's still hanging around?"

He angled his head toward the nearest of the film posters hung on the wall. "That's the second reason."

She followed his gaze. "I don't get it."

"When you know a man's secret passion, you know his greatest weakness."

Baffled, Elizabeth studied the poster more closely. An enigmatic Humphrey Bogart and a sultry Lauren Bacall were posed in a tense scene. The title, *Dark Passage,* was scrawled in red across the bottom.

She looked back at Jack. "So Tyler Page likes film noir. How does that help you find him?"

"He isn't just a fan of old movies," Jack said. "He actually produced a new one."

"I don't understand."

Jack went to the table and hefted a book from an untidy stack. It had a black and white cover. Elizabeth noticed the word *noir* in the title.

Jack opened the book and removed a glossy little brochure that had been carelessly stuck between the pages. "I found this last night when I came looking for Page." He handed the pamphlet to her.

The picture on the front featured a seedy-looking private eye, complete with trench coat and gun in hand, standing in a dark alley. The cold light from a neon sign above a nearby tavern cast his profile into sharp chiaroscuro. The words "Mirror Springs Annual Neo Noir Festival" were printed down one side of the picture in yellow ink.

Elizabeth looked up. "What's this all about?"

"Like I said, Tyler Page made a movie." Jack jerked a thumb at one of the posters. "That one over there, to be specific."

"You're kidding." Elizabeth walked toward the poster to get a closer look.

Although the artwork paid homage to classic poster design, she saw now that it was a contemporary image. It featured a sultry blond actress with fine, sculpted features and eyes that had seen far too much of the dark side of the world. The woman wore a figure-hugging, low-cut gown and held a gun at her side. She gripped the weapon with casual ease, as though accustomed to its weight.

The phrase "Once you start running in Fast Company you can't stop" was written in slashing red script across the top of the poster.

Elizabeth read the rest of the poster quickly. *Fast Company*. Starring Victoria Bellamy. Produced by Tyler Page.

She glanced up. "So?"

"Take a look inside the brochure," Jack said. "One of the movies scheduled to be premiered at the Mirror Springs festival is *Fast Company*."

She opened the brochure and flipped through the list of films until she saw the title: "*Fast Company*. Produced by Tyler Page."

She raised her eyes to meet Jack's. "It takes money to produce a film, even a small, independent one like this. Did Page have that kind of cash?"

"Good question." He gave her an approving smile. "I happen to know someone who is very good with computers. I asked him to see if he could get a look at Page's bank transactions during the past year."

"That doesn't sound real legal."

"Stealing the results of his employer's secret research project wasn't real legal, either. At any rate, it looks like Page went through a lot of money in recent months. Mostly for expenses associated with the film. But judging from the amount, I doubt that he could have underwritten all the costs of *Fast Company*. I'm guessing there were other investors."

She frowned. "But Page got the credit as producer?"

"Yes. Who knows? Maybe he was the biggest investor. My computer whiz also picked up on the fact that, in addition to funding *Fast Company* during the past year, Page cleaned out his bank account two days ago. Furthermore, wherever he is at the moment, he did not use his credit cards to get there."

"You had your whiz check Page's credit-card records, too?"

"Figured I might as well make a thorough job of it."

Elizabeth grimaced. "Leaving the pesky little legal issues aside, I have to admit that it does look as if Page planned his recent disappearance."

"Damn right he did." Jack's eyes gleamed with brooding anticipation. "But I think I know where he's going to turn up next."

She realized he was looking at the brochure in her hand. She waved it once. "This film festival?"

"Yes. Page poured everything he had into *Fast Company*. I doubt if it's much of a film. Just a small, independent production. We're not talking big-budget Hollywood blockbuster here. Probably won't ever be screened anywhere else in the world except at the Mirror Springs festival. But I've done a lot of research into Tyler Page during the past few hours, and I can tell you one thing for sure."

"What's that?"

"No matter what else is going on in his life, Page will find a way to attend the premiere of *Fast Company*. That film is the culmination of all his fantasies. He sees himself as a player. For one week, at the Neo Noir Festival, he'll get to live his dream. Who could resist an opportunity like that?"

Understanding dawned. Elizabeth hurriedly checked the dates on the brochure. "It says the festival starts this Saturday. This is Wednesday."

"I'm leaving for Mirror Springs on Friday morning," Jack said. "That little SOB is going to show up there. I can feel it. And when he does, I'm going to be there waiting for him."

The grim promise in his words sent a chill down her spine. "Jack, maybe we should call the police in on this."

"You know as well as I do that calling in the cops wouldn't do any good. This is white-collar crime. Nobody calls the cops in on this kind of thing. The goal is to recover Soft Focus, not send Page to jail. One whiff of the police and we'll never find him in time to get the crystal back for the Veltran presentation."

"I hate to admit it, but you're probably right."

She was only too well aware that nine times out of ten, businesses did not call in the police in situations such as this. The fear of bad publicity, alarmed clients, and panicked investors was more than enough to make any corporation think twice before going to the authorities.

"The way I figure it, we've got two shots at finding Page," Jack said. "Either he'll contact me to let me make an offer to buy back Soft Focus, or else he'll show up at the film festival. I'm betting he'll do both."

"I'm not so sure, Jack. For heaven's sake, you're a business executive, not a private investigator. What makes you think you can find Page?"

"Go easy on the boundless admiration and unqualified support, will you? I'm not sure I can handle so much wide-eyed flattery from my client's biggest creditor."

She told herself she would not respond to that. She hated it when he made her sound like a brass-brassiered Valkyrie. She was never more acutely aware of her own femininity than when she was in Jack's vicinity. He, on the other hand, had as much as made a public announcement to the effect that he thought she was capable of sinking the *Titanic*.

Very deliberately, very carefully, she refolded the brochure and dropped it into her shoulder bag. She gave him a steely smile. "You make an excellent point, Jack. I am your biggest creditor. As such, I've got a vested interest in the recovery of the specimen. I'm going to go to Mirror Springs with you."

His eyes narrowed. "I don't think so."

"If Page does offer to let you ransom the crystal, you're going to need cash. Lots of it. No bank will loan you the money. Excalibur doesn't have the reserves, and I seriously doubt that you possess those kinds of personal financial resources. Face it. You're going to need the Aurora Fund."

"I can handle Page on my own."

"Maybe. But I don't intend to let you do that. Think of me as your credit card. You're not leaving home without me."

He studied her for a moment. "There are some serious logistical problems involved here."

His air of forced patience set her teeth on edge. "Such as?"

"Mirror Springs is one of those exclusive little boutique resort towns in the Colorado Rockies. Every hotel and motel in the area has been booked for months for the festival. You won't be able to get a room at this late date."

"Really?" She smiled blandly. "How did you find a room?"

He made a casual movement with his hand. "Called a friend of mine who's a vice president with one of the big hotels here in town. He pulled some strings with his second ex-wife. She manages a hotel in Denver. She pulled some strings with the concierge at a place called the Mirror Springs Resort. But even with all that, I had to pay triple the usual rate."

"I'm sure I can turn up something."

He gave her a wolfish smile that set all the hairs on the back of her neck on end.

"If you insist on going to Mirror Springs with me, I might let you talk me into sharing my room," he said much too politely. His eyes gleamed with challenge. "But you'd have to ask real nice."

"Thanks, but that price is a bit too steep for me." She forced another brittle little smile. "I'm sure I can find something a little less expensive."

She turned on her heel and walked out the door.

Oh, now, that was really mature, Elizabeth. You do have a way with men, don't you?

Chapter Five

Jack heard the soft grunt of breath released, sensed the faint, indescribable disturbance in the air that telegraphed the slashing kick, and glided to the side, turning smoothly away from the blow. The striking foot missed his thigh by inches. If it had landed he would have gone down.

He whirled, seeking an opening in the split second it would take for his opponent to recover from the move. He caught an arm and drew it toward him, taking advantage of the other's forward momentum.

His half brother lost his balance, tumbled lightly to the mat, and grimaced. He got to his feet with easy grace and returned Jack's formal bow.

"That makes three in a row," Larry growled as they walked off the practice floor. "You've been practicing too much lately. No fair."

It was true, Jack thought. He had been spending a lot of what little spare time he possessed these days here at the dojo. The hard physical and mental exercise provided a badly needed outlet. It wasn't as if he had a lot of other ways to work off the stress. Sex, for example, at least with another consenting adult, was out. He'd been living like a monk for six months.

"You almost took me down with that last kick," he said.

"No, I didn't." Larry's dark brows scrunched together. "It's not good for my self-esteem to always lose to my big brother, you know."

"Is that right?" Jack watched a pair of students working at the other end of the dojo. "Who told you that?"

"Read it somewhere in a magazine, I think."

"Larry, I've warned you before about reading those men's magazines."

"I only read the articles," Larry said piously.

"That's what worries me."

Larry grinned. "You think maybe I should concentrate more on the pictures?"

"Nah. Save your energy. I've tried the pictures. Hard work getting anything of a stimulating nature out of them."

"Well, they sure as hell won't substitute for a social life, which is what you've been using them for during the past six months."

"I've been busy." He realized he was feeling defensive. It irritated him to know that he was making excuses.

He also knew they wouldn't go over. Not with Larry. For all his techie qualities, and they were legion, his half brother had a surprising degree of insight and intuition when it came to people.

They had been raised apart and they had little in common except a father. Physically they shared very few traits except the color of their eyes. Larry was a couple of inches taller, with light-colored hair and a face that could have come straight off the silver screen. They had not even met until a few years ago. But the bond between them had been immediate and it had proved to be solid. Larry and Megan and their new infant daughter provided Jack with whatever semblance of a family life he possessed.

Larry gave him a knowing look. "You've had, what? Three dates? And one of those was with Megan's cousin Sandra, so it doesn't count."

"Why doesn't it count?" Jack frowned, trying to recall the details of the date he'd had with his sister-in-law's cousin. They were vague. He thought he could remember a pretty face and a cute, rounded little body. He was pretty sure he had bored her half to death. He knew for a fact that he'd been thoroughly bored that night. His mind had been on other things—namely, whether or not Elizabeth had had a date that evening.

"It doesn't count," Larry said patiently, "because Megan told me later that all you talked about for two hours straight at dinner was the state of the Northwest's economy, after which inspiring conversation, you took her cousin home, left her at her door, and never called again."

"I've been busy," Jack said again.

"Bullshit. You're still carrying a torch for that woman who runs the Aurora Fund, and you know it."

"Larry, modern men do not carry torches. Remember that. It's important. Torch-carrying belongs to another era. It comes from a time when people did stupid things and got away with it because they said that they had done them for love. That excuse doesn't fly anymore."

"You know, one of these days you're going to have to stop lecturing me. I realize you think you have to make up for lost time, but it's not necessary. Really." Larry glanced at him. "So what did you want to talk to me about?"

"Think you could play wizard again and go on the Net to get me some financial background on a man named Dawson Holland?"

The familiar gleam of maniacal curiosity leaped in Larry's dark eyes. "Probably. Why are you interested in him?"

"I'm not sure that I am. But it's a place to start. You know what they say about following the money. Holland put together the investment package that bankrolled a little independent film called *Fast Company*. I want whatever I can get relating to the movie, and that means that I want something on Holland."

"I can tell you one thing without even going online," Larry said. "Whoever this Holland guy is, if he's the one who arranged the financing, he's probably the only one who didn't put any of his own money into the movie. And he'll be the only one who actually comes out ahead. The real investors, the ones who coughed up hard cash, will never see a dime. The only people who make money in films, large or small, are the guys who move other people's money around."

"I've heard that for years." Jack thought about the shrine to filmmaking he had discovered in Tyler Page's little house. "But there never seems to be any shortage of people lining up to finance films."

Larry shrugged. "They're all starstruck. They want to pretend that they're players. Go to the opening-night parties. Hang with the stars and the directors. See their names in the credits. Filmmaking is one of the most glamorous clubs in the world. Lots of people are willing to shell out lots of money to join it."

"I know. Just get me what you can on Holland and the film. Use my cell phone number to reach me. I'll be out of town for a while."

Larry's eyes lit with amused interest. "Don't tell me you're taking a vacation?"

"Not exactly. Know anything about film noir?"

"Those old black-and-white movies from the forties? Gangsters and sleazy private eyes and femme fatales? Live fast, die hard kind of stuff? Sure. I've watched a few of the classics on late-night TV. Some great lines in those old scripts."

"You're way ahead of me, then. But I'm going to learn a whole lot during the next few days at a film noir festival."

Larry studied him. "Are you going to take in this festival alone?"

"No, as a matter of fact, a business associate will be going with me."

"Well, now, isn't that interesting. And just who is this business associate?"

Jack set his jaw. "Elizabeth Cabot."

Larry howled with laughter.

Jack narrowed his eyes. "What's so damned funny?"

"You." Larry gradually subsided to an evil chuckle. "Going to a film noir festival with your own, personal femme fatale."

Chapter Six

"Since when did you develop an interest in film noir?" Louise scowled suspiciously over the rims of her reading glasses. "Hell, you don't even like to go to the movies. I'll bet you can't name the film that won Best Picture at the Academy Awards last year."

Elizabeth stopped in front of her assistant's desk. "You're the one who keeps telling me that I'm working too hard and that I need a vacation. This film festival thing caught my eye. Thought it sounded like a change of pace."

"Change of pace, my left gluteus maximus. This is Louise you're talking to. If there's one thing I know when I see it, it's a line of bull."

Elizabeth grinned in spite of herself. "Sorry. Sometimes I forget how much experience you've had with bull."

In addition to Elizabeth, Louise Luttrell was the only other member of the Aurora Fund staff. Elizabeth had inherited her when she had inherited the Fund from her aunt.

The framed front-page headlines of several yellowing tabloid newspapers arranged behind the desk testified to Louise's former career in journalism. "Woman Abducted by UFO Marries Captors," "Man Eaten by Giant Frog," "Ancient Alien Mummy Awakens." All of the stories carried Louise's byline.

Sixty-something, big-haired, full-figured, and not at all hesitant to state her opinion, Louise functioned as secretary, receptionist, travel agent, adviser, and confidante. She arrived at the mansion promptly at nine every morning and took complete charge of the office wing. Elizabeth sometimes suspected the Aurora Fund would collapse without her.

"Damn straight. Professional bullshit detector, that's me." Louise rolled her eyes in the general direction of the framed tabloids and then peered more closely at Elizabeth. "Talk to me. Tell me what's going on here. Are you up to something stupid?"

There really was no point trying to keep secrets from Louise.

"Probably," Elizabeth said. "But I haven't got a lot of choice."

"Let's have it. I can take it. Hell, I've taken stories involving the alien mummies. I can handle your little tale."

Elizabeth got up out of the high, leather, wing-back chair and crossed the antique crimson, black, and gold carpet to stand at the window. It was one of those rare, spectacularly clear early-fall days in Seattle when the local professional photographers rushed outside to grab pictures of Mount Rainier and the Space Needle to put on postcards and calendars.

From here she could see the downtown high-rises, including the one in which Jack lived. She had spent a lot of nights gazing at that particular concrete-and-steel building. Once or twice she'd dug out Sybil's old bird-watching binoculars to see if she could get a closer look at the thirtieth floor. But the tinted windows had defeated her foray into voyeurism.

She concentrated on the view of the city as she gathered her thoughts.

"Tyler Page, the researcher who developed Soft Focus for Excalibur, has disappeared," she said. "Unfortunately, it looks like he took the crystal specimen with him."

There was a short pause behind her.

"Well, shit," Louise said eventually.

"In a word."

"Just out of curiosity, what kind of potential loss are we dealing with here?"

"If the crystal actually works and Grady Veltran agrees to a licensing agreement?" Elizabeth turned back to face her. "I couldn't even guess. The upside potential is in the millions for Excalibur."

"And we get a chunk of the profits." Louise looked briefly smug. She had shares in the Aurora Fund.

"And if we don't get it back, or it doesn't work, the Fund takes a serious hit," Elizabeth added.

"But it wouldn't go under."

"No, we can certainly survive the loss of Soft Focus. Excalibur, on the other hand, can't. Right now our worst enemy is gossip. There are already a few rumors floating around. If anyone calls for background on the Aurora Fund's position with regard to our client, Excalibur, we are officially not worried. Nothing is wrong."

"Got it. Not worried. Nothing wrong." Louise narrowed her eyes. "In other words, we're in full-blown panic mode. So what's this neo noir film festival in Mirror Springs got to do with finding the specimen?"

"Jack Fairfax has reason to think that Page will show up at the festival."

"Whoa. Hang on, here." Louise's chair squeaked as she leaned back in her chair. She cleared her throat. "Let me get this straight. The egg-sucking, lower-than-a-snake's-belly, conniving, underhanded, two-faced SOB is going to this film festival, too?"

Elizabeth smiled humorlessly. "I can't imagine where you got such a low opinion of Jack Fairfax."

"I got it from you, and you know it." Louise pursed her lips and looked contemplative. "Although I have to admit, I've got a sneaking admiration for the bastard. He must have something none of your other boyfriends have ever had."

Elizabeth glared at her. "What on earth are you talking about?"

"I'm talking about whatever it was he did that made you track him down and throw ice water all over him in front of the stuffiest bunch of corporate honchos in town." Louise smiled. "I've known you since you were a little girl, and that was the first time you've ever let yourself go over the top and stage a genuine hissy-fit scene in public. Too bad Sybil wasn't around to witness it. Nothing she liked better than to see a little female empowerment in action."

"I doubt if she would have approved," Elizabeth said shortly. "Not if she knew why I had staged the scene."

She glanced at the portrait on the paneled wall opposite the desk and felt a twist of chagrin. Sybil Cabot looked down on her with the stern but not unkind intelligence that had been her signature trait. Elizabeth remembered very clearly the day her aunt had called her into her office and told her that she intended to leave the Aurora Fund in her hands.

"You're the only one in the family who has the two things required to make the Fund achieve its full potential, Elizabeth. You've got the financial know-how and you've got the instincts of a gambler. Deep down you're willing to take a few risks, and that's what's needed to make the Aurora Fund work."

She'd had her share of good fortune when it came to taking financial risks, Elizabeth thought. But when it came to her personal life, her luck had been disastrous. For some strange reason it was a lot easier to pick a good business prospect than it was to pick a good man.

Louise squinted. "So you're going to Mirror Springs with Fairfax? Are we talking close physical proximity here?"

Elizabeth steeled herself. "No, we are not talking close physical proximity. We're traveling separately, and we will be staying in separate locations."

"Is that a fact?"

"Yes, it is definitely a fact." Elizabeth paused. "That reminds me. I'm going to need reservations, and apparently the town is full because of the film festival. Think you can find me something?"

"Probably." Louise sat forward and reached for her address file. "Mirror Springs is a popular ski resort, and Lord knows we've got a ton of clients, past and present, who ski. Plus I've got plenty of contacts from the old days in the news business. I'll make some calls. Seems to me one of my editors has a vacation place in Mirror Springs."

Elizabeth looked at the glaring headlines of the framed tabloids. "He's not a space alien or a recently revived mummy, is he?"

"Well, if you're going to be picky about it—"

"You're right. I'll take what I can get."

"So you and Fairfax are going to play detectives, huh?" Louise flipped through her card file. "That should be interesting."

"I did suggest that he call in the cops, but you know how executives are about going to the police on this kind of thing."

Louise snorted. "Nobody calls the cops in on white-collar crime."

"For good reasons." Elizabeth started toward her office. "Let me know when you find a place for me in Mirror Springs. I'll also need airline reservations to Denver and a rental car on the other end."

"Right." Louise paused. "I almost forgot, your brother-in-law called again."

"Merrick?" Elizabeth groaned. "What did you tell him?"

"Same thing I told him the last four times he called. That you were busy."

"Which is the honest truth."

"You won't be able to duck him forever, you know."

"I know. But I can at least duck him for the next few days while I'm in Colorado."

A gleam of speculation appeared in Louise's eyes. "Out of idle curiosity, whose idea was it for you to go to Mirror Springs with Fairfax? His or yours?"

"Are you joking? Mine, of course. He told me he wanted to handle this thing alone, but I told him to forget it. I'm going with him whether he likes it or not."

Louise concentrated hard on her address file. "I was afraid of that."

"Are you crazy?" Milo bounced and twitched his way back and forth across Jack's living room. "You can't take off now. We've got a disaster on our hands."

"The only way to avert disaster is to find Page and that damned crystal." Jack walked out of the bedroom, fastening his cuff links. "Mirror Springs is our best shot."

"I don't like this, Jack. I don't like it one damn bit."

"Neither do I, but it's not like we have much choice. Remember, while I'm gone your job is to keep a lid on rumors and gossip. Officially, everything is under control at Excalibur. Got that?"

"Yeah, yeah, I got it." Milo's face tightened. "Cousin Angela's going to be the tough one. I think she went to see Ms. Cabot again yesterday."

Jack glanced at him sharply. "Any particular reason?"

"How should I know?" Milo spread his hands. "Probably just her regular bimonthly attempt to convince Ms. Cabot to stop backing your every move as CEO. Angela figures if she can get Elizabeth Cabot to turn on you, she'll have enough votes on the board to get rid of you."

So far Elizabeth had backed him at every turn, Jack thought. But an alliance between Angela and Elizabeth was a grim possibility.

Milo stared at him, eyes widening. "You're in a tux."

"Very observant." Jack glanced out the window as he picked up his jacket and shrugged into it.

From here he had a good view of Queen Anne Hill. If he squinted, he could just barely make out the lights of Elizabeth's castle. He had spent more than one night during the past six months sitting alone here in his living room with a glass of scotch, staring at the distant glow. He had told himself that it would be tacky to get a telescope.

And pointless.

A purely scientific experiment with a set of binoculars had confirmed that there were too many plants and bushes on the balcony outside Elizabeth's bedroom to allow for a clear view of the interior.

He wondered if she was dressing for the reception at that very moment.

For the past few days, right up until the disappearance of Soft Focus had distracted him, the business charity function had been the high point on his calendar. Typically he avoided such events whenever possible, but he had been looking forward to this one with the same mix of perverse anticipation and foreboding that he got in the days before an Excalibur board meeting. Another chance to see Elizabeth. Another chance to torment himself with all the might-have-been possibilities. Another chance to fantasize about second chances.

And now fate had dropped a ticking bomb in his lap. The good news was that he was going to spend the next few days working very closely with Elizabeth. It was also the bad news, because they would be working together under the worst possible sort of pressure. He figured he would be lucky to survive with his sanity intact.

"Why the hell are you in a tux?" Milo demanded. "You're not going to a party tonight, are you? You're supposed to leave for Mirror Springs tomorrow morning."

"I told you about the charity reception."

Milo's jaw dropped. "You're still going to attend? After everything else that's happened?"

"I don't think it would be a good idea to skip it." Jack glanced at his watch. "Failing to show up would add fuel to the rumors that are already circulating. We can't afford that. In business, perception is all. Never forget that, Milo."

"Huh." Milo's thin face crunched into a darker frown. "I'd sure like to know how those rumors got started."

"So would I." Jack picked up his keys. "But we don't have time to investigate the leak now. We'll deal with it after we get Soft Focus back."

Milo trailed after him toward the door. "Tell me the truth, Jack. Do you really think you can find Page?"

Jack glanced at him as he opened the door. A wave of empathy went through him. Milo had a lot on his young, inexperienced shoulders.

"I'll find him, Milo."

Chapter Seven

Hayden Shaw looked out across the glittering ballroom. "Fairfax just walked in. That raises two possibilities. Either the rumors about trouble at Excalibur were wrong or . . ."

Elizabeth raised one brow. "Or?"

"Or else they were true and both of you are playing it cool tonight so that people will *think* they're wrong."

Elizabeth surprised herself with a low chuckle that she thought sounded remarkably genuine. "I can tell you this much: Jack Fairfax may be cold-blooded enough to put in an appearance tonight even if there were major problems at his company. But I certainly wouldn't be standing around drinking champagne if there were a disaster. I'd be in my office, huddled in front of my computer with a large cup of coffee, and I'd be tearing out my hair."

She had wanted very much not to attend the charity event tonight, but she knew that it would send the wrong message to those who, like Hayden, had picked up hints of trouble at Excalibur. Obviously Jack had followed the same logic. She doubted that he was enjoying himself any more than she was.

She wondered if he had noticed her standing here with Hayden and, if he had seen her, whether or not the sight of her chatting with his archenemy annoyed him. If it did bother him, she knew that he would not reveal it. Jack could play poker with the devil.

Why did she even care if he was annoyed? she wondered. *Stupid question.* She was in that strange mood again, the one she always plunged into a few days before she knew that she was to see Jack. The days preceding a regularly scheduled board meeting at Excalibur were always bad. The peculiar mix of emotions was just as predictable as certain other recurring biological functions.

She wondered what Jack would say if he knew that the thought of being in his company triggered a severe form of PMS in her.

An entire week together. Good grief, how could they possibly do it?

She was accustomed to estimating the odds, but she could not even begin to guess whether or not they would throttle each other before they found Tyler Page.

Hayden surveyed her neat chignon appreciatively. "You look lovely tonight."

"Thank you."

Hayden lowered his voice to a husky drawl. "The dress is pretty terrific, too."

She pretended not to notice his gaze sliding appreciatively over the long line of her spine left exposed by the backless black gown. Hayden was interesting, very successful, and, with his warm brown eyes, dark hair, and good facial bones, about ten times better looking than Jack Fairfax. He was also a few years younger. But the last thing she wanted to do tonight was flirt with him.

Jack's seemingly offhand question about Hayden's marital status yesterday morning had made her uneasy. Just as he had no doubt meant it to do, she thought. Typical of Fairfax to slip home a zinger just when she was starting to convince herself that she could get interested in Hayden.

She had told herself that she would ignore Jack's comment on the divorce, but she had known that would not be possible. Like a number of other people she knew, she had been under the distinct impression that Hayden's divorce was, indeed, final. But once Fairfax had raised the question, she was obliged to double-check the facts.

Sure enough, a discreet inquiry through her lawyer this morning had elicited the information that Hayden's divorce was still pending. There were no children involved, but apparently the battle over the division of the assets had turned extremely messy. Elizabeth did not want to get anywhere near the scene of the accident.

In all fairness, she could not accuse Hayden of having lied to her. She just hadn't asked the right question. Then again, it was a little awkward to ask a person point-blank if his divorce was officially final, especially when he had yet to ask you out on a real date. Thus far all of her encounters with Shaw had been quasi-business meetings.

But lately the atmosphere between the two of them had begun to alter quite subtly. She could not pinpoint the exact moment when she had realized that Hayden was giving off the kind of signals that said he was interested in something more than a business connection. She was still not certain that she was reading him right.

The reason she could not be sure of what was going on was that she was unwilling to ponder the depressing subject of her love life. She was still licking her wounds from the skirmish with Jack.

Things were not improving on that front, she thought. If anything, they were getting worse. Her awareness of him was preternaturally high. She had not needed Hayden to tell her that Jack had arrived in the ballroom a few minutes ago; the tingling on the nape of her neck had provided her with the same data. She was afraid the uncanny sensation was some sort of primitive prelude to a fight-or-fornicate response.

She could not seem to take her eyes off him, so she did her best to observe him without being obvious about it.

The tux did nothing to mute the edgy quality that was so much a part of him. If anything, it enhanced the air of fiercely controlled sexuality he exuded. The warmth that unfurled deep inside her at the sight of him was as irritating as it was disturbing. She watched him stop to speak to some men gathered near the buffet table. He appeared to be monumentally unaware of her.

"You know," Hayden murmured, "just because this is a business affair doesn't mean that you and I have to discuss the economy."

She flicked a glance at him. "I hadn't noticed that we were discussing the economy."

"We weren't. Just trying to get your attention." He gave her a rueful grin. "It came to my attention that you were concentrating on Fairfax, you see."

"Why is that surprising? I've got a hefty stake in Excalibur. I always keep an eye on my investments."

He gave a short, surprisingly harsh laugh. "If a woman watched me the way you're watching Fairfax, I'd like to think that she was contemplating something other than whether or not I could make a lot of money for her."

She smiled politely and set down her glass. "Now you know the awful truth about me. The bottom line is everything!"

"Maybe. Maybe not." He studied her intently. "You're not an easy woman to figure out, Elizabeth. But speaking of Excalibur, did you check out those rumors I mentioned?"

"I did, and everything is under control at Excalibur."

"Glad to hear it. Well, then, can I talk you into a dance?"

"Some other time, perhaps. I'm here to work tonight."

"All work and no play . . ."

"I'm afraid you're a little late with the warning. Too much work has already made me a very dull CEO."

His eyes gleamed suggestively. "Bet I could fix that little problem with a nice long weekend at the coast. What do you say to taking off on Friday and coming back very, very late on Monday?"

She had been right about the signals. She gave an inward sigh, wrenched her covert gaze off Jack, and turned to give Hayden a bland smile.

"Funny you should mention this weekend," she said. "I'm going to be out of town. A little vacation time. My secretary tells me that I need it badly."

He gave her a hopeful grin. "Any chance you might want some company for at least a couple of days of your vacation? I could do with a little time off myself."

He was going to force her into a corner, she realized. Better to deal with it now and get past it. She met his eyes. "I understand that your divorce is not yet final, Hayden. I don't do long weekends with married men."

He grimaced. "Ouch. I get the point. Would it make any difference if I told you that the divorce should have been final several months ago? That the only reason it isn't a done deal is because Gillian is the vindictive type?"

"Nope. It wouldn't make any difference at all." She transferred her small gold evening bag to her other hand and made to move off. "Excuse me. I see some Aurora Fund clients. I'd better go say hello."

"Sure." Something hard flashed in his eyes. It was gone in an instant, replaced by a wry expression. "One of these days I'll get through this damned divorce, you know. Even Ringstead's lawyers can't hold it up forever. We can talk about a long weekend then."

"We'll see," she said, deliberately vague. But something told her that there would never be any long weekends with Hayden.

She dutifully made her way through the crowd, greeting clients and potential investors in the Fund. Her invisible radar screen kept her clear of Jack. She caught glimpses of him now and again. Once she saw him lounging against the bar, a glass in one hand, chatting with an attorney she recognized.

He glanced toward her at that precise instant, as if he had known that she was looking at him. He raised his glass a couple of inches in a mocking salute and turned back to his conversation. For the next forty minutes, however, he managed not to cross her path. It occurred to her that he was going out of his way to avoid her, too.

Shortly after eleven she glanced at her watch and told herself that she had concluded the minimum of socializing the event demanded. She needed some sleep before the flight to Mirror Springs. She smiled at a portly, retired banker who was waxing enthusiastic about his new boat. The man was obviously in love with his most recent acquisition. She wished him happiness and slipped away to collect her coat.

When she emerged from the cloakroom, she turned and went down a quiet, carpeted hall, avoiding the more heavily traveled path to and from the ballroom. She sensed a presence behind her just before the woman spoke.

"If you're smart, you'll stay away from him."

Elizabeth froze at the raw venom in the voice. Then she turned slowly around. A small, elegantly made-up woman dressed in a very chic, very expensive red silk suit and stiletto heels stood in the hall. She appeared to be in her mid-thirties. Her pale blond hair was cut in a sleek line that highlighted her heart-shaped features. There were fine, tightly drawn lines at the corners of her mouth.

"Have we met?" Elizabeth asked carefully.

"Sorry. Allow me to introduce myself. I'm Gillian the Bitch."

"I beg your pardon?"

"Don't you recognize the name? I'm surprised. I understand Hayden always calls me that." Gillian's smile was so brittle, it was a wonder it did not shatter. "I'm his wife."

"I see." Great. A perfect way to end the evening.

"In spite of the impression Hayden may have given you, I am not his ex-wife. Not yet, at any rate. I won't give him that satisfaction until Daddy's lawyers have gotten back everything he took from me."

"This really isn't any of my business." Elizabeth made a show of glancing at her watch. "I'm on my way home. If you'll excuse me . . ."

Gillian's eyes narrowed. "My daddy is Osmand Ringstead."

Elizabeth needed no further details. Ringstead was the very powerful, very reclusive, very rich, and very politically connected head of Ring, Inc. From the Ringstead family compound he commanded a large, closely held business empire. He was rumored to be contemplating political office. No wonder Hayden was having problems getting his divorce to go through on his terms, she thought. Few people could go up against the Ringstead power and money and hope to win.

"Okay, I'm impressed," she said. "Now can I go?"

"I saw Hayden talking to you," Gillian said, her eyes bleak. "I know how he operates. Has he invited you to go on a long weekend to the coast?"

Elizabeth managed to conceal her start of surprise. "I don't know what this is all about, Mrs. Shaw. But I can assure you, I have no personal interest in your husband."

"Let's hope for your sake that you're telling the truth." Gillian took a step closer. "Because I'm going to ruin him before I'm finished with him. He won't have a dime left. I'll get everything. *Everything*. Daddy promised me."

There was more than rage in Gillian's voice, Elizabeth realized. There was pain. She suddenly felt very sorry for the other woman.

"Believe me, the last thing I want to do is get caught up in your private affairs, Mrs. Shaw."

"This divorce is going to be a train wreck, I promise you. Hayden won't get away with trying to walk out on me."

"As I said, this is none of my business. If you'll excuse me, I'm going home."

"He lied to me." Hot tears appeared in Gillian's eyes and spilled down her cheeks. "The bastard lied to me right from the start. I trusted him. I loved him. Daddy liked him. But all Hayden wanted was my money and Daddy's connections. He used me."

Elizabeth longed to turn and run, not walk, in the opposite direction. But she could not bring herself to leave the woman sobbing alone in the hall. She pulled some tissues from the pocket of her coat and went toward Gillian.

"Here, take these." She thrust the tissues into Gillian's hand. "There's a women's lounge right around the corner. I just came from there. It was empty. Would you like to go inside?"

"He made a fool out of me," Gillian blurted into the tissues.

"I know the feeling." Unable to think of anything else to do, Elizabeth patted her gently on the shoulder. "Maybe a glass of cold water?"

"Stay away from him. He'll only use you."

"I have no interest in your husband, Mrs. Shaw."

"I saw the way he looked at you tonight." Gillian blotted her eyes. "I know he wants you."

"I don't want him," Elizabeth said gently.

"I don't believe you." Gillian lowered the soaked tissues. Her voice rose. "Of course you want him. Just like I did. Until I found out what he was really like, that is."

Elizabeth was about to argue the point when she felt the familiar tingling. Simultaneously a lean, dark figure appeared in the hall behind Gillian.

"Ready to go home, honey?" Jack walked toward her with assured arrogance. His tone was unmistakably intimate, bordering on the possessive. "It's getting late, and we've got a long trip ahead of us tomorrow."

At the sound of his voice, Gillian raised her head sharply and quickly blotted away the rest of her tears. "Oh, damn. This is so embarrassing."

Elizabeth looked past her at Jack. Unseen by Gillian, he raised his brows and smiled with cool, knowing amusement. He was coming to her rescue, and he knew she didn't like it. He also knew full well that she was in no position to refuse his help.

"I'm ready, Jack." She managed a bright little smile. "I was just having a word with Mrs. Shaw. Have you met her? Gillian, this is Jack Fairfax."

"Gillian and I know each other," Jack said with surprising gentleness.

"Hello, Jack." Gillian blinked away the rest of her tears and gave him a watery smile. "Sorry about the scene."

"Forget it."

"I heard you took over Excalibur a few months ago. How are things going there?"

"We've been busy." Jack took Elizabeth's arm, casually proprietary. "But Elizabeth and I finally managed to clear our calendars for the same week. We're going on vacation tomorrow. I think we both need one, don't we, honey?"

Elizabeth kept her smile fixed in place, but it wasn't easy. "We certainly do."

"I don't understand." Watery confusion glittered in Gillian's eyes. She glanced from Jack's face to Elizabeth's and then back again. "You're going away together?"

"That's right," Jack said. "Been looking forward to it for weeks."

"I see." Gillian looked as if she was having a problem assimilating the data. "I hadn't realized that you two were seeing each other."

"We've kept it quiet." Elizabeth gave Jack a warning smile. "For business reasons."

"Are you going to the coast?" Gillian asked.

"No." Jack tightened his fingers on Elizabeth's arm. "We're going to a resort in the Rockies. No fax, no phones, no E-mail. Just the two of us alone in the woods. But we've got an early plane to catch, so I'm afraid you're going to have to excuse us."

"Yes, of course," Gillian murmured. She blotted her eyes one last time and gave Jack a warm, tremulous smile. "Have a good time."

"Thanks. We intend to do just that."

He turned Elizabeth and steered her down the hall toward the lobby.

Neither spoke until they walked outside and came to a halt beneath the bright lights that illuminated the hotel's front entrance.

"Don't look back. She followed us into the lobby," Jack said.

"I'm not surprised. She's very upset."

"It will look better if we share a cab," Jack said.

Elizabeth said nothing, just gave a clipped nod, acknowledging the suggestion. He was right. If Gillian was watching them, it would be better if they left together.

Jack signaled the doorman, who raised a whistle to summon the next cab in line. When the door opened, Elizabeth slipped quickly into the rear seat. Jack got in beside her. The door closed.

The back of the cab suddenly seemed like a very small, very intimate space.

Elizabeth gazed straight ahead through the window as the taxi pulled out onto the street.

"I suppose I should thank you," she said stiffly.

"Don't worry, I'm not expecting you to go overboard."

She groaned and settled back into the seat. "Thank you."

"You're welcome," Jack said.

"What happened back there was a little awkward."

"I sort of figured that," he said.

"You were right. The divorce is not final."

Jack slanted her an enigmatic glance. "Told you so."

She controlled her temper with an effort of will. "Yes. You did, didn't you?"

He did not respond immediately. She glanced warily in his direction and saw that he was looking out the side window of the cab into the night. The weak glare of a streetlight glanced off the strong line of his cheekbones and jaw, leaving his eyes in deep shadows.

"I heard Angela paid you a visit this week," he said after a while.

The change in topic surprised her. "Angela generally comes to my office twice a month. What about it?"

"What did she want this time?"

Elizabeth thought about the unpleasant scene that had taken place three days earlier. Angela Ingersoll Burrows was a tall, striking, formidable woman. Her marriage of fifteen years had ended abruptly when her fifty-three-year-old, mild-mannered husband had stunned everyone by running off with his twenty-two-year-old secretary. Left with a teenage son to raise, Angela now focused most of her time and attention on making certain that her only offspring received what she considered his fair share of the family inheritance. The family inheritance consisted solely of the assets of Excalibur.

"We talked about her usual concerns," Elizabeth said as diplomatically as possible. "She wants to see Excalibur sold or merged. She's convinced it's the only way her son will ever see a dime out of Excalibur."

"What did you tell her?"

"The same thing I tell her every time she comes to see me."

Jack watched her from the shadows. "Which is?"

She flexed her fingers around the edge of her evening bag and kept her voice very flat. "Which is that you are Excalibur's best hope and that, therefore, her son's best chance of coming into a significant inheritance from Excalibur rests with you."

There was another short, heavy silence. Jack shifted slightly in the seat, seeming to settle deeper into the shadows.

"You backed me," he said.

"Yes."

"You always do. Not just when it comes to dealing with Angela but on the board, as well." He sounded as if he were making an observation about rain in Seattle. It was expected, it was routine, it was predictable. Still, it warranted comment. "Why?"

She was almost amused by the question. "You and I have our differences, but I've never quarreled with the fact that you are very good at what you do. If Excalibur has any chance at all, it lies with you."

"In other words, your decision to back my decisions as CEO is just a business move on your part," he said neutrally.

"What else could it be except a business move?"

"Damned if I know," he said. He looked at her. "We've both got a mutual interest in recovering Soft Focus. Since you insist on coming along for the ride—"

"I'm not along for the ride," she said tightly. "I'm a full-fledged partner in this thing."

"All right, partner, what do you say we try to cooperate until we get our hands on that damned crystal?"

"Define cooperate."

"I figure it's like porn," Jack said. "You know it when you see it."

Chapter Eight

The timbered house was designer rustic. With its burnished wooden walls, steeply sloped roofline, and expansive windows angled to capture the view, it looked like something off the cover of a high-end resort-and-travel magazine. Night had fallen, but there was sufficient golden light pouring through the windows onto the deck to illuminate a hot tub. It looked large enough to hold half a dozen people, provided they were feeling friendly. There was a massive, high-tech, state-of-the-art stainless steel outdoor grill next to the tub. Thickly padded loungers and a table completed the outdoor furnishings.

And this was just the outside.

Trust Elizabeth to land digs like these on short notice in a sold-out town.

Jack glanced again at the covered hot tub. An image of Elizabeth sitting naked in the bubbling water flashed across his brain. He took a deep breath of the very crisp, impossibly pure mountain air and counted backward from ten. When he got to zero he realized he was still semi-erect. He was also a little light-headed. He reminded himself that it took a while to adjust to the altitude.

He forced his attention away from the hot-tub fantasy and concentrated on the problem at hand. No matter how he played it, he was going to look less than brilliant. He dropped his duffel bag in front of the door and banged the brass, bird-headed knocker. This was not going to be easy.

He planted one hand against the wall while he waited for Elizabeth to respond and studied the view. The lights of the expensive condos and homes that climbed the hillsides above the village of Mirror Springs twinkled in the night. Down below he could see the glow of the shops and restaurants housed in the carefully restored Victorian-era business district. The brightest lights of all were those that marked the entrance of the Silver Empire Theater, one of the focal points of the film festival activities.

"Who is it?" Elizabeth's voice was muffled by the heavy wooden door.

He steeled himself. "Jack."

There was a short pause. He made the mistake of holding his breath again. Then he heard the sound of the dead bolt being disengaged. The door opened.

Elizabeth stood in the cozy glow of the fire. She was dressed in a black cowl-necked sweater made of some soft, cuddly-looking material. It fell to a point just below her hips. In addition to the sweater she wore a pair of snug black velvet leggings. Her dark hair was brushed straight back and secured at the nape with a silver clasp.

She gazed at him with that cautious, watchful expression that made him want to grind his teeth.

"What are you doing here?" she asked. "I thought we agreed that we would meet for dinner somewhere in the village after we each got unpacked. You said we could go over our game plan then."

"A problem has arisen."

The caution in her eyes turned to suspicion. "What kind of problem?"

"When I tried to check in at the resort I was told that there were no rooms available."

"So?"

"So," he said very deliberately, "I haven't got a place to stay."

Suspicion congealed into accusation in her gaze. "You said you knew some people who could pull some strings to get you a room."

"The strings broke."

"I see." She propped one shoulder against the doorjamb and folded her arms beneath her breasts. "What do you expect me to do about it?"

He glanced through the doorway at the high, vaulted ceiling and the expansive, warmly furnished great room behind her. A cheerful-looking fire burned in a handsome stone fireplace. He could see a staircase that led to two sleeping lofts that overlooked the central room.

He cleared his throat. "I thought maybe you could let me share this place."

"Now, why would I do that?"

"Because we're supposed to be cooperating." He switched his gaze back to her. "Look, I'm sorry about this, but the whole damn town is filled to capacity. The people at the hotel said there was absolutely nothing else available anywhere nearby. I promise I won't leave my socks lying around on the floor, and I'll try to remember to put the seat down in the john."

She deliberated a moment longer, her eyes cool and enigmatic. Then, with a small, resigned groan, she straightened away from the jamb. "I should have known something like this would happen. Okay, you can share this place. There are two bathrooms. You can do whatever you want with the seat in yours."

"Thanks." A heady sense of relief and anticipation swept through him. Probably just the altitude again. He'd get acclimated soon. "I owe you."

"You certainly do." She stepped back to allow him to enter.

She made him feel the way Dracula must have felt when he wangled the invitation to cross the threshold, he thought. He picked up the duffel and went through the doorway.

He glanced around at the gleaming wooden floors, the deep-pile rug in front of the fire, and the plush, leather furnishings. "I don't see a stuffed moose head mounted on the wall. Shouldn't there be a moose head?"

"If you want a moose head, you'll have to supply it yourself."

"That's okay, I'm adaptable. I can make do without the moose head."

She gave him a brief, reluctant smile that hit him straight in the gut because it brought back memories of all the radiant smiles he'd received from her B.D.: Before the Disaster.

She gestured toward the stairs. "I've already settled into the loft on the left. You can have the one on the right."

"No problem." He crossed the room to the stairs before she could change her mind. "Just give me a few minutes to unpack. Then we can drive into the village to grab a bite to eat. I may have screwed up with my hotel arrangements, but I think I can redeem myself."

"Really?" She sounded distinctly skeptical. "How?"

He glanced back over his shoulder as he started up the stairs. "I've kept Larry busy for the past couple of days gathering background info on the other people involved in *Fast Company*."

"Who's Larry?"

"The computer whiz I told you about. He's also my half brother."

She looked surprised. "I didn't know you had a half brother."

"I've got two of them. It's sort of complicated." He reached the landing, turned right, and set the duffel on the bench at the foot of the bed. "Anyhow, I told Larry to concentrate on the money people, but I also had him give me anything else he could dig up on the writer, the actors, the director, and everyone else involved in the film."

"And?"

"And, not surprisingly, they're all scheduled to be here in Mirror Springs this week." He unzipped the duffel. "I figure we should be able to track down some of them. Maybe one of them can give us a lead on Page."

"The town is crammed with people. How are we going to find the people involved in *Fast Company*?"

He dropped a folded shirt on the bed, walked to the railing, and looked down at her. "Thought we'd start by attending a party scheduled for tomorrow night."

"A party?"

"The guy who's throwing it is the film's real moneyman. His name doesn't appear in the credits, but he's the one who structured the financing package for *Fast Company*. His name is Dawson Holland."

She was starting to look intrigued. "Interesting."

"There's more." He folded his arms on the railing. "Holland's wife is Victoria Bellamy."

Elizabeth frowned. "The star of the film?"

"Right. What do you want to bet she's the reason he backed the picture in the first place?"

"So that she could star in it?"

"Why not?" Jack straightened and went back to the duffel bag. "He wouldn't be the first man to finance a film in order to give the woman he loved a role in it."

"No, I guess not." Another pause. "How do you suggest we get into this party without an invitation?"

"Easy. If anyone questions us, we'll just tell them the truth."

"Which is?"

"We know the producer," Jack said. "Tyler Page."

*The interior of the Reflections café exuded a chic, contempo-*rary ambience in spite of its Victorian-era bones. Elizabeth glanced around as she took her seat. Like virtually everything else in Mirror Springs, the restaurant glowed with the expensive, golden aura associated with glossy travel-magazine ads.

A fire crackled on the huge hearth. The light gleamed on a lot of wooden surfaces and cast intimate shadows. The diners all looked as if they had just flown in from L.A. or New York. Pleated black trousers, slouchy linen jackets, and black shirts unbuttoned far enough to show off a lot of chest hair were prevalent. So were sleek little black dresses. Those who weren't wearing black were in denim.

This wasn't the Hollywood studio crowd, Elizabeth reminded herself. These were the independent and fringe filmmakers and their fans; people devoted to the kind of small, arty films that would never appear at the mall multiplexes. She knew enough about the independent film business to know that festivals such as the Neo Noir event here in Mirror Springs constituted the only venues for the vast majority of the small, low-budget pictures made by this group.

There was something oddly touching about the passion and enthusiasm she heard in the conversations taking place at nearby tables.

". . . incredible imagery in her stuff. She uses the language of film to create a completely separate reality . . ."

"Very Chandleresque, of course. Great visual style. No real narrative closure . . ."

". . . couldn't get away with letting the killer live in the old days. The Production Code was very strict. The murderer always had to die in the end . . ."

Elizabeth looked across the table at Jack. She had probably made a huge mistake when she had agreed to let him share the house with her. But what was she supposed to do, given the circumstances? She watched him wrap a strong, long-fingered hand around the glass of zinfandel that had just been placed in front of him. Machiavellian fingers, she reminded herself. She must not forget that.

He noticed her staring at his hands and cocked an inquisitive brow. "Something wrong?"

"No." She picked up her menu.

"You notice anything strange about this town?" he asked.

She tried a sip of her Chardonnay and then carefully set down the glass. "You mean like the fact that the sidewalks are spotless and there are no signs of any homeless people and every other business in town is either a cute restaurant or an art gallery?"

"Yeah. Like that."

She shrugged. "Best zoning ordinances money can buy, I imagine."

Jack nodded. He watched her for a moment over the rim of his glass. "So you want to talk about it?"

"The Mirror Springs zoning laws?"

"No." He paused very deliberately. "Us."

She felt as if all the air had just been sucked out of the room. A direct confrontation was the last thing she had expected. But then, this was Jack Fairfax. Expect the unexpected.

"No," she said very carefully.

He held her eyes. "We're going to have to work closely together for the next few days. Might help if we clear the air."

What was going on here? In her experience men generally avoided this kind of conversation. She took a couple of deep breaths and told herself to stay focused.

"What's to clear?" She was pleased with the way that came out. Casual. Cool. Uncaring. Downright heartless. "There's no reason to dig up the past. I prefer to let it stay buried."

She must have got the tone right, because Jack's eyes hardened. His voice, however, was steady. Relentless.

"Let's get one thing straight," he said coldly. "What happened at Galloway, Inc., was not personal. Morgan hired me to design the acquisition strategy, and that's what I did. I'm a consultant, Elizabeth. I do stuff like that all the time."

Just like that, all her good intentions went out the window. The outrage, anger, and raw hurt that she thought she had successfully suppressed suddenly threatened to erupt like lava through ice. She had to fight to keep her voice from shaking.

"No, you do not do stuff like that all the time, Jack. I did some checking after I found out who you really are."

"Who I really am?" He gave her a derisive look. "You make it sound like I've got a secret identity."

"As far as I'm concerned, that's what it amounted to. As I said, I did some research and I discovered that the Galloway deal was definitely not your usual kind of job. You went after that company like a shark. Don't you dare sit there and tell me it wasn't personal."

"It was business."

"You destroyed Galloway. A lot of people got hurt in that takeover, including the nice old lady who had given them all jobs in her firm."

"People lose jobs in a takeover," he said, still doggedly patient. "It's a fact of life. Look, I know that Camille Galloway was an old Aurora Fund client, and I know that your brother-in-law worked for her. I'm sorry about that. It was just one of those things."

"It wasn't just one of those things. Camille Galloway was more than just another client. She was an old and very good friend of the family. She used to feed me cookies and milk when I was a kid. She gave my brother-in-law, Merrick, a job when he needed one badly."

"You make her sound like Saint Camille."

"She was a very nice old lady who had worked hard all of her life to build something to leave to her only son, Garth. When you ripped her life's work to shreds, you tore the heart out of her. And I mean that almost literally. In case you don't know it, Camille died of a heart attack a few months after you savaged her company."

"I know." His voice was low and grim.

She clutched her glass very tightly. "What happened at Galloway was personal and it was damned scary."

"Scary? That does it." He leaned forward abruptly, folding his arms on the table. "You know what? You're right about what happened at Galloway. It was personal. I did go after the company."

"I knew it." But there was no satisfaction in the confirmation, she discovered. If anything, she only felt more glum.

"I went to Morgan, told him I could give him his competition on a silver platter, and he agreed to hire me to handle the takeover."

"Why? What did Camille Galloway ever do to you?"

"Listen up, Pollyanna. You think I'm a shark? Sweet, kindly Mrs. Galloway could have given me lessons."

"What are you talking about?"

"Five years ago she ripped off a nineteen-year-old kid who happened to have developed a brand-new and extremely clever software program. It was designed to make very sophisticated financial projections based on very limited data. Within one year of application, Galloway's profits nearly doubled. The kid never saw a penny more than the measly five thousand dollars Camille Galloway paid him for the software. I wanted her to pay for ripping off the kid, and I made sure she did. That's what the Galloway deal was all about."

Something in his tone gave her pause. Jack was dead serious. "Can you prove that she ripped off this kid?"

"Nope. The contract she got him to sign was one hundred percent legal. Couldn't take her to court. I approached her, asked her to set up a royalty or licensing agreement with the kid. She laughed in my face." Jack shrugged. "So I destroyed her company."

A chill went through her, all the way to her toes. "Where did you get your facts? How do you happen to know this so-called kid you say Galloway cheated, and why do you care that he got ripped off in the first place?"

"The kid was my half brother Larry."

She absorbed that in stunned silence while she searched his eyes for the truth. After a while, she slumped back in her chair. "Your brother."

"Yeah."

"The one you told me about? The one who pulled up the information on Dawson Holland and the other people involved in *Fast Company!*"

"Uh-huh."

She stared at him. "You brought down an entire company for the sake of revenge?"

"I prefer to think of it as justice."

"I'll bet you do. Sounds a heck of a lot more civilized, doesn't it?"

"Part of my deal with Morgan was a licensing contract with Larry on the software. He now gets royalties."

"I see." She took a fortifying sip of wine. "It was a family thing."

Jack looked slightly taken aback. Then he frowned. "I guess you could say that."

"And it *was* personal."

"Yes, it was personal."

She remembered what he had said about going after Tyler Page, even if it turned out to be too late to retrieve Soft Focus. "Words like *revenge* and *reputation* figure rather strongly in your vocabulary, don't they?"

He said nothing; just looked at her.

She sat forward again. "You knew who I was when you came to me for the funding for Excalibur, didn't you?"

"Of course I knew who you were. You were the head of the Aurora Fund."

"Don't try to slide around this. I meant that you knew the Fund had connections to Camille Galloway and that I was highly unlikely to provide financial backing to the . . . the . . ." Unable to summon a suitable epithet, she waved a hand.

"Egg-sucking SOB?" Jack supplied helpfully.

"To the *person* who had destroyed my former client and family friend."

He drummed his fingers on the table once and then exhaled slowly. "I make it a point to research the people I do business with. I knew that Galloway had once been one of your Fund's clients. I knew there was a personal as well as a professional relationship between your aunt and Camille Galloway. I didn't know your brother-in-law worked there, though. Does that count?"

"Don't you dare try to make a joke out of this. The point is that you knew all about the Fund's connection to Galloway but you never bothered to bring up the subject, did you?"

"It had no bearing on our deal," he said quietly.

"You can tell yourself that, if it makes you feel any better. But don't waste your time trying to convince me. The truth is, you didn't tell me who you were because you knew that if I found out that you were the consultant who engineered the takeover of Galloway, I would never have agreed to sign a contract with you. Admit it."

"Like I said, what happened at Galloway had nothing to do with us."

"How would you have felt if you had been in my shoes and discovered that I had omitted a few piddling little details concerning the destruction of one of your former clients?"

"Elizabeth—"

"Don't bother. We both know the answer." She smiled grimly. "You know something, Jack? Maybe I could be convinced that you felt you had a right to even the score with Galloway because of what happened to your brother. I've got family, too. I understand how your sense of loyalty to Larry could make you do something that dramatic. And I accept the fact that you didn't know that your actions cost my brother-in-law another job—"

"Another job?"

"Never mind. The point is, maybe I could have been talked into making some allowance for the fact that you were bent on avenging your brother, although I could never approve of the way you went about it."

He raised his eyebrows in mockingly polite encouragement. "But?"

She hated it when he gave her that superior, all-knowing look. "But you can't expect me to ignore the fact that you didn't tell me that you were the man behind the Galloway takeover before you asked me to back your plans at Excalibur."

"You mean before we went to bed together, don't you?" He looked at her. "That's what you can't get past. The fact that we had sex before you found out I was behind the Galloway deal."

She lifted her chin. "That was a factor, yes."

He contemplated her in silence for a while.

"Know what I think?" he finally asked.

"What?"

"I don't think this is just about me. I think you're equally pissed at yourself. Maybe even more than you are at me."

"What on earth are you talking about?"

"You're mad at yourself because you think you got suckered. You think I used sex to get what I wanted from you, and you blame yourself because you think you fell for a line." He turned one hand, palm up. "You feel like a fool. So naturally, you blame me. Simple psychology."

She stared at him in openmouthed amazement. "When did you take up the study of psychology?"

"I've had a lot of time to think about what went wrong between us. Six whole months, to be exact."

She felt as if she'd just been blindsided. "I'm surprised you bothered to try to analyze our relationship."

"We didn't have a relationship. We had a very short-lived affair."

"A one-night stand."

"Could have been an affair," he said. "You're the one who ended it after one night."

"Because I found out who you were. Lord only knows how long things would have gone on if Hayden Shaw hadn't told me—" She broke off abruptly, but it was too late. The damage was done.

"Figures." Jack just nodded once, as if she had confirmed something he'd already concluded. "I've been meaning to ask you who told you that I was the consultant behind the Galloway deal. Had to be Hayden."

"Don't blame the messenger."

"I'll blame whoever I damn well want to blame." He turned his attention to the menu. "Let's order and then let's change the subject. This has turned out to be one of those conversations I wish I'd never started."

She picked up her menu and opened it with a snap. "Nothing like clearing the air to improve interpersonal communications."

"Yeah, that's what I always say, too." He looked at her over the top of the menu. "Just one more thing before we put this topic to bed. So to speak."

She eyed him warily. "What now?"

"I would like to state for the record that I do not now, nor have I ever, sucked an egg."

Chapter Nine

"Wow. Victoria Bellamy looks exactly like she does on that poster of *Fast Company."* Elizabeth sounded awed.

Jack was surprised. The thought of Elizabeth being starstruck was almost funny. He followed her gaze across the room and spotted Victoria.

The blonde moved between clusters of guests with the languid elegance of a mermaid gliding among small schools of dull, ordinary fish. It was eleven o'clock and the large house was thronged, but it was easy to keep track of Victoria in the crowd. For one thing, she was one of the few who weren't wearing black. She was dressed in a pale, ice-blue, liquid satin dress with a low, draped neckline that could have come straight out of a late-1940s couturier's salon. Her platinum hair fell in a series of waves that framed her fine-boned features. Her mouth was full and heavy with lipstick. Her lashes were weighted down with mascara. Diamonds glittered in her ears and around her throat.

"So she looks like she does on the poster." He paused, taking a closer look. "Except that I don't think she's wearing a gun tonight. What did you expect?"

He took stock of the crowd as he spoke. The glass-walled room in which they stood was crammed with people. It looked like everyone who was anyone at the film festival was here tonight. Dawson Holland obviously was a player in this backwater niche of the film industry.

The decor was simple. It consisted largely of huge movie posters—most of which were black-and-white scenes from *Fast Company*—hung from the ceiling. The majority of the strikingly lit shots featured Victoria Bellamy. There was a lot of cute, clever-looking food around, and a bar had been set up near the entrance to the deck. When he had picked up the drinks earlier, Jack had noticed that the labels being poured were all first class.

"I don't know." Elizabeth paused, frowning slightly, as though trying to sort out her thoughts. "I guess I wasn't expecting her to be quite so beauti-ful or so glamorous in person. This isn't Hollywood, after all. But she looks like she really could be a star."

"The fact that she looks like a star doesn't mean that she can act."

"That's true," Elizabeth admitted.

Jack leaned a little closer to her under the pretext of reaching for a handful of nuts. He was very conscious of her standing next to him. He caught the faint whiff of a spice-and-flower-scented perfume and felt his in-sides tighten.

When she had come downstairs earlier dressed in a sexy little slip of a dress, her hair caught up in an elegant twist, he had wanted to break some-thing, anything to relieve the frustration. Sharing the house with her for a week was going to be hard. Maybe the hardest thing he'd ever done. *Stay fo-cused,* he thought. *Get the job done.*

"Look at the way heads turn when she walks through the room," Eliza-beth said.

Jack glanced back at Victoria, who had stopped to talk to a thin, intense young man with short, curly hair and horn-rimmed glasses. "She's beautiful. Beautiful people get looked at. Fact of life."

"You don't appear to be as impressed as most of the other men in this room," Elizabeth mused.

"I'm impressed." He munched nuts. "But I'm not interested."

"There's a difference?"

"Big difference."

Elizabeth eyed him thoughtfully. "Explain."

He stopped chewing nuts while he grappled with that.

"I don't know if I can," he said eventually. "All I can tell you is that she looks great but she also looks like she knows she looks great. Whatever she's got doesn't translate into sexy. Not for me, at any rate."

"Hmm."

He groped for another way to explain. "She looks cold. Like she's got ice water in—" He stopped in midsentence.

Elizabeth's smile could have frozen a tropical sea. "You were saying something about Victoria Bellamy looking cold, I believe. Would you care to elaborate on that point?"

"Don't think so." He seized another handful of nuts.

"Would you describe her as an ice princess, the way you did me?" Eliza-beth assumed an expression of gentle concentration, as if trying to clarify a point. "Or would that be overstating the case? After all, you don't really know the woman that well. It might be too soon to categorize her as an ice princess."

"Damn." Why did this kind of thing always happen to him whenever he tried to conduct a civilized conversation with her? he wondered glumly.

"Tell me, Jack, do you think the problem is that there really are a lot of ice princesses in the world? Or is it just something about you that affects women that way?"

"We're here for a reason," he said very evenly. "Maybe we better get to work."

"You're changing the subject."

"Damn right." He took her arm and steered her toward another buffet table. "We'll work the room the same way we did at that charity function the other night."

"It would be too much to expect Page to show up here at the party, wouldn't it?"

"Given my luck lately, yes. But it's not beyond the realm of possibility. From what I can tell, Page loved the idea of being in the film business and everything that went with it. Being here tonight might be important to him."

"If you spot him, you might want to make sure I don't strangle him," Elizabeth said.

The writer said his name was Spencer West, and Elizabeth could tell immediately that he'd had one too many tequila sunrises.

"High concept," he announced, slurring the second *c* in concept. "That's what it's all about. You gotta have high concept or you're dead in Hollywood."

"I see." Elizabeth did her best to infuse acute interest and admiration into her voice.

Spencer was very slender and painfully intense. He had curly hair, and he wore horn-rimmed glasses. His unconstructed linen jacket hung from his thin, slightly hunched shoulders. He seemed nice enough, she thought. But after an hour of trying to cultivate conversations of this nature with people who were total strangers, her patience was starting to shred.

"You gotta be able to state the whole concept in a single sentence." Spencer gulped more of his tequila sunrise. "One goddamned lousy little sentence."

"Sort of like an advertising slogan."

"Exactly." He looked morosely pleased at her perception.

"Must be tough."

"Hollywood scriptwriting is for morons who don't have any vision and who don't care that everything they do is going to get turned over to some committee to rewrite. I've got vision. That's why I do independent stuff."

"What was your vision for *Fast Company*?"

Spencer paused for dramatic effect. " 'Once you start running in fast company, you can't stop.' It became the tag line for the film."

Elizabeth nodded. "An unhappy ending, I take it?"

Spencer frowned. "A *realistic* ending."

"Right. Realistic. There must be a lot of pressure on a scriptwriter like yourself."

"Awesome pressure."

"I imagine everyone involved with a film has an idea or two he or she wants to contribute," Elizabeth said delicately.

Spencer snorted in disgust. "More than an idea or two. You wouldn't believe what I went through with the script for *Fast Company*. Everyone tried to get into the act. Shit, I had to completely rewrite the female lead for Vicky."

"Vicky?"

Spencer gave her a quizzical scowl. "Vicky Bellamy. Dawson's wife."

"Oh, sure. Vicky." Elizabeth smiled brightly. "Why did you have to rewrite the part?"

Spencer gave her a look that told her she had just asked either an incredibly stupid or an astonishingly naive question.

"I had to rewrite it because her husband is Dawson Holland," he said with extravagant patience. "Holland held the purse strings on *Fast Company*. He put together the finance package that bankrolled the film just so his wife could star in it. Naturally, he got whatever he wanted. Or, in this case, whatever Vicky wanted."

"I see." Elizabeth smiled weakly. "Actually, the only reason I'm here tonight is because I'm a friend of one of the investors."

Spencer contrived to look both cynical and knowing. "The money guys."

"Yes." Elizabeth searched for an opening. "Did any of them try to influence the script the way Vicky and Holland did?"

Spencer made a face. "Some of 'em hung out on the set a lot. Made nuisances of themselves. One tried to put his two cents in a couple of times, but I ignored him. I mean, what does a guy like that know? He was just some little nerd from Seattle who wanted to pretend he was a player."

Elizabeth choked on a swallow of her mineral water. She sputtered wildly. "From Seattle, you say?"

Spencer took another swallow of his tequila sunrise. "Guy named Page. Tyler Page."

"Oh, yes, the producer."

Spencer rolled his eyes. "Page got the credit, but Dawson Holland was the one who put the deal together. Takes a lot of cash to make a film, you know, even a small one. There are usually several investors."

"But Page got sole credit on *Fast Company*. I wonder why."

Spencer looked bored. "Probably put up the biggest chunk of cash. Or maybe he did a deal with Holland. Who knows? Some of those investors will do anything to get their name in the credits."

Without warning, Victoria Bellamy swam out of a nearby shoal of guests. "Spencer."

Her voice was as glamorous as the rest of her, Elizabeth thought. Husky, low, throaty. Lauren Bacall in *The Big Sleep*. She watched Victoria exchange air kisses with Spencer.

"Nice party, Vicky," Spencer said.

"So glad you could make it." Victoria turned to Elizabeth with an inquiring look. "Introduce me to your friend."

Spencer's eyes glazed for the moment. It had probably just occurred to him that he didn't know her name, Elizabeth thought. She smiled at Victoria and extended her hand.

"I'm Elizabeth. A business associate of one of the money people. I hope you don't mind, Ms. Bellamy."

"Please, call me Vicky. Everyone else does." Vicky's laugh was low and rich. "Of course I don't mind. I just love money people. And their business associates. Are you here for the entire festival?"

"Yes. I'm very excited about the whole event." Vicky didn't seem to care that she hadn't gotten a last name to go with the first name. Elizabeth recalled the book she had scanned on the plane from Seattle. "Noir is such a fascinating genre. The way light and shadow is used as a visual metaphor is so distinctive. And the classic films did such an incredible job of catching the essence of modern moral ambiguity. And the use of the dark urban landscape—" She broke off. "Well, it's *the* quintessentially American style, isn't it?"

Vicky smiled. "Don't forget the Western."

"You're absolutely right. Westerns and noir film are both uniquely American."

"Amazing," Vicky mused.

Elizabeth wondered if she'd overdone it. "What's amazing?"

"Most money people don't talk about film like that."

"I'm just a friend of one of the investors," Elizabeth said smoothly. "I'm attending the festival because I'm a film buff."

"Who's your friend? The one you said was an investor?" Vicky asked.

Elizabeth took a breath. "Tyler Page. You probably met him in the course of making *Fast Company*."

"Yes, of course I met Tyler." Vicky smiled. "He was a rather sweet little man. He liked to hang around the set whenever possible. I think he had stars in his eyes. Didn't he, Spencer?"

Spencer gave an elaborate shrug. "All the money guys have stars in their eyes."

Vicky gave a husky laugh. "Given the fact that most of them will never see a dime in profits, I think it's only fair to allow them a few dreams. Don't you agree, Elizabeth?"

"Dreams are important," Elizabeth said. "Sometimes that's all you get."

Vicky smiled. "That sounds like a line from one of Spencer's scripts. Maybe you'd like to read the script for *Fast Company*."

"I'd love to read it," Elizabeth said quickly.

"I'm sure Spencer could get you a copy." Vicky looked at him expectantly.

Spencer looked up from his tequila sunrise. "What? Oh, sure. Copy of the script. Got one with me. I'll get it for you before you leave, Elizabeth."

"Thanks," Elizabeth said. "I'd appreciate that."

Spencer rocked precariously on his heels and looked at Vicky. "How's it going on the stalker front? I heard about the incident at the spa the other day."

Vicky grimaced. "I wound up with a lot of red paint on my clothes, as usual. It's the third time the bastard has struck in the past month. I think Dawson is getting worried."

Elizabeth stared at her. "You're being *stalked*?"

"Some idiot has decided that I'm the incarnation of a biblical harlot. He started stalking me about a month ago." Vicky made a circular motion with her finger near her ear. "A real loony."

"Good grief," Elizabeth whispered. "I can't imagine anything more terrifying than being stalked."

Vicky's jaw tightened. "It is a little scary, I admit. Dawson is more concerned than I am."

"What are the police doing about it?" Elizabeth demanded.

"There's not much they can do. The police chief here in town is a man named Gresham. He's very nice and very earnest, but the fact is, he's got a very small force and it's not exactly high-tech or state of the art. This week it's probably overwhelmed with the crowd that's in town for the festival."

"Maybe Dawson should hire a bodyguard for you," Spencer suggested with an odd look. "He can afford one."

"He's mentioned it," Vicky said vaguely. "But I've asked him to hold off for a while. I really hate the thought of having to have a bodyguard. I'm hoping the police will catch him before we have to go that route."

"Good luck," Spencer mumbled into his drink.

"Thanks." Vicky stepped back. "Well, if you'll excuse me, I'd better keep circulating. Enjoy yourselves."

Spencer watched her disappear into the crowd. Elizabeth noticed that several other men and one or two women did the same. She thought about what Jack had said earlier and decided to run Spencer through a test.

"She's really beautiful, isn't she?" Elizabeth asked casually.

"Yeah," Spencer replied. "The amazing thing is that she's not a half-bad actress. Not Hollywood material, but not bad."

"I feel sorry for her. That stalker stuff must be very frightening."

Spencer gave a short bark that was probably meant to be a laugh. "I wouldn't worry too much about Vicky and her stalker if I were you."

"What do you mean?"

"Five will get you ten that it's all a publicity stunt. Probably dreamed up by Vicky herself."

Elizabeth felt her jaw drop. "Are you serious?"

"Sure." Spencer seemed amused by her reaction. "Hey, this may not be Hollywood, but this is still the movie business, lady. For someone like Vicky Bellamy, publicity is interchangeable with blood in her veins."

"That sounds a little cold."

"You kidding?" Spencer drained his glass. "I'll bet Vicky has to drink antifreeze in her orange juice every morning to keep herself from freezing solid."

*"The thing about noir is that it all hinges on vision and light-*ing," Bernard Aston declared. "You gotta have vision and lighting."

"And money," Jack said.

He glanced around the room, searching for Elizabeth. He hoped she was having better luck than he was. Thus far he had talked to a lighting technician, a member of the camera crew, and two people who claimed to have had walk-ons in *Fast Company*. None of them seemed to know or care about Tyler Page. He had finally managed to track down the director, but Aston wasn't proving any more helpful than the others.

Bernard was short and heavy, and he had left his designer denim shirt unbuttoned a little too far down his chest. The silver ankh dangling in the sparse gray hair that covered his midsection and the straggly ponytail did nothing to enhance the image Jack suspected he was trying to project.

"Lining up the money is the producer's problem. As the director, I gotta stay focused on vision and lighting," Bernard explained.

"Sure. But with Dawson Holland handling the financing, you had the luxury of staying focused, didn't you?"

"Shit. Holland was a pain in the ass right from the start. He made it clear that the main condition for financing *Fast Company* was the female lead for Vicky. It wasn't easy making her look good, I can tell you that. Woman can't act her way out of a paper bag."

Jack glanced up at one of the huge posters that dangled from the high ceiling. "She looks pretty good in that shot."

"Vision and lighting." Aston removed the olive from his martini and popped it into his mouth. "Vicky was a pain in the ass, too. Never made it in Hollywood, you know."

Jack suspected that Vicky was not the only one present tonight who had failed to make it in Hollywood.

He was formulating a question that would lead to the subject of Tyler Page, when Aston glanced past him and raised his martini in a careless salute.

"Nice party, Holland," Aston said.

"Don't thank me, thank Vicky. She handles things like this. Glad you could make it, Aston."

Jack turned very casually at the sound of the dry, cultured voice. He took in Dawson Holland with a quick glance, measuring him against the information Larry had supplied.

At fifty-seven he was more than twenty years older than his wife, but if Larry hadn't supplied the age factor, it would have been tough to guess. He had refined, ascetic features and a judicious amount of silver in his hair. "Distinguished looking" was the phrase that most people would probably come up with to describe him, Jack thought. Holland moved with the athletic ease of a man who took care of his body. He was wearing a black silk shirt and black trousers, but he somehow managed to carry off the look without appearing too painfully L.A.

He looked at Jack and smiled slightly. His gray eyes were politely quizzical. "Don't believe we've met."

"Jack Fairfax." Jack held out his hand. "And no, you didn't invite me. My date and I crashed your party. Our only excuse is that we know the producer. Or at least, the guy who got the credit in the film. Tyler Page."

"No problem, Jack." Holland's handshake was as solid as a banker's. "Business associates of people who pour money into films are always welcome here. Are you interested in getting into the game yourself?"

"I don't know." Jack glanced meaningfully at the posters. "Looks expensive. And I hear the independent film business is a real crapshoot from a financial point of view."

"Tell me about it." Dawson's chuckle was easy, unforced. "But there's nothing quite like the final product, eh, Aston?"

"No." Aston's eyes gleamed briefly. "Nothing else in the whole damn world like making pictures."

"Are you and your friend here for the festival, Jack?" Dawson asked.

"My friend likes old movies." Jack shrugged. "So we're here for the whole week."

"Your friend has good taste." Dawson winked. "Besides, it usually pays to please the ladies."

Jack glanced across the room and saw Elizabeth. She was chatting earnestly with a young man in glasses.

"Some ladies are a lot harder to please than others," he said.

Chapter Ten

Dawson lounged back against the pillows and watched Vicky come out of the turquoise and white tiled bath. She wore the robe she had brought back with her from Paris last month. It was made of heavy maroon silk decorated with elaborately stitched flowers. Her hair was piled on top of her head.

She had removed her makeup. Even without it she was still stunning. His two previous wives had both been beautiful, but neither of them could hold a candle to Vicky.

He felt the familiar heaviness between his legs. He knew that a lot of men never got past Vicky's beauty. The fools never noticed the razor-sharp brain. But he had noticed. That was why she was with him instead of some other man. Vicky traded on her beauty, but she had only disdain for men who could not see beyond it or who did not care what lay beneath the surface.

He thought fleetingly about the redhead in L.A. last month. He could not recall her name, just the nice tits. *Not nearly as nice as Vicky's.* He gave a small inward sigh and wondered again why he bothered with the one-night stands. None of the other women he had been with during the past two years since his marriage to Vicky meant anything to him. They were nameless and faceless. When he came with one of them, he usually fantasized that he was with Vicky.

Why the hell did he waste his time with the others when he had a woman like this in his bed? he wondered. It was a question that had begun to bother him more and more frequently during the past few months. Maybe he should see a shrink, he thought.

He watched Vicky sit down on the white velvet chair in front of the dressing table and cross her long legs. One high-heeled slipper dangled.

"I thought it went well tonight," he said. "You were spectacular, as always."

"Thank you." She swung one ankle absently and met his eyes in the mirror. "We may have a problem with the stalker thing, though."

"Why do you say that?"

"I think people are starting to conclude that it's just a publicity stunt. Spencer West mentioned it. I could tell that he had his doubts, and I'm pretty sure he's not the only one. Maybe it's time to end it."

"Let's let it run through the festival. The local paper gave you several column inches after the last incident. So what if a few people suspect it's a stunt? No big deal. We'll get our money's worth out of it."

She smiled. "You mean *your* money's worth."

"My pleasure, I assure you. If it helps to advance your career, I consider it a worthwhile investment."

Vicky's smile faded. She regarded him with a somber, considering look. "You're very good to me, Dawson."

"I enjoy being good to you, my dear."

She uncrossed her legs, stood, and unbelted the silk robe. She wore nothing underneath.

Dawson felt himself grow rock hard. "Damn, but you're beautiful."

She smiled again, turned out the light, and came to him in the darkness. When she took him into her mouth he felt as though he had been swept up and roiled in a tidal wave. With the others he had to do all the work. But Vicky made love to him with the skill of a trained courtesan. All he had to do was lie back and give himself over to the thrill of the experience.

His questions about the fling with the redhead in L.A. evaporated. Vicky would never know about the others, he promised himself as she flowed across his body. He was always very careful.

He liked to think that he practiced discretion out of consideration for her. She was his wife, after all. She deserved at least that.

Just before the powerful orgasm seized him and shook him until he was limp, he thought about the way Jack Fairfax had studied one of the posters featuring Vicky in *Fast Company*. There had been a calculating look in his eyes. Probably imagining what it would be like to have Vicky in his bed.

Fairfax would never know the answer to that question, Dawson thought, because, unlike his first two wives, Vicky did not cheat.

Her priorities in life had been obvious from the outset: She craved the financial security his money provided, and she wanted to star in films. Although she could act her way through an orgasm as well as any woman he had ever known, he was almost certain that she had no great personal interest in sex. It was simply the commodity she offered in exchange for what he could give her.

She was expensive, but she was worth it. He'd had a lot of women in his bed, but never one like Vicky.

Later, just before he collapsed, exhausted, from the sex, he wondered again why he bothered with the others.

Chapter Eleven

Jack settled deeper into the simmering waters of the hot tub. The steam that rose from the surface was invisible in the darkness, but he could feel the cloud of warmth that enveloped the pool.

He had not turned on any lights when he had come downstairs a few minutes ago. He had left the underwater lamps inside the tub off, too. The only illumination on the deck came from the cold glow of the moon and the stars.

He stretched his arms out along the edge of the tub on either side and leaned back to contemplate the late-night sky. It was after two in the morning. He and Elizabeth had returned to the house shortly before one.

As far as he could tell, she had gone straight to sleep, which, for some obscure reason, irritated him. How could she drop off so easily while he lay there staring through the glass at the night-shrouded mountain? The answer was all too obvious. The fact that he was in a bed a short distance away from her didn't affect her one damn bit.

He had eventually concluded that he might be able to think more clearly out here in the hot tub. He got some of his best ideas in the middle of the night, he reflected. But there was some risk involved, because he had also been known to come up with some of his dumbest ideas at night. Take the decision to start an affair with Elizabeth before he told her that he had been the man behind the Galloway takeover. Six months ago, that brilliant idea had come to him shortly after three in the morning.

He listened to the muted hum of the hot-tub motor and the soft bubbling of the churning water. The only other sound was the faint sighing of nearby tree branches.

It occurred to him that for most of his adult life he had taken for granted his ability to focus on a specific goal. His father, Sawyer Fairfax, had once told him it was a gift, like being able to write music or paint pictures. It was like anything else, Sawyer had told him. Use it or lose it. Jack had used it.

His big mistake six months ago, he decided, had been trying to concentrate on two goals simultaneously: Elizabeth and Excalibur.

He had lost the first and was precariously close to losing the second.

He heard the sliding glass door open behind him.

"Jack?" Elizabeth's voice was sharp with curiosity. "What in the world are you doing out here?"

"Thinking."

"Oh." There was a short pause. "Give me a minute. I'll join you."

"I'm not sure that would be a good idea," he said softly. Much too softly for her to hear.

She vanished back inside the house. A light came on upstairs. A short time later she reappeared. Jack watched her walk toward him through the shadows. She was enveloped in a fluffy white toweling robe.

A surge of heat went through him as she undid the sash of the robe. She should have turned off the light before coming back down here, he thought. There was just enough glow spilling from the upstairs windows to enable him to see her.

If she expected him to simply ignore her while she climbed into a hot tub with him, she could damn well think again.

She slipped out of the robe, revealing the one-piece bathing suit she wore. So much for his fantasy of getting naked with her in a hot tub.

She frowned at him as she climbed cautiously into the tub. "Care to share the joke?"

"No."

"Why not?"

"Because it's on me."

She gave him another quick, unreadable look and then settled down on one of the benches. In the shadows he could see the water frothing around the gentle swell of her breasts, but everything beneath the surface was concealed. He would have to use his imagination, he decided. Then again, maybe that wasn't such a terrific idea, either.

"Couldn't sleep after all?" he asked.

"I did for a while. But I woke up a few minutes ago and started thinking." She tilted her head back against the edge of the tub. "We didn't make much progress tonight, did we?"

"I wouldn't say that. We identified a lot of the people who knew Tyler Page on the set of *Fast Company*. One of them might be able to give us some idea of where he is now."

"Mirror Springs is filled with people. If he's staying somewhere in town, he must have made his reservations weeks ago. Maybe we should—"

"Forget it. I had Larry check out that angle first. There's no record of a Tyler Page registered at any hotel, motel, or bed-and-breakfast in town or anywhere nearby. If he's here, he's hiding under another name. And according to Larry, he's still not using his credit cards."

Elizabeth pondered that for a moment. "If he made reservations several weeks back under an assumed name and booked them without using a credit card or check, he must have planned to steal the specimen some time ago. This wasn't a spur-of-the-moment thing."

"Nope. Looks like the little SOB planned it for quite a while."

"All this crafty, detail-oriented plotting doesn't quite fit with what you've told me about his personality. You said he was absentminded and something of a slob. Except when it came to his work."

"Maybe he considered the theft part of his research and development of the crystal," Jack said. "Gave the project the same kind of attention he gave his work."

"Or maybe he had a little help," Elizabeth suggested quietly.

Jack groaned and settled deeper into the tub. "I've been trying not to think about that possibility. If there's more than one person involved in this thing, it's going to get much more complicated."

"But it is a possibility."

"Yeah, it's a possibility. But on the positive side, there's no one else mysteriously missing from the lab where Tyler Page worked. He seems to have had no close friends or relatives."

"What about a lover?"

Jack grunted. "Everyone who knew him at Excalibur says he didn't have a love life. Didn't seem to be interested in women."

"Men?"

Jack shook his head. "Or men, either. All he cared about was Soft Focus and making movies."

She closed her eyes. "We might not find him, Jack."

He flexed his fingers around the edge of the tub. "We'll find him. He'll turn up here at the festival. He won't be able to resist."

"You're very sure of that, aren't you?"

"Like I said, when you know a man's greatest passion, you know his greatest weakness. *Fast Company* is Page's passion. Sooner or later, he'll turn up. I still think he'll try to sell the crystal back to me."

"What makes you so sure?"

"There's nothing else he can do with it except sell it. I'm his best potential buyer."

She opened her eyes and looked at him. "A couple of days ago you made some comment about not letting Tyler Page ruin your professional reputation. But what will you really do if we don't get the specimen back in time for the Veltran presentation?"

"I'm committed to saving Excalibur," he said evenly.

"And your reputation."

"And my reputation," he agreed.

"You picked a hard one this time, Jack. But most of them have been hard, haven't they?"

He glanced at her. "What are we talking about now?"

"The kind of work you do. I did some checking during the past six months. Excalibur isn't the first small, family-held company you've tried to save. Why?"

What was this all about? he wondered. Why was she getting so intense? "Turning around companies like Excalibur is what I do."

"Maybe, but I would have figured that you were too smart to waste your time with a company facing the kind of odds Excalibur is facing."

"I like the odds."

"Even if you get Soft Focus back, you can't be sure the firm will have the resources to take it to market."

"If we get it back, I can get it to market."

"Why don't you cut your losses and go find another client?"

He looked at her across the foaming water. "I don't walk away from a client after I sign the contract."

"That brings up another question. I made some calls. Asked some people I know about some of your past contracts. I noticed a pattern."

"What the hell is this? Have you spent the past six months setting up a file on me?"

"I didn't spend the *entire* time setting up the file," she said. "Just some of the time."

He was dumbfounded. She'd made a file? On him? He didn't know whether to be angry or wary or flattered.

"Well, hell," he finally said neutrally.

"I noticed that you almost always sign on with small, struggling, closely held or family-held companies. The contract you signed with Morgan to strategize the Galloway takeover was an exception to your usual pattern."

He looked up at the stars. "I needed a company the size of Morgan to make it happen. A small operation wouldn't have had the resources or the incentive to do the job."

She smiled thinly. "And you were bound and determined to have your revenge on Galloway, weren't you?"

He said nothing.

"Tell me," she said, "why do you only work for small, privately held firms? I would think that, generally speaking, the larger the company, the bigger the payoff for a turnaround consultant. Everyone knows about those golden parachutes executives in your position usually get when they take the helm of a major firm. Even if the companies go under, they routinely walk away with huge bonuses in addition to their salaries. But you don't sign contracts like those."

"You know that for a fact, huh?"

"Your business life history is in my file."

"Huh." A file. On him.

"Care to explain?" she prodded.

He chose his words with caution. "I like working with the small family-helds. I have greater control. More opportunity to affect the outcome. And there are no stockholders to appease."

She gave him a look of mingled amusement and disbelief. "You're telling me that you actually prefer dealing with squabbling family members like the ones on the Excalibur board?"

Her wry tone made him grin briefly. "I'll admit that handling the Ingersolls, especially Angela, is a challenge. Want to know a deep, dark secret?"

"What's that?"

"There have been times during the past six months when I've been damned glad you forced me to give you a seat on the board."

She gave him a knowing look. "You've used me to back you up, haven't you?"

"Yeah."

"Nice to know I haven't been a complete and unmitigated thorn in your side."

"I didn't say you weren't a thorn in my side, just that you've been a useful thorn."

She studied him for a while. "So it's the challenge and the sense of control?"

"Now what are you talking about?"

"The reasons why you almost always work for the little firms. You like the challenge and the control you have in those kinds of turnaround situations."

"Like I said, it's what I do."

"How very macho." Her mouth curved slightly. "The modern equivalent of the hired gun back in the days of the Wild West. Loyal to your employer come hell or high water. When the job is done, you ride off into the sunset."

He did not respond.

"I think there's more to it than that, Jack," she said very softly.

"Mind telling me why we're having this conversation?"

"Probably because it's after two o'clock in the morning." She paused. "Maybe I shouldn't have come out here."

"Maybe not."

She stood up abruptly in the churning water. The wet bathing suit clung, sleek and snug, to her slender waist and full hips. "This discussion appears to be deteriorating. I think I'll go back to bed."

He watched her climb out of the hot tub. "You really have a file on me?"

"A nice thick one." She pulled on her robe. "I just hope for both our sakes that you're as good as your track record says you are."

She turned and walked toward the darkened doorway.

"Yeah, me too." He stood up, strode through the frothing water to the tub steps, and climbed out.

"For heaven's sake, Jack."

He paused in the act of wrapping the towel around his waist and glanced toward the doorway. "Now what?"

She stared at him for a few seconds. Then she looked quickly away.

"Nothing." Her voice sounded oddly muffled.

"What the hell is wrong?"

"I didn't realize—" She had her back to him. "I mean, just assumed that you were wearing a bathing suit, too."

"Why would I wear a suit? Hell, I didn't even bring one with me."

"You should have said something," she shot back on a rising note.

"Yeah, well, just make a note and put it in my file. 'Doesn't wear swim trunks in hot tubs.' "

He went to the control panel and flipped off the hot-tub switch. *Give her plenty of time to run,* he told himself.

But when he turned around he saw that she was still standing in the darkened doorway. She was facing him again, her arms crossed very tightly beneath her breasts. She watched him with brooding, unreadable eyes.

"Sorry," she said very stiffly. "I overreacted."

"Don't worry about it." He shoved his hand through his steam-dampened hair as he walked toward her, scattering a few stray drops. "We're both under a lot of pressure here."

"Yes." She frowned, as if that were a particularly new and worrisome concept, one she had not considered until now. "That's true, isn't it. We'll each have to make allowances."

"You make allowances. I'm going to bed." He started past her through the doorway.

"Jack?"

He stopped and turned to look at her. She was so close that he could have touched her. So close that he could take her into his arms. Close enough to allow him to see the haunted look in her eyes.

"What is it?" he asked softly. "Worried about how we're going to get through the week together?"

"No."

"Well, three cheers for you." He moved closer and planted one hand on the sliding glass door frame above her head. "I'm sure as hell worried about it."

"Why?" She lifted her chin, but she did not try to duck away beneath his arm. "Because you're afraid I'll freak out every time I see you sitting in the hot tub?"

"No." He leaned closer. "Because every time I see you, I want to pick up where we left off six months ago."

"Why would you want to do that? You called me the Ice Princess, remember?"

"I was pissed off at the time."

"And now you're no longer pissed off?"

"I'm still pissed," he said, thinking about it. "But that doesn't mean I don't want to pick up where we left off six months ago."

Her lashes veiled her eyes. "That would be very stupid."

"Very." He kept one hand braced against the frame and used the other one to cradle her stubborn chin. "But I've been known to do stupid things."

"Probably not this stupid."

"Don't bet on it."

"Things could never be the same," she said very distinctly. "Not now."

Images of their one night together flashed through him. He remembered his own driving urgency. He had been blind-sided by his reaction to her that night. Accustomed to making love the same way he did business, with absolute control and attention to detail, he knew that he had screwed up badly. He had been utterly oblivious of the small, telltale signs that should have warned him that he was moving too quickly. Hell, if he was honest with himself, he had to admit that even if he had been aware of them, he probably could not have slowed down much. Not that first time. But he knew her failure to find satisfaction in his arms had cost him dearly. The morning after, she had learned that he was the man behind the Galloway deal. There had been no second chances in bed.

"The last thing I want," he said in a very low voice, "is for things to be the same as they were that first time between us."

"Jack—"

"You have my personal guarantee that next time things will be very, very different."

She cleared her throat. "You're missing the point here."

"Don't think so." He lowered his mouth until it was only an inch or so above hers. "I notice that you're not running, screaming, into the night."

"Should I?" she said in a hushed voice.

"Let's find out."

He covered her mouth with his own.

And the rush hit him. Just as hard and fast as it had six months ago. But he was ready for it this time; braced to withstand the high winds at the heart of the tornado. This time he would get it right. This time he would stay in control.

He held himself in check, drawing out the kiss, searching for the response he wanted. She did not pull away. But neither did she throw her arms around his neck. He leaned in closer. He could feel the firm curves of her small breasts beneath the robe. She was still a little damp from the hot tub.

Her hands went to his shoulders. She parted her lips slightly.

He suddenly got the nasty feeling that she was testing him and maybe herself as well. She was willing to dip one toe into the sea, but this time she was not about to dive in headfirst the way she had six months before.

Desperation threatened to sweep through him. He realized then that he had been nurturing a fantasy. In the back of his mind, he had convinced himself that, given another chance, he could ignite the fires in her. But what if he had been wrong?

He took his hand away from the door frame, wrapped his arms around her, and pulled her close. She made a small, muffled sound—not a protest, but not exactly a sigh of surrender. Nevertheless, he was certain that he could feel the first flicker of a genuine response.

He deepened the kiss. She leaned into him. Relief and anticipation surged through him.

"If this is a test," he whispered against her mouth, "I'm going to do whatever it takes to pass."

He knew at once that he'd lost the moment. She stiffened, and pushed herself slightly away from him. Her eyes were inscrutable in the shadows. "Thanks for the warning."

He put one hand back on the door frame above her head and gripped it hard. It was either that or pull her back into his arms again. He knew that would not be a good idea.

"What's the matter?" he asked. "Decide to run, screaming into the night, after all?"

"I'm going to walk, not run. And I don't think it will be necessary to do any screaming." She slipped under his braced arm and moved deeper into the shadows of the living room, heading toward the stairs.

She was leaving, heading back to bed. Alone. He felt cold claws close around his gut. There would be no second chances tonight.

"How long are you going to continue punishing both of us for what you think I did to you six months ago?" he asked.

She paused at the foot of the stairs and turned to glance at him over her shoulder. In the darkness he could not see the expression on her face.

"You know, I would have thought that you were busy enough this week looking for Soft Focus, Jack. But if you really feel the urge to take on yet another challenge, I suggest you try something a little more exciting than a repeat of the seduction of the Ice Princess."

"You think I want to start over because I see you as some kind of challenge?"

"Yes. That's exactly what I think."

"That's not how it is."

She did not move. "What do you want from me?"

"Another chance."

"Why?"

"Because I want you and I think that you want me. Or was I imagining what just happened during that kiss?"

She said nothing, just stood there watching him for an eternity. Then, without a word, she went up the stairs and disappeared into the darkness of the landing.

He let out the breath he had not realized he had been holding, closed his eyes, and flexed one hand into a fist. *No second chances*.

"Jack?" Her voice floated softly down from the loft.

He opened his eyes and looked up with an effort. She was leaning slightly out over the railing. He could see the pale outline of her white robe.

"What now?" he asked.

"I'll think about it."

The phone burbled, shattering his fitful sleep. He opened his eyes and glanced at the clock. Four-thirty.

The phone squalled again.

He groped for the receiver, found it, hauled it across the pillow.

"This is Fairfax."

"It was very clever of you to come to Mirror Springs, Mr. Fairfax. But there was no cause for concern. You were on the list. You would have been notified of the location in due course."

He was suddenly very wide awake. "What list?"

"The list of people invited to the auction. I wouldn't dream of conducting the sale of Soft Focus without you."

"When? Where?"

"Relax, Mr. Fairfax. You will be notified of the time and place. Meanwhile, as long as you're in town, you may as well enjoy the film festival. Have fun."

"Who are you?"

"Me? I'm the auctioneer. Oh, by the way, there's no need to waste your time pushing *69. This call is being made from a pay phone."

There was a click and then silence.

The light came on. Jack propped himself against the pillows and watched Elizabeth hurry into his loft. Her hair was tumbled around her face. She fumbled with the sash of her robe.

"Who was it?" she asked anxiously.

"Called himself the auctioneer. Said I'm on the list of people who will be invited to bid on Soft Focus."

"*Bid* on it. You mean there's going to be an auction?"

"Sounds like it."

She grimaced. "So much for your theory that you might be able to ransom the crystal. An auction could really drive up the price."

"Yes."

She met his eyes. "Was that Tyler Page on the phone?"

He thought about the mechanically distorted voice on the other end of the line. "Could have been anyone."

Chapter Twelve

Eden sits at the dressing table and regards her own stunning image in the mirror. She wears silver stiletto heels and a cheap, imitation silver lamé dressing gown. The lapels and cuffs of the gown are trimmed with fake fur. Her makeup turns her face into a beautiful, enigmatic mask.

Behind her, the cold flashing light of a neon sign is seen through the room's single window. Harry, obviously distraught, paces nervously back and forth in front of the window.

HARRY: "The cops think I killed your husband. They're getting ready to arrest me."

EDEN: "That's too bad."

HARRY: "How can you act so goddamned casual? I'm going to go to jail for life if you don't help me."

EDEN: "I'm kind of busy at the moment."

HARRY: "For God's sake, Eden, I'm innocent. You know that."

EDEN: (gazes thoughtfully into the mirror)
"Innocent. How do you spell that? With one n or two?"

HARRY: (stops pacing and swings around to stare at her with an expression of mounting disbelief and horror)
"Who the hell cares how to spell 'innocent'?"

EDEN: "I always have to look it up, you know. Hard to remember how to spell a word when you're not exactly sure what it means."

There was a smattering of applause as the film clip abruptly ended. The lights came up, revealing the four panelists seated at the long table in front of the hotel meeting room.

"Our thanks to Bernard Aston, the director of *Fast Company,* for providing us with that clip," the moderator said. "The character of Eden is a great example of the modern femme fatale in neo noir film. We're lucky to have the star of the film, Victoria Bellamy, here with us on our panel today."

Under the cover of another round of light applause, Elizabeth leaned toward the young woman seated beside her. "You did a fantastic job with the makeup. Perfect noir look."

"Thanks." Christy Barns looked first startled and then gratified by the compliment.

Elizabeth had met the young makeup artist who had worked on *Fast Company* at the Holland reception. Christy was no more than twenty-three or twenty-four at the most, a thin, sharp-featured woman with long red hair. This morning when Elizabeth had spotted her going into the workshop titled "Femme Fatale: Women in Noir Film," she had made a spur-of-the-moment decision to sit next to her.

While the rest of the panelists—which, in addition to Vicky, included the author of a book, a self-proclaimed therapist, and a film critic—were introduced, Elizabeth did a quick survey of the audience. There was no sign of a short, balding little man with horn-rimmed glasses and a furtive air. It would have been too much to hope that Tyler Page would be drawn to the panel, she thought, even if it did feature some advance clips from *Fast Company* and one of the film's stars.

"The female lead of the classic noir film is the spider woman," the moderator continued. "The dangerous temptress with her own agenda, the mysterious, sexually aggressive female who threatens every man. She manipulates, seduces, and destroys. Ultimately, she is unknowable. A force of nature that both attracts and repels."

Seated at the end of the table, Vicky smiled drolly and picked up her microphone. "Speaking as an actress, I can tell you that she's also a lot of fun to play."

The audience chuckled appreciatively.

The author frowned and seized the second microphone. "The femme fatale character is at the heart of noir. In my new book, *Dark Worlds: A History of Film Noir,* I demonstrate that, in one guise or the other, the female lead subverts the patriarchal establishment. She uses the power of her sexuality to lure men to their ruin. When we think of the femme fatale archetypes, we think bitch-goddess or black widow."

Elizabeth tuned out the panelist and thought back to Jack's grim mood at the breakfast table an hour ago. Not content to wait for the auction, he had announced that he was determined to forge ahead with his plans to try to locate Tyler Page. She knew that the thought of having to pay for the return of Excalibur's property galled him. She did not blame him.

But she was also fairly sure that his unpleasant mood owed its origins to more than just the four-thirty A.M. phone call from the auctioneer. He had not taken rejection well last night. She wondered if he now considered her a bitch-goddess or a black widow. Either one was preferable to Ice Princess, she decided. At least bitch-goddesses and black widows sounded more interesting.

One thing was certain. Jack was never going to know how difficult it had been for her to walk away from him after that scorching kiss. It had taken every ounce of willpower she possessed to climb those stairs.

Another chance? Was that really what he wanted from her? And what, in the name of heaven, had made her dangle the possibility in front of both of them? For six months she had told herself she would never trust him again. But what she had discovered in the course of checking out his business track record had made her question some of her assumptions about him. Your run-of-the-mill ruthless corporate shark who was smart enough to rescue companies on the brink concentrated on large corporations. Turnaround specialists as good at their jobs as Jack obviously was, piled up fortunes working for the big companies. They rarely wasted time trying to save small firms.

Curiosity had been plaguing her for months. That was the reason she had succumbed to the temptation to try to push Jack into explaining himself last night. She should have known better, she thought. He was not the kind of man who spilled his deepest secrets in a hot tub.

At the front of the room, the therapist grabbed the microphone. "The femme fatale is an archetype that clearly embodies the threat of the overcontrolling mother figure."

Vicky smiled again and leaned toward her microphone. "Eden is a lot of things, but she's definitely not maternally inclined."

The audience chuckled. The therapist glared at Vicky.

The author leaped into the opening. He had obviously fallen victim to the ancient publicity maxim "whenever you're interviewed, make sure that the title of your book gets mentioned at least three times."

"In my book *Dark Worlds: A History of Film Noir*, I argue that the overcontrolling mother figure is a gross simplification of the extraordinarily complex role of the femme fatale."

"Eden's not complex," Vicky drawled. "She's very simple, really. All she cares about is her own survival. Nothing else matters."

The film critic and the therapist both made desperate bids for the second mike, but the author had it in a death grip.

"In my book *Dark Worlds: A History of Film Noir*, I devote several chapters to explaining the varied roles of the femme fatale character."

Unable to get hold of a mike, the therapist raised his voice. "It's important to realize that the femme fatale comes from a seriously dysfunctional background. Obviously sexually abused as a child, she seeks to manipulate others with sex."

"No, no, no. You don't understand the role of archetypes," the critic yelled toward the microphone, which was still firmly in the grasp of the author. "They go much deeper than the limited concepts of modern psychological theory."

Elizabeth glanced at Christy. The young woman was starting to look bored.

The author gave the film critic a baleful glance. "In my book *Dark Worlds: A History of Film Noir*, I give several examples of how different actresses have portrayed the femme fatale. Claire Trevor, for instance—"

The therapist finally managed to wrestle the mike out of the author's fingers. He started to drone on about the impact of dysfunctional childhoods on the characters.

Elizabeth turned to Christy. "I think I've had about enough of this.

Would you like to go somewhere and have a cup of coffee? I'd really like to talk to you about makeup techniques."

Christy brightened. "Sure. Why not?"

Forty-five minutes later, seated in the window of a small, heavily ferned coffee shop, Elizabeth discovered that she now knew far more about film makeup than she had ever intended to learn. It hadn't been hard to get Christy to talk about her craft. The hard part was finding a way to make her stop.

"I can see that a film such as *Fast Company* is completely dependent on getting the right look with makeup." Elizabeth surreptitiously glanced at her watch and wondered if Jack was having any better luck in the producers' workshop he had attended.

"Hardly anybody understands that." Christy dunked her biscotti into a mug filled with a lot of steamed milk and a shot of espresso. "Everyone thinks you get the effect just by using black-and-white film, but that's not true. I had to do a lot of research to get that edgy look for the actors. Eyebrows are absolutely key, you know."

"Vicky Bellamy appears to be a natural for that style."

Christy rolled her eyes. "In more ways than one."

"What do you mean?"

"She was always real particular about everything, including her makeup. Used to drive me nuts. Always telling me I hadn't got the arch of the eyebrows right or complaining because I didn't do her eyes the way she wanted them. Like I hadn't studied the classic films myself."

"Well, actresses are famous for being temperamental."

"Yeah, I guess." Christy grimaced. "And given the fact that her husband bankrolled the film, she got to do pretty much what she wanted on the set."

"Speaking of bankrolling the film," Elizabeth began cautiously. "Did you ever happen to meet the producer?"

"Dawson Holland? Yeah, sure."

"No, the one whose name is listed in the credits. Tyler Page."

"Oh, him. The nervous, mousy little guy who was always hanging around? Yeah, I met him."

"That sounds like Tyler," Elizabeth said. "I'm a friend of his. I've been looking for him ever since I got to Mirror Springs, but I haven't run into him."

"Hard to find anyone in this crowd right now unless you know where he's staying."

"Unfortunately, I don't know." Elizabeth paused. "I take it you haven't seen him?"

"Uh-uh."

"Did you talk to him much on the set?"

"You kidding?" Christy rolled her eyes again. "He had to be at least fifty or sixty. And he was shorter than me."

"I see."

Christy's eyes widened. "Hey, you're not Angel Face, are you? If so, I'm real sorry. I didn't mean to insult him or anything."

Elizabeth held her breath. "Angel Face?"

"That's what he called her. I heard him talking to her on his cell phone once. He went behind the makeup room to make the call. Guess he wanted to be private, but those walls are as thin as cardboard."

"You overheard the conversation?"

"Yeah. Kind of embarrassing. He really had it bad." Christy paused. "It wasn't you?"

"No. I'm a friend of Tyler's, but not his girlfriend. How could you tell he had it bad for Angel Face?"

Christy grimaced. "Just the way he talked to her and all. Sounded like he was reading lines from a low-budget script."

"What did he say?"

"Like I said, he called her Angel Face. Said she had to know that he would do anything for her. I think he promised her that they would be together forever once this was over."

"Once what was over?"

"The filming of *Fast Company* I, guess." Christy shrugged. "I forget the rest. It wasn't exactly memorable."

"So you never saw his girlfriend?"

"Nope. Just heard him talking to her that one time. Why?"

"It occurred to me that if I found her, I might be able to find him. So you don't know what she looked like, I take it?"

"Can't help you there. But I can tell you that he was crazy about her, whoever she was." Christy frowned in thought. "I remember thinking it was kinda weird, though."

"What was weird?"

"Him calling her his Angel Face."

"What's so strange about that? A little sappy maybe, but—"

"No, no, you don't get it," Christy said impatiently. "*Angel Face* is the title of a classic noir movie starring Robert Mitchum and Jean Simmons. It was one of the films I studied so that I could get the look of the makeup right for *Fast Company*!"

"What about it?"

"Well, see, Jean Simmons plays the femme fatale who ends up destroying everyone around her, including Mitchum's character. Just seemed sort of strange that a guy who was into noir the way Page is would call his girlfriend Angel Face. Not exactly a compliment, you know. I mean, the lady in the film was a psychopathic killer. He had to know that."

Dawson Holland looked out at the audience. He smiled wryly. "This panel has done its best to tell you about the pitfalls of getting involved in the production of an independent film. When it comes to reliable methods of losing money, financing a film ranks right up there with walking into a casino and throwing cash into a slot machine." He paused meaningfully. "I can't help but notice that a lot of you are still here, however."

The crowd that had filled most of the seats at the producers' seminar laughed. Standing at the back of the room, one shoulder propped against the wall, arms folded, Jack watched Dawson as he summed up the comments of the panel.

"Any film is a huge financial risk. That goes double for small, independent films, because there are no studios with deep pockets to stand behind you and absorb losses," Dawson said. "Bottom line is, if you can't afford to lose your money, stay out of the business."

"But what if a major studio picks up your film and gives it national distribution?" someone asked.

Dawson shook his head. "That's the big dream, but in reality, it almost never happens. True, you might find your film on the bottom rack of a video store someday, or it may be screened at a festival such as this one. Sometimes you can make a little in the foreign market. But realistically speaking, odds are that the only payoff you'll ever see is your name in the credits."

Someone else spoke up. "But isn't there a lot of important, experimental work being done by independent filmmakers these days?"

One of the panelists snorted. "Important, experimental work and a dollar won't even buy you a cup of cappuccino. If you're going to get into the business of making movies, do it because you love film, not because you expect a return on your investment."

"My colleague speaks truth," Dawson said. "One last word of advice." He paused for effect. "On the off chance that your film actually does turn a profit, always remember the mantra of this business: Make sure your contract states that your payoff comes in the form of a percentage of the *gross* profits, not the net. For as sure as the sun will rise tomorrow morning, I can assure you that there will never be a net profit."

The audience broke into more laughter and desultory applause. As far as Jack could tell, no one looked the least discouraged by the hard facts of life concerning the independent film business. *Everyone wants to make movies,* he thought as he turned to leave the seminar room. The enthusiasm, excitement, and anticipation that animated the crowd of would-be producers was painful to behold.

Tyler Page had been gripped with this same fever, Jack reminded himself. Probably planned to use the profits from the sale of the crystal to finance another film.

Talk about stupid.

Then again, any man who could make a fool of himself the way he had last night with Elizabeth wasn't exactly in a position to scoff at another man's doomed dreams.

He walked out of the seminar room and started down the wide, windowed hall that led to the lobby of the Mirror Springs Resort. He glanced at his watch and saw that he was ten minutes late. Elizabeth had promised to meet him at noon for lunch.

"Well, Fairfax?" Dawson fell into step beside him. "Did we succeed in discouraging you?"

Jack snapped his thoughts back and glanced at Dawson. "You did a good job of laying out the downside of independent filmmaking. If it's such a great way to lose money, how come you're still involved in the business?"

Dawson put his hands into the pockets of his jacket. Comfortable. Sure of himself. "Like I said, you've got to love filmmaking. Nothing else like it on the face of the earth. And, of course, there's Vicky."

"Right. Vicky."

"My wife is very, very important to me, Jack," Dawson said. "I would do anything to make her happy. And what she likes to do is act in films."

"So you make her dreams come true, is that it?"

"It's a small price to pay for the pleasure of her company." Dawson paused. "Is the charming Miss Cabot an aspiring actress?"

"No."

"Your interest in filmmaking is personal?"

"You could say that."

"Then you have much in common with the others in that seminar. In real life they're dentists and stockbrokers and business executives."

"And research scientists."

"I beg your pardon?"

"The producer of *Fast Company*, Tyler Page, worked in a high-tech lab in Seattle."

"Ah, yes, Page." Dawson nodded absently. "I believe he did mention that he lived in Seattle. But he didn't say much about his professional life."

"He must have poured a ton of money into *Fast Company* to get his name in the credits as the producer."

"He made it clear at the outset that he did not want to share the credit. He said he wanted the film to be his movie. He was willing to put up the money to pay for the privilege."

"What about the other investors?"

Dawson shrugged. "None of them was willing to put up the same kind of money."

Jack felt his professional curiosity stir. "So tell me, how do the investment partnerships work for the guy who puts the package together?"

"Someone in my position, you mean?"

"Something tells me you don't take the same kind of risks that the other investors take, do you?"

"I do get a commission for my work," Dawson said. "It's one of the standard expenses of the partnership." He broke off as a figure suddenly loomed in his path.

The stranger scampered awkwardly backward, hands raised in front of Jack as if to ward him off. The man was of medium height. His head had been completely shaved to expose a lot of pink scalp. His clothing consisted of a black turtleneck, black trousers, and low, black boots. There was a silver ring in one ear. His eyes were concealed behind a pair of stylish sunglasses that were entirely unnecessary in the dimly lit hotel hallway. Jack wondered if the man wore the glasses in an effort to add a dramatic edge to what was otherwise a soft, round face.

"Future noir," the man intoned.

Jack did not slow his pace. "Huh?"

"Future noir." The man continued to backpedal along the corridor in front of Jack. "Gothic realism. The dark night of the soul in a dark future. Think moral ambiguity. Think murder for passion's sake. Think the eternal femme fatale. All against a black-and-white, futuristic background."

"Would you mind getting out of my way?" Jack took another look at his watch. "I'm meeting someone in the lobby."

Dawson chuckled. "Allow me to introduce you to Leonard Ledger. He's a filmmaker. Like a number of other people here, he's looking for someone to finance his next film."

"Dark Moon Rising," Leonard said.

Jack eyed him curiously. *"Dark Moon Rising?"*

"That's the working title," Leonard explained. "I see it as the classic noir story told against a black-and-white future. Incredible lighting effects. Minimal sets. All angles, lines, and shadows."

Jack nodded. "And you need money."

Leonard continued to walk backward. "This is very high-concept stuff. The kind of film the major studios will pick up for distribution. They'll kill for a film like this."

"I'll get back to you," Jack said. He glanced at Dawson. "That's the right phrase, isn't it? I'll get back to you?"

"Obviously you were born for this business." Dawson looked amused.

Jack turned back to Leonard. "Excuse me," he said. "I think I mentioned that I have an appointment?"

"Sure, sure." Leonard reluctantly sidled out of Jack's path. "I've got a script. I'll get it to you. You're gonna love it."

Jack kept walking. Leonard's voice gradually receded into the background.

"Get used to it," Dawson advised. "Now that you've been spotted as a potential source of money, you're going to meet a lot of Leonard Ledgers."

"I'll watch where I step," Jack said.

He was about to ask another question concerning the financing of *Fast Company* when he turned the corner and walked into the elegantly rustic lobby of the Mirror Springs Resort.

He spotted Elizabeth right off. She was standing near the massive stone fireplace. She was not alone. The man leaning intimately over her, obviously engaged in close conversation, was Hayden Shaw.

"Son of a bitch," Jack said very quietly.

Chapter Thirteen

"I'm sorry about the misunderstanding." Hayden's mouth thinned. "And on behalf of my soon-to-be ex-wife, I apologize for whatever Gillian said to you at the reception. She's not happy with the proposed settlement. Her father's lawyers told her that they could get more money out of me, but it's not going to happen."

Elizabeth tried to peek over his shoulder to see if she could spot Jack coming out of the meeting-room hallway. "I really do not want to discuss your divorce, Hayden."

He leaned in a little closer, very intense. There was something vaguely familiar and slightly unsettling about the way he zeroed in on his target, she thought.

"You need to know that for all intents and purposes, I'm a free man," he said.

"Not quite." She gave him a pointed look. "And even if that were true, it's not important to me because it has no bearing on this situation. You didn't come here to see me or because you've suddenly developed a keen interest in low-budget filmmaking."

"You underestimate yourself."

She frowned as a thought struck her. "How did you get a room in this place? This town has been booked for months."

He made a dismissive movement with one hand. "No big deal. I know the general manager here at the resort."

"Pulled some strings, did you? Well, you wasted your time."

"What do you mean?"

She glared at him, exasperated. "Stop playing games. You're here because of those rumors you heard about Soft Focus, aren't you?"

"Is that why you're here with Fairfax?" he countered. "Keeping an eye on your number-one investment?"

"That's none of your business."

"Gillian found me in the crowd at the reception after you and Jack left." Hayden grimaced. "She was gloating. Couldn't wait to tell me that you and Fairfax were going off on a vacation together. But I know damn well that you wouldn't suddenly decide that you wanted to jump back into bed with the bastard who played you for a sucker six months ago. You're too smart to fall for his line again."

"You're right about one thing: I'm smart. Smart enough to know that you're here because of Soft Focus, not because of me." The pieces of the small puzzle clicked into place. "Damn. You were invited, weren't you?"

He gave her a politely quizzical look. "Invited to what?"

"You know what I'm talking about."

He exhaled slowly, his gaze speculative. "There's no reason we can't join forces and work together. Together we can outbid Jack. Without you, he hasn't got much in the way of resources."

Her worst fears were confirmed. Hayden had been invited to the auction. She clenched her hand around the strap of her shoulder bag.

"Give me one good reason why I would want to hurt my client by bidding against him," she said.

Hayden smiled slowly. "Revenge?"

She stared at him, mouth open, for a few seconds. He was serious, she realized. "Hurt Excalibur just for the sake of a little revenge? Good grief, Hayden, do you think I'm an idiot? I'm a businesswoman, remember? My job is to keep my clients profitable. The simple fact of life is that the Fund doesn't make money unless they do."

He glanced around with deliberate casualness and then bent his head in a seemingly intimate gesture. "If Soft Focus has even half the potential I've heard it has, there are other ways to make money with it besides leaving it in the hands of a struggling little R & D firm that will probably get swallowed up by the first big company that comes along."

A chill went through her. "I can't believe I'm hearing this. In fact, I refuse to believe it. You aren't suggesting that I sabotage my own client? Not for something as empty and meaningless as revenge?"

Hayden's eyes hardened. "There's nothing empty and meaningless about it."

She searched his face. "What did Jack ever do to you to make you hate him so much?"

Hayden did not reply. His attention had shifted to a point just behind her. Elizabeth did not need him to tell her that Jack was coming toward her. The familiar prickle of awareness had already wafted across the back of her neck.

She turned and saw him cut through the crowded lobby with fluid, cold-blooded grace. There was no doubt that she and Hayden were his target. His face was disturbingly expressionless.

"Looks like your business associate has arrived," Hayden said. His eyes held a malicious gleam. "And he doesn't look happy to see me. Think about my offer, Elizabeth."

Jack came to a halt just behind Elizabeth's shoulder. He was close. Too close. She could feel the possessive aura that he flung around her like an invisible cloak. It was annoying, but she told herself that this was not the time or place to make an issue of his politically incorrect attitude. The last thing she wanted to do was pump up the level of testosterone in the vicinity. It was already much too thick.

Jack looked at Hayden. "I had a hunch you'd show up sooner or later."

"I always did like to go to the movies."

"Just make sure that all you do is watch," Jack said. He glanced at Elizabeth. "Let's go. We're late."

His hand closed around her arm. She considered digging in her heels and then reminded herself that the last thing she wanted was a scene.

"Where are we going?" she asked, grimly polite. "I thought we were supposed to have lunch here in town."

"We're going back to our place," he said, laying a not-so-subtle emphasis on the *our.* "I've got some work to do."

She forced herself to smile at Hayden. "See you later."

"Yeah," Hayden said coldly. "You will."

Elizabeth allowed herself to be drawn toward the front of the lobby. An attendant jumped to open one of the heavy plate-glass doors.

Outside, the snapping air and the too-bright sunlight slapped Elizabeth in the face. She pulled her sunglasses out of her purse.

Jack already had his dark glasses in his hand. When he put them on, his already stony expression became bleak and menacing.

"Where's he staying?" he asked without preamble.

That was not the question she had been expecting. "What difference does that make?"

"A lot." He turned his head. He was looking at her, but his own eyes were concealed behind the sunglasses. "Hard to get a room here in Mirror Springs, remember?"

Belatedly she realized where he was going with the question. She frowned as the implications hit her. "Hayden said he had a room here at the resort."

"Amazing." Jack's mouth twisted laconically. "Wonder how he got it on such short notice."

"He said he pulled some strings."

"Bullshit."

"Do you really think so?" She felt a stab of icy amusement. "Seems to me I recall you telling me something similar not too long ago. Guess his strings must have been better than yours, though. They didn't break."

Jack ignored that. He came to a halt on the passenger side of the car and looked at her through the dark lenses. "Be interesting to find out just when Hayden made his reservations."

"Why?"

"Because if he made them anytime before last Tuesday night, it would mean he knew in advance about the plans to steal the specimen." Jack yanked open the car door. "Maybe he even helped plan the theft."

The sharp, crisp air made Elizabeth pull her jacket more snugly around herself. "If you're thinking of wasting a lot of time investigating Hayden, I'd advise you to save your energy. I'm almost positive he didn't know about the theft until he heard the rumors late Tuesday. I think he's here because he was invited to the auction." She slid into the car seat.

Jack just stared at her for a long moment.

"Damn," he said very, very softly.

A fresh wave of unease shot through her. "What?"

"I wonder who else was invited."

The car door shut with a distinct and very final-sounding *ker-chunk.*

Elizabeth watched Jack walk around the front of the car and get in behind the wheel. Who else had been invited to the auction? It was a disturbing question.

Jack put the silver-gray rental car in gear, reversed out of the slot, and drove toward the parking lot exit.

"Look, if Hayden's here for the auction," Elizabeth said, "at least it means that he wasn't involved in the theft." She did not know just why that was important, but it was.

Jack grunted. "That make you feel better?"

"Yes."

"Why?"

She propped her elbow on the window ledge and braced her chin on her hand. "I sort of like him. I guess I just don't want to find out that I've been completely wrong about him—" She broke off quickly.

But not quickly enough.

"You don't want to discover that you were wrong about him, *too*." Jack did not take his eyes off the road. "The way you were wrong about me? Is that what you were going to say?"

"As Aunt Sybil would say, I think it's time to change the subject."

Jack's jaw tightened into a hard line. "It's possible that Hayden was involved in the theft, but now he's here for the auction because things went wrong."

"What are you talking about?"

"Think about it. Maybe Hayden orchestrated the theft with Tyler Page's cooperation. But what if Page decided afterward that he didn't need Hayden to help him sell the crystal? What if he's got his own agenda?"

"You're suggesting that there was a falling-out among thieves? And now Hayden is trying to find Tyler Page and the crystal?"

"Just like us."

Elizabeth watched the mountain road unfurl in front of the car's hood. "I think we may have an even bigger problem on our hands."

Jack shot her a brief glance. "What's that?"

"Before I ran into Hayden at the resort, I had an interesting conversation with a young woman named Christy. She was the makeup artist on *Fast Company*."

"And?"

"And she thinks that Tyler Page was madly in love."

Jack greeted that with a short, undiplomatic snort of disgust. "Page? In love? Give me a break."

For some reason his complete disdain annoyed her. "Why is that so unbelievable? It might explain why he stole Soft Focus. He's obviously got an obsessive passion for film. Maybe he's got an obsessive passion for a woman, too. Maybe he stole the crystal for her sake."

"Are you saying you think Tyler Page stole Soft Focus so that he could sell it for a bundle of cash he could use to impress a woman?"

"Christy overheard him talking on his cell phone to someone he called Angel Face. He promised her that when this was all over they would be together forever."

Jack took his gaze off the road just long enough to throw her a quick, curious look. "You really think that there's a woman involved in this?"

"Page loves film noir. You know what they say about life imitating art. What if he's fallen for a femme fatale type? Someone who seduced him and encouraged him to steal the specimen so that they could run off together into the sunset? It might explain his bizarre behavior."

Jack drove in silence for a while. He was concentrating again. She could almost feel him processing the data in his brain.

"Don't think so," he said eventually.

"Why not?"

"That kind of thing might work in the movies, but in real life a man doesn't throw away everything he's worked for most of his life, for the sake of a woman. For the sake of a fortune, yes. For the sake of a fortune to spend on his films, yes. But not for a woman."

Elizabeth settled deeper into her seat and folded her arms. What was the matter with her? Had she actually started to wonder if Jack had a secret romantic streak?

Jack's cell phone rang just as Elizabeth finished cutting the last of the tapanade, lettuce, and tomato sandwiches she had hastily put together for lunch. He set down the two bottles of springwater he had removed from the refrigerator and took the device out of his pocket.

"Fairfax here." Pause. "Don't worry about it, Milo. My instructions were to call with any updates. What have you got?"

Elizabeth listened absently as she carried the plate of sandwiches around the long, granite counter that separated the kitchen from the living area of the house.

"Is Durand sure?" Jack's voice was suddenly charged with intensity. "How the hell did Kendle ever get hired in the first place? No, don't answer that. I know how he got onto the Excalibur payroll. Nobody bothered to check out his references, right? Tell Scott in HR that he's going to have some explaining to do."

Elizabeth put the sandwiches down on the table.

"Forget it," Jack growled into the phone. "It's a little too late for that. Did Durand say anything else about Kendle?"

There was another short pause.

"Huh." Jack walked to the window and stood looking out at the mountains. "Interesting. No, it's nothing important. Just . . . interesting. What about the Vanguard of Tomorrow thing?"

There was another tense silence while he listened.

"Nothing at all in the media? Sounds like we lucked out. Nice work, Milo. Yeah, you said all the right things to Veltran's people. Good work . . . Yeah, we're getting close. We'll find it, Milo. Call if anything else develops."

Elizabeth almost smiled at the cool, calm, wholly unwarranted assurance in Jack's voice. The man in charge, she thought. Make everyone think you know what you're doing and they'll follow you anywhere.

Jack ended the call and pocketed the phone. He looked across the room and saw her watching him. "Remember that group that trashed the Excalibur lab?"

"Vanguard of Tomorrow?" She took a seat at the table. "What about it?"

"They haven't come forward to take the credit or responsibility or whatever it is that kind does take when it smashes private property." Jack sat down across from her. "Apparently they didn't contact the press or go on their Web site to brag. I find that sort of curious, don't you?"

A deep sense of foreboding went through her. "I hope you're not going to tell me that you think the trashing of the lab had something to do with the theft."

"I don't know. I suppose Page could have gone back to the lab the night after he stole the crystal in an effort to conceal the loss for a while. Give himself time to get safely out of town."

"But you discovered that Soft Focus was missing a few hours before the lab got trashed. You went to see Page and found that he was already packed and gone."

"True. But it was just random chance that I checked up on the crystal when I did Tuesday night." Jack reached for a sandwich. "Page couldn't have had any way of knowing that I'd find out so quickly that it was gone. It would have been reasonable for him to assume that it wouldn't be missed until the following day or even later. For him, the biggest danger at that point was that I might call in the cops."

Elizabeth thought about it. "If you had done that, they would have been strongly inclined to blame the theft on the Vanguard of Tomorrow nuts."

"Right." Jack took a bite and chewed reflectively. "The vandalism would have sent the authorities off in the wrong direction. A nice distraction, if it had been needed. Not a bad backup strategy. There's something else."

Elizabeth's sense of premonition grew stronger. "What is it?"

"Milo said that the reason we couldn't dig up a next-of-kin on Ryan

Kendle is because his résumé was fake. Phony ID, phony addresses, the works. The police are trying to find out who he really was."

Very slowly she put down her sandwich. "It happens. People often lie on résumés."

"Uh-huh." Jack took a swallow of the bottled water. "Sometimes they lie because they've got a criminal record."

"Maybe he did. You mentioned that the cops said he was involved in the drug scene. They said he was killed in a drug deal gone bad."

Jack looked at her across the table. "The homicide detective working on the case told Milo something else."

"What?"

"They scrounged up a witness. A drunk transient sleeping in a doorway. He didn't actually see the shooting, but he said he thinks he heard Kendle talking to someone just before the shots were fired."

"Someone?"

Jack hesitated briefly. "A woman."

A woman. Elizabeth thought about what Christy Barns had said about a female character named Angel Face. *The femme fatale who ends up destroying everyone around her.* She flexed her fingers to try to rid herself of the prickling sensation. "You're not thinking that Kendle was somehow connected to the theft, are you?"

"As of right now I'm leaving all options open—including the possibility that there is a woman involved."

"But, Jack, this is white-collar crime, remember? People don't get killed in white-collar crime."

"There are exceptions to every rule."

Elizabeth steeled herself against the trickle of unease. She looked at Jack and said nothing.

He frowned. "What are you thinking?"

"I'm thinking that a man like Tyler Page probably wouldn't encounter too many femme fatales in his line of work."

"Trust me, there are no femme fatales employed at Excalibur. Company policy." Jack paused, suddenly very thoughtful. "Unless . . ."

"Unless what?"

"There is one woman connected with Excalibur who has been trying to force the company to shift its course," he said deliberately. "Angela Ingersoll Burrows."

Elizabeth turned that over a few times in her mind. "I don't think so.

I've talked to her a lot during the past few months. I admit that, given the right circumstances, she could qualify as a femme fatale. She's attractive enough for the part, and she's certainly obsessed with protecting her son's future, so she's got motive, but—"

"If she thinks that sabotaging the Soft Focus project might assure a sale or merger of the company—"

Elizabeth shook her head. "No. Not if we're talking violence or, God help us, murder. Besides, I can't see her setting out to seduce Tyler Page. However . . ."

"Yeah?"

She took a deep breath. "I can think of one place where Page might have met a real live femme fatale."

Jack watched her very intently. "Where?"

"On the set of *Fast Company*."

Jack was silent for a moment. "Are you talking about Victoria Bellamy?"

"The thought crossed my mind, that's all." Elizabeth shivered. "But it doesn't make sense. I mean, she's an actress, not an industrial spy. What would she know about an exotic, high-tech material, much less how to make a profit on it?"

"Probably not a lot," Jack conceded. "But Dawson Holland might. We'll know more about him when Larry finishes checking him out."

"Probably a waste of time."

"Not like we've got a lot else to do."

"I've got something else to do." Elizabeth helped herself to another sandwich. "I've got a real, live film script to read."

Shortly after midnight she heard him go softly down the stairs. She had finished the script for *Fast Company* a few minutes earlier and turned out her light to go to sleep.

When she heard the hushed footsteps, her first thought was that Jack was heading for the hot tub. Then she heard the front door open and close quietly.

"Oh, damn." She sat bolt upright and shoved aside the bedding. He wouldn't dare. Not without telling her.

But outside she heard the sound of one of the car engines turning over. Jack was leaving.

She knew, with a terrible certainty, exactly where he was headed. Panic shot through her. She scrambled out of bed and grabbed her jeans.

Chapter Fourteen

He sat in the darkness near the window and waited. The cold moonlight slanted through the blinds, layering shadows on the hotel-room carpet. He studied the icy grid pattern and thought about the past.

After a while he opened the small bottle he had taken from the minibar. He rarely drank scotch, generally only when he was facing a brick wall.

The scotch was appropriate tonight. Not just because of the brick wall he was about to confront, but because his father had favored scotch. And this was all about his father.

The door opened. A wedge of harsh corridor light angled across the floor. Hayden stood silhouetted in the doorway.

"We need to talk," Jack said from the shadows near the window. "Come in and close the door. This won't take long."

"What the hell are you doing here? How did you get into my room?"

"Swiped a master key from housekeeping."

"Shit. You haven't changed, have you?" Hayden closed the door. He did not turn on the light. "A real chip off the old block."

"I didn't come here to talk about the past."

"No? Then why are you here?" Hayden crossed the room to the minibar. Opened it. Reached inside. Small bottles clinked. "Are you really that worried that I might get Elizabeth into bed?"

"Leave Elizabeth out of this."

"No can do." Hayden closed the minibar door, straightened, and walked to the chair opposite the one Jack occupied. He flung himself down into it. The grid of moonlight shafted across his face. He lifted his own small bottle of scotch in a mocking toast. "She's a part of it now. That's your fault, not mine."

"She's got nothing to do with what happened. Leave her alone."

Hayden looked amused. "What is it with you and Elizabeth, anyway? Can't quite figure it out."

"You don't have to figure it out. It's none of your business."

"You know, when I told her that you were the guy behind the Galloway deal, I thought sure she'd yank your funding. Didn't realize you already had her name on the contract." Hayden took a swallow from the bottle. "Your timing, as always, was damn near magical."

"I told you to leave Elizabeth out of this."

"It was too late to screw up your funding, but it wasn't all for naught, was it? Your little fling together ended kind of fast. A real blaze-of-glory thing." Hayden chuckled. "The scene at the Pacific Rim Club is legend in certain segments of the Seattle business community."

"That's enough, Hayden."

"Do you think that you maybe went a little over the top when you called her the Ice Princess, though? Not very gentlemanly to kiss and tell."

Jack was mildly amazed that the little bottle of scotch did not fracture in his hand. "Shut up."

"You might as well have written her name on the men's room wall at the club: 'For a good time you definitely do not want to call Elizabeth the Ice Princess.' "

"I said, *shut up.*"

"Word must have gotten around that she's no fun in bed. She hasn't dated much in the past six months. Tell me, just out of curiosity, is she really a frigid fuck?"

The bars of silver light on the floor were suddenly too bright. They blazed with the intensity of magnesium flares. The lines of shadows between them were as dark as the far side of the moon. Nothing in the room looked quite right.

Jack came up out of the chair, impelled by an adrenaline rush. He hurled the half-empty bottle aside, grabbed Hayden by the lapels of his jacket, and hauled him up out of the chair.

"You've pushed your luck as far as you can tonight," Jack said very softly. "One more word about Elizabeth and I will take you apart."

"Cool. I can see the headlines now. 'Excalibur Exec Jailed for Assault.' That kind of PR will certainly make future clients think twice about hiring you."

Jack shoved him up against the wall. "Do you really believe that I give a damn about the publicity?"

There was a short, brittle pause. Hayden stopped smiling.

"You're a little out of control here, Jack. Not your style."

"Yeah, but you know something? It feels sort of good."

Hayden narrowed his eyes. "If you didn't come here to talk about Elizabeth, why the hell are you here?"

The room stopped looking like a scene from a noir film. The shadows became normal again. Jack forced himself to relax his grip on Hayden's jacket. He dropped his hands and stepped back.

"The Vanguard of Tomorrow crowd," Jack said.

Hayden frowned as he removed his jacket. "The radical group that trashes high-tech facilities? What about it?"

Jack walked to the window. He looked down into the shadows that concealed the river that tumbled out of a nearby mountain canyon. "It tore up one of the Excalibur labs late Tuesday night or early Wednesday morning. But it hasn't come forward to claim the incident."

There was the smallest of hesitations before Hayden said, "So?"

"So I can't help but wonder if maybe VT had nothing to do with it, after all. But maybe you did."

There was a short silence behind him.

"Prove it," Hayden said.

"I don't have to prove it. If I decide you did it, that will be enough for me."

"What the hell do you think you can do to me even if you do manage to jump to that totally false conclusion?" Hayden asked. He sounded mildly curious.

"You don't want to find out."

"Are you threatening me?"

"Think of it as a promise." Jack turned to look at him. "Excalibur is my client. The Ingersolls are good people. I won't allow you to hurt them just to get at me."

"I had nothing to do with the trashing of the lab." Hayden's voice sharpened. "I didn't even know about it until now. You can't pin that on me. If you're thinking of going to the cops, forget it."

"I'm not going to the cops." Jack walked toward the door. "Not yet. But if I find out that you've let your desire for revenge push you into hurting a lot of innocent people, I won't protect you."

"I don't need your goddamned protection. I've never needed it."

"One other thing." Jack twisted the doorknob. "I realize that you're in Mirror Springs because you think you can get your hands on Soft Focus. I'm not sure yet just what role you're playing in this little film script we seem to be acting out here. But I'll tell you this much: You better make damn sure that you don't try to use Elizabeth to get what you want."

Hayden gave a short, sharp, edgy laugh. "Why do I have to follow that rule? You sure as hell didn't follow it, did you?"

Jack said nothing. He opened the door and stepped out into the hall. He closed the door, went down the corridor to the elevators, and leaned wearily on the call button. While he waited for the cab to arrive, he caught a glimpse of his reflection in the mirror that decorated the opposite wall. His father's eyes looked back at him.

"It hasn't been easy cleaning up the mess you left behind, you son of a bitch," he said to the image in the mirror.

The elevator doors slid open with a soft hiss. He got into the cab, descended to the lobby, and walked out into the cold, moonlit night.

He crossed the parking lot to where he had left the car. He did not see Elizabeth bundled up in her long, black, down-filled coat until he was almost on top of her.

"I've had enough of your games, Fairfax." Her eyes glittered furiously in the shadows. "I want some answers. You owe me that much."

He looked at her and thought about what Hayden had said. *You might as well have written her name on the men's room wall at the club.*

"Yes." He ran his hand over his face once and then let it fall to his side. "I owe you that much."

She replaced the bottle of cognac in the kitchen cupboard, picked up the two glasses she had poured, and carried them out into the firelit room. She paused near the low, square coffee table and looked at Jack.

He stood in front of the hearth, one hand braced against the mantel, and stared into the flames.

Silently, she handed him one of the glasses. He scowled at it, as if he had to concentrate hard to pull his attention back from the fire. After a moment he took the glass from her fingers.

"You went to the hotel to confront Hayden, didn't you?" she said quietly.

He shrugged and took a swallow from the glass.

"Why?" She studied his face. "What did you hope to accomplish?"

"I don't know." He slowly lowered the glass. "It's a long story."

"We've got all night."

He met her eyes. She realized that, for the first time since she had met him six months ago, he was allowing her to catch more than a fleeting glimpse of what lay beneath the surface. What she saw was daunting.

"My father was Sawyer J. Fairfax. He was a brilliant corporate strategist. Made a fortune in mergers and acquisitions during the last boom. His specialty was the hostile takeover of small, closely held companies. In his time, he destroyed countless little family businesses simply because he knew how to make a lot of money doing it."

"Go on."

"He was good at making profits and he was also very good at living a lie. He died while on a business trip to Europe. I was twenty-four at the time. Swear to God, until the day of the funeral, I assumed that I was his only son. So did my mother."

Elizabeth frowned. "You didn't know about Larry?"

"No." Jack looked at the cognac in his glass. "Turns out Larry and his mother didn't know about me, either. They lived in Boston. They were aware that my father was married and that he did a lot of traveling on business."

"That accounted for all the absences."

"Right. But none of us had a clue that there was a third son. Not until he showed up for the reading of the will."

Elizabeth drew a sharp breath. "Not—?"

"Yeah. Hayden."

"Good grief. Talk about a shock."

"Hayden didn't come to the funeral. His anger at Dad runs so deep that he blames Sawyer's lies for his mother's suicide. Unfortunately, Dad died before Hayden could get his revenge." Jack paused. "But that still leaves me."

Elizabeth closed her eyes. "I see."

"I was named executor in Dad's will. I got the job of untangling his legal, financial, and personal affairs. There were several pending lawsuits. Some incredibly arcane business deals that had to be closed out. And then there were all those people he had hurt along the way. All the small businesses he had crushed. All the families he had ruined."

Some answers clicked neatly into place. Elizabeth opened her eyes. "That's why you've committed yourself to protecting small, family businesses. You're trying to compensate for all the damage your father did."

He sipped his drink. "Don't get the wrong impression here. I'm not the altruistic type. I've carved out a market niche for myself, and it just happens to be very profitable."

She let that go. "Tell me the rest of the story."

"Like I said, unraveling my father's business affairs wasn't easy. But that wasn't the hard part."

"What was?"

"The family stuff."

"Of course." She watched him for a long moment. "The family stuff is always the hardest part."

"I will say one thing for Dad. He treated us all equally in his will. Larry is the youngest of his sons." Jack's mouth curved briefly. "We have almost nothing in common, but we get along fine."

"But you and Hayden are very much alike, aren't you? You've both got smart, savvy instincts when it comes to business. You've both got an amazing ability to focus on a goal or a problem. Good grief, now that I think about it, you've both got the same taste in clothes and food."

Jack's expression hardened. "We're not exactly twins, separated at birth."

"No," she agreed readily. "You certainly don't look anything alike."

Jack gave her a laconic look. "If that's a polite way of implying that Hayden is better looking—"

"He's not better looking," she said brusquely. "Just different looking."

"Very diplomatic." Jack shrugged. "I can't help it if I take after my father. As I was saying, Larry's mother is one of those sweet, nurturing types. I don't think she was all that surprised to learn that I existed. But Hayden's mother wasn't so understanding. She knew that Sawyer was married, but she had always believed that he would one day divorce his wife and marry her. She didn't know about me."

"Hard enough to discover that the man you loved had not only died before he got the divorce he had promised, but that he also had a son he had forgotten to mention."

Jack took another taste of the cognac. "Vivien Shaw went into a severe clinical depression after Dad died. For some reason she fixated on the idea that my existence was a bigger betrayal than the fact that Sawyer had never gotten the divorce. In the end, she took pills. A lot of them."

"And Hayden transferred his anger at Sawyer to you."

"He agrees with his mother's version of events—the one in which I was the favored child and he got the shaft." Jack downed the last of his cognac. "He hates my guts."

"There's an old saying to the effect that family feuds are the worst kind of feuds."

"I can testify to that."

"Why does Hayden use a different last name?"

"He was raised in a small town in California. His mother called herself Mrs. Shaw. He grew up with that name. He still uses it. Another way of getting back at the Fairfax family, I guess."

"I see." She hesitated. "What did Hayden have to say tonight? Did he admit he'd been invited to the auction?"

"We didn't discuss the auction," Jack said.

She stared at him. "I don't understand. What else was there to talk about?"

"I went to see him because it occurred to me that he might have been responsible for the trashing of the lab."

"What?"

Jack looked irritated by her incredulity. "I figured that he might have allowed his hostility toward me to spill over onto my clients."

"There's a term for that."

"Collateral damage," Jack said dryly.

"No." She shook her head quickly. "Impossible. I can't believe Hayden would go that far."

"How the hell would you know what he's capable of doing for the sake of revenge?"

Elizabeth turned and began to pace the room. "I can't see him doing thousands of dollars' worth of damage to the Ingersolls' lab just to get even with you. It doesn't fit with what I know about Hayden Shaw."

"Don't be too sure how much you know about him." Jack watched her through narrowed eyes. "Why do you think he's been working so hard to get you into bed?"

"To annoy you?" Anger surged through her. She did her best to conceal it behind a mocking smile. "Now who's being undiplomatic?"

Jack's profile was all hard, inflexible planes and angles. "It's obvious that he went after you because he wanted to use you against me."

"You mean it wasn't my drop-dead gorgeous body and sexy eyes that made him fall at my feet?" She heaved a dramatic sigh. "That's right, go ahead and rip apart my little fantasy of being a femme fatale."

"Damn it, Elizabeth, I'm trying to explain—"

"Here I thought I had two men competing for my favors and it turns out that not just one, but both of them, used me to further their own agendas."

Jack watched her with steady intensity. "I didn't tell you that I was involved in the Galloway deal because I knew you would misinterpret everything."

She smiled a little too sweetly. "And your brother didn't mention that his divorce wasn't final because he was afraid I'd get the wrong impression."

"Don't," Jack said very evenly, "compare me with Hayden."

She ignored that. "You know, I really hate being caught in a war zone." She set the empty glass down very hard on the table. "It's hard on the ego."

He took a step toward her. "Elizabeth—"

"Maybe I'll just invest in a nice collection of high-class erotica and some interesting mechanical devices designed for personal use and forget about trying to have a real relationship."

He came toward her. She refused to give in to the urge to retreat. When he was close enough for her to feel the heat of his body, he stopped. He did not touch her.

"I don't recommend that approach," he said.

She tilted her head. "You've tried it?"

He raised one hand and slid his fingers slowly around the nape of her neck. "I used a manual technique instead of mechanical devices, and the erotica wasn't exactly high-class, but, yeah, I tried it."

Whispers of awareness stirred her senses. She tried to suppress them without success. It was always like this when he touched her, she thought. Sorcery. That was the only rational explanation.

"What happened?" she asked, wishing she did not sound so breathless.

"Not much." His thumb traced a small pattern against her throat. "Not until I used my imagination."

She dampened her lower lip with the tip of her tongue and then swallowed. "What did you imagine?"

"You. With me."

A fine time to get light-headed from the altitude, she thought. The night she had opened the door and found him standing there on the deck she had known what *might* happen. Last night when she had left him with that faint, dangling promise, she had known what *would* happen. Sooner or later. But for some strange reason, she had assumed that it would be later.

"Let me get this straight," she said very carefully. "You imagined my face on the models in some porn magazine?"

"Not just your face." He bent his head and brushed his lips lightly, invitingly, across hers. "I imagined everything else, as well."

She shuddered. "Was I wearing leather and steel studs and stiletto heels? I always wanted to wear that kind of an outfit."

"In my imagination," he said against her mouth, "you weren't wearing anything at all."

Without warning he deepened the kiss. His arms closed around her, crushing her gently. She put her hands on his shoulders and sank her fingers into the sleek strong muscles there.

"Jack."

"I've been going crazy." His lips burned against her throat. "Out of my mind."

She shut her eyes and inhaled the scent of his body, savoring the heady, indescribable essence of him. Waves of excitement swept over her. She felt his hands on the buttons of her shirt. A moment later the garment was on the floor. His palms closed around her breasts. In her haste to get dressed so that she could follow him, she had not bothered with a bra.

"I was right," he muttered against her mouth.

"About what?"

"About the feel of you." His thumbs moved across her nipples. "I spent a lot of time trying to recall exactly how soft you were."

She took her hands off his shoulders, pushed them beneath the bottom edge of his pullover, flattened them against his chest. "I wasted a lot of time thinking about how you look without a shirt."

"We both wasted six damned months."

"I'm not so sure they were wasted."

"I am."

He moved abruptly, scooped her up in his arms, and lowered her to the rug in front of the hearth. She heard the flames snap and crackle. The warmth of the fire enveloped her as Jack tugged off her jeans. But that was nothing compared to the heat of his eyes.

He put one hand on top of the triangle of curly hair at the apex of her thighs.

"Since when did you stop wearing underwear?" he asked.

"I was in a hurry tonight."

His mouth curved in a devastating grin. "So was I."

She discovered exactly what he meant a moment later when he unfastened his own jeans and removed them. He had not bothered to put on a pair of briefs. But he had thought to carry a condom in his wallet, she noticed.

He came to her at last, pinning her beneath him. She gasped when she felt his fingers slide between her legs. The deep, low-level hunger that she had learned to live with during the past few months sharpened without warning. She was suddenly ravenous. She felt herself grow moist and she knew that she had dampened his fingers. He groaned heavily and took one nipple into his mouth.

She sighed and slid her hands down the length of his spine, savoring the muscled contours of his back. His hand moved on her, exciting and at the same time maddening. He stroked gently, inside and out. Everything tingled and then tightened. She sucked in her breath as anticipation spiraled out of control. She clung to his shoulders, nibbled on his ear, and demanded more.

"I told you that this time I'd get it right," he whispered.

He moved slowly down the length of her body, leaving a trail of warm kisses along the way. But she did not realize his destination until she felt his mouth on her in an electrifyingly intimate kiss.

"Jack." She clutched at his hair.

He paid no attention, intent instead on what he was doing to her. Nobody, she thought, could focus on a project the way Jack could. She was wound so tightly now that she was afraid she would explode. She threaded her fingers into his hair and tugged. Hard.

He did not stop.

"Jack, *please.*"

The sweet tension was almost unbearable now, but he did not pause. She wanted to scream, but she could hardly catch her breath.

"Jack, so help me, if you don't—"

And then the climax hit her, wave after delicious wave of sensation. A thrill ride unlike any other she had ever taken. She could do nothing except hang on for the pulse-pounding trip.

Before it was over, Jack made his way back up her body, eased her thighs more widely apart, and used one hand to guide himself into her.

She had been so certain that she had not forgotten a single detail about their one night together six months ago. But she had been wrong. When she felt him push slowly, inevitably into her she realized that she had failed to recall precisely how hard he was and just how much of him there was when he was fully aroused.

And then, at last, he was inside. He pushed deep, filling her completely.

He lowered his head to kiss her throat. "I told you that if I ever got a chance to take this test a second time, I'd do whatever it took to pass."

Chapter Fifteen

He pushed the pause button and leaned forward to study the frozen frame. Vicky was spectacular in this scene, he thought. It was the one in which Eden plotted with her lover, Harry, to murder her brutal husband. The lighting was exquisite. It glinted on her elegant cheekbones and deepened the shadows around her eyes. She was so beautiful. So haunted. So desperate. She absolutely had to win the festival's Best Actress Award.

He continued to study the scene with a critical eye while he munched on the hamburger he had prepared on the outdoor grill. He must remember to clean up after he finished, he reminded himself. *She* had provided him with this beautiful house. She had also made it clear that she expected him to keep things picked up while he stayed here. She did not approve of his casual bachelor ways. He tried to please her, but it wasn't easy. She was very demanding. Very temperamental. Lately her mood swings seemed to be getting more dramatic. But then, she was under a lot of pressure. He understood. He was tolerant.

She was so beautiful, the most beautiful woman he had ever met. She could have had any man she wanted. He knew that she did not love him, not the way he loved her. Few could love the way he loved—with passion, conviction, total devotion. Few would throw away everything for the beloved one, as he was in the process of doing.

But she needed him. Ah, yes, she needed him. No one else could give her what he could give her, the gift she valued above all others: vengeance.

His ability to bestow that prize gave him a more secure hold on her affections than any other man could ever hope to have.

He finished the hamburger and absently brushed some crumbs onto the floor. The titles of a couple of classic films came to mind. He whispered them aloud to himself there in the darkness, because he thought they summed up his present situation quite nicely.

"I'm *On Dangerous Ground*. And there is *No Way Out*."

Perfect. It was the reason he loved film noir. It described his life.

After a while Tyler Page pressed another button on the remote control. The video of *Fast Company* snapped back into motion on the small screen. The voices of the actors echoed softly in the room.

> *"Some things you do for the sake of love, Harry. Some you do for the sake of revenge. Doesn't matter which reason you choose, you know. Either way, in the end, everyone thinks you're crazy."*

Chapter Sixteen

He awoke when the moonlight angled across his face. He opened his eyes and looked up through the high windows. The circle of silver was brilliant against the late-night sky. He was warm and comfortable. Satiated was a better word, he decided. The ideal word, in fact.

Elizabeth stirred in his arms, stretching languidly. The blanket he had snagged off the back of the sofa earlier fell to her waist. She must have noticed him gazing at her bare breasts, because she reached down to tug the large square of striped wool back to her throat.

"The rug's a little rough, isn't it?" she said.

"A little."

Common sense warned him that this would be a good time to keep his mouth shut or at least a good time not to ask questions. To ask questions would be to tempt fate. He had gotten lucky tonight. Few people got second chances. He should give thanks for his good fortune and keep his mouth shut.

Instead, he turned on his side, propped himself on his elbow, and looked down at her.

"Why?" he asked.

She gazed up at him. The only light in the room came from the fire and the moon. Her eyes were veiled by her half-lowered lashes. "Why is the rug rough?"

"You know what I'm asking. Why now? Tonight? What made you decide to give me another chance?"

"I told you I'd think about it." She shrugged. The blanket shifted again. She adjusted it. "I thought about it."

"It was because I told you about Hayden and the past, wasn't it?"

"Does it matter?"

He watched her face closely. "It matters."

"Why?"

"Because as much as I want you, I don't want any mercy fucks from you."

Her eyes widened in shock. "For heaven's sake, Jack—"

"I don't want you sleeping with me because you've decided I'm on some kind of noble quest to right the wrongs my father committed and because I've got a problem with a half brother who is out for revenge. Hell, I don't want you feeling sorry for me."

Her eyes narrowed. "If I slept with every man I've ever met who came from a dysfunctional family, I'd be an extremely busy woman."

Her tone brought him up short. Was he getting a little obsessive here?

"I guess that's true," he said.

She touched his bare shoulder, her fingers light and gentle on his skin. "I didn't sleep with you because I felt like doing you a favor. I don't do those kinds of favors."

"I know that." He was definitely showing indications of obsessive behavior, he decided. It was time to pull back, close down, put up some barriers. But he couldn't seem to stop himself. "So why did you do it?"

She wrapped her arms around his neck. Her smile was slow and sensual and filled with a hint of smug satisfaction. "I did it because I've been wanting to do it again with you for six very long months. I was pretty sure we'd get it right this time. And we did."

"You're saying this is all about sex?"

"Not just any sex." She scowled playfully and tapped an admonishing finger against his mouth. "Very, very good sex."

A wave of heat tightened his body. "I won't argue that point."

"Good. Because I don't feel like arguing." She pulled him down to her, kissing him quickly, invitingly, before he could ask any more questions.

The familiar rush went through him. He forgot about everything else except the taste and feel of her. He bent his head to kiss the curves of her breasts, but paused when he realized that she was pushing insistently at his shoulders.

He grinned and obediently rolled onto his back, curious and intrigued now. She came down astride him, circled his wrists with her fingers, and pinned him to the rug. There was a delightfully wicked, erotic challenge in her eyes.

"Is this a new game?" he asked.

"You spent the past six months reading men's magazines in your spare time. I spent the past six months reading women's magazines in my leisure time."

Holding his wrists against the rug, she began to move against him. The insides of her thighs were smooth and firm. He was already hard, but he got harder.

He looked up at her. "Does this involve little velvet whips?"

"Do you mind?"

"Not as long as we get to take turns."

"I don't know about taking turns. I think I like this position."

"Me too," he said. "Those women's magazines must have been very cutting edge, editorially speaking."

"They were." She kissed his flat nipple. "Very politically correct, too."

"Politically correct? Ah, you mean the lady on top. That's good. I can go with politically correct on occasions like this."

She smiled again and bit his ear.

He laughed softly, savoring the torment.

"My turn," he said after a while.

"Not yet," she said.

She kissed him again. Heat roared through him.

"Now," he said.

Very gently he flipped her onto her back, reversing their positions, and lowered his head to take her mouth.

"Wait," she said just before he entered her. "What about the little velvet whips?"

"We'll get to those," he promised softly.

It was only later, when the first gray light of dawn appeared in the high windows, that he realized that she had deliberately distracted him. It had been an effective tactic, he reflected. But the bottom line remained clear. He still did not know why she had ended the standoff that had kept them apart for six months.

He told himself it did not matter. But a part of him knew that it did matter. A lot.

He had been so sure that if he got a second chance with her in bed everything would be okay.

He was profoundly grateful that he had been given an opportunity to get the sex part of the equation right at last.

But now that that hurdle was past, he sensed the problem was not yet solved. Something was still missing.

What the hell did he want from her?

*The Mirror could have served as a set for a scene from a clas-*sic film, Elizabeth thought. The atmosphere of the crowded nightclub was dark and hazy, heavy with a sense of languor and seedy decadence. Antique mirrors of all shapes and sizes hung on the walls, creating a disorienting series of cloudy reflections.

Not exactly Rick's place in *Casablanca*, but close enough.

On the small stage a sultry redhead clad in a form-fitting gown stood in the spotlight. She delivered a torchy love song in a rich, husky voice that was slightly rough around the edges.

With a little imagination one could picture Bogart sitting at a corner table, a drink in front of him, thinking about Paris.

Jack had chosen the club after making a few inquiries. Not that there were a lot of choices. Mirror Springs was trendy, but it was, nevertheless, a small town. It could sustain only a handful of night spots. The Mirror was generally acknowledged to be the hottest of the lot.

Jack had bet that it would attract the most prominent festivalgoers. He had been right, Elizabeth thought, glancing around. Everyone who was anyone was here tonight. Vicky Bellamy and Dawson Holland held court at a table near the stage. Elsewhere in the gloom, Spencer West, the writer, was downing tequila sunrises at a steady rate. He was surrounded by a group of very serious-looking people dressed in black who were also drinking heavily.

It had been Jack's decision to come here after they had attended the screening of an extremely forgettable festival entrant titled *Stranger in an Alley*. Everybody died in the end.

Elizabeth leaned partway across the small, candlelit table and pitched her voice to a level just above a whisper. "I don't want you to think that I lack faith in your executive planning ability, but are you sure you know what you're doing?"

"Trust me." He did not look away from the singer. "It has always been my experience that nothing loosens up a logjam like a little cash."

"You're not talking about a little cash. You're talking big bucks here."

"It'll be worth every cent if it gets us to Page before he pulls off his auction."

"But, Jack—"

He switched his attention from the singer to her. In the bluesy light his face was etched in shadows. She could feel the relentless determination humming through him.

"It's not like we have a lot of options here," he said. "Time is running out."

"I still say he'll show up at the awards ceremony or at the premiere of *Fast Company*. That gives us two chances to nab him."

"If this works, we won't have to depend on trying to spot him in the crowds at the ceremony or the screening." Jack broke off, eyes narrowing as his gaze shifted to someone or something behind her. "There goes Ledger. Looks like he's headed toward the men's room. If you'll excuse me, I've got an appointment."

Elizabeth winced. "Charming venue for a business conversation."

"Don't knock it." Jack was already on his feet. "I've done some of my most important deals in the men's room."

"Why in a rest room, for heaven's sake?"

"Size does matter."

She glared at him, uncomfortably aware of the heat rising in her cheeks. She silently gave thanks for the dim lighting. Jack slanted her a knowing grin and glided off through the maze of small tables. In the faint, flickering glow of the candles he was a lean, imposing figure. A man of mystery. She lost sight of him when he disappeared into a dark hallway. The sign over the entrance was done in purple neon letters that spelled out the words "Rest Rooms."

A figure moved out of the shadows and halted near the chair Jack had just vacated.

"I hate to see a lady sitting alone," Hayden said. "Mind if I join you?"

Jack followed Leonard Ledger into the men's room. A quick glance showed that they were alone in the facility. There were mirrors in here, too. The three antique framed squares of reflective glass that hung in a row above the washbasins appeared quite ordinary. But he couldn't say the same for the wide strip of mirrored glass set into the wall behind the urinals. The inset mirrors were positioned precisely at groin level. Any man taking a leak would find himself gazing down at the reflection of his own penis.

Which was exactly what Leonard Ledger was doing. In fact, Ledger seemed happily riveted by the scene he was viewing.

Jack took a closer look and noticed that the mirror behind the urinals had been designed to reflect a larger-than-life image. Maybe the designer should have etched a warning on the glass: "Caution: Objects in mirror may be smaller than they appear."

Jack reached back and flicked the lock on the door. At the sound of the faint but unmistakable click, Leonard glanced over his shoulder. When he saw who stood there, his slightly perplexed expression lightened instantly.

"Jack. Hey, what a coincidence," Leonard said brightly. "I was planning to catch up with you tomorrow. Got a copy of the script for *Dark Moon Rising* for you."

"Is that right?"

"You're in luck. I happen to have it with me tonight. You can take it home to read. You're gonna love it."

"How badly do you need money for your film?"

Leonard rolled his eyes, shook twice, and stuffed himself back into his pants. "Are you kidding?" He yanked on his zipper. "If money is the mother's milk of politics, it's the life's blood of filmmaking. There's never enough cash."

"Never enough?"

Obviously fearing that he had made a serious misstep, Leonard rushed into words of urgent reassurance. "Which doesn't mean I don't know how to stick to a budget. Don't worry about that angle. I guarantee I'll bring *Dark Moon Rising* in on time and under budget. No problem."

"I'll take your word for it. I'm interested in investing in your picture."

Leonard's shaved head glowed pink with enthusiasm. "Fabulous. You won't regret this, Jack. *Dark Moon Rising* is going to be big. Very, very big. And we haven't even talked about the foreign distribution possibilities. Sky's the limit there. Trust me."

"You can tell me about the distribution possibilities later. Right now I want to go over the terms of our arrangement."

Leonard blinked. "Terms?"

"I'll sign on as an investor for *Dark Moon Rising* if you help me find a man."

Leonard's mouth was already opening to accept the deal. But he closed it again very quickly and cleared his throat.

"A man?" he repeated neutrally.

"Yes."

"Well, hey. Don't get me wrong here." Leonard held up his hands, palms out. "I got no problems with your sexual orientation. Personal thing, y'know? It's just that I'm not sure I can help you out in this area. I mean, I'm not exactly Mr. Matchmaker, see? I could maybe introduce you to some people I know, but—"

Jack smiled. "Forget the matchmaking. I'm not looking for a date. I'm looking for a guy who stole something from me."

Leonard looked more wary than ever. "What did he steal?"

"That's not important. What's important is that I find him as soon as possible."

Fresh alarm blazed across Leonard's face. "We're not talking drugs or anything like that, are we? I don't want to get involved—"

"No drugs. Nothing illegal. Nothing dangerous. This was high-tech industrial theft. White-collar crime."

"Sounds like you need the cops."

"Nobody ever calls the cops on this kind of crime."

"Oh, yeah. I've heard that. Bad publicity, huh?"

"Right."

Leonard frowned. "You check the local hotels for this guy?"

"Yes. He's not registered anywhere here in town."

"But you're pretty sure he's around?"

Jack thought about the phone call he had received inviting him to attend the auction. "He's here somewhere. What I need is someone who knows who's who behind the scenes here in Mirror Springs."

Leonard looked wise. "Someone who knows the players."

"Whatever." It was hard to think of any of the low-budget independent filmmakers he'd met here at the festival as Hollywood-style *players,* but Jack decided not to comment. He didn't want to insult Leonard. "If I give you the name of a guy who helped produce a film called *Fast Company,* think you could find him?"

Leonard's eyes narrowed. "Maybe. If he's hanging around. Is that all you want me to do?"

"There is one other small thing."

Leonard uttered a world-weary groan. "I was afraid of that."

Jack smiled slightly. "It's not so hard. I just want to be sure you keep this low-key, understand? I'm trying to find this guy, not scare him off."

Leonard relaxed, happy again. "Got it. Don't worry, I won't take out an ad in the *Mirror Springs Gazette.* What's the name of this dude you're looking for?"

"Tyler Page."

"Never heard of him." Leonard flipped one hand in a vague gesture. "He can't be very big in the business."

"He's not. But he's got ambitions."

"Doesn't everyone? Okay, I'll see what I can turn up." Leonard frowned. "How do I get in touch with you?"

"You can call me at either of these two numbers." Jack took a card out of his pocket and scrawled the number of the house where he and Elizabeth were staying and his cell phone number. He handed the card to Leonard. "Day or night. Remember, try not to make waves. He'll disappear on me if you screw up. And I will lose all interest in *Dark Moon Rising* if that happens."

Leonard glanced at the card and then looked up. Some of his initial enthusiasm had faded. "You really want to find this guy bad, don't you?"

"Yes." Jack went to the door and unlocked it. "I do."

"Hang on." Leonard hurried to follow him out of the rest room. "I'll get that script for you."

Jack paused at the door. "Mind washing your hands first?"

"I think I'd better make it clear that I'm a noncombatant in your little war with Jack," Elizabeth said.

"Innocent bystanders get hurt when he's in the vicinity." Hayden smiled grimly across the table. "But you already know that, don't you?"

"What is this all about, Hayden?"

"Soft Focus."

"I don't intend to discuss that subject with you again."

He ignored that. "You're here for the auction. You're Jack's checkbook. He won't be able to afford to stay in the bidding without the Aurora Fund to back him up."

"Go away, Hayden."

"I didn't get a chance to finish making my pitch yesterday. We can both make a killing on this if we work together."

"This conversation is starting to bore me."

He leaned closer, his eyes gleaming in the candlelight. "Talk to me, Elizabeth. Work with me."

"Why should I?"

"Because you can't trust Jack. You know that. Come in with me on this and I'll make it worth your while. You have my personal guarantee."

"What, exactly, do you want me to do?"

"Nothing."

"I beg your pardon?"

He grinned, a fleeting smile that reminded her of Jack. "I just want you to agree not to back him at the auction. He can't outbid me on his own."

"I thought I made it clear that as far as I'm concerned, I've got a vested interest in Excalibur. I'm not interested in taking a financial hit for the sake of revenge."

"You disappoint me, Elizabeth. I pegged you as a woman of passion and imagination."

"A lot of people make that mistake."

"If it's only the money that's standing in the way, I can take care of that. My company is worth ten times as much as Excalibur and it has its own R & D projects, remember? At least two are guaranteed to hit big. I give you my word that if you help me out here, I'll cut the Aurora Fund in for a piece of the action."

She studied him. "I know he's your half brother, Hayden. He told me the story. I don't want to get involved in a family quarrel."

Hayden stared at her. Then his eyes hardened. "Shit. What's the matter with you? He's using you. Can't you see that?"

"What I see," she said gently, "is that your need for revenge is eating you up inside. On top of the unresolved issues you've got with the past, you're going through a difficult divorce. That's undoubtedly added a lot of stress."

"Don't analyze me. You don't know a damn thing about my past except what Jack chose to tell you. And you can bet that was a pack of lies. As for my divorce, you haven't got a clue. No one does. You can't even begin to understand what it's been like dealing with a spoiled little girl who thinks her rich daddy can give her anything she wants."

The sudden gritty anger in his voice alarmed her. "Hayden—"

"Jack was smart enough to slip out of the noose before Ringstead could tighten it around his neck. I'll give him credit for that. But I got caught."

"What on earth are you talking about?"

"Didn't Jack tell you that he used to date my almost-ex-wife? Jack and Gillian. Cute, huh?"

"Oh, dear."

"She picked him because *Daddy* liked him, you see. Ringstead decided that Jack had what it took to control Ring, Inc. But fool that I was, I convinced her that Daddy would like me even better. And you know what?" Hayden's mouth twisted with savage self-mockery. "He did."

Elizabeth groaned. "You stole Gillian away from Jack?"

"It wasn't hard." He tightened one hand into a fist on top of the small table. "Now I know why."

"Why?"

"Because Jack had already figured out that the whole fucking family was poison. He probably laughed himself sick on my wedding day. And he's laughing even harder now, knowing how much it's going to cost me to squirm out of the Ringstead trap."

"You can't blame Jack for the fact that you married Gillian Ringstead. Deep down, you know that." Impulsively she touched his clenched hand. "You've obviously got issues with the past, but you won't settle them by trying to avenge yourself on your brother."

"*Half* brother." Hayden got to his feet with a quick, violent movement. "And I will destroy him, Elizabeth. The way his father destroyed my mother. For your own sake, I hope you're not standing too close when it happens. Believe it or not, I really don't want to see you get hurt."

He turned and strode off toward the entrance of the club. On stage the singer launched into another haunting ballad, a tale of love and risk. Elizabeth did not recognize the song, but she knew the wistful, melancholic feeling it produced all too well.

> "Better yes than no,
> Better to take the fall,
> Better some kind of love than no love at all."

She let the music drift over her, feeling safe as long as it stayed on the surface. And then, without warning, it was inside her. She tightened her grip on her glass as the song stirred memories of last night.

She had made a pact with herself. She had vowed to concentrate on the physical pleasure and the satisfaction she had found in Jack's arms. *Keep it all on the surface this time.* But the singer was reaching deeper with her music, stirring more dangerous embers.

Getting beneath the surface.

In an effort to shake off the disturbing twist in the pit of her stomach, she glanced toward the purple neon sign that marked the rest rooms. There was no sign of Jack. How long did it take to make a deal in a men's room?

She glanced at her watch. When she looked back at the dark hallway again, she caught a glimpse of blond hair piled high on a gracefully held head. Vicky Bellamy was heading toward the women's room.

On impulse, Elizabeth got to her feet. She slung her small evening bag over her shoulder and made her way through the shadows toward the purple neon sign. She tried to think of a clever way to engage Vicky in a conversation in the ladies' room. *Loved your comments on the Femme Fatale panel. By the way, did you seduce Tyler Page to get him to steal a secret research specimen of a high-tech material for your husband?* Not exactly subtle. On the other hand, the approach had the virtue of being direct and to the point.

The walls of the hallway had been painted a very dark shade of purple. In the dim light they appeared almost black. Beneath the neon sign, the corridor branched off in opposite directions. A plaque on the wall informed her that the men's room was to the left. She glanced in that direction. The door was firmly closed. Jack was apparently still engaged in his business conference. The women's room was to the right.

She went down the short hall and opened the door. There were three stalls inside, all painted purple. There were no feet showing beneath any of the stall doors. The rest room was empty.

She backed out of the small room and rechecked the configuration of the hallway. There was one other way out that did not lead back into the main room of the club. She went to the third door and twisted the knob.

She found herself standing on a small loading dock.

A draft of cold night air hit her in the face. There was a single, bare bulb glowing weakly overhead. She peered into the shadows and saw a service road and a small employee parking lot. A large metal garbage bin loomed to her right. The odor of rotting garbage and stale booze was faint but detectable.

There was no sign of Vicky Bellamy, but she caught the sound of muted voices nearby in the darkness.

She closed the door behind her, wrapped her arms around herself to ward off the crisp mountain chill, and went down the loading-dock steps. Should have brought her coat, she thought. It was freezing out here. Then again, who could have guessed that Vicky Bellamy would sneak out of the club via the rear entrance?

A sudden, jolting possibility occurred to her. What if Vicky Bellamy really was involved in the theft of Soft Focus? What if she had chosen tonight to run off with Tyler Page and the crystal while Jack was doing his deal in the men's room?

No, that made no sense, Elizabeth thought. There was supposed to be an auction. If Vicky was mixed up in this mess, she was unlikely to leave until she got her hands on the money.

She couldn't just stand here and do nothing, Elizabeth decided. Slowly, she began to prowl along the line of dark vehicles. If someone asked her what she was doing, she could always say she had just stepped outside for a breath of fresh air.

She tried to appear casual as she moved from car to car, peering into the front seats. There was enough reflected moonlight to allow her to see large, bulky shapes. If Vicky was sitting in one of the vehicles, she would be able to see the outline of her body.

The body was not behind the wheel of one of the vehicles. It was lying on the ground near the rear tire of an aging Ford.

Elizabeth stared at the outflung arms, so pale in the moonlight. She opened her mouth to scream, but no sound came out. She took an instinctive step back toward the safety of the nightclub's rear door.

Then she made herself move forward again. With a sense of great dread she crouched down and started to check for a pulse.

"Are you—?" Stupid question. Of course the woman was not all right. She looked very dead.

A brilliant light flashed on, blinding her, just as she reached out to check for a pulse.

"Don't touch her," a man yelled furiously out of the shadows. "It took me half an hour to set up this scene."

Elizabeth's nerves were already strained to the limit. The man's irate shout was too much. She shrieked in startled outrage and leaped back, fetching up hard against the fender of the car.

"What . . . what . . ." She had to force herself to take a deep breath. "What the hell do you think you're doing?"

"Making a movie." Vicky Bellamy sounded dryly amused.

Elizabeth whirled around. She still had spots in front of her eyes from the effects of the sudden bright light, but she could make out Vicky's figure. The actress stood in the darkened space between two parked cars. The moonlight turned her hair to silver.

"Sorry about that." The man who had yelled at her did not sound sorry. He sounded annoyed. He moved into the light, displaying a sophisticated handheld camera. "Didn't mean to scare you. But you almost screwed up the scene."

The body on the ground stirred. "Can we finish this? It's getting damned cold down here."

"Yeah, sure. Just don't move, okay?" The man with the camera hurried back to his post behind the lights.

Someone else adjusted the long arm of a microphone.

Vicky chuckled. "They're participating in the contest."

"What contest?" Elizabeth asked.

"The Noir on the Fly contest," Vicky explained. "It's an annual tradition at the festival. Participants get some film stock and equipment and are challenged to script, shoot, and edit a short film during the week of the festival."

"I see." Elizabeth was relieved to note that her breathing was returning to normal. "The body on the ground was awfully realistic."

"Nothing is ever what it seems in the movies," Vicky said very softly. "Or in real life. It might be a good idea if you remembered that."

Elizabeth stilled. Surely she had not imagined the note of warning embedded in the words. "Thanks, I'll keep it in mind."

"It's a little chilly out here, isn't it?" Vicky turned and started back toward the loading dock. "You should have brought your coat."

Determined not to be left behind, Elizabeth hurried to catch up. "I wasn't planning to stay outside very long."

"What were you planning to do?" Vicky asked.

"I just wanted to get a breath of fresh air." Elizabeth groped for some plausible details to flesh out her thin story. "We're sitting in the nonsmoking section, but you know how it is. The air is never really great when there's a smoking section nearby."

"Yes," Vicky said. "I know how it is. But if I were you, I wouldn't stay out here too long. Normally, the crime rate in Mirror Springs is almost nonexistent. But this week there are a lot of strangers in town. You never know what might happen."

A shiver that had nothing to do with the chilled night air sent a trickle of alarm down Elizabeth's spine. She kept her smile in place with willpower alone. "You're certainly full of good advice tonight, Ms. Bellamy."

"I hope you'll pay attention. I don't usually waste my breath on advice, but I thought I'd make an exception in your case."

"Why?"

"I'm not sure." Vicky's smile was enigmatic. "Maybe it's the way you look at your friend, Jack Fairfax."

"Why is that important?"

"It's not important. Not really. It's just that once, a long time ago, I wanted to look at a man like that."

"What way is that?"

"As if you're wondering if you should let yourself fall in love with him." Vicky gave another throaty laugh. "My advice on that point, by the way, is don't."

Elizabeth stumbled against a small stone she had not noticed on the pavement. She sucked in a sharp, painful breath and quickly caught her balance.

"Are you by any chance trying to warn me off?" she asked bluntly.

Vicky gave her a long, considering glance. "A lady with a past has nothing to lose. But a woman with a future can't be too careful."

Elizabeth came to a halt and said nothing. Vicky went up the three steps to the back door, opened it, and disappeared inside the club without looking back again.

Now what the heck was that all about? Elizabeth wondered. She stared at the closed door of the club for a while longer and then the cold began to penetrate. She jerked herself out of her reverie and started toward the steps. So much for her big plan to pin Vicky down on the subject of Tyler Page.

The back door of the club opened without warning.

"Elizabeth?" Jack's voice sliced through the shadows. "What the hell are you doing out here?"

"Don't snap at me like that. I've already had a major scare tonight."

"What's going on?" Jack came swiftly forward and took her arm. He glanced at the filmmaking going on in the parking lot. "What the hell are those people doing out there?"

"Making a film. Some sort of festival contest." She glanced at him. "How did you find me?"

"Vicky Bellamy stopped me in the hallway and told me that she'd seen you step outside. Something about getting some fresh air."

"That's not quite how it happened. She came out here first. I followed her."

"Followed her?" Jack swept the dark landscape with a quick, assessing gaze. "Why?"

"Well, I did have a clever little plan in mind. I was going to see if I could trick her into admitting that she was involved with Tyler Page. But things didn't quite work out."

"What happened?"

"Vicky gave me lots of sound advice instead," Elizabeth said dryly.

Jack looked blank. "Advice?"

"Yep. And then she said something really, really interesting."

"What was that?"

" 'A lady with a past has nothing to lose. But a woman with a future can't be too careful.' "

"What's so interesting about that?"

"For starters," Elizabeth said, "it's a direct quote from the script for *Fast Company*."

"So?"

"So Vicky is one of a very small number of people who could possibly know that I had a copy of the script and might recognize the quote. She was the one who suggested I read it, in fact."

Jack eyed her curiously. "What's your point?"

Elizabeth turned around to watch the filmmaking in the distance. "I think she was trying to give me a warning."

Jack was silent for a long moment.

"Now why in hell would she do that?" he asked very quietly.

Maybe it's the way you look at your friend, Jack Fairfax. . . . Once, a long time ago, I wanted to look at a man like that.

"I don't know," Elizabeth said.

"Well, damn. Maybe you were right about her being Tyler Page's femme fatale. If she was trying to warn you off, then we have to assume that she's in this up to her phony blond hair."

"Yes."

"Why give herself away? And why try to get rid of you? If she knows anything about this deal, she knows you hold the purse strings for Excalibur."

"Yes," Elizabeth said. So many questions.

"And why would she think that some bad dialogue from *Fast Company* would be an effective warning?" Jack asked.

"Maybe because of what happens to the naive, not-so-bright female character who falls for the guy the femme fatale wants."

"Okay, I'll bite," Jack said. "What happens to her?"

"She gets killed."

Chapter Seventeen

"Stop it." Elizabeth threw her hands up. "Not another word. I've had all the arguing I can take for one night. I am not going back to Seattle, and that's final."

Jack stood motionless in the center of the rug, the very spot where he had made love to her last night, and watched her sweep recklessly around the room. Her anger created a palpable if invisible wake.

When the argument had exploded into full flame a few minutes ago, she had had her arms locked tightly beneath her breasts. But now, as the momentum gathered, her hands were sometimes in the air, sometimes stuffed into the back pockets of her snug velvet jeans. Never still.

He tried for a semblance of calm, soothing logic. It was only a facade, and he knew it. Underneath he could feel an unholy mix of rage and tension and something that was uncomfortably close to fear simmering. *If anything happens to her . . .*

He paused midway through that thought, unwilling to complete it. The truth was, he did not know how he would react if anything happened to Elizabeth. He might go a little crazy—make that a whole lot crazy.

He pulled himself up short with an effort of will. He would not go down that road. There was no point. It would be a clear case of overreaction. This was not some film noir script come to life. This was high-tech theft. White-collar crime. People didn't get hurt in this kind of thing. Not usually, at any rate.

But that did not mean it could not get nasty.

"She threatened you," he said for what must have been the thirtieth time. "We have to take it seriously."

"She did not threaten me." Elizabeth gave him a fulminating look. "Not exactly. She tried to warn me off. I think."

"It doesn't make sense. If she's in this, she knows who you are. She knows you've got the Aurora Fund checkbook and she knows that you can shell out big bucks for Soft Focus on behalf of your client. Why try to scare you off before the auction? Unless—" He broke off abruptly, thinking it through.

"Yes?" Elizabeth looked at him from the other side of the room. "Unless what?"

"If Vicky is involved in this, then it's probably safe to assume that Dawson Holland is also involved."

"Probably."

"Okay, for the sake of argument, let's say that assumption is true. It still leaves us with at least two possibilities. Number one: Vicky and Dawson were the strategists behind the theft of Soft Focus."

"Which fits in very nicely with my Vicky-as-Tyler-Page's-femme-fatale theory."

"Or," he continued deliberately, "possibility number two: They're here in Mirror Springs for the same reason we are. The same reason Hayden is, for that matter."

"Because they've been invited to attend the auction?"

"Right. Think about it. There aren't a lot of folks Page can risk inviting to his auction. He's a lab man, a loner. He doesn't move in the kind of circles where he'd be likely to meet high-rolling investors who would wink at the idea of bidding on a stolen item that can only be safely resold overseas. That crowd is definitely on the sophisticated side. If there's one thing Page is not, it's sophisticated."

"I take your point." She pursed her lips, eyes intent. "He would know about you and me, of course."

"Worldly sophisticates that we are," Jack muttered.

She ignored him. "He probably also knew about your long-standing rivalry with Hayden and could have guessed that your brother would be eager to bid up the price of Soft Focus."

"Right. And the one other person we know for sure he's come in contact with lately who might have enough money and few enough scruples to take part in this kind of deal is Dawson Holland."

Elizabeth frowned. "That would give us a motive for Vicky trying to warn me off tonight. She might be attempting to help Dawson by scaring off some of the competition."

"Yeah." He thought about it. "That does make some sense. I like it better than your femme fatale theory."

"That's because there is no romance in your soul." She shot him a withering glare. "You just can't envision a man taking the sort of risks Tyler Page is taking for love, can you?"

He was startled by the accusation in her voice. "I'm just trying to be realistic."

"Yeah, right." She halted abruptly. "You know what our real problem is?"

He raised his brows. "You want an annotated list?"

"I'm serious. Our problem is that we don't have enough information."

He raised his eyes to the high, vaulted ceiling and asked for patience. "No shit."

"We need to know more about Vicky Bellamy and Dawson Holland."

"I told you, I'm having Larry check out Holland."

She started toward the phone on the end table. "You asked your brother to check out Holland from a financial angle, right?"

"Far as I can see, that's the only angle that matters here."

"Maybe." She picked up the phone and punched in some numbers. "Maybe not."

He glanced at his watch. "It's after midnight. Who are you calling?"

"My assistant, Louise. She spent twenty years working for the tabloids. She has all kinds of contacts in the entertainment industry. She might know someone who—" She stopped, listening to whoever had answered the phone. Surprise flashed across her face. "I'm sorry, I must have dialed the wrong number. I'm calling for Louise Luttrell."

Jack walked to the window and looked out at the twinkling lights of Mirror Springs.

"Yes, I'll hold on a minute," Elizabeth said in muffled tones. "Louise? Who in the world was that? What do you mean, an old editor from out of town called? How old?"

Jack glanced over his shoulder, amused by the disconcerted look on Elizabeth's face.

"No, of course I didn't think you lived in a convent. I just wasn't expecting a man to answer your phone, that's all. Not at this hour, at any rate." Elizabeth glanced at Jack, saw that he was watching her, and turned her shoulder to him. "Uh, well, no, I'm not, actually. There was a slight problem with Jack's reservations at the resort, so he had to stay here and—"

She stopped speaking again and started to turn pink. Jack could hear the cackle of hysterical laughter on the other end of the line clear across the room. He smiled to himself.

Elizabeth cleared her throat and started to speak very quickly. "If you don't mind, Louise, I'm calling on a business matter. I want you to see what you can dig up on a small-time actress named Victoria Bellamy and her husband, Dawson Holland. I think they've both hung around the fringes of the film business for years and they're major figures here at this little festival."

Jack waited until she had finished her conversation with Louise and hung up the phone.

"That should get us some useful information," she said, turning back to face him. "Louise knows how to dig up the dirt on just about anybody. I should have thought of this yesterday."

"It's not a bad idea," he said.

"Gee, thanks for that glowing endorsement."

"Speaking of problems, I'd like to get back to our earlier topic."

"Which one?"

"You. Here in Mirror Springs."

She leaned against the back of the sofa, braced her arms on either side of her hips, and gave him a fierce look. "Don't even think about trying to convince me to leave."

"Elizabeth, I've got enough to worry about without having to wonder if Vicky is going to continue her little campaign to scare you out of town. It could get vicious. I don't want to take any chances."

"What you're really saying is that I've become an additional complication for you."

He spread the fingers of one hand wide. "You've been complicating my life since the day we met."

"You seem to have coped," she said a little too sweetly.

"Maybe. But this situation is getting messy."

"Well, you'll just have to deal with it, because I'm not cutting out now." Elizabeth gave him an oddly thoughtful expression. "Besides, she may come after you next."

He smiled. "You think Vicky will try to scare me off?"

"Not necessarily." Elizabeth studied him intently for a long moment. "If she's really into the role of the femme fatale, she might decide to try to seduce you instead."

He blinked. Then he gave her a wolfish grin. "That possibility worries you?"

"Yes, it does." She glowered at him. "Talk about complications. If Vicky sweeps you off your feet, we'll have real problems on our hands."

He laughed softly. "Fat chance."

Elizabeth smiled dangerously. "Are you saying you wouldn't be tempted if a woman like Vicky Bellamy came on to you?"

"Yeah, that's what I'm saying, all right. I was never good at juggling women. It's always a lot more difficult than it looks. At the moment, I've got my hands full."

"Are you talking about me?"

"Of course I'm talking about you. See any other women in the vicinity?"

She hesitated. "No."

"I thought I'd made it clear that there hasn't been anyone else for the past six months."

She turned her back to him and stood looking out into the night. "You've been busy with Excalibur."

He studied the rigid line of her graceful spine. The proud way she carried herself drew him like a magnet. "Not so busy that I couldn't have taken time to get laid if I'd wanted it or needed it badly enough. A good CEO knows how to set priorities."

"I see."

"What about you?"

"I've been pretty busy, too," she said, very offhand. "A few business dinners. That's about it."

Hayden's mocking words came back to him. *You might as well have written her name on the men's room wall at the club: "For a good time you definitely do not want to call Elizabeth the Ice Princess."*

He walked across the room and came to a halt immediately behind her. He did not touch her. "Hayden told me that it's my fault you haven't had any serious relationships for the past six months."

"Your fault?" Her voice rose in sharp outrage. "Good grief. Does he actually believe that I've been carrying the torch for you and you alone for six whole months?"

He winced at the derisive tone. "Not exactly. He thinks that after that blowup in the Pacific Rim Club, you got saddled with a certain, uh, reputation."

"I see. The Ice Princess thing?"

"Hayden implied that the title may have scared off a few of your date prospects."

She gave a short, ladylike snort. "Do you really think I'd want to date any man who got scared off that easily?"

He studied the arrogant tilt of her chin and smiled. He had definitely been wrong about the ice part, he thought, but not about the rest of it. There was something innately regal about her.

"No," he said.

"Look, we're getting a little off track here. We were talking about Vicky and Dawson Holland."

"I need to know," Jack said simply.

"What, exactly, do you need to know?"

"Was it the fallout from that scene at the club that put a damper on your social life?"

She exhaled deeply. "Brace yourself, Jack. Believe it or not, there were one or two men who worked up the nerve to ask me out after you announced to the world that I was frigid. What's more, I got the distinct impression that they were interested in more than just a friendly chat about what the Fed will do with interest rates."

He forced himself to ignore the sarcasm. He drew his finger across her bare nape. "So why haven't you been dating?"

"I've been busy." She turned slowly around to face him at last. There was steely determination in her eyes. "About Vicky Bellamy—"

He knew that he had pushed her as far as she was willing to be pushed. Reluctantly he dropped his hand to his side. "If you won't talk about packing your bags and heading back to Seattle—"

"I won't even discuss it," she said crisply. "I'm not going anywhere. You need me, Jack."

He looked at her and felt everything inside him focus one hundred percent on her. He put his hands very carefully around her neck. He used his thumbs to tip up her chin.

"I won't argue with that," he whispered.

Something in her eyes softened and deepened. "What a relief." She raised her mouth for his kiss.

This time they made it upstairs to his bed before he got her out of her jeans.

Later, after she had fallen asleep beside him, he lay back against the pillow, one arm behind his head, and silently asked the other question, the one he had not asked earlier.

Do you need me?

Dawson picked up the two balloon glasses and handed one to Vicky. "It's time for another assault from our stalker."

"I don't think it's working," Vicky said. "Everyone has concluded that the whole stalking thing is just a PR stunt. Even the masseuse at the spa asked me yesterday if it wasn't just a publicity gimmick."

"It's your fault. You're not acting sufficiently terrorized when he strikes."

Vicky swirled the liquor in the glass. "Maybe it is my fault. But I want to call it off. At least until the festival is over. Please, Dawson. This is an important week for me. I want to enjoy it."

He hesitated and then decided to relent. "You're right. This is your big week. I suppose we can cancel our stalker for a while."

She gave him a glowing smile. "You are so good to me, Dawson."

He looked at her. She was wearing the white peignoir tonight, the one that made her look like an innocent acolyte from some medieval cloistered retreat. She knew how much he liked this game, he thought. Hell, she knew everything there was to know about his sexual tastes. She had studied him, devoted herself to learning what pleased him in bed. She could have been the perfect mistress. Instead, she was the perfect wife. His wife. Every man he knew envied him. Every man who saw Vicky wanted her. But as long as he could afford her, she was his.

So why *did* he need the other women? he wondered. What was he looking for when he spent himself inside those faceless, nameless bodies? None of them could hold a candle to Vicky. If he tried to explain his problem to a shrink, the guy would think he really was nuts.

Vicky smiled as she sank down onto her knees in front of him.

The fabric of her white gown settled around her in graceful folds, brushing the tips of his shoes. She looked up at him from beneath her lashes, a novice kneeling at the feet of her chosen instructor, eager to learn the mysteries only he could impart.

He felt himself grow hard. It was as if she worked some magical spell on him. He did not have to do anything. She always did all the work. She was the aggressor, even when they played the acolyte game. How many men would kill to be in his place?

She put her fingertips on his knees and opened his legs. His robe fell open. She leaned forward, lips parted.

A short time later, on the brink of abandoning himself to the white-hot climax, he opened his eyes for a split second. He looked down at the top of Vicky's golden head and had a revelation. Suddenly he knew why he still needed the other women.

He sought them out because he needed reassurance. From time to time he needed to confirm his own manhood in the oldest, most fundamental way. He needed to prove to himself that he was still the one in control.

Because when he was with Vicky he knew that he was not in control. Like some exquisitely trained geisha, she gave him everything and at the same time she gave him nothing of herself. He could own her, but he could not truly possess her.

She was smart. He was a little worried that she might be even smarter than he was. But lately what disturbed him the most was that she was always in complete command of herself. She never drank too much, never ate to excess, never truly surrendered to the pleasures of sex. He was almost certain now that she was frigid.

As far as he could tell, she had no weaknesses other than her desire to act in films, and even when it came to that she drew the line. Acting was important to her, but not so important that she would have been willing to sacrifice everything for an acting career. Perhaps that was why she had never made it in Hollywood.

The blinding truth hit him.

Sometimes she scared the hell out of him.

*Elizabeth stood on the sidewalk outside a small shop that fea-*tured expensive handmade jewelry and pretended to study the display of one-of-a-kind necklaces behind the window. But her attention was on the faint reflection of Vicky Bellamy, who was walking into a clothing boutique on the opposite side of the street.

Tailing someone was proving to be a lot more boring in real life than it looked in the movies, Elizabeth thought. Either that, or Vicky just had a lot of dull stuff on her schedule today.

She couldn't complain, though. It had been her idea to follow Vicky around this morning. Jack had warned her that it would be a waste of time. He had remained at the house to make phone calls to Milo Ingersoll and to Larry. When she had left him he had been deep into a conversation with his brother. The topic had been Dawson Holland's recent business activities.

Jack had looked up from the phone and frowned when he noticed that she was heading for the door.

He'd put one hand over the receiver and said, "Don't do anything stupid."

She'd made a face and walked outside to her car.

Finding Vicky in town had been easy enough. Elizabeth had consulted the festival schedule, noted an actor's workshop that featured her quarry on a panel, and simply waited.

When the panel had concluded, Vicky had promptly gone shopping. An hour had passed and she was still cruising through the trendy boutiques and shops that lined the main street of Mirror Springs.

The small downtown district was crowded with festival-goers who were taking a break from screenings and workshops, but it was not difficult to keep track of Vicky. Dressed in a winter white turtleneck, flowing, wide-legged white trousers, and a long sweep of dashing white coat, she stood out like a beacon amid the sea of black and denim. Not just wanting to be noticed, Elizabeth thought. Needing it. Craving it. Living the part of Victoria Bellamy, Actress.

Or just making it easy for someone to follow her?

She was so intent on Vicky that she did not sense the presence of the large, burly man who had moved into her personal space until he spoke.

"Lizzie? Hey, talk about luck, huh? I was just about to drive out to your place."

She started at the sound of the too-familiar voice. Her gaze snapped from Vicky's reflection to that of the man standing beside her. At the sight of him she felt a small sigh unfurl within her.

Her brother-in-law always reminded her of a good-natured, eager-to-please St. Bernard. There was something refreshingly innocent and endearing about him. It was almost impossible to resist his friendly, engagingly unhandsome face. His red hair and cheerful blue eyes gave him a look of honesty and sincerity that she knew was utterly genuine.

He was actually quite brilliant. Grand schemes and plans bubbled forth from him in a seemingly endless fountain of cleverness. On top of everything else, he was an utterly devoted husband and a proud father of three.

Too bad he was such a screwup, she thought fondly. The downside of Merrick was that something inevitably went wrong whenever he tried to implement his great ideas. In the years since he had married her sister, Rowena, he'd had at least a dozen jobs, tried three times to start his own business, and lost a lot of money in the stock market.

Definitely a screwup, but he was family. That made him her screwup.

After her initial jerk of surprise, a fatalistic sense of resignation went through her.

"What are you doing here, Merrick?"

"Kind of obvious, isn't it?" He smiled his slightly canted smile, the one that curved a little more on the right than it did on the left and made his eyes crinkle slightly. "I came here to find you, Lizzie. Since when are you into this film noir stuff, by the way?"

"I don't believe this." She swung all the way around to face him. "You *followed* me to Mirror Springs?"

"Just got here." He scrubbed his face with his hand. "Been a long trip. Caught a red-eye to Denver and then had to rent a car and drive that damned mountain road. I thought I'd stop for some coffee here in town before I looked up the address of the place where you're staying. Lucky I spotted you when I left the café. I was just on my way back to my car when I saw you standing here."

She tightened her hands into fists inside the front pockets of her down coat. "How did you get my address here in Mirror Springs?"

"Called Louise. She gave it to me."

"I'll have to speak to Louise."

"What the heck's going on, Lizzie?" Merrick cocked his head. "You've been avoiding me for the past month. You didn't return any of my calls. Then I arrive in Seattle and find out you've left town to attend a film festival, of all things. And what's all this about you being here with some guy named Fairfax?"

Elizabeth sorted through the flood of questions and picked the one that had the simplest answer. "I am here with Jack Fairfax."

Merrick's red brows came together in a troubled frown. "I didn't know you were seeing anyone special these days."

"You and I haven't talked a lot lately, Merrick. We've both been busy."

"Who is he?"

"Fairfax? Among other things, he's the CEO of Excalibur Advanced Materials Research. The Aurora Fund has a heavy investment in the company."

Merrick's eyes widened in alarm. "You're sleeping with a client?"

She ground her teeth. "I prefer not to use the phrase 'sleeping with a client.' Sounds tacky."

"Geez, I'm sorry, Lizzie. It's just that that kind of thing's not your style. Sort of a shock to hear that you're, uh, fooling around with a client."

"He's not exactly a client. Well, technically speaking, he is, I guess." She angled her chin. "I prefer to think of him as a business partner."

"Sure, sure, call him whatever you want. So what's the deal? Is this serious? Rowena's going to have a million questions when I tell her."

"Merrick, I really don't want to talk about this. My personal life is my own affair. Tell me what you want and then you can leave."

He looked crushed. "You make it sound like I only come to see you when I want something."

"We do seem to have our most intimate chats when you're looking for someone to back one of your projects."

"That's not the way it is, and you know it," he said earnestly. "We're family, Lizzie."

"I know, I know." She smiled ruefully. He was right. They were family. "What is it this time? I better warn you I'm not putting another dime into frozen methane hydrate technology. You can get methane out of the back end of a cow a lot cheaper than you can by drilling through the ocean floor."

Merrick looked briefly distracted. A familiar light appeared in his blue eyes. "Methane hydrates are the fuel of the future, Lizzie. An enormous natural gas resource. That company I invested in was just a little ahead of its time, that's all. Sometime in the next five years someone will make that drilling technology financially viable."

"I think I can wait."

"Actually, that wasn't why I tracked you down," he said quickly. "I want to talk to you about this computer security lock idea I've got. It's a completely new approach. Mechanical instead of a software design, see? What's more, it's perfect for the new light-based technology."

"Excuse me, Merrick." She stood on tiptoe to peer over his broad shoulder. "You're standing in my way."

She spotted Vicky emerging from the doorway of the clothing boutique. Sunlight glinted on the actress's dark glasses as she turned and walked along the sidewalk to a white Porsche parked at the curb.

"I've got a business plan this time, Lizzie," Merrick continued. "I've also talked to some computer guys. Real hackers and crackers. They say my idea looks good. But I need some backing—"

"I'm a little busy at the moment, Merrick."

"I'll lay it on the line." He drew himself up. "We both know my track record is not real good. I've got nowhere else to turn. You're my only hope."

"Uh-huh." Elizabeth started to edge around him. "Call me when I get back to Seattle, okay?"

Down the street Vicky got into her white Porsche and pulled away from the curb.

"Damn," Elizabeth muttered.

"Lizzie?" Merrick frowned. "Is something wrong?"

Elizabeth contemplated running back to where she had parked her own car and following the other woman. But that did not sound promising. Vicky was probably on her way home.

So much for her budding career as a private eye, Elizabeth thought. Resigned to the inevitable, she turned back to Merrick.

"All right." She started along the sidewalk. "Let's go someplace and talk."

Relief erased the incipient concern on Merrick's face in an instant. His boundless optimism snapped back into place. His eyes brightened with excitement as he fell into step beside her. Elizabeth suppressed another sigh. She knew that look. He was sure everything was going to be all right now. She would come to his aid with the Aurora Fund and he would rush recklessly forward with his blue-sky dreams.

"All I need this time is a small commitment from the Fund," Merrick assured her. "Seed money. Just enough to get the attention of some other potential investors. You know how it is. Money follows money. Once other people know that the Aurora Fund is in on the deal, they'll want a piece of the action. The idea is great. Guaranteed return on your investment. But it will take a little time to get it up and running."

"That's what you said the last time."

"I know. But this time things are going to work for me, Lizzie. I can feel it."

"That's what you said the last time," Elizabeth repeated. But she said it under her breath.

Merrick looked up with a frown when the man's shadow fell across the fender of the car. "Do I know you?"

"The name's Hayden Shaw." Hayden smiled at him. "I saw you talking to Elizabeth Cabot a few minutes ago."

Merrick removed his hand from the car door handle and turned around with a quizzical expression. "You know Lizzie?"

"I'm in business in Seattle. We're both members of the same club. You a friend of hers, too?"

"I'm her brother-in-law. Married her sister, Rowena." Merrick stuck out his hand. "Name's Merrick. Merrick Grenville."

Hayden's smile widened slowly as he shook hands. "What a coincidence. Are you here for the festival?"

"This film thing?" Merrick grimaced. "No. I just came in for the day to see Lizzie. Gotta get back to Phoenix tonight."

"If you can spare fifteen minutes, I'd like to buy you a cup of coffee."

"Thanks, but I'm in kind of a hurry. Long drive back to the airport."

"This won't take long." Hayden clapped a hand on his shoulder. "I think you'll want to hear what I have to say."

"What's this all about?"

"It's about your sister-in-law's relationship with Jack Fairfax."

Merrick frowned. "You know the guy?"

"Yes," Hayden said. "I know him very well. And there are a few things I think you should know about him, too."

Chapter Eighteen

Jack saw Elizabeth the moment that she walked into the restaurant. He glanced at his watch and frowned. She had kept him waiting twenty minutes for lunch. She was never late.

Almost never.

"What happened?" He got out of the booth and took her coat. "Get lost following Vicky Bellamy around town?"

"Shush." Elizabeth scowled as she sat down on the other side of the table. "For heaven's sake, lower your voice."

"Sorry."

"You think I'm wasting my time watching her, don't you?"

"Uh-huh. I'm going to learn a lot more from Larry than you will playing private eye. So why are you late?"

"Not because of Vicky. My brother-in-law, Merrick, showed up out of the blue."

Merrick Grenville. The brother-in-law who had lost his job when Morgan had swallowed up Galloway. Damn. He did not need this particular complication, Jack thought. Not now.

"Grenville came all the way here just to see you?" he asked warily.

"He wanted to talk business." She opened her menu with a tense, jerky little motion. "I spent an hour and a half with him. He left a few minutes ago. Said he had a plane to catch."

"What did he want?"

Her jaw tightened. She did not look up from the menu. "It was just a personal conversation. Family stuff."

"In other words, he wanted money."

"Like I said, it was a personal conversation," she said tightly.

He reached out and removed her menu from her fingers. It wasn't easy. She tried to hang on to it. When she was finally forced to release it and meet his eyes, he did not like the mix of emotions he saw in her face.

"Did you tell him about me?" he asked bluntly.

"He knows I'm staying with you, yes."

"Don't play games with me, Elizabeth. Did you tell him that I was the consultant behind the Galloway takeover?"

She reached across the table, seized the menu, and yanked it back out of his hand. "The subject did not arise." She bent over the list of appetizers as though seeking divine portents.

"In other words, you didn't tell him. He doesn't know you're sleeping with the man who took Galloway apart."

She did not look up from the menu. "I didn't think it was any of his business."

"Why didn't you tell him about me?"

"I think I'll have a salad," she said. "I'm not very hungry for some reason."

He leaned partway across the table. "Why didn't you tell him about me?"

She closed the menu. Her Ice Princess mask was firmly in place. "Because I knew it would upset him and I was not in the mood for a scene. Now, can we please change the subject? Did you have any luck talking to Larry?"

"You're afraid to tell him about us, aren't you? You think he'll conclude that I'm using you."

Anger flared in her eyes, melting the ice in a flash of blue-green fire. "I told you, I want to change the subject."

"How long do you think you can keep our relationship a secret from your family?"

"I wouldn't exactly call what we have a relationship."

"What would you call it?"

She narrowed her eyes. "At the moment, I suppose it could be classified as a business fling."

"Business fling, huh?" Anger shafted through him. "How would you define 'business fling'?"

"Gosh, I'd say it looks pretty much like any other kind of fling to me. Limited in both scope and duration."

"You think that what we have going between us will burn itself out so quickly that you'll never have to explain me to your family? Is that your big plan?"

"We don't have time for this," she said through her teeth. "We've both got another priority, remember? What did you find out from Larry?"

He wanted to argue. He wanted to make her admit that what they had together was not limited in scope or duration. He wanted to force her to tell her family about him.

But one look at the stubborn determination in her eyes and he knew he would get nowhere today. The waiter arrived to take their order. Jack sat back, took a deep breath, and concentrated on the problem of Soft Focus.

When the waiter disappeared, Jack met Elizabeth's eyes across the table. "Larry had some more background data on Holland's business dealings. The guy's had his financial ups and downs in the past, but that's not unusual for a high roller. The most interesting piece of news is that he's chalked up some big losses in the past year. Took a huge position in an international hedge fund that went belly-up."

Elizabeth looked thoughtful. "That is interesting. I wonder if he plans to use Soft Focus to recover."

"Maybe. But to do that, he'd have to take it out of the country." Jack reached for a chunk of the focaccia bread that the waiter had left on the table.

"I suppose it goes without saying that there's been no sign of Tyler Page?"

"No. The little worm seems to have vanished from the face of the earth."

The waiter returned with the salad Niçoise that Elizabeth had ordered and a plate of grilled salmon. Jack picked up his fork. He got one bite of the salmon before he saw Elizabeth stiffen. Her gaze went to a point just behind his shoulder. Her mouth parted on a soft, wordless exclamation.

Adrenaline pumped. He put down his fork. "What is it? Do you see Page?"

"No, I—" She broke off. "Jack, wait, don't get up."

But he was already on his feet, turning to see who it was she had spotted in the crowded restaurant.

He stepped straight into a swinging fist. He had about half a second to see it and turn away in an arc that harmonized with the direction of the moving fist. The result was that the blow clipped him on the side of the jaw and slid off into thin air. But he had been caught off balance. He lurched to the side and came up hard against the end of the booth.

"Merrick!" Elizabeth sounded both furious and horrified. "What do you think you're doing?"

Elizabeth knew the guy, Jack realized. Wonderful. Instinct warned him not to defend himself. He would come off looking like the aggressor, and women always took a dim view of that kind of thing. He reached out, grabbed the back of the seat, and made a show of trying to steady himself.

A startled hush had fallen. Every eye in the restaurant was directed at the three of them.

Great. Another restaurant; another scene. Somehow, Jack thought, he just knew Elizabeth was going to blame him again even though he had made no move to retaliate to the unprovoked attack. He took in the sight of the large, redheaded, red-faced man who loomed in front of him. Merrick was breathing heavily, fists clenched. Jack glanced past him and saw Hayden hovering at the entrance of the restaurant.

Hayden caught his eye, gave him an icy smile, and flipped a one-fingered salute. Then he turned and walked outside.

"What the hell do you think you're doing with my sister-in-law?" Merrick demanded in a voice that shook with righteous indignation.

Jack cautiously touched his jaw while he contemplated the various possible answers to the question. "Funny you should ask. I was just telling Elizabeth that she really ought to introduce me to her family."

"I already know who you are, Fairfax. You're the bastard who took down Galloway."

Elizabeth was on her feet. "Merrick, please. Don't say another word."

"Do you know who this is, Lizzie?"

"I know who he is," she got out in a half-strangled voice. "We are in the middle of a restaurant, and everyone is staring at us. I do not want to hear another word from either of you. Is that clear?"

"Sure clear to me," Jack said.

Merrick pressed his lips tightly together and watched Jack as though he were a snake that might strike at any instant.

Jack cautiously checked his teeth with his tongue. Everything seemed solidly in place. He didn't taste any blood. His lucky day.

Elizabeth opened her purse, removed a handful of cash, and tossed it down on the table. Then she hitched the strap of her purse up onto her shoulder and looked at each man in turn.

"You will both follow me out of here and you will not speak until we are outside." She started toward the door without a backward glance.

Jack looked at Merrick. "After you."

Merrick hesitated, and then he turned with an awkward motion and stalked out of the restaurant in Elizabeth's sizzling wake.

Heads swiveled to follow the trio. Elizabeth and Merrick went through the front doors without looking at the hostess, who stood at her post, clutching a stack of menus as though they were bibles she could use to ward off vampires and demons.

Jack took pity on her.

"Don't worry," he said as he went past the stunned woman. "It's a family trait. You get used to it after a while."

He went out the door and saw Elizabeth and Merrick standing on the sidewalk. He caught the tail end of the low-voiced quarrel.

"Shaw told me the whole story," Merrick said. The words were muffled and tight with fury. "How Fairfax seduced you into backing Excalibur and then humiliated you in front of half of Seattle."

"It wasn't exactly *half* of Seattle," Elizabeth said stiffly.

Jack glanced at her. "If that's your idea of setting the record straight, I think I'd better handle this myself."

They both turned to glare at him.

Jack sighed. "Why don't you go back to the house, Elizabeth? Merrick and I will take a walk down by the river and sort this out."

"Oh, no, you don't," Elizabeth said. "I am not about to leave the two of you alone. I will not tolerate any more stupid, macho, chest-beating scenes."

"Coming from the lady who poured a full pitcher of ice water over my head and called me an egg-sucking son of a bitch in front of *half* of Seattle, that's almost funny," Jack said.

Elizabeth glowered at him. "I am not going to let the two of you go off alone together."

"I give you my word we won't kill each other." Jack opened her car door. "Get in."

"I have absolutely no intention of leaving."

"This is something Merrick and I need to discuss alone," Jack said patiently. "Your presence will only complicate the issue."

A flicker of uncertainty appeared in her eyes. She glanced at the stone-faced Merrick. He said nothing.

"I don't think this is a good idea," Elizabeth insisted.

"Trust me," Jack said softly.

She hesitated a couple of seconds and then got behind the wheel. She took out her sunglasses, put them on, and sat there, frowning at him.

"Drive carefully," Jack said. "You're a little upset, so pay attention to the road, okay?"

"I am perfectly capable of driving safely."

"Glad to hear it." He shut the car door and stood back.

She shoved the key into the ignition and pulled away from the curb with only the slightest screech of burning rubber.

Jack looked at Merrick. "Let's go for a walk."

Elizabeth tossed the keys down onto the hall table and slammed the door closed. It was all she could do not to scream with frustration. What else could possibly go wrong?

She stalked into the kitchen, grabbed the kettle, and turned on the faucet. It was as if some malignant force was determined to jinx every attempt to recover the crystal. Or maybe the force was just bent on screwing up her relationship with Jack. Either way, the result was the same. She was no closer to getting her hands on Tyler Page and the crystal, and no closer to resolving the thorny questions embedded in her affair with Jack.

Why had Merrick chosen this week, of all times, to show up asking for money? It was her own fault, she thought. She should have returned his phone calls before she left Seattle. She groaned as she set the kettle on the stove. Aunt Sybil would have told her that that's what she got for trying to avoid a problem.

The phone rang just as she was pouring the boiling water over the loose green tea in the pot. She reached for the kitchen extension with her free hand.

"Hello?"

"I'm calling for Jack Fairfax." The voice was low, urgent, male. "Tell him it's important."

She heard voices in the background. They sounded like they were coming from a sound track. "Who is this?"

"Just get him, will you? I gotta talk to him. He's expecting my call. It's a business thing, y'know?"

Intuition kicked in. "Is this Leonard Ledger, by any chance?"

There was a short pause on the other end of the line.

"I gotta talk to Fairfax."

"Jack isn't here right now. Can I take a message?"

"Uh, no. No, I gotta talk to him myself. I'll try his cell phone."

"I think I hear his car in the drive," Elizabeth said smoothly. "Do you want to hold on, Mr. Ledger?"

"Yeah, sure," he said automatically. "I'll hold on."

She smiled as he confirmed his identity. Who said she couldn't play the role of the private eye. "Sorry, Mr. Ledger. It wasn't his car, after all."

"Damn. Okay, I'll try his cell phone."

There was a sharp click in her ear as Leonard hung up. She replaced the receiver and studied the teapot for a long moment. After she thought she had given Leonard enough time to make his call, she poured a cup of tea and started to reach for the phone again. It rang just before she touched it.

She answered quickly, expecting to hear Jack's voice.

"Hello?"

"I'm sorry about that scene in the restaurant," Hayden Shaw said quietly. "Just wanted you to know there was nothing personal in it."

"Nothing personal?" She heard her voice rise in renewed fury. "It was one hundred percent personal. What is it with you and Jack, anyway? You're not a stupid man. I can't believe you're going to let this ridiculous vendetta ruin your life."

"You don't understand, Elizabeth."

"Damn right." She hung up the phone.

*   *   *

"Shaw told me about what you did to Lizzie." Merrick stood at the
edge of the river and gazed out over the tumbling water. "How you lied to her
to get her to renew the funding for Excalibur. You seduced her to get what you
wanted. You used her. Humiliated her. I oughta beat the crap out of you."

"I didn't lie to her," Jack said. "And what happened between us six
months ago wasn't a seduction. It was the start of a serious relationship."

Merrick shot him a look of angry disbelief. "A serious relationship?"

"I admit things have been a little rocky from time to time, but we're still
together." He thought about the monthly board meetings. "We've been seeing each other on a regular basis."

"Bullshit. You're using her. She hasn't had a serious relationship since
she broke up with Garth Galloway."

An ominous cloud of gloom settled around Jack like a fog. "Garth Galloway? As in Camille Galloway's son? The chief financial officer at Galloway?"

"Yeah." Merrick shoved his hands into his coat pockets. "Elizabeth was
engaged to him."

"Engaged. To Camille Galloway's son." He was caught in some sort of
doom loop, Jack thought. Every time he made some progress, he was faced
with another disaster. "Figures."

Merrick scowled. "What do you mean?"

"Forget it. Why did she break up with Galloway?"

Merrick sighed. "She told everyone that the stress of the hostile
takeover put too much strain on their relationship. And it was true, as far as
it went. After you demolished her company, Camille blamed Garth for leaving the firm financially vulnerable. Garth blamed everyone in sight for his
failure. He got angry, and then he got depressed, and then he started sleeping with someone else."

"I see." Jack looked at the fast-moving water. "I didn't know that Galloway was engaged to Elizabeth."

Merrick gave him a derisive look. "Would it have made a difference?"

He hesitated, thought about Larry, and then shook his head. "No."

"I didn't think so. In the end, she confronted Garth with his infi-
delity and broke off the engagement." Merrick paused a grim beat.
"Garth then told her that the only reason he had gotten engaged to her
in the first place was because his mother had wanted the match.
Camille liked the idea of having the Aurora Fund in the family, you see.

She thought that it would make a nice, ongoing financial cushion for her company."

Jack felt his insides turn cold. "In other words, Galloway wanted to marry her for her money."

"He wanted to use her," Merrick said evenly. "The same way you did. But I'll give Garth Galloway credit for one thing. He didn't humiliate her in a public scene in front of her friends and colleagues."

"Do you think she loved him?"

"Well, sure." Merrick frowned. "I mean, she was engaged to him, right?"

"If you say so."

"Of course she was in love with him." Merrick hunkered deeper into his coat. "She got over him eventually, but it was hard on her for a while. And then you come along a second time and screw up her life all over again."

"Believe it or not, I didn't mean to screw it up this time."

Merrick gave him a dark look. "So what's the deal between you two?"

"I've been trying to figure that one out for six months."

"Come up with any answers?"

"No."

"Well, let me help you get some context here," Merrick said. "It's real simple. You need the backing of the Aurora Fund to keep Excalibur going, so you're sleeping with the lady who writes the checks. What's going to happen when you no longer need her money?"

"Beats me," Jack admitted. What would he do when he no longer had that tenuous link with her?

"I don't get it. This whole thing just doesn't make sense." Merrick eyed him for a few tense seconds. "There's something else going on here. What is it?"

"Nothing that concerns you."

"Like hell. She's family. I've got a right to know—"

The cell phone rang, silencing Merrick. Grateful for the interruption, Jack quickly removed the small instrument from his jacket pocket.

"Fairfax here."

"This is Leonard Ledger. You know that guy you were looking for? Tyler Page?"

Jack stilled. "I'm listening."

"I think I've got a lead on him."

"Where is he?"

"I can't talk now. Come to my hotel room tonight, okay? Make it around eleven-thirty. I gotta go to some screenings, and then I gotta have drinks with some people who are interested in investing in my film."

"Ledger, if you expect me to shell out hard cash for your next project, you'd better come across now—"

"You never told me this guy was trouble." A whining note infused Leonard's words. "I can't afford to piss off certain people, y'know? I gotta be real careful here."

"Listen, Ledger—"

"Room three-oh-five. The Mirror Springs Resort. Eleven-thirty. Don't bother coming around earlier. I won't be here."

The phone went dead.

"I don't like this, Lizzie." Merrick shoved his fingers through his hair and slanted a suspicious look at Jack. "I don't like leaving you here alone with him."

Jack, occupied with making coffee in the kitchen, did not look up from his task.

Elizabeth summoned up a reassuring smile for Merrick. "Don't worry about me. I can take care of myself."

Jack did pause briefly at that comment. He glanced at Merrick. "My advice is to listen to her. She's an adult. She's smart. She knows what she's doing. She's also real stubborn. Take it from me."

Merrick stabbed his fingers through his hair again. "There's something about this whole damn situation that doesn't ring true."

"If I tell you the truth, will you give me your word that you'll keep your mouth shut?" Elizabeth asked him.

Jack shot her a quick, warning glare. "Elizabeth—"

"It's okay, Jack," she said quietly. "I trusted you earlier when you said you wanted to talk privately to Merrick. Now you'll just have to trust me."

Jack subsided, but he did not look thrilled.

"I knew it." Merrick turned eagerly back to Elizabeth. "Something is going on. What is it?"

"What do you think it is?" Elizabeth smiled blandly. "It's business, of course."

Relief flashed across Merrick's face. "That makes more sense. I knew that you were way too smart to fall for another jerk."

Elizabeth was very careful not to look at Jack. "I appreciate your faith in my intelligence, Merrick."

"But what the hell kind of business are you doing here in Mirror Springs? Don't tell me it's got something to do with the film festival."

"Indirectly," Elizabeth said smoothly. "We're trying to put together a deal with someone who is attending the festival. He wanted to spend the week here. We wanted to get together with him, so we're here, too."

"Huh." Merrick's brow puckered slightly. "If it's business, why did Shaw give me that song and dance about the two of you being involved in an affair?"

"Hayden Shaw is pursuing the same prospect we are," Elizabeth said. "He's got his own reasons for wanting to put a spanner in the works."

Merrick slanted another suspicious glance at Jack. "So how come you and Fairfax are both staying here together?"

"There's a severe shortage of accommodations in town." It occurred to Elizabeth that she'd had to make this excuse a lot lately, first to Louise and now to Merrick. "When Jack arrived he was told his reservation had been lost. He didn't have a place to stay. I let him share this place. There's plenty of room."

Merrick eyed the twin sleeping lofts. "Not a lot of privacy."

"We're careful," Jack said from the kitchen.

Merrick frowned at him and then turned back to Elizabeth. "What kind of deal are you two putting together that involves both Excalibur and the Aurora Fund? Licensing agreement?"

"Something like that," Elizabeth said. "I really can't tell you any more than that. Lot of money involved. If we close the deal, the Aurora Fund stands to make a huge return on its investment."

"I see." Merrick was definitely wavering now.

Elizabeth decided to take advantage of his growing uncertainty. She looked pointedly at her watch. "It's getting late, Merrick. You've got a long drive ahead of you if you're going to make your plane. Rowena will be waiting."

A pang of anxiety lit Merrick's eyes. "I know."

"I'll walk you out to the car," she said gently.

She crossed the room and opened the front door. Cold, crisp air wafted into the room. Merrick looked at the open door and then at Jack.

"Business, huh?" he said, obviously wanting to be convinced.

"You heard Elizabeth." Jack flicked the switch on the coffee machine and lounged back against the edge of the counter. "Business."

"No other reason she'd be here with you," Merrick muttered.

"Right," Jack said without any inflection. "There's no other reason why she'd be here with me."

Merrick turned slowly and walked through the door past Elizabeth.

She followed him out onto the deck, closed the door, and went down the steps beside him to where his car was parked in the drive. She could feel the uneasy tension in him and was touched.

"It's all right, Merrick. Everything's under control." Mentally she crossed her fingers.

"If you say so." He stopped beside the car and looked at her. "You'll call me if you need me?"

She held her blowing hair out of her eyes. "I'll call you if I need you."

"Rowena and I are here for you, Lizzie. Always. You know that."

"I know." She put her arms around him and hugged him tightly. He was solid as a rock and, as long as you didn't look at the financial aspect, just as dependable. He would always be a dreamer, filled with plans and ideas that would probably never quite work out the way he had envisioned, but she knew that if she ever needed him, he would be there. Just as she knew that her sister would always be there.

He hugged her back, a big, brotherly, bearlike embrace. Then he patted her on the shoulder with one broad hand and opened the car door. He wedged himself in behind the wheel and looked up at her.

"I'll send a revised copy of my business plan to your office."

She sighed. "Thanks. I'll get to it as soon as I get home."

Optimism glowed in his eyes. "Thanks. I'll tell Rowena everything's all set."

Elizabeth reminded herself that some things were more important than making money. Family was one of those things.

"I'll call you next week," Merrick promised.

He closed the car door, put the vehicle in gear, and drove down the drive to the tree-lined road.

Elizabeth watched until the car disappeared. After a while she turned to find Jack standing in the open doorway behind her.

"You're going to give him the money, aren't you?" he asked neutrally.

"Probably." She started up the steps. "Don't worry about it, Jack. It's not your problem. The Fund has a special account for family loans. Aunt Sybil was very farsighted."

"You're not doing him any favors. He'll never learn how to handle his business affairs if you keep bailing him out."

She brushed past him. "Like I said, it's not your problem."

He followed her back into the house, closed the door, and stood in front of it as though he would block the exit if she tried to make a run for it.

"I didn't know you were engaged to Garth Galloway," he said.

She opened the refrigerator. "Would it have made any difference?"

There was a long silence behind her. She finally glanced at him.

"Your brother-in-law asked me the same question."

She raised one brow. "Well?"

He did not reply.

"Didn't think so," she said.

She walked behind the granite counter and opened the refrigerator. "What do you say we have a sandwich? We never did get to eat lunch today."

"Elizabeth, I didn't even know you when the Galloway deal went down."

"No, but you knew there were a lot of innocent people who were going to get hurt."

His jaw tightened. "It happens in business. You know that."

She looked out the window as she took some feta cheese out of the refrigerator. There was some yellow in the trees on the hillsides, she noticed. The aspens were starting to turn color. In a short while they would ignite the mountains in a blaze of gold.

"Damn it, Elizabeth—"

"Speaking of business," she said, picking up a knife, "why don't we talk about ours? It certainly beats raking up old history. Tell me, what do you think Leonard Ledger meant when he told you that he did not want to make certain people mad?"

"I don't know." Jack abandoned his guard post in front of the door and came to stand on the other side of the counter. He picked up his unfinished coffee. "That's one of the questions I want him to answer tonight. Elizabeth, about your brother-in-law—"

"I'm sorry he hit you this afternoon." She rinsed off the tomato under running water. "It's not like him at all. He's really a gentle man. He must have been extremely upset. Are you okay?"

Jack hesitated. She held her breath.

But Jack must have realized that he was fighting a losing skirmish. He was too good a strategist not to know when to retreat.

"Don't worry, I'm not going to sue," he said.

"That's a relief." She smiled very brightly. "I'm not sure the Aurora Fund's insurance would cover that kind of lawsuit. You might bankrupt us."

Jack watched her over the rim of his cup. "Wouldn't want to do that."

"Of course not." She started to slice a plump, red tomato. "The Fund wouldn't be of much use to you or Merrick if it got wiped out in a lawsuit, would it?"

Jack was silent for a long moment.

"No," he said eventually. "It wouldn't."

Elizabeth saw the drop of blood before she felt the sting. "Damn."

"What happened?"

"Nicked my finger with the knife."

He set down his cup and walked around the end of the counter. He turned on the faucet and grasped her wrist.

"I read about a situation like this once," he said, holding her injured finger under the cold running water.

"What kind of situation?"

"You know, princess pricks finger. Drop of blood appears. She falls under a spell. Gets awakened by a kiss from a frog."

"A frog? Not a prince?"

"Don't you know anything about fairy tales?" Jack turned off the faucet. "The frog doesn't turn into a prince until after she kisses him back."

Chapter Nineteen

"What d'ya mean, he died of natural causes? You murdered the guy, Verna. You shot him down in cold blood."

"If you knew Joey the way I knew Joey, you'd know that getting himself murdered was the most natural thing in the world that coulda happened to him. Besides, it beat the alternative."

"Yeah? What was the alternative?"

"I coulda married him. But my better nature prevailed."

"Better nature?"
"I don't believe in torture. Not even for guys like Joey."

The black-and-white images faded to black on the screen and the credits for *Natural Causes* began to roll. Leonard Ledger's name appeared as director. A smattering of applause broke out in the crowded theater.

Elizabeth leaned toward Jack, who was sitting next to her in the balcony. "It looked like the whole movie was shot in a kitchen. I could swear that section of the tunnel wall where Joey gets it was a refrigerator door."

"Got to give Ledger credit for being able to work within a limited budget," Jack said as the lights came up.

Elizabeth's eye was caught briefly by an elegantly gilded figure that projected outward from a stately column. The Silver Empire Theater was a beautifully restored Victorian treasure. According to the brochure she had read, it had originally been built as an opera house. No expense had been spared. It was adorned with red velvet seats, crimson curtains, chandeliers, and elaborate giltwork.

It had been constructed in the late eighteen hundreds when silver and gold had flowed in bright, shiny rivers out of the Colorado mountains. Newly rich miners had competed to show off their wealth and hastily acquired culture by investing in such emblems of civilization as opera houses, theaters, and spas. Privately, Elizabeth thought that the grand Silver Empire looked a little odd here in the middle of a town that had once been a mining camp and was now a ski resort, but she had to admit that the theater did have a certain charm.

Jack appeared to be oblivious to his ornate surroundings. He shifted forward in his seat and rested both arms on the balcony railing. She realized that he was studying the crowd streaming out of the seats below, a hunter waiting for prey to break cover. He was searching for Ledger's face. It had been his idea to try to locate the filmmaker at the screening of *Natural Causes* and follow him back to his room at the Mirror Springs Resort. His inability to get Ledger on the phone had made Jack increasingly restless all evening.

She was just as eager to find out what Ledger had to say, Elizabeth thought. But for the past two hours, she had been aware of a gathering sense of deep unease that she could not explain away. It was Jack's fault, she told herself. The dark anticipation in him was indeed affecting her nerves.

She was starting to wonder exactly what he would do if he did find Tyler Page. How could he force the other man to turn over Soft Focus? Threats? Violence? Jack could be intimidating when he chose. He would be quite capable of scaring Dr. Page to death.

"It's eleven o'clock," she reminded him quietly. "Only another half hour to go. It doesn't matter if you don't see Ledger here. We'll catch up with him soon enough."

"I don't like the way he's set this up." Jack continued to scrutinize the crowd down below. "A little too melodramatic for my taste."

"He's a filmmaker who makes movies in his kitchen. What do you expect?" Elizabeth got to her feet and collected her coat. "Come on, let's go. By the time we get the car, drive to the resort, park, and find his room, it will be eleven-thirty."

"You're right." Jack did not take his eyes off the crowd below as he stood. "Let's get out of here."

They joined the tide of people on the red-carpeted staircase that led down to the lobby. Elizabeth caught a fleeting glimpse of Vicky Bellamy and Dawson Holland, but neither appeared to notice her or Jack.

A number of filmgoers milled around outside on the sidewalk, waiting for the midnight performance of another festival entry, a low-budget picture titled *Truth Kills*. Snatches of film-speak floated in the air.

". . . like, total mastery of the language of film, man, you know?"

". . . The guy's a master with a camera, especially handheld work. Can frame a perfect shot on the fly."

". . . got a fabulous script, but so far, no backers . . ."

". . . completely misinterpreted the symbolism of the gutter scene . . ."

The theater crowd thinned quickly just beyond the brilliant marquee lights. But as she and Jack walked through the parking lot Elizabeth saw another oasis of bright light and a small cluster of people gathered around it. An air of concentrated activity surrounded the scene.

"They're making a film over there," Elizabeth said. "Must be one of the groups in the contest."

"They'd better not have blocked the exit with their equipment," Jack replied, barely looking up. "I'm not going to miss that meeting with Ledger just because somebody has decided to shoot a movie in the parking lot."

Elizabeth studied the scene more closely. "The exit is clear. They're working in the space next to it. Must be a murder mystery. See, there's a body on the ground."

"Every film we've seen since we got here has had a dead body in it." Jack dug his keys out of his pocket. "Murder seems to be a staple of the genre."

"Of course it is. Haven't you learned anything this week? Noir is all about the dark underbelly of modern life. It's a reflection of urban decadence and moral ambiguity. It came so naturally to American filmmakers in the forties that they didn't even realize they were creating a genre. The French had to come up with the name for it."

"Don't start." Jack opened the car door and bundled her inside. "I am not in the mood for another lecture on film noir."

"I can tell."

Jack closed the door, walked around the car, and got behind the wheel. He pulled out of the parking space with smooth, economical skill and pointed the vehicle toward the exit.

Elizabeth lowered her window to watch the filmmaking going on at the far end of the lot. There was a figure sprawled on the pavement. Two actors dressed in black masks stood over the "body." One held a length of metal pipe. The other grasped an extremely realistic-looking pistol. A man with a handheld camera hovered over the scene. A woman fussed with what appeared to be sound equipment.

"Okay, people," a paunchy man in a billed cap shouted. "Let's do it again. This time I want the beating to go on a little longer before Calvin pulls the trigger. This is the guy who supposedly double-crossed his partner and slept with his wife, remember? We're talking revenge here. Let me feel it."

Jack drove out onto the street. Elizabeth sat back and raised the window.

"Kind of chilly out here to be making movies," she observed.

"From what I can tell, these independent film people don't let anything get in the way of making movies."

Elizabeth thought about that. "There's something rather endearing about artists who are so passionate about their art."

"You call that art?"

She smiled. "Given that you are about to sign on as a producer for something called *Dark Moon Rising,* I would think that you'd take a more open-minded approach to the subject."

"I've seen enough here this week to know that filmmaking is a business, not an art."

"Hah. I'll bet you'll take an entirely different attitude when you see your own name in the credits."

"I doubt it, but tell me, Elizabeth, will you attend the premiere of my film with me?"

For some reason the invitation caught her off guard. Probably because it implied a future for the two of them, she thought. She hadn't realized that Jack had been thinking that far ahead. She certainly had been trying to avoid the subject.

She cleared her throat. "It, uh, generally takes quite a while to make a film and get it screened. Even a little independent film. Leonard probably won't get his movie premiered until the next neo noir festival. That's a whole year from now."

"Right." Jack slowed for the turn into the Mirror Springs Resort parking lot. "So is it a date?"

He was serious, she thought. He was talking about a date next year. As if he expected them to still be involved in a relationship twelve months from now. She noticed that she was breathing shallowly, the way she did when she was tense or anxious. Or scared. Or excited.

"We'll see," she said quietly.

He parked the car in a slot and ripped the keys out of the ignition with sharp, controlled motion. "I love it when you're so decisive."

"Okay, okay, it's a date." Exasperated, she yanked hard on the door handle. "If you actually do produce a film, I'll attend the premiere with you."

"Be nice to me," he said in a voice that was heavily shaded with wicked innuendo, "and maybe I'll let you have a walk-on."

"Does this offer involve a casting couch?"

His eyes gleamed. "It sure does."

"Let's go see Ledger." She opened her car door quickly and leaped out.

Jack climbed out from behind the wheel and joined her. Together they walked toward the lights of the resort lobby. A young man in a red shirt, black bow tie, and black trousers opened the door.

The lobby was nearly deserted except for the front-desk staff. Jack did not stop to use the house phone to call Ledger. He headed straight for the elevators. She had to quicken her pace to keep up with him.

He said nothing as they rode the elevator to the third floor and stepped out into the hushed corridor. Elizabeth could feel his anticipation. Adrenaline was flowing through her veins, too, but the sensation made her deeply uneasy. She should have been excited about the prospect of getting a lead on Tyler Page, she thought. Instead, she was aware of a gathering sense of dread.

"Do you think he's found Page for us?" she asked as they went down the hall to room 305.

"He'd better have something useful. Ledger won't get a dime out of me if I find out he's wasted my time with some vague story about having seen Page around town."

They came to a halt in front of room 305. Elizabeth heard the faint sound of a television set emanating from inside. Jack raised his hand to knock.

Elizabeth glanced down and saw the card key sticking out of the slot. "Jack, wait."

He followed her gaze and frowned when he saw the key. "Why in hell would he leave it in the door?"

"It happens sometimes." Elizabeth swallowed. "If a person has other things on his mind, he might forget about the key in the lock."

"Huh." Jack knocked three times, very quietly, very deliberately.

There was no response.

Elizabeth felt the unease twist more tightly in the pit of her stomach. "I don't like this."

"No kidding." Jack slid the key in and out of the slot in a single, smooth motion, unlocking the door. "I was just thinking the same thing."

He opened the door and pushed it inward. The only light came from the flickering images on the television screen. Elizabeth braced herself, although she did not know what she was tensing against. She tried not to think of all the films she had seen in which the hero and heroine keep a midnight appointment only to discover that the person they were going to meet had been murdered moments before they arrived.

The television set was louder now. A video. She recognized the dialogue immediately. Leonard Ledger's *Natural Causes.*

". . . I trusted you, Verna."

   "Big mistake. I'm attracted to men with brains. I could never fall for a guy who was dumb enough to trust me."

It was obvious from where she stood that the room was empty. Elizabeth breathed a small sigh of relief. Then she glanced at the bathroom door. It stood ajar. The interior of the smaller room was dark.

Jack flipped the switch on the wall. "Ledger? Are you here?"

The only response came from the television set. Elizabeth stared at the bathroom door. Jack met her eyes. Then he took a step forward, reached around the edge of the doorjamb, and turned on the light inside the small room. He eased the door inward, revealing the tub, commode, and basin.

Empty. Elizabeth exhaled deeply.

"What's the matter?" Jack gave her a humorless smile. "Expecting a body in the tub?"

"Weren't you?"

"The possibility crossed my mind. We've obviously seen one too many movies in the past few days." He opened a nearby closet. There were no clothes hanging inside. No body, either.

Elizabeth took a closer look inside the bath. There were some wet towels on the floor but none of the usual male travel accoutrements. No razor, toothpaste, or condoms.

She walked farther into the main room and watched Jack open a drawer beside the bed.

"Anything inside?" she asked.

"No." Jack straightened. His face was grim. "The bastard's gone. Packed up and left. Took off so fast, he forgot his key in the lock."

"The question is, why?"

"I can think of one very likely reason." Jack studied the room with brooding eyes. "Someone else offered him more money than I did."

"*. . . You set me up, Verna.*"

The voices on the small screen were annoying. Elizabeth glanced around for the clicker and saw it lying on the bed next to a videotape box. She picked up the small instrument and silenced the TV. Then she took a closer look at the plastic tape container.

"He left this behind." She plucked the box off the bed and saw that there was a tape inside. She removed it and glanced at the hand-scrawled title. *"Betrayal."*

Jack put out his hand. "Let me see that."

She gave it to him. He took it and went toward the armoire that housed the hotel room's entertainment equipment.

"What are you doing?" she asked.

"What does it look like I'm doing? I'm going to play the tape."

"For heaven's sake, why?"

"This is the only thing left in the room, and it was left in plain sight."

She stared at him as he removed the previous tape and fed the tape into the slot. "You think Leonard Ledger wanted you to find that tape?"

"It seems like a reasonable conclusion under the circumstances."

Jack punched a button. There was a soft, mechanical whir. New black-and-white images appeared on the television screen.

The scene was grainy and obviously shot by an amateur, but Elizabeth had no trouble making out the setting. She was looking at the door of a hotel room. It appeared to be an inexpensive establishment. Portions of the carpeted hall were visible. As she watched, she saw a maid push a cart past the closed door and disappear.

Another figure walked into view. Hayden Shaw.

Elizabeth's sense of foreboding went ballistic. Her stomach was a solid knot of tension now. She watched Hayden remove a card key from his pocket, open the hotel room door, and vanish inside.

"Jack, what's going on here?"

"I don't know yet." Jack did not take his eyes off the screen. "But the plot is starting to look interesting."

Another man bustled into camera range. He was short with a round face and a nervous air. The top of his head was completely bald. What hair he had left was too long and tied in a straggly ponytail. Gold, wire-rimmed glasses gleamed on his face. He wore a baggy black linen jacket and pants and a lot of gold chains. He clutched a briefcase.

Jack whistled softly. "Tyler Page."

Elizabeth watched Page knock twice. The door opened almost immediately. Page disappeared inside.

"That bastard," Jack said very quietly. "I knew he was in this somewhere."

"Page? But we already guessed that he was involved."

"I'm talking about Hayden." Jack gazed enigmatically at the screen. "I knew that he hated me. Just didn't realize how much."

Elizabeth did not know what to say in the face of such overwhelming evidence of betrayal. She could only imagine what it would feel like to find out that your own blood kin would do something like this to you. She touched Jack's arm. He did not seem to notice.

Nothing else happened on the screen for a while. But the camera never wavered. Elizabeth wondered if the photographer had hung around to catch the two men leaving the hotel.

Another minute or two passed. Elizabeth glanced back toward the door.

"Someone could walk in on us at any minute, Jack. Why don't we take the tape back to the house and finish watching it there?"

"You're right." He started to walk toward the television to retrieve the tape.

But just as he reached out to punch the button, a third person walked into view on the film.

At first Elizabeth did not recognize herself.

And then she did, and the floor seemed to fall away beneath her feet. Her hands suddenly felt as if she'd plunged them into ice water. The tingling was so sharp, it hurt.

She almost stopped breathing altogether when she saw herself walk to the hotel room door and knock twice.

No. Impossible.

On the small screen the hotel door opened. Elizabeth watched herself enter the room where Hayden Shaw and Tyler Page waited.

The video ended with shocking suddenness.

She remembered the title. *Betrayal.*

"It won't be much longer now," she said in that warm, husky voice that sent exciting little chills down his spine. "Then we can be together. Think of it, Tyler. Paris. Rome. Madrid. The world will be ours."

"Yes." Tyler Page held the phone to his ear with one hand. He used his other hand to dig more potato chips out of the bag.

The house was dark. The only light in the room came from the video playing on the television screen.

He munched chips and watched Bette Davis in *The Letter*. *So good when she's bad.*

"Tyler?"

"I'm here, Angel Face."

On screen Davis, in the role of Leslie Crosbie, shot her lover in a jealous rage.

"We must not see each other until this is finished. You understand that."

"I understand," he said.

"It's hard on both of us."

"Yes," he said. "Very hard." And it was also becoming a bit boring. He felt as if he'd been sitting here alone in this house forever.

"Goodbye, my darling."

"Farewell, My Lovely." He hung up the phone and stared at the screen. He knew what would happen. Leslie Crosbie would go free in court, but

she would die in the end. The Production Code had to be satisfied. She had
to pay for her crime.

He wondered if he would eventually have to pay for his crime, too.

He reached into the bag for another potato chip.

He thought about Angel Face. He had sacrificed everything for her. He
had exchanged all that he had once held dear for the woman who held him
in thrall. When it was finished, there would be no going back.

No Going Back. A shudder went through him.

No Going Back.

Deep down inside he knew that he was already starting to miss his
pleasant routine at the lab. Life had been so simple there. People tolerated
his little idiosyncrasies. They left him alone with his work. He also missed
the peace and quiet of his little house. At home no one pestered him about
dishes in the sink or crumbs on the carpet. He could leave his dirty laundry
on the floor for weeks if he wanted.

But *she* didn't approve of that kind of behavior. When this was over and
they were finally able to be together, he would have to become Cary Grant
for her. Debonair, articulate, clever, and above all, fastidiously neat. It was
a daunting thought.

It would be worth it, he assured himself. She was his *Gilda,* his *Laura,*
The Woman in the Window, The Lady in the Lake.

But sometimes she scared the hell out of him. Maybe that was why he'd
bought the gun a few weeks ago.

Elizabeth could no longer bear the silence. She was choking
on it. She jerked her gaze away from the view of the narrow, winding
road and looked at Jack. He seemed wholly absorbed in his driving. It
was as if getting back to the house they shared was the only thing that
mattered.

He had said nothing since they had left the resort. Not one bloody
word. On the other hand, she reminded herself, neither had she.

The shock was only now beginning to ebb. A rush of clean, hot anger
was sweeping in to take its place. She could deal with this now. She *would*
deal with it.

"What are you thinking?" she asked.

Jack frowned, as if he had forgotten that she was sitting there beside
him. He turned briefly toward her and then returned his attention to the
twisting pavement ahead.

"I was thinking about that video we found," he said.

"What, precisely, were you thinking about it?"

"Mostly I was wondering who planted it there in Ledger's room for us to find."

She folded her arms tightly beneath her breasts and stared at the trees. "Someone who wanted you to think that Hayden, Tyler Page, and I all conspired to steal Soft Focus."

"Believe it or not, I had figured out that much." He slowed for a sharp turn. Halfway through it, he accelerated smoothly. "The question is, who would want me to have that information, and why now?"

"The information is false," she said very evenly.

"Sure it is. But that only makes the list of people who might have planted the video in Ledger's room longer than it would have been if the tape was for real."

For a split second she did not think she had heard him right.

She turned as far as the seat belt would allow. "Wait a second. Are you telling me that you don't believe what you saw on that videotape?"

"Give me a break." He kept his eyes on the road, but his mouth twisted in cold amusement. "We are surrounded by several hundred professional filmmakers and video experts of all kinds. In addition, there are upwards of a couple thousand serious film buffs in the immediate vicinity of Mirror Springs, any one of whom probably knows how to fake a piece of videotape. Of course I don't believe what I saw on the tape."

The great, icy monster that had sunk its claws into her insides released its grip so suddenly, she was surprised she did not take flight. Okay, so he had dismissed the evidence on the video on technical grounds. So what? He had refused to believe it. That was the important thing.

"I see." She could not think of anything else to say.

He gave her a quick, searching look. "Are you okay?"

"I'm great," she said softly. "Fine and dandy."

"When we get back to the house, I'm going to call Larry again. He's had enough time to come up with more information."

"I'll call Louise, too."

"Maybe if we get it all down on paper and take a look at it, we might come up with a new angle—" He broke off on a half-muttered groan of resignation and took his foot off the accelerator. "Damn. Not another one. We don't have time for this."

"What's wrong?" Elizabeth asked. Then she followed his gaze and saw the bright lights and the van that partially blocked the thin ribbon of pavement.

The door on the driver's side of the van was flung wide. In the glare of the beams a motionless figure could be seen draped across the steering wheel. Blood gleamed. There seemed to be a lot of it.

Equipment was scattered around the edge of the scene. Elizabeth saw two light stands anchored by sandbags. Only one of the lights was switched on. There were also some cables and a generator.

A man with a camera balanced on his shoulder moved about restlessly, apparently lining up his shot. He had his back to her, but when he stepped briefly into the circle of light she saw that he was dressed in a black denim, waist-length jacket and black jeans. He had a billed cap pulled down low over his averted face. The half-circle of shiny metal that decorated the heels of his chunky black boots glinted when he moved.

"Another body, another movie." Jack sounded irritated. He braked to a stop.

"They're probably involved in the contest," Elizabeth said.

"They've got a hell of a nerve blocking the public road like this."

"Be fair, Jack." Fair? Heck, she could be downright generous tonight. Jack hadn't believed the video in Ledger's hotel room. Life was good. "I'm sure they weren't expecting any traffic on this stretch. Not at this hour of the night."

"Kind of a small crew." Jack undid his seat belt and opened the door. "I only see two people."

He climbed out of the car and walked toward the van.

Elizabeth opened her own door and got out.

"How much longer are you going to be?" Jack asked as he drew closer to the van.

The photographer did not turn around. He stayed hunched over his camera, concentrating on lining up the shot of the bloody scene inside the van. "Gonna be a while. Mind cutting your headlights? They're messing up the shot."

"Sorry," Jack said. "We can wait a few minutes, but that's all. We're in a hurry."

"Screw you, we're makin' a movie here." The man gestured toward the sandbagged light stands and the carefully positioned van. "Took us an hour to set up this shot."

"If you just shift that one light stand," Jack suggested, "I can get around the van."

A ripple of unease trickled through Elizabeth. "Let them get their shot, Jack," she said urgently. "We can wait a few more minutes."

He paused and stared back at her. In the glare of the headlights, she could see his alert, questioning look.

"Please," she said tightly. "Come back to the car. We don't want to get in the way of their art, do we?"

He hesitated, but to her profound relief, he asked no questions. "No, sure wouldn't want to get in the way of art," he said.

At that moment, the actor draped over the wheel stirred and raised his head. His features were hidden behind the mask of phony blood that covered his head and face.

"Hey, a woman," he called out cheerfully. "We can use her in the shot. How about it? Wanna be in pictures, lady?"

Elizabeth opened her mouth to tell him that she was not interested in taking up an acting career. But she stopped when she saw that the photographer had set down his camera. He took a step toward the light stand.

"Touch my equipment and I'll have you arrested," he yelled at Jack.

Jack gazed back over his shoulder. "I'm not going to touch your stuff. We'll give you a few minutes to finish the shot."

"We're gonna finish this, all right." He broke into a run, charging toward Jack. "Come on, Benny."

Benny scrambled out of the van and started after his pal.

"Jack," Elizabeth screamed. "Behind you."

Jack had already whirled around to face the two men rushing toward him.

The cameraman reached Jack and swung a fist in a short, brutal arc. Jack sidestepped the punch. The artfully bloodied actor grabbed his arm and pulled him off balance.

Jack went easily to the ground. Too easily, Elizabeth realized. He took the actor with him. The other man hit the pavement hard. Jack landed on top.

"Hold him." The cameraman danced agitatedly around the pair. "Hold him, goddammit."

Elizabeth ran toward the van.

"Stay back," Jack shouted at her.

She kept moving toward her goal. She got her first good look at the cameraman's face when she went past him. She saw that the bill of his cap and the deep shadows had concealed the ski mask he wore.

The cameraman lashed out at Jack with a booted foot. Jack rolled off the actor, who took the blow in his ribs.

"Shit," the actor screamed, clutching at his side. "Shit."

Elizabeth saw that Jack was back on his feet, closing with the cameraman. She reached the nearest light stand and seized the spindly metal upright.

"My lights," the actor shouted. He sounded more alarmed now than he had when he took the kick that had been meant for Jack. "Don't touch my lights."

She yanked at the metal stand. The light fixture mounted on top wobbled and crashed to the ground, exploding on contact with the pavement. A length of metal came free in her hand. She swung it in a wide arc as she turned back to the mêlée.

The actor screamed, an agonized, keening sound that echoed forever. *"My lights."*

Elizabeth ignored him. She saw Jack turn aside from a heavy blow that glanced off his shoulder. He stuck out a foot, grabbed the cameraman's wrist, and tugged.

The cameraman flew forward, landing on his belly with a hoarse grunt. Jack started toward him.

The actor was screaming curses at Elizabeth. She turned and saw him lunge toward her. She swung the light stand again, catching him on his arm.

"Put down my stuff, you bitch."

He tried to grab the length of metal out of her hands. She skittered backward, wielding the upright as if it were a long sword.

"Don't touch her," Jack shouted at the actor.

He turned away from the cameraman and launched himself at the actor.

The cameraman lurched to his feet. Apparently concluding that he'd had enough, he dashed for the driver's side of the van.

"Wait for me, goddammit." Abandoning the attempt to recover the light stand, the actor halted in midcourse, whirled around, and barreled toward the passenger side of the van.

Jack grabbed him as he shot past.

"No, no, *no*." The actor's artificially bloodied features crumpled in grotesque despair. He did not even struggle in Jack's grasp.

The van's engine roared to life. The headlights flashed. Wheels screeched on the pavement. The vehicle careened off into the night, rear doors clanging.

"Bastard." The actor sagged. "Lousy, stinking bastard."

A stark silence descended on the scene. Elizabeth stood frozen on the white line. She looked at Jack.

"Are you all right?" he asked tersely.

"Yes." She realized she still held the length of metal. It was quivering in her grasp. Very carefully she carried it to the side of the road and set it down. "Yes, I'm all right. What about you?"

"I'm fine." He looked at his captive. "You want to tell me what the hell that was all about? Or shall I just go ahead and call the cops?"

"Huh?" The actor squinted through his mask of fake blood. "Cops?"

"That was the next thing on my to-do list," Jack said.

"But he said there wouldn't be any cops." The actor sounded aggrieved now. "He said this was one of those white-collar crime gigs. He said nobody ever called the cops if things went wrong."

"What, exactly, went wrong?" Jack asked.

The actor looked sullen. "I dunno. Ollie offered me five hundred cash if I would give him a hand tonight. Now look what's happened. The light's ruined. It'll cost a hell of a lot more than five hundred to replace."

Elizabeth walked slowly forward. "What's Ollie's last name?"

"Dunno. He just goes by Ollie."

"What's he do for a living?" Jack asked.

"He's a stuntman. Got kicked outta the big studios for drinking on the job."

Elizabeth stopped next to Jack. "What's your name?" she asked gently.

"Benny. Benny Cooper." Benny searched her face. "It was just supposed to be a warnin', see? That's all. We were just supposed to rough him up a little and tell him to pack his bags and get outta town."

"That's it?" Jack asked. "That was the whole message? Leave town?"

"Yeah." Benny heaved a deep sigh. "But it all went wrong. Ollie said nobody would call the cops if it did."

Jack smiled coldly. "This is your lucky day, Benny. Ollie was right."

Fifteen minutes later Jack parked the car in the drive and cut the ignition. Elizabeth made no move to get out. She sat gazing blankly through the windshield.

"Another warning," she said. "Do you think this one was also from Vicky Bellamy and Dawson Holland?"

"Maybe." Jack did not open his door either. He sat beside her, staring pensively at the front door.

"Maybe we should have called the cops, Jack."

"If we do," he said very neutrally, "this whole thing will blow up in our faces. Everyone involved will disappear. We can probably kiss off any chance of finding Tyler Page or the crystal."

"True."

"Not much the police could do about what happened tonight, anyway," he continued in a judicious tone. "Except let us file a report."

"By the time we did that and got an officer out to investigate, it's highly unlikely that there would be any evidence left anyway."

"True," he agreed.

They sat in silence for a few more minutes.

"Amazing how two intelligent people like us can sit here in the middle of the night and rationalize not going to the police in what is obviously a clear-cut case of assault," Elizabeth said eventually.

Jack opened the car door. "We didn't get to be hotshot CEOs for nothing."

Chapter Twenty

Elizabeth pulled up the collar of her white robe, opened the glass slider, and stepped out into the night. The well-chilled air made her catch her breath. Words like *clean and fresh* and *invigorating* took on new meaning at this altitude, she thought.

She looked toward the hot tub. There was enough moonlight for her to see Jack. He reclined on one of the benches, arms stretched out along the curved sides of the tub. The water swirled around his chest. His head was back, his eyes closed.

"Are you sure you're all right?" she asked.

"Yeah." He opened his eyes and looked at her. "Thanks to you. Nice trick with the lights. Certainly got Benny's attention. We were lucky."

"How's that?"

"Ollie and Benny are obviously just a couple of smalltime guys connected to the small-time film business, not professional rent-a-thugs." Jack touched his ribs.

"You're sure you don't want to go to the emergency room?"

He grunted in disgust. "I'm sure."

"Thank goodness you've studied the martial arts."

"My father signed me up for lessons when I was eight years old. Larry said that he got signed up at about that age, too. I wouldn't be surprised if Hayden was also sent off to a martial arts instructor at the age of eight. Dad tended to do things in a very methodical way. I've kept up with my instruction over the years. For the exercise. Never actually used the moves for real until tonight."

"I wonder if Hayden is getting any warnings," Elizabeth mused.

"That," Jack said slowly, "is an excellent question. There is, of course, another possibility."

"What?"

"He may be the one who sent those two after me tonight. Maybe he's got his own plan to cut down the competition."

"Don't look now, but your paranoia is showing."

"Huh."

"Jack, pay attention. Read my lips. If you don't believe that scene of me walking into the hotel room to meet with Tyler Page, you can't take the scene of Hayden going into that room seriously, either."

Jack closed his eyes and leaned his head back against the edge of the tub again. "The fact that you're not involved doesn't mean that Hayden isn't."

"You're letting your personal feelings get in the way of sound logic. If Hayden was involved in a conspiracy with Tyler Page, why would he hang around the Mirror Springs Resort? He'd take Soft Focus and catch the next flight to Amsterdam or Berlin or the Middle East."

"Revenge is no fun if your target doesn't know you pulled it off."

"Hayden had nothing to do with the theft." She sat down on the edge of the tub and dangled her bare feet in the warm water. "He's here for the same reason we are. The auction."

"You can't be certain of that," Jack said.

"Yes, I can. On the day he arrived, and again the other night at The Mirror, while you were carrying out high-level negotiations in the men's room, he suggested that I use the Aurora Fund to back him instead of you when the bidding started."

Jack slitted his eyes. "Son of a bitch. Why didn't you tell me?"

She shrugged. "I didn't want to add any more fuel to the fire that's already burning between you two."

"Son of a bitch," Jack said again. "You should have told me."

"I made an executive decision."

"Damn it, Elizabeth—"

"The point is," she said firmly, "he wouldn't have approached me like that if he wasn't here for the auction. I'm telling you, he didn't steal the specimen. He's here to bid on it."

Jack looked as though he wanted to argue the point, but he changed tactics instead. "Last Tuesday night, the night Hayden took you to dinner and told you he'd heard the rumors about Soft Focus, did he tell you *how* he'd gotten the news?"

"To tell you the truth, I was so stunned by the possibility that Soft Focus was gone that I'm not sure I picked up all the details." She summoned up a mental image of her dinner with Hayden. "But now that I think about it, I'm almost certain he just said something about having received an anonymous phone call."

"Not exactly original. I'm surprised he didn't come up with something a little more high-tech, like a mysterious E-mail message or a fax."

Elizabeth shrugged. "Actually, when you stop and think about it, a call from a pay phone is still the simplest, surest way of delivering a message that you want the recipient to get. And it's easy enough to disguise a voice."

"Yeah."

She looked at him. "Earlier this evening you suggested that we sit down with everything we've got and try to put the pieces together. I think that's a good idea."

"So do I. But not tonight. I need some sleep before I tackle that project."

"Me, too."

He settled deeper into the water. "Are you going to just sit there twiddling your toes in the water, or are you going to get into the tub?"

"Would you answer a question before I decide?"

"As long as it does not involve extensive use of logic or rational thinking. I'm not at my best at the moment."

"It's a simple question." She paused to gather her nerve. "Earlier, before we ran into those two thugs on the road, you said that you didn't buy the video of me joining Hayden and Tyler Page in that hotel. You said you didn't put any credence in it because it could have been faked by any number of people."

"So?"

"But you were not so quick to dismiss the possibility that Hayden and Page might have gotten together to conspire in that hotel room."

"So?" he said again.

This was getting painful, Elizabeth thought. But she could not stop now. "So I was just wondering why you found it easy to throw out the evidence against me?"

"The only motive you would have for arranging the theft of Soft Focus would be revenge."

It was her turn, she realized. "So?"

"Elaborate, carefully plotted revenge involving coconspirators and extensive cover-ups and a lot of outright lies is not your style."

"Oh." She pondered that briefly. "What is my style?"

He opened his eyes and gave her a fleeting grin that showed some of his excellent teeth. "Toe-to-toe and to the point is your style. Ice water in my face in a fancy restaurant is your style. Calling me an egg-sucking SOB in front of a hundred people is your style."

She groaned. "I'm never going to live that down, am I?"

"Not if I have anything to say about it."

"Do you think my style of revenge is sort of boring and predictable?"

"Nothing about you is boring."

"But predictable?" she pressed.

"Only in the most attractive way," he assured her.

"I suppose I'll have to be satisfied with that." She studied him closely. In the darkness it was impossible to see beneath the surface of the foaming water. "Are you wearing a swimsuit this time?"

"Funny you should mention that."

"You're not wearing one, are you?"

"When it comes to some things, I, too, have a tendency to be predictable."

"But never boring," she said softly.

She untied the sash of her robe and let the garment fall from her shoulders. When the cold air wrapped itself around her bare skin she sucked in her breath and quickly slipped into the hot water.

Jack smiled slowly as she sat down beside him on the submerged bench. "You've given up wearing swimsuits in hot tubs, I see."

She put a hand on his bare thigh. "I wouldn't want to become too predictable."

She traced a slow, circular pattern slowly up the inside of his leg.

He captured her hand and raised it above the surface to his mouth. He watched her through half-closed eyes as he kissed her wet fingers. She saw the dark hunger in him, and her insides were suddenly hotter than the water in the tub.

He bit gently down on her thumb, then nibbled a bit on her knuckles. She sighed softly and settled closer against him. Very deliberately he drew her palm back beneath the churning water and curved her fingers around him.

He was fully aroused, taut and hard. Gently she tightened her grasp. A shudder went through him.

"The most predictable thing around here is my response to you," he whispered against her lips. "Just like the sunrise."

She opened her mouth for him. He drank deep. After a time she decided to try his own tactic against him. She sank her teeth into his lower lip. He endured the gentle assault for a moment and then groaned, muttered something unintelligible, and pulled her across his legs. He kissed her deeply, with a thoroughness that sent delicious little shock waves through her.

She twisted against him and stroked him slowly, digging her nails gently into his damp shoulders. Beneath her hip she could feel his fierce reaction to her touch. He was straining against her thigh.

His hand slid down her spine to the cleft of her buttocks, and then his fingers were between her legs. When he prodded her gently open with his thumb and forefinger, a surge of exultant energy zapped through her. The liquid heat welled up inside. Irresistible. Unstoppable. Too late she realized the climax had taken her by surprise.

"Jack."

"Don't fight it." He kissed her throat and forged deeper. "There's plenty more where it's coming from."

The strident jangle of an alarm bell cut into a dream of endless hallways and crisscrossing corridors that ended in blank walls.

The alarm was unnecessary, an annoying distraction that only made everything worse.

She did not need the shrill ringing to warn her of the danger. She was all too well aware that they were both in jeopardy. She had to con-

*centrate. She had to think clearly, logically. How was she supposed to
do that with that bloody bell going off in her ear?*

Elizabeth came awake abruptly, blinked at the dull sheen of a cloudy sky
visible through the windows. She groped for the telephone, found it, got it
to her ear.

"Hello?"

"My, my, someone woke up on the wrong side of the bed this morning,"
Louise said cheerfully.

"Save the cutesy stuff, Louise. I'm not in the mood." She felt Jack slide
one leg between her calves and tighten his arm around her. *Get a grip. It was
just a dream.* "What have you got for me?"

"I'm not sure yet," Louise admitted. "Probably nothing. But I talked to
a couple of people who know some people who have covered the film festival circuit for years. There are film festivals everywhere these days. Used to
be just places like Cannes and Santa Fe, but now every town that's got a
theater holds a festival."

"Could you get to the point, Louise?"

"Sure. Point is Dawson Holland has hung on the fringes of the film
crowd for years. Likes to sleep with aspiring actresses. Still does, even
though he's married again."

"What?" Elizabeth sat up very quickly against the pillows. "He sleeps
around, even though he's married to Vicky Bellamy?"

"Yep. But no one special. Different woman every time. What can I say?
The guy likes to get laid. But he doesn't seem to get serious about any of the
ladies who engage his affections for an evening of fun and frolic. Faithful in
his fashion, you could say."

"To Vicky?"

"For the past eighteen months, at any rate," Louise agreed.

"They've only been married for a year and a half?"

"Uh-huh."

"Hmm." Elizabeth wondered if Vicky knew or cared about the other
women. "Anything else on Holland?"

"Uh-huh." Louise paused for effect. "He was married twice before he
met Vicky Bellamy."

"I know that much. Not all that unusual, especially in his crowd."

"Ah, but do you know that he's a widower twice over?" Louise said
softly.

Elizabeth saw that Jack was watching her intently. He had caught the drift of the conversation.

"Natural causes?" Elizabeth asked carefully.

"Nope. Car accidents. The first wife was killed nearly twenty years ago. The second one went off a cliff eight years ago. And here's the really interesting part. Holland inherited a lot of money both times. The first wife left him several thousand shares of high-tech stock that coincidentally took a huge jump in the months just before she died."

"What about the second wife?"

"Oddly enough," Louise said dryly, "he had taken out a very large insurance policy on her shortly before her death."

Elizabeth tightened her grip on the phone. "Was there an investigation?"

"Sure. According to my source, the insurance company sent out an investigator, but he couldn't prove anything. The company paid off."

Elizabeth went cold. "Is Vicky rich in her own right?"

"Nope. I checked. No family money. Seems to have lived by her wits, as they used to say in the old days, for most of her life. I couldn't dig up too much on her, but there was no indication that she had money of her own." Louise shuffled through some more notes. "But it might be interesting to see whether or not Dawson Holland has taken out an insurance policy on her."

"Creepy thought," Elizabeth said.

"Dawson Holland appears to be a professional creep."

"And maybe something worse, if you're right about the two dead wives."

"Like I said, there was no proof in either case. But my source tells me that there's probably more than coincidence involved." Louise paused. "I think that's all I've got for now. Want me to keep digging?"

"Yes." Elizabeth drummed her fingers absently against Jack's shoulder. "Call me right away if you find anything else."

"Will do." Louise paused. "So how's it going with the egg-sucking son of a bitch?"

Elizabeth felt herself turn very warm. She stared intently out the window, avoiding Jack's eyes. "Fine. Just fine."

"He's there, isn't he? Right there in bed with you."

"I've got to run, Louise."

"I hesitate to inquire, but my old journalistic instincts demand to know." Louise cleared her throat. "Is there anything extra special about doing it with an experienced egg-sucker?"

Elizabeth hastily slammed down the phone.

Jack gave her a politely inquiring look. "Well?"

"Do you think Larry could use his computer to find out whether or not Dawson Holland has taken out an insurance policy on Vicky Bellamy?"

"Probably." He propped himself on his elbow. "What have you got?"

"A very nasty feeling."

Two and a half hours later, Jack put down the phone and looked at her. There was a cool, calculating expression on his hard face.

Elizabeth picked up her coffee. "What did Larry say?"

"He said that your hunch was right." Jack walked behind the counter and helped himself to coffee. "Dawson Holland took out a very large policy on Vicky about four months ago."

A shiver ran through her. "Did he confirm that the deaths of Holland's first two wives were suspicious?"

"There's nothing in the records to indicate that the first death was anything other than an accident." Jack took a swallow of coffee. "And the insurance company did pay off on the second death. Officially there's no indication of foul play, but . . ."

"I'm listening."

"But in the months before each death," Jack continued softly, "Holland had experienced severe financial losses. The first time he was able to recover because of the stock he inherited from his wife. The insurance policy on Mrs. Holland Number Two pulled him out of the red the second time."

Elizabeth met his eyes. "The last time Larry called he said that Holland had experienced some serious money problems in the past few months, didn't he? Something about taking a big hit in a hedge fund?"

"Yes." Jack's brows rose. "What are you thinking?"

She paused a moment longer to contemplate the idea that had just occurred to her.

"I'm thinking," she said, "that one good warning deserves another."

Chapter Twenty-One

Vicky watched Dawson in the mirror as he walked out of the bathroom. The effects of his last facelift were wearing off, she noticed. He was getting soft around the jawline. He was still slender, but no amount of time spent with his personal trainer could give him the hard, fit body of a younger man again. The slackness of age was overtaking him rapidly.

She wondered what the other women saw in him. After all, he was never with any of them long enough for them to get their hands on his money. Did they really fall for his vague promises? Were they silly enough to believe that he could get them into films?

She couldn't blame them. She had believed him for a while back at the beginning, but she knew the truth now. When she had first met him, Dawson had had the money to make himself a player, but he'd had no real interest in the Hollywood game. He stayed strictly on the fringes of the film business because it gave him access to starlets and pretty little wannabes who could make him feel young. But she knew now that he would never risk serious money on a major film.

And lately there wasn't as much serious money to risk. She did not know all the details. Dawson was very secretive about his assets, but she was no fool. She knew that he was in trouble. She was fairly certain he would recover. He seemed to have the Midas touch, after all. But in the meantime, she suspected that he was getting by on his charm and his track record.

But even after he had recouped his finances, she knew there would be nothing more for her than a series of smalltime roles in low-budget films like *Fast Company.* Perhaps she had known the truth all along. She usually prided herself on her realistic approach to life, but she had to admit she was guilty of deluding herself when it came to her desire to act.

What the hell, everyone was entitled to a weakness.

Dawson's was pretty, brainless women. She was amused by the great lengths he took to conceal his meaningless affairs from her. She found it oddly touching in a perverse sort of way. He was no doubt afraid that she would leave him if she found out about the others.

She could hardly assure him that he had nothing to fear on that front. To do so would be to give up much of her power over him. And power was the only true currency in a relationship. She had learned that lesson long ago.

"Tomorrow night's the big night, my dear." Dawson adjusted the collar of his black silk shirt in front of the other mirror. "Excited?"

"A little."

He smiled at her. "Relax. I know you're going to win."

"Do you really think so?"

"No question about it." He chuckled as he turned away from the mirror. "I'm afraid that *Fast Company* won't win Best Neo Noir Festival Film, but the judges can't possibly overlook your performance in it. You were fantastic."

"Thanks to you."

She rose from the dressing-table chair and went to the closet. It gave her an excuse not to have to look at his soft, smiling face.

She hated it when he smiled the way he was smiling now. It struck her as a paternal smile. The sort of smile her father had given her on the mornings after the nights he had come to her bedroom. A smile founded on lies and secrets that could not stand the light of day. It was a smile that had long ago frozen her to the bone. She knew that she would never thaw.

She took down an ice-pale blouse and a pair of pale blue trousers, concentrating very hard so that the image of her father's smiling face was no longer superimposed on Dawson's blandly handsome features. It took an effort, but she managed.

"What are your plans for the day?" Dawson asked with idle, husbandly interest.

"I thought I'd go to the spa. I feel like a massage and a soak in one of the pools." She turned around and gave him her brightest smile. "Dawson, about tomorrow night—"

"There is no doubt but that you'll win, my dear."

She gave him an amused glance. "Don't tell me that you've bribed the judges."

"There was no need," he said gallantly. "They would have to be incredibly dense not to see how good you are in *Fast Company*. Going to wear the white and silver gown?"

"Yes."

"Excellent. You look wonderful in it."

She hesitated. "Dawson, you did tell Ollie that the stalker stunts are finished, didn't you? I don't want him splashing paint on me tomorrow night, of all nights."

"Of course I told him, my dear." Dawson smiled. "Publicity is all well and good, but I certainly wouldn't allow him to ruin your big night."

"I appreciate that." She relaxed, went to him, and kissed him lightly, provocatively on the mouth.

She was a good actress, she thought. Too bad no one else knew just how very good she was.

She was good enough, for example, to conceal the fact that she sometimes saw the ghost of her father's features on Dawson's face when they had sex. It was the reason why she always went out of her way to be the seducer rather than the seduced. As long as she was in control of the game, she held the power.

And power was everything—the only thing that guaranteed survival.

Jack studied the neatly organized items on Dawson Holland's desk. A plump pen trimmed with tiny bands of gold was positioned to the side of an old-fashioned, leather-bound writing pad. A laptop computer and a two-line telephone completed the simple work scene.

He had kept his plans to search the Holland home to himself. He'd had a feeling that Elizabeth would have fretted if she'd known what he intended to do. He didn't have any great hopes of turning up a fabulous clue, especially now that he had discovered that he couldn't get anything off the computer, but he was short on options. He had no intention of cooling his heels until Tyler Page chose to conduct the auction.

He eyed the laptop in frustration. He had already attempted to download at least a portion of the contents onto a floppy disk, but he'd quickly discovered that the machine was password protected. Unfortunately, he hadn't been able to bring Larry along to deal with little snags like that.

He was reaching for one of the desk-drawer pulls when he heard the car in the drive.

Fifteen minutes ago he had watched from the depths of the nearby woods as Vicky and Dawson had both left the house in separate vehicles. Perhaps one of them had forgotten something and turned around to get it.

He heard the vehicle stop.

Not good. He was pretty sure he could deal with the cops, but he did not relish the prospect of trying to explain to Elizabeth how he'd come to get arrested for breaking and entering.

He crossed to the bank of windows that formed the south wall of the bedroom and looked down through a crack in the blinds. A well-worn pickup stood in the driveway. Not Vicky's white Porsche or Holland's high-end SUV.

As he watched, a middle-aged woman got out of the truck. She hurried toward the side door, keys in her hand. The housekeeper, Jack thought.

He breathed a small sigh of relief.

Then he heard her enter the too-quiet house. A moment later, she was on the stairs.

Damn.

He swept the room with a quick glance. None of the obvious hiding places appealed. The closets and the bathroom were too risky. There wasn't enough space under the bed.

It would have to be the deck. There was no way down to the ground, but he had noticed a storage locker under the eaves. With luck the housekeeper was not coming upstairs to retrieve an item from the locker.

He grasped the handle of the glass slider and pulled the door open. Cautiously he stepped out onto the deck and shut the door again.

He went to the storage locker. The door was latched but not padlocked. He opened it cautiously and peered inside. A hose lay coiled on the floor. Next to it was a folded chaise longue and a watering can. There was room enough for him.

He slid into the locker and closed the door. The shadows closed around him. He stood listening intently.

The housekeeper did not stay long. A short time later, the pickup trundled off down the drive.

He opened the locker door and started to move out onto the deck. The edge of his running shoe brushed up against an object.

He glanced down and saw three small cans of paint stacked neatly next to the hose.

Red paint.

Elizabeth paused beside the padded lounger. "Mind if I join you?"

Vicky Bellamy, fresh from a massage and swathed in a turban and a thick, white robe, opened her eyes. If she was surprised to see Elizabeth standing over her, she did not show it.

"Be my guest."

"Thanks." Elizabeth set down the fruit smoothie she had bought from the spa's refreshment bar and took the lounger next to Vicky's.

She glanced quickly around to make certain that no one else was within hearing distance. Fortunately, the array of tiled, hot spring-fed pools were quiet at this hour. There was only a handful of people in the elegantly re-stored spa. Most were wrapped in robes, as she and Vicky were. A few were seated on the steps in the deep tubs. Attendants in white uniforms bustled back and forth between the various therapy rooms, offering several kinds of massage, mud wraps, and facials.

"The other night outside The Mirror, I got the distinct impression that you were trying to give me a warning," Elizabeth said. "Was I right?"

Vicky closed her eyes. "You can take it any way you like."

"Fine. I'm going to go with my intuition. You were trying to warn me off. Which means that you know who I am."

"You're the head of the Aurora Fund."

"And you're married to Dawson Holland," Elizabeth said quietly.

"What does my husband have to do with this?"

"I think he's here for the same reason that Jack and I are here. Maybe you're also here for the same purpose. We've all come to Mirror Springs to attend an auction."

"I have no idea what you're talking about. I'm here for the film festival."

"You know," Elizabeth said, "some men just aren't good at marriage. I hear that Dawson Holland is one of those men."

Vicky opened her eyes at last. She fixed Elizabeth with an assessing, catlike gaze. "I know that he was married twice before he met me, if that's what you mean. I know that he has affairs. I don't have a problem with those facts. And they're certainly none of your business."

"Did you know that both of his wives died in car accidents and that Dawson came into a lot of money on each occasion? Were you aware that the insurance company was suspicious of the second death? Did you know that Dawson took out a very large insurance policy on you a few months ago?"

Vicky's beautiful face was an enigmatic mask. "Why are you telling me this?"

"Like I said, you gave me a warning. I thought I'd return the favor. I'll admit that my warning isn't nearly as clever and subtle as yours was, but then, I don't have a script. I'm ad-libbing."

Vicky studied her for a long moment. Then she smiled coldly. "You're sleeping with Jack Fairfax."

"Is that important?"

"Not to me." Vicky closed her eyes again. "But it does make me question your judgment as well as your motive for giving me your little warning about Dawson. I know what Fairfax did to you, you see. Dawson told me how he suckered you into giving him the financial backing he needed to salvage that little company he's running back in Seattle."

"Dawson knows about what happened in Seattle?"

Vicky smiled. She did not open her eyes. "Apparently it's common knowledge in certain circles."

Elizabeth watched a bather go down the steps into one of the wide, chin-deep pools of hot, crystal-clear springwater. The faint odor of the mineral-rich waters filled the large, colonnaded chamber. Soft dripping and splashing sounds echoed gently against the white and blue tiled walls.

"Is that why you gave me your warning the other night?" she asked eventually. "Do you feel sorry for me because you think I've let myself fall for a man who is taking coldblooded advantage of me?"

"Naïveté can be quite charming, Elizabeth. But it comes with a very high price tag."

Chapter Twenty-Two

It took three tries before he could make the card key work in the slot. He finally got into the darkened hotel room. He went straight to the minibar. When he removed the miniature bottle of scotch he noted with disgust that his hands were still shaking.

"Shit."

He could still feel the unpleasant prickles created by the slowly evaporating adrenaline. His insides were ice cold. He felt light-headed.

It had been close. So damn close that he knew he would probably have nightmares for a while. In his head, he could still hear the sucking rush of air as the car swept past only inches away. If he hadn't glanced back over his shoulder at that precise instant . . .

If he hadn't reacted with blind instinct; if he hadn't relied on the reflexes the martial arts training had given him . . .

He did not want to think about what had almost happened, but he could not get the images out of his mind. The windows of the steel-colored rental car had been tinted. He had not been able to see the driver's face. But that did not matter. He knew who drove a steel-gray rental car here in Mirror Springs.

He downed the scotch and went to the window. He stared into the thickly wooded river canyon while he waited for the liquor to melt the ice in his gut.

His mother had been right. His half brother detested him. But until tonight, Hayden thought, he hadn't realized that Jack hated him enough to try to kill him.

"I can't believe it." Elizabeth stormed across the landing that separated her sleeping loft from Jack's. "Are you totally nuts? You went to their house? Searched their *bedroom?*"

"What can I say?" He opened the closet and took out a fresh shirt. "Seemed like a good idea at the time."

She stared at him, momentarily speechless with shock and outrage. Under any other circumstance she would have enjoyed watching him change clothes. She had never seen another man who looked so interesting without a shirt. But the shock of hearing that he had spent the afternoon committing an act of breaking and entering while she had been at the spa with Vicky overwhelmed everything else, including the sight of his bare chest.

"You could have been arrested," she blurted.

"I doubt it." He shrugged into the shirt and started to fasten the buttons. "Holland doesn't want the police dragged into this any more than we do."

"You can't be certain of that." She realized she had begun to wave her hands in the air. Never a good sign. "Jack, you ran a terrible risk."

"Take it easy. No harm done."

"Is that so? Well, if it wasn't such a risk, why didn't you tell me what you planned to do before you did it?"

He glanced at her as he rolled up the cuffs of his shirt. "Because I knew you'd have a fit."

"I've got a right to have a fit. Good grief, when I think of what might have happened. And it was all for nothing. Absolutely nothing."

"Not entirely." He managed to look offended. "I told you, I found some red paint."

"Big deal," she shot back. "We already suspected that the red-paint stalker routine was a publicity hoax. It's not connected to the theft."

"Maybe. Maybe not."

She folded her arms and glared at him. "What's that supposed to mean?"

"I'm not sure," he admitted. "But it occurs to me that if Dawson Holland is thinking about getting rid of wife number three, making her the victim of a stalker might be one way to handle the problem."

Elizabeth swallowed. "You're right. It would certainly make a change from car accidents."

"Yes, it would." Jack walked toward her. "What did Vicky say when you told her about Dawson's history of bad luck with wives?"

"She was cool about it." Elizabeth turned away. "I got the impression that she thinks I'm not real bright when it comes to men."

Jack came up behind her. His hands closed over her shoulders. "She said that because you're with me?"

She cleared her throat. "Something along those lines, yes."

"What about you, Elizabeth?" His voice was very even, completely without inflection. "Do you still think I made a fool out of you six months ago? That I used you?"

She gazed straight ahead, very conscious of the weight and heat of his hands. "This isn't a good time for this kind of discussion."

"Did you love Garth Galloway?"

"Garth?" Stunned by the unexpected question, she stepped quickly out from under his hands and whirled around. "What in the world does he have to do with any of this?"

"Your brother-in-law said you loved Galloway but that you found out after the takeover that he had only asked you to marry him in order to please his mother. Merrick told me that Camille Galloway wanted the Aurora Fund in the family."

Elizabeth groaned. "Merrick talks too much."

"Is it true?"

"Does it matter?"

"Yes," Jack said. "It matters."

She eyed him suspiciously. "Why?"

"Because it makes me wonder just how badly you got hurt by what happened two years ago and how much you blame me for it." His gaze was intent and steady. "It makes me wonder if you think Vicky's right about you being not too bright because you're sleeping with me. It makes me wonder if—"

The muted rumble of his cell phone sounded, cutting off the rest of his words. An impatient expression flashed in his eyes. Then he reached for the phone lying on the end table.

"Fairfax here," he said brusquely, his gaze still on Elizabeth's face.

His expression turned to stone as he listened to whoever was speaking on the other end of the connection. He said nothing at all in response. A few seconds later, he ended the call and just stood there, looking at her.

A rush of anxiety swept through Elizabeth. "What's wrong?"

"That was Hayden." Jack drew a long breath. "He thinks I tried to kill him sometime late this afternoon. From what I can gather, someone almost succeeded in running him down with a car at about the time I was returning from the Holland place."

"This is a waste of time," Jack said as he followed Elizabeth off the elevator.

"Quit whining." She led the way down the hotel corridor to Hayden's room. "You've already made your position clear. But I still say we've got nothing to lose."

She came to a halt in front of Hayden's door and knocked. Behind her, Jack loomed, grim-featured.

Hayden opened the door. He looked surly and resentful. But Elizabeth got the impression he had been in that mood before he realized who was standing in the hall.

He gave Jack a disgusted look and then pointedly ignored him. He studied Elizabeth.

"What are you doing here?" he asked.

Elizabeth caught the scent of alcohol on his breath. He'd been drinking, she realized, but he was not yet drunk.

"I think it's time the three of us talked," she said.

"I'm more than willing to talk to you," Hayden drawled, "under the right circumstances. But I haven't got a damn thing to say to Jack."

Elizabeth flattened a hand on the door and pushed firmly inward. "Unless you like being played for a sucker, I think you'll want to cooperate with us."

Hayden fell back, scowling. "What's this about being played for a sucker?"

"Someone's playing some unpleasant games," Elizabeth said. "You aren't the only victim."

She walked into the room. Jack followed without a word and closed the door.

"Sit down," Elizabeth said to both men. "Try to deal with this as adults. Hayden, we need some answers from you."

Hayden sprawled in the chair and looked mutinous. "I don't see why I should tell you a damned thing about what I know or how I came to know it."

Jack said nothing. He just stood gazing stoically out the window.

Elizabeth sighed. This was even harder than she had imagined. She could only give thanks that none of her family relationships had taken this terrible turn. She made a mental note to transfer a nice, fat sum from the Aurora Fund into Merrick's account the moment she arrived back in Seattle. It was worth every penny to know that, whatever else happened, she had family she could depend on in a crunch.

"Someone is handing out warnings," she said to Hayden. "It sounds like you got one earlier today. We got one last night."

"What are you talking about?" Hayden muttered.

"Two thugs waylaid us on the road and tried to beat up your brother."

"Half brother," Hayden said automatically. "And I don't believe a word of it. He looks fine to me."

"It's the truth," Elizabeth snapped. "You may not trust Jack, but I think you know that you can trust me."

"Yeah? How do I know that?"

Elizabeth just looked at him. He had the grace to turn a dull red. She noticed a room-service tray in the corner. There was a large pot of coffee and some sandwiches on it. She found a clean cup on top of the minibar and crossed the small space to help herself to the coffee.

"We think that someone who is here in Mirror Springs for the auction has decided to try to scare off some of the competition," Jack said from the window.

"Someone such as yourself, maybe?" Hayden's jaw tightened. "I'm sur-

prised you used a car, Jack. Next time try a gun. Hit-and-run with a car usually leaves some trace evidence."

"If you really think I tried to run you down," Jack said, "go to the cops."

"With what?" Hayden growled. "I can't prove a damn thing, and you
know it. But I saw the car. Silver gray. Just like that rental you're driving."

"There must be a couple of hundred silver-gray rentals in town this week."

"Stop it." Elizabeth slammed down her cup. "I will not tolerate these
stupid accusations. Jack had nothing to do with whatever almost happened
to you this afternoon, Hayden."

"Is that so?" Hayden gave her a politely inquisitive look. "Were you with
him all afternoon? Can you vouch for his whereabouts at approximately four
o'clock?"

Jack turned his head and gazed at her with laconic amusement. She
knew exactly what he was thinking. She had been on her way home from
the spa at four o'clock. He had not been with her. He had been driving back
from Holland's house.

"Jack was not with me," she admitted quietly. "But I know that he would
never do what you've suggested."

"How can you be so damned sure of that, given what he did to you?"
Hayden asked.

"What are you? Crazy?" She looked at him, amazed at how deep his bitterness had gone. "Grow up. Jack might be a little ruthless when it comes
to business, but—"

"A *little* ruthless." Hayden uttered a short, sharp laugh. "That's a joke,
and you know it. Look what he did to Galloway. Hell, look what he did to
you six months ago. I can't believe you've bought his line of bull. You always
struck me as smart, Elizabeth. At the very least, I would have thought that
you were intelligent enough to learn from your mistakes."

"And I think you're too smart to let the anger and bitterness of the past
blind you to the facts," she retorted. "No, I didn't like what Jack did at Galloway, but at least I now know why he did it. He was trying to get justice for
your brother Larry. Given the same set of circumstances, I might have done
something similar."

Jack gave her a quick, surprised look over his shoulder. But he said
nothing.

"I'm not sure what that says about you," Hayden drawled. "I heard you
were engaged to Garth Galloway and that the stress of the hostile takeover
wrecked your relationship. Didn't that mean anything to you?"

"Garth wasn't exactly a paragon of honor and manly virtue. He only wanted to marry me to help his mother get her hands on the Aurora Fund," she said.

Hayden snorted. "I'll bet Jack told you that."

"No," she said quietly. "Garth told me that himself. He was very, very clear on that point."

A short, awkward silence fell. Hayden's mouth was a grim line.

"Sorry," he said after a while. "I know how it feels to have someone lie to you like that. And how it feels to fall for the lie hook, line, and sinker. I really thought that Gillian—Hell, never mind. It doesn't matter now."

"You're right," Elizabeth said. "It doesn't matter now. What matters is that you stop blaming Jack for everything that's ever gone wrong in your life and start dealing with reality. We've got a problem here. It could be a lot more serious than any of us first thought."

Hayden eyed her morosely. "What's more serious than almost getting killed in a hit-and-run accident?"

Jack finally turned away from the window. "Actually getting killed in a hit-and-run accident."

Hayden blinked. "What's that supposed to mean? Are you threatening me?"

"No," Jack said quietly, "I'm not threatening you. I'm telling you that there's an outside chance that this situation could turn dangerous. Elizabeth and I think that Dawson Holland is here for the auction. If that's true, we've all got to watch our backs. Some people are convinced, for example, that he might have arranged the murder of his first two wives in order to collect on an inheritance and some insurance."

"Dawson Holland?" Hayden stared at him in disbelief. "The guy who's involved in all this film stuff? Where the hell did you get the idea that he's here because of Soft Focus?"

"His wife gave me the idea," Elizabeth said.

Hayden frowned. "She actually mentioned the specimen and the auction?"

"Well, no, but she sort of implied that it might be a good idea if I got the heck out of Dodge. And last night, after we were stopped on the road, one of the thugs admitted that he had been hired to, quote, 'deliver a message.' "

"This is bullshit." Hayden levered himself up out of his chair. "Pure bullshit."

"In addition to the warnings," Jack said coolly, "there is a possibility that the trashing of the Excalibur lab might be connected to the theft."

"Hard to see how," Hayden said.

"The Vanguard of Tomorrow crowd doesn't want to claim responsibility. They've certainly been eager enough to take credit for their vandalism in the past. So we have to wonder if there could be another reason for the break-in. Given that it occurred within hours after Soft Focus disappeared, I think we can assume that it might have been done in an attempt to distract attention from the theft."

Hayden scowled. "You're starting to sound like some kind of conspiracy nut." But he appeared reluctantly thoughtful now.

"And there is one other outstanding matter that has not been resolved to our satisfaction," Elizabeth said very quietly. "A man is dead."

That got Hayden's attention. "What the hell are you talking about?"

"A lab tech named Ryan Kendle was murdered the night the lab was trashed," Jack said. "The cops think that he was killed in a drug deal. But it turns out he was working at Excalibur under an assumed identity."

"Probably because he was involved in the drug scene," Hayden muttered with exaggerated patience. "Maybe he had a history with the law. You know it's not uncommon for someone to fake a résumé."

"A few details maybe, but not an entire identity."

"It happens."

Jack shrugged. "Yeah. It happens. And I admit there is no direct connection between Kendle and Tyler Page. Kendle didn't even work in the same lab. But I don't like the coincidence."

Elizabeth went to stand behind the nearest chair. She gripped the back with both hands. "The point here is that it's possible this thing is escalating beyond the normal parameters of high-tech, white-collar crime. In which case it would behoove all three of us to stick together."

Hayden threw a sour look at Jack. "Forget it. I offered you a deal, Elizabeth, but it sure as hell doesn't extend to Jack."

"I'm not interested in going into partnership with you, either," Jack said. "But you're here. That means you're involved. Tell us what you know about this mess, Hayden."

Hayden hesitated and then shrugged. "Even if I felt like helping you out, which I don't, I couldn't. I don't know anything useful. I'm here because I got a phone call inviting me to an auction. That's it."

"Has anyone contacted you since you arrived?" Elizabeth asked sharply.

"Once. The night I got here. I was told that I would get a call just before the auction was scheduled. That was all." Hayden's mouth thinned. "Until someone tried to run me down tonight, that is."

"It wasn't me," Jack said. "But I will give you a warning, Hayden. If, by some bizarre chance, you do get your hands on that specimen, I'll tie you up in court for years even if I have to pay for it out of my own pocket. You'll never be able to use the technology in your own labs."

Hayden gave him a beatific smile. "Jack, Jack, you just don't get it. I don't give a damn about Soft Focus. All I care about is keeping it out of your hands long enough to kill the deal you've set up with Veltran."

Elizabeth frowned. "You know about the Veltran presentation?"

Jack took a step toward him. "Who told you?"

"The same person who called to invite me to the auction," Hayden said. "Guess he wanted to make sure I'd have a good incentive to take part in the bidding. Timing is everything here, isn't it? If you don't get Soft Focus back by the presentation date, you might as well scrub the whole project."

"Tyler Page." Jack glanced at Elizabeth. "He's the only one who could have known about the timing of the Veltran presentation."

"We've known all along that he was the thief," Elizabeth said. "Nothing new there." She looked at Hayden. "One more thing. Did you ever meet with Tyler Page in a hotel room?"

"Hell, no, I've never met the guy anywhere. Didn't even know he existed until I got that phone call telling me that a specimen of a crash-research project at Excalibur had disappeared."

Elizabeth traded glances with Jack. He shrugged but did not say anything.

She looked at Hayden. "Think about what you're doing here. If you keep us from making the Veltran presentation, it won't be just Jack who gets hurt. Excalibur will go down the tubes, too. A lot of innocent people will be put out of work. A family heritage will be destroyed."

"You know what they say about making omelets," Hayden murmured. "Gotta break a few eggs."

"What a perfectly disgusting thing to say." Elizabeth picked up her purse. "Jack was right. You're so obsessed with your need for revenge that you're willing to do something stupid and vicious. And you've got the nerve to accuse your brother of being ruthless."

"How the hell can you defend him after the way he screwed you over not once, but twice?" Hayden demanded.

"My differences with Jack stem from the Galloway takeover," she said tightly. "I didn't like what happened two years ago and I didn't like the way he handled it. But I can understand his motive."

"To make a nice profit," Hayden drawled.

Elizabeth threw her hands into the air, beyond exasperated now. "I told you, he did it for your brother Larry's sake."

Hayden's expression tightened again. "You might be willing to buy that story, but I'm not."

"Why don't you pick up the phone and ask Larry for the truth?" Elizabeth suggested through her teeth. She looked at Jack. "I've had enough of this. Let's get out of here."

"Whatever you say." He followed her to the door.

Neither of them looked back at Hayden as they went out into the hall. They waited for the elevator in silence. When the cab arrived, Elizabeth stepped inside. Jack followed.

She gazed determinedly at the closed doors. "That was my fault."

"Your fault?"

"That scene with Hayden. I'm sorry about it. I honestly thought I could talk some sense into him. I didn't realize he would be so . . . so rigid."

"Told you so."

"Yes. You did mention it once or twice."

Jack exhaled slowly. "He hates me, Elizabeth."

"I agree that something is eating him up inside and he's projecting it outward, focusing those feelings on you. But I don't think he really hates you."

"Has anyone ever told you that your naïveté is quite charming at times?"

"Vicky mentioned it this afternoon. She seemed to think it was an unfortunate character flaw."

Jack smiled slowly. He caught her chin on the edge of his hand and leaned down to kiss her briefly, a quick, hard, hungry kiss that left her slightly breathless. She gazed at him, wide-eyed.

"What was that for?" she asked.

"For championing my honor and my integrity back there in that hotel room."

She flushed. "Don't be ridiculous. We both know you didn't try to scare off Hayden by nearly running him down this afternoon."

"I know it." Jack's eyes gleamed. "But how can you be so certain? You weren't with me."

"That kind of thing just isn't your style," she said brusquely. "You might confront him. You *did* confront him, in fact. But you wouldn't use scare tactics, especially not the kind that could result in physical injury or . . . or worse."

"Not my style, hmm?"

"What's so funny?" she demanded.

"Nothing. It's just that I recall saying something very similar to you after we watched that video."

Silence fell again. Elizabeth said nothing as they walked through the lobby and out into the resort parking lot. She waited until she was in the car and Jack was behind the wheel.

"About Garth Galloway," she said quietly.

He paused, his hand on the ignition. He glanced her way, his eyes concealed behind his sunglasses. "What about him?"

She gazed straight ahead at the row of parked cars in front of her. "For the record, Garth and I had begun to have problems before you launched your assault on Galloway. I suspected that he, well, it's not important now."

"You knew that he was seeing someone else?"

"Yes." She cleared her throat. "What I'm trying to say is that the engagement would have ended even if the takeover had never occurred. I delayed the inevitable because I didn't want to abandon Garth and Camille while they were under siege. It just didn't seem right, somehow. They were old friends of the family. I had known them both for so long, you see."

Jack folded his hands on top of the steering wheel and stared out over the hood of the car. "You didn't answer my question. Did you love him?"

"Whatever it was I felt for Garth, it was founded on lies and errors in judgment. My judgment. As Vicky Bellamy once told me, nothing is ever quite what it seems in the movies or in real life."

He turned with unexpected speed, whipping around in the seat, catching her by the shoulders, hauling her toward him. "Don't give me that bullshit. *Did you love him?*"

She went very still, hardly daring to breathe. "Back at the beginning? Yes, I loved him. Is that what you wanted to hear?"

His jaw tightened. She could see her own reflection in the lenses of his glasses.

"No," he said. "It's not what I wanted to hear. But I had to know the truth."

"Stop it," she ordered gently.

"What?"

She touched his taut jaw with her fingertips. "Garth killed my love for him before you came on the scene, Jack. You've got some things to answer for because of what you did to Galloway, but wrecking my engagement is not on the list. You don't have to assume responsibility for destroying the great love of my life, okay?"

"Was it the great love of your life?"

"No." She hesitated. "It was nice while I thought that it was real. But looking back, it never was great."

He did not move for a long moment, just sat there studying her intently from behind the shield of his sunglasses.

"I told you once that if I had to do the Galloway deal again, I would," he said, as if he wanted to be certain she understood.

"I know. Because of your brother Larry."

He looked as if he wanted to say something else but changed his mind. He bent his head and kissed her instead.

It was a different kind of kiss, unlike any of the others she had received from him. There was a deeply buried hunger in it, not for sex, she realized, but for something else. Something more. Absolution?

Whatever it was, she sensed the need and could not resist the appeal. She put her arms on his shoulders and kissed him back, not with the fire and passion that his kisses usually induced in her, but softly, gently. Offering him the forgiveness he seemed to be searching for in the embrace.

He wrapped her close against him and held her very tightly. It was a long time before he released her, turned the key in the ignition, and drove out of the parking lot.

He said nothing, but she saw the grim, unyielding plane of his jaw and she knew a sense of failure. He had not gotten whatever it was he had wanted from her.

If it wasn't forgiveness he had been seeking, what had he been searching for in that kiss?

Shortly before eight the following evening, Elizabeth took her seat in the first row of the balcony and watched the festivalgoers arrive for the awards ceremony. It had been her idea to attend this evening. She was convinced that Tyler Page would want to be here to see if his film or Vicky Bellamy won an award. Jack had agreed that it was possible Page would break cover for the event.

She glanced at him as he took the aisle seat beside her. He wore an expensively cut, deceptively casual jacket, black pullover, and black trousers. His attire was similar to that of a number of other men pouring into the theater, but unlike the majority of them, he looked as if he really did wield power and control. It wasn't a question of money or industry influence, she thought. It was that impression of self-mastery that radiated from him. That was what made him both dangerous and compelling.

She was still wondering what she had misunderstood about the kiss in the resort parking lot yesterday. One thing was for certain: She was not about to ask for explanations. Jack had made it obvious that his only concern was his mission to find Tyler Page.

She studied his hard profile as the other ticket-holders streamed down the aisles to their seats. During the drive to the Silver Empire Theater this evening, he had been silent. He had handled the car and the narrow, winding road with his usual flawless precision and control, but she had sensed the cold determination in him. She had known that the scene with Hayden had disturbed him, but she was somewhat surprised by the return of this chilling reserve.

Just like the old days, she thought. She had seen a lot of this attitude during the past six months.

"Are you going to stay in this mood all evening?" she asked pleasantly.

"Depends."

"On what?"

"On whether or not Tyler Page shows up."

"It wasn't wondering if Page would show that turned you surly tonight," she reminded him. "It was that conversation with Hayden last night. Want to talk about it?"

He frowned and turned briefly to look at her. She was startled to see a flash of surprise in his eyes.

"No," he said.

She sighed. "That is so typical."

He slanted her a brief, derisive glance. "Of the male of the species?"

"No, of you, in particular. You always act like this when things don't go just the way you planned them."

"Like what?"

"Like *this*." Bright little flashes of crimson danced before her eyes. Her nails. He had her waving her hands again. She checked the telltale movement and quickly folded her fingers neatly in her lap. "You go all distant and cold and watchful. It makes it difficult to carry on a meaningful conversation."

"Really? I hadn't realized that we were involved in a meaningful conversation."

Anger sparked through her. She covered it with a steely smile. "You know, a shrink could have a field day analyzing the relationship between you and your brother."

"I doubt if any therapist would touch our case."

"Why not?"

Jack's smile was devoid of all amusement. "Because neither Hayden nor I would ever pay anyone real money to analyze us. And I can't see any therapist worth his or her salt doing the job for free. Can you?"

"No. Especially if he or she knew that the clients weren't interested in the results."

The film clip from Fast Company, the audience was told, was a scene that took place three-quarters of the way through the movie. The dramatic lighting gave Vicky Bellamy's spider-woman character a luminous glow. It wasn't Rita Hayworth in *Gilda,* or Lauren Bacall in *The Big Sleep,* Elizabeth thought, but it wasn't bad.

Unfortunately, the dialogue wasn't *Casablanca,* either.

"But I didn't kill him. Eden, for God's sake, you've got to tell the cops the truth."

"I make it a habit to never tell the truth, Harry. I believe in living a simple life, and the truth always seems to complicate things."

Under cover of the enthusiastic clapping that followed the clip, Jack leaned toward Elizabeth.

"We're wasting our time. He's not here. I've checked every damn seat in the house."

"I don't understand it," she whispered. "How could he stay away? He might not have expected *Fast Company* to win Best Picture at the festival, but what about Vicky?"

"I told you that you were putting too much stock in the theory that Page is a victim of passion."

"I still think he's here somewhere," she insisted.

"The ceremony is almost over. Only Best Actress and Best Film left. If Page is here, he'll probably try to leave just before the houselights come up."

"Then it's time for my fallback plan," Elizabeth said briskly. "Ready?"

Jack hesitated, then reluctantly got to his feet. Elizabeth collected her coat and followed him up the darkened aisle. A moment later they emerged into the plush, red and gold upstairs lobby. It was empty except for a couple of idling ushers and the waiter lounging behind the wine bar.

"You're sure you want to do this?" Jack asked.

"It's not like we have a lot of other options," she reminded him.

"All right. You take this exit. I'll take the other one."

He turned to the left, as though he intended to go to the men's room. Elizabeth hurried in the opposite direction toward the women's room.

Once in the dimly lit hall she kept going past the door marked "Ladies," all the way to the emergency exit. She was relieved to see that it was not equipped with an alarm.

She glanced over her shoulder to make certain that no one was watching her. Then she opened the door. Unlike the lush Victorian lobby, the stairwell was starkly utilitarian. The harsh, fluorescent lighting revealed a set of concrete steps. She grasped the handrail and went quickly down to a door marked "Exit." When she pushed it open, the brisk night air swirled around her.

Outside she huddled into her coat and walked swiftly down the alley toward the back of the theater. When she got there she saw a small parking area. Jack stepped briefly into the weak yellow glare of the single streetlamp that illuminated the rear of the theater. He raised a hand to let her know that he had seen her. Then he moved back into the shadows on the opposite side of the building.

She pulled up the collar of her coat and prepared to wait. The plan was simple enough, she reminded herself. She would watch the emergency exits on this side of the theater. Jack would watch the exits on the other side. Between the two of them they would be able to see anyone leaving via one of the side doors.

Jack had bought into the scheme with something less than enthusiasm, and only after she had pointed out that they would be within easy hailing distance of each other. He considered the vigil a waste of time.

Minutes ticked past at a relentlessly slow pace. Elizabeth scrunched deeper into her coat and clenched her gloved hands inside her pockets. Eventually the dull, muted thunder of applause broke out inside the theater. The Best Actress Award. She wondered if Vicky had won.

Next up would be Best Picture.

A few minutes later, muffled applause again echoed through the old theater building. Elizabeth tensed in expectation and peered into the alley. If Tyler Page had attended the ceremony, he would no doubt try to leave quickly and quietly now that it was over. With any luck, by a side entrance. She watched the alley door, waiting for it to open.

There was another rumble of applause inside the theater. The ceremony was over. Still the alley door did not open. Frustration rose inside her. She had been so sure of her analysis of Page's motivation. The man had done what he'd done for love of Vicky Bellamy, his femme fatale. How could he bring himself to miss his lover's big night?

People were leaving the theater now. She heard laughter and conversation from the vicinity of the front entrance. But the emergency exit door on her side of the building did not budge.

She sensed Jack and turned to see him coming toward her. With his coat collar up and his face hidden, he looked like Humphrey Bogart in *The Maltese Falcon*.

"Give up?" he asked.

"Not yet. Maybe he decided to wait until the theater is empty. He could be hiding in the men's room or a utility closet." She took one hand out of her pocket and made a shooing motion. "Go back to your post."

"Face it, he didn't show."

"I still think—" She broke off as the roar of a motorcycle engine split the darkness behind her.

She and Jack both turned quickly toward the sound. A single headlight beam pierced the night. Elizabeth realized that the motorcycle was racing along a service road behind the theater. As they watched, it turned into the small parking lot where she and Jack stood.

"What the hell?" Jack took her arm and hauled her deeper into the darkness near the wall. "Don't move," he said in her ear.

She obeyed, standing very still in the circle of his arm.

The motorcycle flashed past the pool of shadows where they waited. The driver did not appear to notice them. He drove down the narrow alley on the right side of the building toward the entrance of the theater. The vehicle was not moving at a great speed, but the engine was revved to a loud, full-throated roar.

Once the motorcycle had gone safely past them, Elizabeth felt Jack release his hold on her. Together they stepped out into the alley to watch the bike zoom toward the street.

When the cyclist passed beneath the yellow bulb above the exit door, Elizabeth caught her breath. The pale light glinted malevolently on a black helmet that effectively concealed the driver's face. Metal studs gleamed on a black leather jacket and, very briefly, on the metal trim that decorated a familiar-looking black leather boot.

"Jack." She grabbed his arm and tugged him forward in the wake of the cycle. "It's the other guy who tried to beat you up the other night. Ollie, the one that got away in the van."

"How do you know?"

"His boots. Come on. Something's going to happen, and I bet it's going to involve Vicky."

He did not argue. Together they ran down the alley in pursuit of the motorcycle. Elizabeth silently cursed her high heels.

The cycle had reached the brightly lit front entrance of the theater. It slowed. Elizabeth saw the driver raise one hand. He was holding something in his gloved fist. A cylinder-shaped object.

At that moment Vicky Bellamy appeared. Her white and silver gown glowed in the brilliant marquee lights. Dawson was a short distance behind her, smiling proudly. He paused to speak to a man in a dark coat.

The driver of the motorcycle made a throwing motion with his arm. A stream of liquid arced through the air.

"Whore. Scarlet woman. Jezebel."

Vicky screamed, a high, cresting shriek of mingled anger and fear, as the red paint splashed across her gown.

"For God's sake, somebody stop him," Dawson shouted.

As if there were anything that anyone could do, Elizabeth thought. It had all happened too fast. The driver gunned the motorcycle's engine and careened off into the night. The crowd of theatergoers gazed, dumbfounded, after him.

Elizabeth limped to a halt beside Jack, breathing hard.

Vicky's voice rose to a theatrical wail above the murmurs and exclamations. "Dawson, look what he did. Why does he hate me? Why does he call me those terrible names?"

Dawson put his arm around her shoulders in an unmistakable protective movement. "I'm going to talk to the police again, my dear. There must be something they can do. Whoever he is, he's sick and he's dangerous. I'm afraid he's growing bolder."

Jack took the cognac bottle down out of the cupboard. He watched Elizabeth kick off her sadly scuffed high heels and flop lightly down on the sofa in front of the fire. The skirt of her slim black gown rode high on her thigh. It occurred to him that she had very pretty feet—elegantly arched and incredibly sexy, especially when sheathed in a pair of black hose.

And to think he'd never considered himself a foot man.

He heard a sharp clink and winced when he realized he'd struck the edge of one glass with the neck of the cognac bottle. *Clumsy.*

Out of the unholy mix of murky emotions that had been screwing up his thought processes lately, at last emerged one he knew that he could comprehend. It glowed like a homing beacon. Bright, obvious, riveting. That was the nice thing about sex. It wasn't complicated.

He allowed his eye to follow the long line of Elizabeth's neatly curved legs to the point where her thighs disappeared beneath the hem of her dress. He felt his blood heat.

She scowled at him as he finished pouring the cognac into two glasses. He remembered that she had berated him earlier for being in a surly mood. So much for sex not being complicated. He groaned softly. With Elizabeth, everything was complicated.

"There was something strange about what happened outside the theater tonight," she announced.

"There's something strange about this whole damn setup." He picked up the glasses and walked around the corner of the granite counter. "I feel like we're in one of those films where everything keeps turning out wrong and the characters get sucked deeper and deeper into a quagmire of disaster."

"I know what you mean." Her eyes traveled to the bound script lying on the coffee table. "Sort of like the plot for *Fast Company.* But I meant that there was something weird about Vicky's reaction tonight."

He stopped beside the sofa and handed her one of the glasses. "Why do you say that? Looked like a pretty straightforward publicity gimmick to me. Beautiful star victim of crazed fan."

"Her initial scream sounded genuine."

"She's an actress, remember?"

Elizabeth turned the glass of cognac in her hands, studying it. "The scream sounded for real. But a few seconds later, she sounded like an actress again. *Why does he hate me? Why does he do these things to me?* Kind of phony. And Dawson sounded even phonier when he talked about going to the cops again because the stalker was getting bolder."

Jack snorted. "I think it's a good bet that Holland has not gone to the police about the so-called stalker. If he had, good old Ollie would have been out of a job by now. He's not smart enough or fast enough to avoid getting caught."

"And if everyone's right about the stalker incidents being a publicity gimmick, Dawson wouldn't want to have the police looking too closely into the incidents anyway. But that's not my point."

Jack noticed that her brows were etched in a frown of deep concern. "You're worried that the stalker thing is part of Dawson's plan to get rid of a third wife, aren't you?"

Elizabeth twisted restlessly on the sofa. "It's just that I got the impression that Vicky wasn't expecting to have red paint thrown at her tonight. I wonder why not. After all, she must be involved in the planning of the stalker incidents. They'd have to be choreographed ahead of time, wouldn't they?"

"If you were after maximum publicity, yes."

"You know what?" She met his eyes across the top of the cognac glass. "I think something went wrong tonight. Vicky recovered fast, but I'd be willing to bet that she didn't expect the stalker to strike."

Jack thought back to the scene at the theater entrance. Holland folded protectively around his wife, warning everyone in earshot that the stalker was getting bolder. "Dawson expected it."

"Yes."

They looked at each other for a long moment. Jack exhaled slowly.

"You've warned Vicky. There's nothing more that you can do. And we could be wrong about Holland."

"I know." She sat up on the edge of the sofa and put the cognac glass down on the table. "There's something else that's worrying me. I still think that Tyler Page is madly, passionately in love with his femme fatale. What's going to happen when he discovers that Vicky doesn't intend to run off with him after the auction of Soft Focus? Because I sure can't see her throwing away everything for poor Dr. Page."

Jack groaned. "Please don't tell me that you're starting to worry about that little bastard. He's the one who created this mess, remember?"

Elizabeth's expression grew more troubled. "He's obviously a man of intense passions. Something tells me that he won't take Vicky's rejection well. Not after he's sacrificed so much for her. He could make himself . . . difficult."

"How?" Jack asked dryly. "By going to the cops? Not a chance. Like everyone else involved in this thing, he's not about to drag the police into it. He could end up in jail if this deal goes public."

"I can't help but think of Page as a victim of passion."

"Victim? The little shit stole Soft Focus." Jack set his glass down very forcefully on the mantel and left it there. He started across the room toward Elizabeth. "If you're going to feel sorry for anyone, feel sorry for us. If we don't find him and that damned crystal, Excalibur will go out of business, my professional reputation will be in the toilet, and the Aurora Fund will lose a hell of a lot of money."

"I'm very aware of the business and financial implications," she said stiffly. "That's not the issue."

"The hell it's not." He reached down, closed his hands around her shoulders, and pulled her to her feet. "This is no time to lose sight of the main objective."

"I know."

The anxiety in her eyes irritated him. "Do me a favor. Don't go all soft and sentimental about Tyler Page—or Vicky Bellamy, either, for that matter. Both of them can take care of themselves. They don't deserve your sympathy. You know something?"

"What?"

"You've got a bad habit of feeling sorry for people. Page, Vicky, your brother-in-law, Camille Galloway. Hayden. Hell, yesterday afternoon in the parking lot you felt sorry for me. Where does the list stop?"

Her chin came up fast. "It stops with you." She turned away from him with a sharp, angry movement. "I can see where you got the idea that I'm the world's easiest pushover. After all, I'm sleeping with you, aren't I?"

He stiffened. "That's got nothing to do with this."

"It has everything to do with it." She spun around, eyes alight with anger. "You think I'm a wimp or an idiot, or both."

"Damn it to hell, that's not true and you know it. *I just don't want to be on your feel-sorry-for list.*"

She blinked. For an instant he thought she was going to throw something at him. Then, quite suddenly, the fires of battle faded. He was not sure he liked the closed, speculative expression that took their place any better. Fires of battle he understood. This look was much more complicated and therefore much more dangerous.

She folded her arms. "If you don't think I'm a wimp or an idiot, what do you think?"

His blood chilled. What had gone wrong? He was losing control of the situation again. Why in hell did this kind of thing always happen whenever he tried to talk to her about something other than business? He groped for a way to get the conversation back on track.

"You once asked me what I would do if I failed to recover the crystal for Excalibur," he said.

"You told me that you would liquidate the company for the Ingersolls and track down Tyler Page."

"Right. I'm real clear on those two points. But what about us?"

She went very still in front of the fire. "Are you asking me if I'm interested in continuing our affair after whatever happens"—she waved a hand—"happens?"

"Yes." He watched her, aware that inside he was coiled so tightly he was afraid he might snap. "That's what I'm asking."

She did not take her eyes off the flames. "Don't you think it's a little too soon to be making any long-range decisions in that direction?"

Shit. Now what the hell was he supposed to say? He tried to plow forward, afraid that he was sinking deeper with each step. "What I think is that we're both attracted to each other. We've fought it for six months."

Her mouth twitched. "We haven't exactly been fighting it this past week."

"You've got to admit that what we've been doing for the past few days is pretty convincing evidence that we wasted a hell of a lot of time during the past six months."

She put one hand on the mantel. Her lipstick-red nails glowed like rubies in the flickering light. "You know something? I've been thinking about what's been happening between us since Soft Focus disappeared."

Hope ignited in him. He took a step toward her and then stopped. "Me too."

She contemplated him thoughtfully. "We've been thrown together under a highly abnormal set of circumstances. We're both under a lot of stress this week. We're two single, healthy people forced to share the same space. We're united in a mutual goal."

"I'm probably going to hate myself for asking, but just where are you going with this?"

She began to tap her nails against the mantel. "I'm saying that, what with everything that's happened during the past few days, it's quite possible that we have both experienced an artificial sense of bonding."

"Is that what you call it? Bonding?"

She pursed her lips. "It seems obvious to me that sex may be our bodies' natural way of relieving the tension in what is, after all, a highly unnatural situation."

"There is nothing unnatural about it." His jaw tensed. "Or artificial, either, for that matter."

"I don't think we should read too much into what's been going on between us during the past few days."

"You're calling this a one-week stand?"

"What else can we call it?" She swung around to face him. "Don't you understand? We won't really know how we feel about each other until we're back in Seattle. We need to try having a normal relationship before we can decide what this is all about. It's possible that what's happened between us here in Mirror Springs is just one of those things."

The fierceness that had been gnawing at his insides all evening welled up once more. He took another step toward her. "I already know that I want us to continue sleeping together after we return to whatever passes for a normal life back in Seattle."

"I think we should go very slowly here. Neither of us should put pressure on the other."

"Why the hell not?"

She eyed him with an unreadable expression. "Well, for one thing, I've got a rather poor track record when it comes to choosing the right man."

"I knew it. You don't trust your feelings for me." He smiled slowly. "Who would have thought that the Ice Princess would be such a coward?"

Anger flared in her eyes. "Don't you dare call me a coward just because I want to make sure that this whole affair amounts to something more than a one-week stand."

He gathered her into his arms. "What are you afraid of, Elizabeth?"

"I'm not afraid of anything." She put her hands on his shoulders, holding herself away from him. "I just don't intend to make any more mistakes where you're concerned."

"For six months we've been stuck together like a couple of staples in a jammed stapler."

"Oh, that's a romantic image."

He ignored her. "Now we're sleeping together, which, for my money, is a lot more comfortable. What's wrong with this picture?"

"Nothing, as far as this week goes," she shot back. "It's comfortable, all right. But I refuse to be pushed into making a sweeping decision about what will happen when this business with Soft Focus is finished. I don't want to go too far out on a limb."

"When are you going to realize that we've already gone too far out on this branch? You can't turn back now any more than I can."

She opened her mouth. He realized she was going to continue to argue. He also knew that he was out of words. He kissed her quickly, swallowing her indignant protest with a kiss.

She made a muffled, exasperated sound.

"Okay, okay," he muttered against her mouth. "No commitments beyond this week. I'll take what I can get and shut up."

She tilted her head back against his arm. "Will you really? Shut up about it, I mean?"

"It might be a one-week stand, but it's the best week I've had in six months, even if I have lost my client's only tangible business asset and very possibly my own career." He lowered the zipper of her gown to her waist. "Which only goes to show how miserable the last six months have been."

"A couple of jammed staples?" she mumbled a long time later.

"I'm a CEO, not a scriptwriter."

Chapter Twenty-Three

She still didn't trust him. Or maybe she just didn't trust herself. Either way, the result was the same. He had a problem.

Jack punched up the pillow behind his head so that he could study the dull glow of a cloudy mountain dawn. Beside him, Elizabeth slept soundly, the sweet, lush curve of her derriere settled against his hip. He had called her a coward, but he knew the truth. The tension between them was all his fault, not hers. He had really pissed in his chili six months ago.

The bottom line was that he'd gotten exactly what he'd told himself he wanted: a second chance with Elizabeth in his bed.

Be careful what you wish for . . .

She was willing to have an affair, or at least a one-week fling, but she was not about to commit to anything more. Not yet, at any rate. He had a sudden vision of finding himself back in Seattle and discovering that she intended to see other men while she waited to find out exactly how she felt about him.

The bleak mood that had crowded in on him during those rare hours when he had not been working during the past six months threatened to settle on him again. But this time he could not escape to the dojo. This time his problem was lying right here beside him.

Somehow he had to make her see that what they had was worth working on—worth a commitment.

He tried to step back mentally and view the situation the way he would any other kind of business problem. He needed a strategy. He was usually pretty good at strategies.

The phone rang, cutting into his swirling thoughts. It was the house phone, he realized. Not his cell phone. Elizabeth stirred beside him as he groped for the receiver.

"Fairfax here."

"I'm calling for Elizabeth Cabot."

For a split second he didn't recognize the low, sultry voice. Then it hit him. He sat up suddenly. "Vicky Bellamy?"

There was a slight pause before she said, "May I please speak with Elizabeth?"

"Sure. Right." He shook Elizabeth gently. "For you."

She opened her eyes and yawned. "Who is it?"

He put his hand over the mouthpiece. "Vicky Bellamy."

She snatched the phone from him.

"This is Elizabeth."

Jack listened intently to the silence while Elizabeth listened to Vicky. He saw her expression change from surprise to cool and shuttered.

"I can handle it," she said crisply. "I'm really not as naïve as everyone seems to think. Why did you call?"

More silence.

"I understand." Elizabeth turned toward Jack. "I can promise you that he won't."

Another pause.

"Yes, of course. I'll be there." Elizabeth gave the phone back to Jack.

He tossed it down onto the end table. "What did she want?"

Elizabeth sat up amid the tumbled sheets and wrapped her arms around her updrawn knees. "She wants to talk. Privately. She doesn't want Dawson to find out that she's meeting with me."

Anticipation pumped through him. "How the hell is she going to arrange that?"

"She's got it all figured out," Elizabeth said thoughtfully. "I got the impression that she spent a lot of time planning this before she called me. I wonder why."

"Should be interesting." Energized by the new turn of events, he threw back the covers and got to his feet. Then he remembered something. "What did she say to you when you first took the phone?"

"Hmm?" Elizabeth sounded distracted as she reached for her robe.

"Your answer was 'I can handle it.' What was the question?"

"Nothing important." Elizabeth tied the sash. She did not look back at him as she walked toward the bathroom. "She just asked me if I knew what I was doing sleeping with you."

She disappeared into the bathroom. Jack looked at the closed door for a long moment. *I can handle it.*

*The only lights in the empty interior of the Silver Empire The-*ater were the dimly glowing fixtures located at the ends of the aisles. The details of the ornate ceiling were lost in the darkness overhead. The rows of velvet seats marched down the sloping floor, a regiment of hulking, headless robots frozen in formation. Steeped in the thick gloom, the heavy crimson curtains appeared as dark as midnight. The thick folds of velvet were drawn closed across the stage, concealing the screen.

"It's a different world when there's no crowd and nothing happening on the screen, isn't it?" Vicky said from somewhere in the darkness.

Elizabeth, poised at the top of one aisle, started slightly at the sound of the other woman's voice. She peered into the depths of the theater, willing her eyes to adjust quickly to the dim light.

"Just isn't the same without the smell of popcorn," she said.

"That can be faked, too, just like everything else in the movies." Vicky rose languidly from an end seat. The pale, smoke-colored pantsuit she wore gave her a ghostly look. "Remember what I told you, Elizabeth. In the movies and in life, things are seldom what they seem."

"It's the same way with business." Elizabeth started slowly down the aisle. "But I assume you didn't ask me to meet you here just to trade philosophical observations on our respective careers."

"No, I didn't." Vicky smiled slightly. "I understand that the Aurora Fund has an old tradition of underwriting business ventures launched by women."

"The Fund has branched out in recent years, but you're right. Aunt Sybil started it with the goal of helping entrepreneurial women get financial backing when they couldn't secure it from other sources." Elizabeth halted when she was two rows away from Vicky. "Did you call me because you want to request funding for a business venture?"

"Something along those lines, yes. I'm changing careers. I'm getting out of the film business."

"I have to say, I'm surprised."

"It's time to move on. I know that better than anyone. Whatever chance I had came and went years ago. I'm too old for Hollywood now, and I've decided I've had enough of the independent film industry."

"You're just going to walk away from your acting?"

"Not bloody likely." Vicky gave a short, harsh laugh. "I've acted all my life. It's the only thing I know how to do. But I won't be doing it in front of a camera anymore. *Fast Company* will be my last film."

"I see. And you want the Aurora Fund to underwrite your new career?"

"Not entirely. Just some of the initial start-up expenses. I've always known this day might come." Vicky hesitated. "I just didn't expect it to come quite so soon. I thought I'd have a little more time."

A chill went through Elizabeth. She tried and failed to read Vicky's face in the darkness. "What are you going to do?"

"I'm going to disappear."

Elizabeth felt her jaw unhinge. "Disappear? For heaven's sake, why?"

"It's time." Vicky gazed out over the rows of velvet seats. "In the old days they used to call women like me adventuresses, you know."

"I've heard the term."

"It was a euphemism, of course. What people really meant was that we used sex to get what we wanted. They said that we lured men into our webs and manipulated them as if they were stupid, mindless creatures who thought only with their balls."

"Femme fatales."

"Yes. Nice work if you can get it, hmm?" Vicky's eyes were ice cold. "But

I can tell you from experience that it isn't as easy as it sounds. For starters, you have to be able to act big time. I mean, you've got to be *good*. Academy Award good."

Elizabeth nodded. "I can see where it would be difficult to live a lie twenty-four hours a day."

"The hard part is not letting your so-called victim know that what you really want to do is run into the bathroom and throw up every time you have sex with him."

"Yes, I can see that would put a strain on a relationship. You were saying something about disappearing."

"I've got good survival instincts," Vicky said. "For the past few months they've been telling me that it was time to move on. I should have done it by now, and I would have if it hadn't been for *Fast Company*. I knew it would be my last film. I wanted to see how it would go over in the independent film circuit. But after last night, I knew I couldn't wait any longer. I've pushed my luck as far as it will go."

"Last night? You mean the red paint incident after the awards ceremony? I thought that was just a publicity stunt. Are you telling me that the stalker is for real?"

"The stalker thing was Dawson's idea. He thought it would help grab some publicity for me during the festival. But last night's assault was not on my schedule. I have a feeling that there may be more incidents like that. One of them will go too far."

"My God." Elizabeth stared at her. "Do you think some nutcase has decided to stalk you for real?"

"Nutcase." Vicky sounded briefly amused. "I wonder if—" She broke off with a shrug. "Doesn't matter, I guess."

"What's going on here, Vicky?"

Vicky seemed to collect herself. She was abruptly all business. "Dawson handles my publicity. As I said, he came up with the stalker concept. He scripted all the incidents. Hired an out-of-work stuntman to carry them out."

"A hulking type named Ollie. Wears black leather boots with metal trim on the heels, right?"

"You know about him?" Vicky's eyes narrowed.

"We had a run-in with him and his pal on the road the other night. They said they had been sent to deliver a warning. We figured it came from Dawson."

"And you ignored it." Vicky chuckled. "Ollie told Dawson that the warning had been delivered. But obviously that was not the whole story. Not if you managed to learn his name. Dawson would not be pleased if he knew that there had been a screwup."

"You said last night's stalker incident was not on your schedule?"

Vicky's full mouth tightened. "Dawson arranged the assault, as usual. But he didn't bother to tell me about it until afterward."

"Why not?"

"He claims that I was getting blasé about the stalker. He said that my reactions were not believable. He thought my acting would improve if I was taken by surprise."

Elizabeth grimaced. "Some surprise. I can imagine how you must have felt when that jerk threw the paint."

"I like to think I rose to the occasion," Vicky said dryly. "But I was furious with Dawson for not warning me. He had promised me that there wouldn't be any more incidents. It was only later that I thought about what you said to me the other day in the spa. I did some checking, and now I'm starting to wonder if Dawson has rewritten the script. Maybe given it a different ending."

Elizabeth drew a deep breath. "Holland did take out a policy on you, didn't he?"

"Yes." Vicky's voice was clipped and emotionless. "A business policy. Taken out by the Holland Group. But Dawson is the Holland Group. After you and I spoke, I went on the Internet. Did some research. Found out that you were right about the deaths of his first two wives. There were rumors and questions, even though Dawson was never officially under suspicion."

"And after last night, you no longer trust him, is that it?"

Vicky laughed softly, harshly. "I don't trust any man. Professional suicide for an adventuress."

"I suppose so."

"I've made my decision. I'm getting out. But it's not going to be simple. Lately Dawson has been acting increasingly possessive. He rarely lets me out of his sight. Right now, for instance, he thinks I'm in the spa. It was the only excuse I could come up with that would allow me to get away from him long enough to see you in private."

"What do you want from me?"

"I'm going to make you a business proposition," Vicky said. "Think of it as an application to the Aurora Fund."

"I'm listening."

"I've got some information to sell."

Elizabeth held her breath. "What kind of information?"

"Call it deep background concerning the provenance of a certain item that is scheduled to go up for auction soon."

Elizabeth reminded herself to breathe. "Go ahead."

Vicky gave her a cool, knowing look. "I'll tell you everything I know about Dawson's other business here in Mirror Springs. I admit it's not a lot. But you and your friend, Jack Fairfax, might find some of it helpful. At the very least, you won't be going into the auction unprepared."

"You think we should be prepared?"

Vicky smiled grimly. "If you plan to go up against Dawson Holland, yes, I think you should be prepared. I don't know what it is that's being auctioned off, but I can tell you that Dawson will do whatever is necessary to get his hands on it."

"Because he needs the money?"

"Not the money. He needs the item itself, whatever it is, to get himself out of some very deep manure."

One could never have too much information before one went into a business negotiation, Elizabeth told herself. "How much do you want from the Aurora Fund to finance your midcourse career change?"

"Don't worry, I'm not going to soak you." Vicky's mouth twisted. "I've got enough in ready cash in my purse to get to Florida. But I'll need a little help after that."

"Good grief, you're planning to leave the *country*?"

"I've learned a lot in my career as an adventuress," Vicky said. "One of the things I've learned is how and where to purchase a new identity. But it will cost me."

"You think it's necessary to hide under a different identity?"

Vicky closed her eyes for a few seconds. Then she opened them and looked straight at Elizabeth. "Let's just say that as long as that insurance policy exists, I'd rather not have Dawson find me."

"I see your point. You want the Aurora Fund to help you finance this new identity, is that it?"

"Think of it as an investment."

Elizabeth pondered the offer for all of two seconds. It really was a no-brainer. "Okay, it's a deal. Tell me what you know about Dawson's business here in Mirror Springs."

"Mostly what I know is that he's desperate," Vicky said bluntly. "And that makes him dangerous. Several months ago he scammed a rather unpleasant group of offshore investors. These are not the kind of people who take you to court to get their money back, if you see what I mean."

Elizabeth shivered. "I see."

"Dawson has never discussed the situation with me, and I've certainly never let him know that I'm aware of his problems. But I think he bought some time for himself by promising to turn over something very valuable in the high-tech field. And I'm almost positive that whatever is going down is supposed to be concluded here in Mirror Springs this week."

"Speaking of warnings," Elizabeth said, "can I assume that the ones Ollie was supposed to deliver to Jack and Hayden came from Dawson, not you?"

"I certainly didn't send Ollie out to deliver any warnings to anyone."

"What about the videotape in Leonard Ledger's hotel room?"

Vicky looked mildly curious. "What videotape?"

"Never mind." That must have come from Dawson, too. An attempt to sow dissension among his competitors. "What do you know about Tyler Page?"

"Other than the fact that he loves film, very little." Vicky met her eyes. "But I do know that Dawson has been looking for him since we got here."

Elizabeth tensed. "Has he found him?"

"No. I assume that Page is the one who stole this piece of high-tech hardware that everyone seems to want?"

"Yes." Elizabeth frowned. "Are you telling me that Holland didn't ask you to seduce Page into stealing it?"

Vicky laughed. She sounded genuinely amused for the first time. "No. I told you, Dawson did not involve me in this thing. I met Page on the set a few times, but all we talked about was *Fast Company*. That was the extent of my relationship with him."

"Is there any possibility that he thinks he stole Soft Focus for your sake?"

"If you're asking me if he had a crush on me, the answer is no."

"You're sure?"

Vicky looked amused. "Trust me, Elizabeth, I know when a man is interested and when he's not. Page was not."

"Damn." So much for her theory about Vicky's being Tyler Page's femme fatale. "Does the name Ryan Kendle mean anything to you?"

"No." Vicky paused. "Should it?"

"I don't know," Elizabeth admitted. "Do you know anything about the trashing of an Excalibur lab?"

"No."

"Guess that's about it," Elizabeth said. "When do you want your money and how do you want it?"

"I've written down the number of a bank account in Florida, and the amount I'll require. Have the money wired into it as soon as you've heard that I've disappeared."

Elizabeth stared at her as she took a folded piece of paper from Vicky. "There's going to be an announcement?"

Vicky chuckled. "I certainly hope so. Pay attention. When you hear about it, just remember what I told you, nothing is ever what it seems in the movies."

"All right." Elizabeth hesitated. "Just one more question."

"Make it quick. I've got to get back to the spa."

"Why did you try to warn me off that night outside the club?"

"Once every decade or so I get this irrational, overwhelming impulse to do a good deed. Just for the hell of it."

"Thoughtful of you," Elizabeth said.

"I should have saved my energy this time. You didn't take advantage of my gentle hint to go back to Seattle, did you? Maybe next decade I'll resist the impulse."

"She's an actress, Elizabeth," Jack said. *"What makes you* think Holland didn't tell her to feed you that entire story?"

Elizabeth shot him a quelling look, silently warning him to keep his voice down.

Not that there was much chance anyone had overheard him, she assured herself. There was only a handful of people browsing through the display of classic film posters in the gallery, and most of them were at the far end of the long room.

She turned back to study the framed poster on the wall in front of her. The creases where it had once been machine folded were still visible. The title, *The Woman in the Window,* was written in lurid yellow script under an image of the stars, Edward G. Robinson and Joan Bennett.

A single glance at the array of noir artwork displayed for sale made it obvious that bright, shrieking yellow ink had been extremely popular with the artists who had produced the posters and lobby cards used to hype the old films. The other dominant colors were bloodred, midnight blue, and black. The heavily saturated hues together with the gritty, suspenseful images combined to give the classic posters their unique look. Guns, dangerous-looking women, and men with 1940s-era hats pulled down low over their cold eyes figured as the most prominent motifs. The prices on the little placards next to the framed pictures indicated that they were pricey collectibles.

Ten minutes after leaving the theater, Elizabeth had found Jack waiting for her in an espresso bar. She had hurriedly dragged him into the gallery to tell him about the interview with Vicky. He had listened, but it was clear he was not entirely convinced.

She glared at him, exasperated. "Why would Dawson tell Vicky to give me so many details about his business dealings? From the sound of it, he's coloring outside the lines."

"Just another tactic designed to try to scare us off," Jack said patiently. "All this stuff about dangerous offshore investors who are threatening his life, et cetera, et cetera, is a little hard to take."

"What about Vicky's plans to disappear?"

"Probably a scam to con some money out of you."

"She was telling the truth, Jack. I could feel it."

He frowned. "Look, all I'm saying is that we can't trust Vicky Bellamy any further than we can trust Dawson Holland. She's the kind of woman who's always got an angle. From what you've just told me, I'd say she's trying to make a little extra cash for herself on the side."

Elizabeth nibbled on her lower lip. "You really think she's trying to scam me?"

"Uh-huh." Jack turned his attention back to Robert Mitchum's grim, world-weary face in a poster for *Out of the Past*. "That's exactly what I think."

"I don't know." Elizabeth moved on to the image of Rita Hayworth posed in sultry invitation against a yellow backdrop in a title card for *The Lady from Shanghai*. "I think she's planning to split."

"She's planning to separate you from some of your money."

"Don't be so negative. Everything she told me about the stalker incidents and those warnings you and Hayden got from Ollie adds up, doesn't it?"

"So what? She and Dawson have probably guessed that we've already figured most of that stuff out for ourselves. And even if she is on the level, you'll notice that she didn't give you any hard information that we can use to find Tyler Page and the crystal."

"That's because she doesn't know where they are." Elizabeth drummed her fingers on the strap of her shoulder bag. "There's only one thing that doesn't quite fit."

"Your idea that she was Page's femme fatale?"

"Yes." Elizabeth gazed at a framed lobby card for *The Big Sleep*. The chemistry between Bogart and Bacall was unmistakable, even in a simple ad for the film. "I was so sure—"

"Look on the bright side," Jack said. "If I'm right about not being able to trust her, your theory that she seduced Page into stealing the crystal remains intact."

"But I do believe her. Which means that there was no woman involved in this, after all." She thought about the report that Ryan Kendle had been overheard arguing with a woman shortly before his death. "Scratch the Kendle connection."

"It was always a damn weak link anyway," Jack reminded her. "The police were sure from the start that he was killed in a drug deal. But I have a hunch that the trashing of the lab is a solid connection. Page probably thought he could muddy the waters that way, just in case I did go to the cops."

"Vicky didn't know anything about that, either."

"Why am I not surprised?"

Elizabeth gazed pensively at Veronica Lake in *This Gun for Hire*. The uneasiness she had been feeling ever since she had left the theater was getting worse. "Well, one thing's for certain. We should get some answers soon."

"What do you mean?"

"If Vicky suddenly disappears, we'll know that she was telling us the truth about her own plans to make a new life for herself."

"Financed by the Aurora Fund," Jack said dryly. "Now, that I can believe."

"Why would you buy that part of her story?"

"Because according to Larry, Holland is really on the rocks again financially. Even if she wasn't afraid that he might be thinking of cashing in the insurance policy he has on her, Vicky would be looking for greener pastures."

The distant, muffled sound of thunder brought Elizabeth awake with a suddenness that left her tingling from head to toe. She sat straight up in bed and blinked at the gray dawn scene outside the window. It took a few seconds for her dream-drenched brain to register the fact that there was no storm.

Jack was already out of bed, padding toward the windows.

"What is it?" she asked.

"Sounded like an explosion of some kind. I can't see anything from this angle." He turned, stepped into a pair of khakis, and headed for the stairs.

Elizabeth scrambled out of bed, seized her robe, and hurried after him. She caught up with him as he opened the downstairs slider and stepped out onto the deck. She winced as her bare feet came in contact with the cold, dew-dampened wood.

"There." Jack pointed toward a plume of smoke that rose skyward in the distance.

She strained to see it. "What on earth?"

"I'm not sure, but from the looks of it, I'd say a car just went off the road into the canyon. It must have gone up in flames. Now the scrub is on fire."

"Oh, my God," she whispered.

Sirens sounded in the distance.

Jack put his arm around her. Together they watched the smoke spiral upward into the dawn.

Elizabeth felt the prickle of tiny goose bumps on her arms. She hugged herself to chase away the chill. It didn't work.

"You okay?" Jack asked quietly.

"Yes." But the prickling sensation did not vanish.

After a while they turned silently and went back indoors. The house was so cold that Jack switched on the gas fire.

An hour later, showered and dressed, Elizabeth paused in the act of slicing some bananas for breakfast and turned on the radio to catch the local news. The local announcer, probably more accustomed to giving ski-condition reports, sounded shaken.

> ". . . *The brush fire caused by the explosion was brought under control almost immediately. Chief Gresham stated that the victim had apparently been thrown from the car and had been swept downstream. A search is under way, but the authorities warn that it will not be easy, given the force of the water in that section of the canyon.*
>
> "*The vehicle has been identified as a white Porsche registered to Victoria Bellamy. Ms. Bellamy has reportedly been stalked in recent weeks by a . . .*"

Elizabeth snapped off the radio and sat down hard on one of the counter stools. She stared blankly at the knife in her hand.

"Jack."

"Right here." He came down the stairs, buttoning his shirt. His hair was still damp from the shower. "What's wrong?"

"I just heard the news. The car that went into the canyon is Vicky's Porsche. There's a search under way for her body. They think she was thrown into the river."

He halted on the last step. "Are you sure?"

"I'm sure."

"Interesting." He crossed the room and took the stool beside her. "You think she really did it? Pulled off a disappearing act?"

"Either that or Holland killed her," Elizabeth said. "Maybe she waited too long. She said she knew that she had been pushing her luck."

Jack looked thoughtful. "I don't think he killed her."

"Why not? It's the same kind of accident that happened to his first two wives."

"Which is why I don't think he's responsible. Holland is smart. He has to know that, given the questions raised by the insurance company last time, there would be a lot of suspicion centered on him if a third wife died under similar circumstances. The last thing he wants right now is to have the police hanging around asking questions about Vicky's death."

Elizabeth's spirits lifted. "You're right. He doesn't want them in the way while he's trying to find Soft Focus."

"There's another point, too. If he had murdered her, he would probably have made it look like an assault by the stalker. Everything was in place for that kind of ending to the story. All he needed to do was throw a little red paint on the car."

"There was no mention of red paint in the newscast." Elizabeth was feeling almost euphoric with relief now. "Jack, you're brilliant."

He smiled faintly. "Your good buddy, Vicky, may have done us a very big favor on her way out the door."

"What do you mean?"

"If she did arrange her own accident, she picked the one surefire way of making certain that Dawson would fall under immediate suspicion. If he's dealing with the cops right now, he's going to have a hard time attending an illegal auction."

"She told me to remember that nothing is ever what it seems in the movies or in real life." Elizabeth smiled. She hopped down off the stool and grabbed the phone. "Excuse me, gotta make a call to Louise."

Jack swung slowly around on the stool, watching her as she punched out the number. "You're going to transfer the money into that account in Miami, aren't you?"

"Yes, I am."

"Damn. I was afraid of that. It's a scam, Elizabeth."

"It's a bargain. And a deal's a deal." She eyed him as she waited for Louise to answer the phone. "I would think that you, of all people, would understand that, Jack. You're the one who wouldn't let me out of the Excalibur contract, remember? Not even after I poured ice water all over you in front of God and everyone in the Pacific Rim Club."

Chapter Twenty-Four

"She took excellent care of her body, I'll say that for her." The masseuse bore down on Elizabeth's shoulders with the heels of her strong hands. "Most people come in here hoping that a soak in the hot pools and a massage will instantly bring back muscle tone and energy. They walk out the door and head straight back to their recliners and their remotes. But not Ms. Bellamy. She worked out every day and watched her diet."

The masseuse poured more warm oil on her hands. Elizabeth stifled a groan as the woman went to work on her lower back. She had made the appointment at the spa with the idea of picking up some local gossip. But shortly after stretching out on the table, she had decided that she really did need the massage. She had certainly been somewhat tense lately.

"Were you her regular masseuse?" Elizabeth asked.

"Yes. She always asked for me when she was in town." The woman sighed. "Hard to believe she's dead."

"Maybe she's not dead," Elizabeth said cautiously. "I hear that they still haven't found the body."

"It can take a while to recover a body that gets washed downriver."

"A terrible accident."

"Well, now." The masseuse lowered her voice to a confidential tone as she began a vigorous kneading motion. "My friend, Ethel, works as a dispatcher at the station. She says that Chief Gresham isn't so sure it was an accident."

"Good heavens." Elizabeth exhaled sharply as the masseuse intensified the pressure. "Do they think the stalker got her?"

"Between you and me, there wasn't any stalker. Ms. Bellamy told me that in confidence one day. Said it was just a publicity stunt. Chief Gresham is no fool. Ethel says he guessed that it was just a PR thing. Holland never filed a complaint."

"What does Chief Gresham think happened?"

"I couldn't say for sure." The masseuse pummeled Elizabeth's buttocks. "But Ethel says he's looking for Dawson Holland as we speak. Wants to ask him a few questions. Apparently Holland's first two wives died in similar accidents."

Elizabeth sagged beneath pounding fists. She buried her face in the little opening provided in the massage table and tried to breathe. "What do you mean, Gresham's looking for Holland? Everyone knows where he lives here in Mirror Springs."

"Didn't you hear? Dawson Holland's housekeeper, Mary Beth, says that Chief Gresham went to the house early this morning to notify Holland of his wife's death. When he went back a couple of hours later to ask him some questions, the place was empty. Looked like Dawson had packed up all of his personal stuff and left town."

Forty-five minutes later, Elizabeth slithered languidly into the espresso shop booth and smiled benignly at Jack. She set the pot of herbal tea and the cup she had picked up at the counter in front of her.

"What's the matter with you?" he asked. "You're glowing a weird pink color."

"Just finished my massage and a soak in the hot spring pools at the spa. You know, I really ought to do that kind of stuff more often. Very relaxing. And informative."

He glanced at the tea as she poured some into the cup. "There's no caffeine in that."

"Nope. Don't want any. It would spoil the afterglow."

He settled back into his seat. "What did you learn?"

"For starters, Dawson Holland has disappeared. Chief Gresham has notified the authorities between here and Denver to watch for his car."

"Yeah, I got that much just sitting here waiting for you. In fact, I'm a
step ahead of the spa gossip. The kid at the counter says it's all over town
that a man who fits Holland's description got on a plane in Denver late this
morning."

"Why are the local cops suddenly so concerned? Gresham jumped on
this kind of quick, didn't he?"

Jack smiled faintly. "Word has it that someone phoned in a tip to the police shortly after Vicky's Porsche went off the road. Suggested that the authorities should ask Holland where he was when the accident occurred and
take a look at how his previous two wives died."

"I'll bet it was Vicky," Elizabeth said.

"I'll bet you're right."

Elizabeth sipped her herbal blend. "Did Larry get a chance to check
that account in Miami?"

"I talked to him just before you got here. So far the money is still sitting
there."

"She probably took an indirect route to Miami to hide her tracks. Lots
of layovers. Weather en route. Could be several reasons why she hasn't
picked up her money yet."

He hesitated, not wanting to destroy her bubble of confidence. "There's
another reason why Vicky might not have collected her money. She might
be dead."

Some of Elizabeth's warm, rosy glow dimmed. "If that's true, we'll have
to talk to the cops. Tell them what we know."

He thought about that for a moment and then shook his head. "Maybe.
But not yet. Chief Gresham is already looking for Holland. Let's give Vicky
a few more hours to pick up her money and get out of the country."

Elizabeth looked at him over the rim of her cup. "Any way you look at
this, one thing's for sure. With Holland gone, the auction is going to be a
very small event. Unless there's someone in the picture we don't know
about yet, Tyler Page is left with only two bidders. You and Hayden."

The phone rang at seven-fifteen that evening. Hayden jumped
at the sound. He was mildly surprised to realize that night had fallen. He

had been sitting in the dark for some time now. Ever since he had finished talking to Larry.

"Hello?"

"The auction will take place at nine o'clock tonight. I will give you the address. No late bidders will be seated."

The click of the hangup was painful in his ear. Hayden slowly lowered the phone. He sat in the gloom of the hotel room for a few more minutes, thinking. Then he picked up the phone again and punched out a number.

*The cell phone sounded just as Jack eased the car into a park*ing slot in the lot across the street from the Silver Empire Theater. Elizabeth whipped around in the seat, her eyes wide with excitement.

"Jack?"

"Take it easy." He switched off the engine and reached for the phone. "Could be anyone. A lot of people have this number." He spoke into the instrument. "This is Fairfax."

"I just got my summons to the auction," Hayden said.

Jack tightened one hand on the wheel and looked at the bright lights of the Silver Empire. The world premiere of *Fast Company* was scheduled to begin at eight-thirty. Elizabeth had insisted on arriving early to watch for Tyler Page.

"Why are you telling me?" Jack asked.

Hayden did not answer that. "Did you get the call?"

"No."

"Place out on Loop Road, about thirty minutes away. Nine o'clock."

"One more time. Why are you telling me this?"

"Wouldn't want you to miss the auction. Not every day a man gets a chance to buy back his own property."

Hayden hung up.

Jack slowly lowered the phone. Elizabeth watched him from the other side of the car.

"What's going on?" she asked.

"Hayden got the call from Page. The auction's scheduled for nine this evening. A place out on Loop Road. About a thirty-minute drive, Hayden said."

"So why haven't you gotten a call?"

"Beats me. Can't hold much of an auction without bidders to drive up the price." Absently he tapped the cell phone against the backseat. He studied the bright lights of the theater marquee. "*Fast Company* starts in half an hour."

"Yes, I know. Forget about my plan to watch for Page. Obviously he won't be in the audience. He'll be conducting the auction."

Jack turned his head to look at her. "Doesn't it strike you as strange that, after everything he put into it, Tyler Page would be willing to miss the premiere of his film?"

For a second or two, Elizabeth said nothing. Then her eyes widened. "What are you thinking?" she asked.

"That maybe you were right all along. Maybe there is a femme fatale in this script."

Hayden opened the door, saw Jack and Elizabeth standing in the hall, and glowered. "What the hell is this all about?"

"Just thought we'd stop by and pick you up for the auction," Jack said. "We're both going to the same place. Might as well use one car. Think of it as a little brotherly togetherness after all these years."

"Screw you."

"Actually, I think we are both about to get royally screwed," Jack said. "Want to talk about an alternative?"

Hayden turned away, but not before Elizabeth glimpsed the weary pain in his eyes.

"No," he said.

"You're not real good with the big-picture thing, are you?" Jack asked. "How the hell did you ever get to be a big-time CEO?"

"Is this conversation going anywhere? If not, I've got plans for the evening."

"Yeah, I know, you're going to attend an auction."

"As a matter of fact, I thought I'd take in a film instead."

Elizabeth stared at him. "What do you mean?"

"I've decided not to bid on Soft Focus." Hayden threw himself down into one of the chairs and looked at Jack with hooded eyes. "It's all yours, brother. Good luck. Not that you should have too much trouble getting it. With Holland and me both out of the running, I doubt you'll face any competition."

Jack closed the door very deliberately. "What made you decide to take yourself out of the bidding?"

Elizabeth smiled slowly. "You called Larry, didn't you? Got the other side of the story."

Hayden gave a massively indifferent shrug. "Odds are, the specimen won't work, anyway. Might as well save my money."

Jack glanced at Elizabeth and then turned to Hayden. "What is this?"

"Hayden is telling you, in his own fashion, that he's changed his mind. He's not going to go after Soft Focus in order to get a little revenge."

Jack looked at Hayden as if he were some odd, new carbon life-form that had just stepped off a spaceship.

Hayden gave another elaborate shrug. "Like I said, Soft Focus probably isn't worth what it would cost me to keep it out of your hands. And it's not like I can use the damn thing myself. Hell, I'm still not real clear on what it's supposed to be able to do. Page, or whoever called me, never went into technical details."

Elizabeth gave him an approving smile. "It's all right, Hayden. You don't have to play Mr. Tough Guy. We all know you're doing this because you've come to realize that taking your revenge against Jack won't change the past. He's not to blame for what happened between your parents. You know he's innocent."

Hayden grunted. "There's nothing innocent about Jack. But you're right. Screwing with his business reputation won't change anything. I'm going home in the morning. I've wasted enough time here in Mirror Springs."

Jack eyed him thoughtfully. "I think someone is going to be very disappointed if you don't show up at the auction tonight."

"Tyler Page?" Hayden gave a short, humorless laugh. "My advice is, don't give him a dime for Soft Focus. Beat it out of the creep. He stole it from you in the first place, didn't he?"

"I don't think Tyler Page is the one who will be waiting for you out on Loop Road," Jack said. He took his cell phone out of his pocket.

Elizabeth glanced at him. "What are you doing?"

"I think it's time we called in the cops."

The isolated cabin off Loop Road was a single-room, one-story log structure. It had the neglected look of a house that has been abandoned for years. In the headlights, Jack could see that the railing on the steps that led to the front door had been broken long ago. Weeds grew wildly in a yard.

A stone fireplace formed one wall, but there was no sign of a fire or any other kind of warmth or light visible through the single front window.

"This is the old Kramer place," Chief Gresham said as he got out of his patrol car. "No one's used it in years." He flicked on his flashlight and gave Jack and Hayden a sour look. "I don't see anyone around. Are you sure about this?"

"No," Jack admitted. He shoved his hands into the pockets of his jacket and looked at the unlit house. "But I couldn't think of any other explanation that fit the facts."

"You should have contacted the authorities right at the start of this thing," Gresham muttered. He started toward the front steps. "Damn corporate suits. Always think you can handle things better than the cops."

Jack looked at Hayden and Elizabeth as they got out of the car beside him. Elizabeth shrugged. Hayden raised his brows but said nothing.

They trekked behind Gresham to the front door. The police chief was a small, wiry man with an aura of competence and command. He might be a small-town cop, Jack thought, but he knew his business.

Gresham had not been thrilled when he had been summoned from home to listen to Jack's version of recent events. But he had not wasted any time taking charge of the situation, either.

Gresham knocked on the front door of the cottage with the butt of the flashlight.

There was no response.

Jack stood with Hayden and Elizabeth. They watched Gresham knock a second time.

"I still think you figured this wrong," Hayden said quietly.

"I hope I did," Jack said.

Gresham gave up knocking and went to the grimy window. He aimed the flashlight into the darkened interior.

"Well, hell," Gresham said softly. "I did not need this."

He went back to the door and turned the knob. The door swung inward. The beam of Gresham's flashlight sliced into the small, dark room.

The light glanced across an outflung hand that lay, palm up, on the floor. Then it skimmed over blond hair that had been stained red with blood. The smell of death was heavy in the air. The woman's forehead had been partially destroyed by the bullet, but there was no doubt about her identity.

Elizabeth gave a muffled cry, put her hand to her mouth, and turned quickly away from the gory scene. Jack put his arm around her shoulders.

"Oh, Christ." Hayden sounded as if he was about to be ill. "It's Gillian. You were right, Jack."

"Not exactly." Jack tried to breathe through his mouth as he stared at the body on the floor. "She wasn't supposed to be dead."

Chapter Twenty-Five

A long time later, Hayden slouched into the booth at the back of the Mirror Springs Resort bar and wrapped his hands around a glass of scotch. "Page probably made that call. He intended for me to be found standing over the body when you arrived, Jack. It would have been perfect. Angry husband kills wife because she's giving him trouble over divorce settlement. He'd have been in the clear."

"Well—" Jack began, looking thoughtful.

"Damn," Hayden interrupted fervently. "If you hadn't come to my room tonight and made me listen to your screwy theory, I'd have been trying to talk my way out of a murder rap tonight."

Jack shook his head. "You had already changed your mind about attending the auction, remember?"

Hayden grimaced. "Yeah, but that was a real last-minute thing. Who could have known?"

Elizabeth shook her head. "Either way, I don't think Tyler Page set it up to make you look guilty. If he really did kill her, as Gresham and everyone else seems to think, he did it in a fit of passion. Probably because he found out that Gillian never intended to run off with him after she conducted her auction."

Jack looked at her. "You're a real die-hard romantic, aren't you?"

"I keep telling you that Page is a man of passion, not a cold-blooded strategist," she said.

"Whatever he is, he's probably a long way from Mirror Springs by now. But, unlike Holland, who got away, I have a hunch the authorities will find Page fast. He doesn't have the skills and the know-how that it takes to hide from the police for long."

Hayden turned to Jack. "How did you figure out that Gillian was the one who had orchestrated the theft and set up the auction?"

"It was Elizabeth who insisted all along that there was a woman in this somewhere," Jack said.

"I thought at first that it was Vicky Bellamy." Elizabeth sipped her mineral water. "But I changed my mind. I had pretty much abandoned the whole femme fatale concept when Jack came up with his own variation on it tonight."

Jack looked at Hayden. "Tyler Page is not the organized type. But whoever had planned the theft and made Page disappear here in Mirror Springs was good at organizational details. For a while I thought Dawson Holland might have been more than just another bidder."

"You thought he had used Vicky to seduce Page and convince him to steal the specimen? Set up the auction?" Hayden asked.

Jack nodded. "Like I told Gresham, Holland had had plenty of contact with Page over the past few months. And according to Larry, he had motive. But it didn't quite fit. Holland was too savvy and too well connected to want to waste time trying to sell Soft Focus here in the States. I figured if he actually had it in his possession, he'd take off for Europe, where the sky would be the limit at an auction."

"And then Vicky more or less confirmed that she thought Holland was here in Mirror Springs for business reasons," Elizabeth said. "She told me that she thought he was planning to get hold of something of a high-tech nature that he could turn over to a consortium of foreign investors."

"Which meant that he was just another bidder," Jack said. "That didn't leave a lot of candidates for the job of organizing Tyler Page and setting up an auction. Tonight when you called me to tell me that you had been given directions for the auction and that it was going to take place during the premiere of *Fast Company,* I started thinking. Finally."

"About Gillian?" Hayden asked.

Jack nodded. "She fit Elizabeth's theories as well as mine. A femme fatale who, through her father, was connected to the high-tech scene. She was smart enough to have picked up the rumors of Soft Focus and understand the potential. She would have known how to go about getting a spy into Excalibur—"

"Ryan Kendle?" Hayden asked. "I heard you tell Gresham about him."

"Kendle probably identified Page as the one person who could most easily steal the crystal. Gillian researched Page, discovered his weakness for filmmaking, and went after him."

"But why did she fixate on stealing Soft Focus?" Hayden asked. "Taking it hurt you, not me."

"You still don't get it, do you?" Elizabeth said quietly.

"Get what?"

"No one will ever be able to prove it now," Jack said. "But Elizabeth and I think that the reason you got the call first tonight was because Gillian intended to kill you."

"Oh, Christ." Comprehension lit Hayden's eyes.

"Jack would have been called later," Elizabeth said. "Because she planned for him to be the one the cops found standing over the body with the smoking gun."

Hayden stared at her. "I knew she hated me because I wanted out of the marriage and Daddy was not happy about that."

"And she hated me because I had also refused to be the son-in-law Daddy wanted," Jack said.

Hayden rubbed his temples. "So she planned to kill me and let you take the rap."

"Can't you see the headlines? 'Long-Standing Feud Between Two Brothers Ends in Murder.'" Elizabeth snapped her fingers. "Just like that, she gets revenge on both of you. One is dead and one goes to jail for murder."

Hayden gave a visible shudder and took another swallow of scotch. "I realized shortly after I married her that she had some serious problems. It got a little scary, to tell you the truth. But even after I filed for divorce I didn't realize that she was capable of murder."

"A real femme fatale," Elizabeth said. "The genuine article."

Hayden winced. "I hate to admit it, but you did try to warn me about her, Jack."

Jack said nothing.

"Gillian used Tyler Page," Elizabeth said softly. "Treated him like a pawn, as if he had no strong passions or emotions."

"And in the end, he killed her," Hayden said.

Elizabeth glanced back over her shoulder as she went through the front door of the house. "Did you realize that Gillian was crazy?"

"No." Jack walked across the room and switched on the gas fire. "I just knew that there was a screw loose somewhere and that it had to do with Daddy Ringstead."

Elizabeth hung her coat in the closet. "How did you end your relationship with her?"

"I thought I'd handled it fairly well. Made it clear that I could never fill her father's shoes at Ring, Inc. Pointed out that I was just a small-time consultant who would never amount to much, et cetera, et cetera. I thought she came to the conclusion that she could do much better than me. And as it happened, Hayden started sniffing around at about that time. He reinforced the idea that I had limited ambitions and prospects."

"She concluded that he would make a better husband to take home to Daddy, is that it?"

"That's it." Jack sank into a chair in front of the hearth and stretched out his legs. "When I realized that Hayden was actually serious about marrying her I told him he might want to think about it some more. But that only pushed him faster toward the altar."

"Human nature. Weird."

"Yeah. Just look at you and me. Talk about a weird relationship."

Elizabeth sat down across from him. "But never dull."

"No." He smiled faintly. "Never dull."

Silence fell. Elizabeth listened to the flames crackling on the hearth for a while. Then she reached up to remove the clip in her hair.

"We both need sleep," she said. "We should go to bed."

Jack watched her hair tumble around her shoulders. "I know."

Elizabeth turned to watch the flames leap. "It's over, isn't it?"

"It's in the hands of the cops now." Jack scrubbed his face with one hand. "Gresham was right. Should have called in the authorities back at the beginning."

"Think they'll catch up with Page before the Veltran presentation?"

"Maybe." He hesitated. "But even if they do find him, it won't do Excalibur any good. The crystal will probably get taken into custody as evidence. Could be months before we get it back. By then, the company will be in bankruptcy."

She hesitated. Then she decided to take the plunge. "I've been thinking."

"What about?"

"Your future."

He smiled faintly. "I won't starve, you know."

"I know. You can take care of yourself." She looked at him. "But would you consider a position in management with the Aurora Fund?"

"You're offering me a job?"

"Well, yes. I guess so."

"Working for you?" he said very carefully.

"Why not? You'd fit in very well."

"The Aurora Fund is a two-person operation. You and your assistant, Louise. Just how would I fit in?"

"You have experience in analyzing small start-up and troubled companies," she said quickly. "You would be terrific at assessing candidates for funding. Or we could even add on a whole new department. In addition to funding new ventures, we could offer start-up and management consulting expertise to our clients."

"Me taking orders from you," he said thoughtfully. "An interesting concept."

She began to grow irritated. "What's the matter? Don't you think you can deal with taking orders from me?"

"Hmm."

Pride twisted inside her. "If you aren't interested, just say so."

He propped his elbows on the arms of the chair and steepled his fingers. "What I'm interested in is something a little more permanent."

She glared at him. "The Aurora Fund is very permanent. It's much stronger now than it was when I took charge. Regardless of what happens with Soft Focus, it will turn a profit this quarter."

"Lucky you," he said.

"Jack—"

He met her eyes. "I wasn't talking about a permanent job. I was talking about marriage."

She stopped breathing for a few seconds. "Marriage?"

"I'm a lot more interested in marrying you than I am in working for you."

She swallowed. Then she swallowed again. "I thought we decided that we needed time," she finally managed to get out in a strangled voice. "We agreed that we wouldn't rush things."

"That was your idea, not mine. I've known what I've wanted for six months."

She gazed into his gleaming eyes. "You have?"

He shoved himself up out of the chair, walked to the sofa, and scooped her up in his arms. "Yes."

"But—"

"Tell you what," he said as he started for the stairs with her in his arms. "When you work up enough guts to take a chance on marrying me, I'll let you know whether or not I'm willing to risk working for you."

"That's a ludicrous bargain, and you know it." She clutched at his shoulders. "For heaven's sake, put me down. You've been through a ton of stress tonight. You must be exhausted. You're in no shape to carry me up a flight of steps."

"Watch me."

"This is no time to show me how macho you are."

"It's not like I've got anything better to do." He reached the landing and turned right into his sleeping loft. "We were both headed for bed anyway."

"You're not going to solve anything with sex, you know."

"Maybe not, but you have to admit that it does help keep us both entertained while we wait to see what you decide."

"I'm trying to have a serious discussion here."

"Sex is more fun."

He walked to the bed and opened his arms. Elizabeth tumbled down onto the quilt. She pushed her hair out of her eyes, looked up, and saw that he already had his shirt off.

"Are you serious about marriage?" she whispered.

"Uh-huh." He unfastened his belt buckle.

She watched with growing fascination as he finished undressing. His erection was full and hard and heavy. She felt the familiar excitement uncoil within her when he put one knee on the bed.

He came down on top of her, caging her within his arms.

"But I'm also very, very serious about sex," he said.

"I can see that," she whispered. She put her arms around him and pulled him down on top of her, relieved to be able to escape into the passion that flared so easily between them.

But she knew, even as he eased himself between her thighs and crushed her into the bedding, that it was only a temporary reprieve.

Marriage?

To Jack?

A long time later, Jack rolled onto his back and hooked an arm around her. "There is another item on the agenda tonight. In the interests of unbridled honesty, there is one more thing you should know about me before you tell me that you'll marry me."

She groaned and raised herself up on her elbow. "Must I brace myself?"

"Maybe. I just thought that I ought to clear up a small misunderstanding under which you have been laboring for the past week."

Her eyes widened. "Don't tell me, let me guess. You are actually independently wealthy, and even if we don't find Soft Focus and even if your professional reputation goes down the toilet, it's okay because you are secretly filthy rich."

"There wasn't any misunderstanding on that point," he said dryly. "I am not secretly filthy rich."

"Oh. Well, in that case, what was it you lied about that first night here in Mirror Springs?"

"I prefer to think of it not as a lie but rather as a slight bit of judicious misdirection," he said.

"About?"

"About the problem with those reservations I told you I had at the Mirror Springs Resort."

She flattened her hand on his chest. "Okay, I've braced myself for the worst."

He settled himself more comfortably against the pillows and regarded her through half-closed eyes.

"The strings I mentioned, the ones I pulled to get a room, didn't exactly break," he said. "My booking was on file when I got to the resort. I told the front-desk clerk that I didn't want the room. He gave it to the person in line behind me, who was profoundly grateful because he had arrived without a reservation."

She drummed her fingers on his chest. "Then you showed up on my doorstep, gave me that tale of woe about not having a place to stay, and begged me to take you in."

He frowned. "I don't recall begging."

"Darn close."

"Darn close," he agreed. "Looking back, I took a hell of a risk. I shouldn't have canceled the reservation until I knew for sure I could talk my way in here."

She pursed her lips and appeared to ponder that admission. "Holding on to the reservation until you knew for sure that I'd fall for your line would definitely have been the savvy, street-smart CEO kind of thing to do."

"Don't know why I didn't think of it," Jack mused.

She stopped drumming her fingers and gave him a smug smile. "I know why."

"Yeah?" He wrapped his hand around the back of her head. "Why?"

She cleared her throat. "It has come to my attention in recent months that you are, at heart, an old-fashioned romantic, Jack Fairfax. A regular Don Quixote."

His hand stilled in her hair. He stared at her, too astonished to speak for an instant. Then he started to laugh.

He laughed so hard, he considered the fact that he did not fall out of bed a near miracle. When he finally recovered, he summed up his opinion of her observation in a single word.

"Bullshit," he said.

"It's true." She appeared unperturbed by his incredulous reaction to her announcement. "You are a knight in somewhat tarnished armor. That's why you feel obliged to atone for some of the damage you think your father did. It's why you consult for small, troubled companies that can't afford you. It's why you never insist on a golden parachute before you sign on to a contract with a firm that is facing disaster. It's why you prefer to work for closely held businesses that have a personal history and a family legacy instead of big, soulless corporations."

He grinned. "Let me get this straight. You think it was this wildly romantic streak of mine that convinced me to take my chances with you that first night here in Mirror Springs?"

"Absolutely. It's the only thing that could possibly explain your taking such a ridiculous risk."

"Huh."

"And that," she announced, "is why I've decided to accept your proposal of marriage."

Some type of rare and extremely precious energy burst through him. If he could bottle it, he would be the richest man in the world, he thought. Then again, it was right there inside him, rushing through his veins, making him lightheaded, creating all sorts of new sensations for him to savor. He didn't need to sell the joy to get rich. He already owned it.

"I'll let you in on a little secret." She bent her head and brushed her mouth across his. "I think it was just as wildly romantic of me to take you in."

"Yeah? Why?"

She smiled. "Because even as I held the door open for you and invited you inside, I was almost certain that you were lying through your teeth."

A tide of heat flooded his veins. Not sexual arousal, he realized, although that was probably somewhere in the mix; something else. Something infinitely more satisfying. She'd taken him in even though she'd suspected that he had given her a line about the hotel room.

He put his other hand into her hair and gently tightened his fingers. "Apparently, I'm not the only closet romantic here. I do love you, you know."

"I love you, too." She started to kiss him and then paused, her gaze growing abruptly thoughtful.

"What?"

"It brings up that old problem, doesn't it?"

"It's up, but it's not that old, and I honestly don't consider it a problem."

"Stop grinning like that." She sat up slowly amid the rumpled sheets. "This is serious. I think."

He put both of his hands behind his own head. "I'm listening."

"All that talk about your little game with the hotel reservations makes me wonder just where Tyler Page stayed while he was here in Mirror Springs. Gresham said that it looked as if Gillian drove in from Denver for the day, remember?"

"Go on."

"But we've assumed all along that Page was here in Mirror Springs. We thought he'd want to be as close to the festival as possible."

"Maybe we assumed wrong."

Elizabeth's eyes gleamed. "Maybe we didn't."

Jack sat up slowly. "What are you getting at?"

"We all agree that Page is not good with the details of daily life. The details of a fake identity are even trickier to handle."

"Gillian must have taken care of that end of things for him."

Elizabeth tightened her hand in the sheet. "The first day I saw Hayden I asked him how he managed to get a room at the resort. He told me that he knew the general manager and had pulled a few strings. He said it very casually, more or less in passing. It's possible that he met the manager somewhere else."

"High-ranking hotel personnel frequently get transferred from one property to another on a regular basis," Jack said slowly.

"But it's also possible that Hayden met him right here in Mirror Springs. Which would mean that this wasn't his first visit."

"It's a popular ski resort in the winter. Hayden skis." Jack paused. "So does Gillian."

"Jack, what if—"

"Hang on." Jack grabbed the phone off the end table. Then he rummaged in the drawer for the small Mirror Springs phone book. "We can put an end to this one way or the other with a call."

He found the resort number and punched it in. Hayden came on the line after several rings. He sounded half asleep and groggy.

"How much more scotch did you drink after Elizabeth and I left?" Jack asked.

"If you think that you can start playing big brother after all these years, forget it. Besides, I had a right. It was a rough night."

"I can't argue with you there," Jack said. "You can go back to sleep in a minute. Right after you answer a question."

Hayden groaned. "Just because you saved my life, don't get the idea that you can call me up in the middle of the night anytime you feel like it. My newfound brotherly gratitude only goes so far."

"Hayden, pay attention here. You told Elizabeth that you got that room there at the resort because you knew the manager."

"Douglas Finley. Nice guy. So what?"

"Have you stayed at the resort in the past?"

"No."

"Damn." Jack's sense of anticipation went flat, but he caught Elizabeth's eye and decided to push a little more. "How did you get to know Finley?"

"To tell you the truth, I don't really know him. At least not personally. I used my ex-in-laws' name to pull some strings with him."

"Finley knows Gillian's family?"

"Yeah. But he didn't know about the divorce. Probably wouldn't have given me the room if he had known about it. Can I ask where in hell this is going? I need my sleep. I got a call from Gillian's father earlier. Ringstead's on his way back from Zurich. A family lawyer is on his way here tonight. I'm going to have to deal with both of them tomorrow."

"Stick with me for a little longer," Jack said. "Are you telling me that Gillian's family vacations in this area?"

"Not her immediate family. But one of her cousins has a place a few miles out of town. Gillian and I used it once or twice."

Jack was amazed that the phone didn't crack in his hand. "Her cousin has a place here?"

"Yeah. But what with the divorce and all, I'm persona non grata with the Ringsteads these days. Figured there was no point asking for the key to the cabin, so I tried my luck here at the resort instead."

Chapter Twenty-Six

The house was invisible from the road, impossible to see until Jack reached the end of the long access lane and turned the corner. Elizabeth sat forward, watching as the headlights splashed across a large, sprawling structure. The windows were dark. There was no car parked in the drive.

"If Page was staying here, he's long gone." Jack switched off the engine and picked up the flashlight. "But maybe we'll find something that will tell us where he's headed."

Elizabeth gave him an uneasy glance as she opened her door. "Chief Gresham is not going to be thrilled when he finds out we came here without consulting with him."

"What with Vicky's car crash and Gillian's murder, Gresham has enough on his hands at the moment. Besides, this is probably just another wild-goose chase. If we turn up anything useful, we'll call him."

"Sure." She slid out, closed the door, and buttoned her long down coat. She gave him a knowing look over the roof of the car. "Right after we set out after Page ourselves."

"If Page is in Europe, there's nothing Gresham can do anyway. But there might be something we could do if we catch up with him before he figures out how to unload Soft Focus in the foreign market."

She shook her head as she followed him toward the house. "That's one of the things I admire about you, Jack. You never give up."

"Giving up is not usually a viable strategic maneuver." He pulled on a pair of leather gloves. "Let's face it, finding a missing lab specimen is not a high priority for Chief Gresham. He's after a couple of murderers. Excalibur's stolen property is low on his list right now. We're the only ones with a vested interest in getting that damned crystal back before the Veltran presentation."

"You don't need to remind me." She took her gloves out of the pocket of her coat and put them on. Then she hurried up the steps to the rear deck and watched Jack test the locks on the door and the nearby windows.

"There's a name for this," she said.

"Breaking and entering." Jack continued around the corner of the deck. "Not our first time. You should be getting used to it by now."

"When we went through Page's house in Seattle, we had a key and a semi-legitimate-sounding excuse. This could be a little trickier to explain."

"I'll deal with it if necessary."

"Spoken like a real CEO."

"A good CEO can talk his way out of anything."

"Or into anything," Elizabeth said. But she said it very quietly.

She tried to ignore the hot-cold feeling in her hands as she trailed after Jack. He was halfway around the wide deck that encircled the big house.

She followed him around the corner and saw that the entire front wall of both stories was a mass of floor-to-ceiling windows. Anyone standing inside would have an expansive view of the mountain. But from where she stood on the deck the dark glass appeared as an impenetrable barrier.

Jack started toward the nearest sliding glass door. Elizabeth cast her own small flashlight around the deck. The beam of light grazed a large, professional-size stainless-steel outdoor grill, two chaise longues, a table, and a hot tub.

"Looks like hot tubs are big here in Mirror Springs," she said. "Everyone's got one."

"After our recent experience I've decided I've got a keen interest in them myself. I'm thinking of installing one when we get home." Jack moved to the next door.

"You live in a condo."

"We could put it in at your place. How about that balcony outside your bedroom?"

She frowned. "How do you know that there's a deck outside my bedroom?"

"I can see it from my front window."

"Not without a pair of binoculars, you can't."

He did not respond to that.

"Jack, were you spying on me during the past six months?"

"I couldn't get a clear view," he assured her. "There were some bushes in the way. You know, you should probably tell your gardener to cut back some of the shrubbery on that balcony. Getting a little overgrown, don't you think?"

She groaned, not sure whether to be outraged or flattered. She was about to tell him where he could stick the excess shrubbery when she noticed that the lid of the outdoor grill was open. An array of cooking implements was scattered across a greasy steel counter that extended out from the side.

"I think someone used the grill recently. Look at all the utensils and the mess on the counter. I wonder if—" She broke off, staring at the dark shape that projected around the edge of the hot tub. Her first thought was that someone had left a shoe out on the deck.

A man's shoe.

Then she saw that the shoe was connected to a pant leg. "Oh, my God. *Jack.*"

He crossed the deck in three long strides and halted beside her. He aimed his own light toward the side of the tub. "Damn."

He walked toward the edge of the small pool, never taking the beam off the shoe.

"Please, God," Elizabeth whispered. "Not another one."

She went slowly forward, wanting to look away from the shoe but unable to do so. It was as if she were under the influence of a terrible compulsion.

She came to a halt next to the large grill, put out a hand, and gripped the counter extension to steady herself. Her fingers brushed against the handle of a long, unwashed cooking fork.

The hot tub was uncovered, but it was not running. The motor was silent, the interior lights off. The surface of the water was still.

Jack walked around the edge of the circular pool and aimed the flashlight at what appeared at first to be a pile of rumpled clothing.

Elizabeth saw a thin, bony-fingered hand. Then she saw the blood that still oozed from the head wound. She was grateful that the man's face was turned away from her. Something glinted at the edge of the light. A stylish, stainless-steel cocktail shaker lay on the deck next to a chair leg. The shaker's lid had been removed, she noticed. The dead man must have been caught in the act of mixing himself a martini.

"Dear heaven." She lowered the light. The beam shined across a dark metal object on the deck. "Jack—?"

He glanced at the gun that had apparently fallen from the man's hand. "I see it."

When she glanced back at the body she noticed the wide, dark stain that had spread out from beneath the head. It could have been water that had splashed out of the uncovered hot tub, but she knew that it wasn't. Her stomach lurched.

She watched, mesmerized, as Jack crouched and felt for a pulse at the throat.

"It's Page, isn't it?" she whispered.

"Yes." Jack stood and started to reach into the pocket of his jacket for his cell phone. "He never made it out of town."

"He must have shot himself after he killed Gillian. Lover's remorse. The poor man. She truly was his femme fatale."

A dark figure moved out of the shadows beneath an awning. A third flashlight winked on. Elizabeth felt a scream rise in her throat. But nothing happened, because she could not seem to get her breath.

"Not suicide, I'm afraid," Dawson Holland said. "The stupid little bastard refused to hand over Soft Focus. He kept saying that Gillian had *betrayed* him and that he would never give me the crystal. He actually had the nerve to pull a gun on me. I had to kill him."

"Why are you still hanging around?" Jack's voice was stunningly even. He did not rise from his crouched position near the body. "Coming on top of Gillian's death and a missing wife, another murder is going to be a little tough to explain, isn't it?"

"I have no intention of sticking around long enough to explain anything to anyone."

"You killed Gillian," Elizabeth whispered. "It wasn't Tyler Page, after all."

"The bitch went crazy on me. Kept ranting on and on about getting revenge." Dawson swung the flashlight beam directly into Elizabeth's eyes.

She staggered back as if he had used a laser. She stumbled against the grill and fumbled wildly to catch her balance. The implements on the counter clattered and clanged. A heavy pan crashed to the deck. It bounced twice and then went still. Jack never took his eyes off her, but he said nothing.

Dawson Holland smiled and swung the light back toward Jack. "I think she's nervous."

"You're enough to make any intelligent person nervous," Elizabeth said.

"And you are an intelligent person, are you not? Do you know, there is something very exciting about clever women. I find them fascinating, especially when they are also beautiful. But in the end, one can never trust them. They always have their own agendas, and that makes them dangerous."

"Speaking of dangerous," Jack said casually, "you've had a real run of bad luck lately, haven't you? First Vicky splits before you can murder her for the insurance money, and then Gillian turns out to be more obsessed with her revenge than with the business of selling Soft Focus abroad."

"Gillian screwed up the whole deal." Dawson's face worked in fury. "She wasn't interested in the money. She only wanted her silly revenge. She used me."

Elizabeth watched him as if he were a cobra. "How did you meet her?"

"She attended a film festival in Sedona a few months ago. Sought me out. Introduced herself. She'd done her research. Knew who I was and that I might be interested in an offshore business venture."

"She needed someone who could give Tyler Page what he wanted so badly," Elizabeth said. "A film he could claim to have produced."

Dawson's mouth thinned. "As I said, she used me. At first it seemed like an ideal partnership. I needed Soft Focus to get some people off my back, and I was preparing to cash in on Vicky's insurance policy anyway. I thought I could kill a couple of birds with one stone here in Mirror Springs."

"But in the end Gillian didn't cooperate, did she?" Jack said.

"The crazy woman hid herself and Page, too. I couldn't find either of them." Dawson's voice rose. "And then you and Shaw showed up. I tried to scare you off, but neither of you budged. Then you sent Ledger out to ask questions about Page, and I had to buy him off."

"Where did you get that video?"

Dawson grimaced. "Gillian had it made weeks ago. Just in case, she said. She wanted to make certain that, if anything went wrong, the evidence would point toward someone else. She was willing to give me a copy, so I took it and kept it. Just in case."

"The authorities think you're on your way to Amsterdam," Elizabeth said.

"I had to pretend to disappear after Vicky staged her accident. I bought the ticket for Amsterdam at the airport this morning. But then I rented a car and drove back here. I had Shaw's hotel room bugged. I knew when he got the call from Gillian. I got to the location first and confronted her."

"She told you where she had hidden Page?" Jack asked.

"The crazy bitch was so excited about her plans for vengeance finally coming to a head that she laughed in my face and told me I could have Soft Focus. She even told me where she'd stashed Page."

"So you shot her dead and came here," Elizabeth whispered.

"Page was about to leave." Dawson grimaced. "The fool was going to try to sneak into the theater tonight to watch the screening of *Fast Company,* if you can believe it. A fortune at stake, and he wants to go see his movie."

"You came here to force Page to hand over Soft Focus, and he refused because he guessed that Gillian had betrayed him with you," Elizabeth said. "And he was right."

In the backwash of the flashlight, Dawson's face was a shadowed mask of fury. "The idiot kept saying that Soft Focus was right in front of my eyes but that I would never find it."

"You figured you could find it, though, didn't you?" Jack gave him a humorless smile. "How long have you been searching for it?"

"I've spent the past few hours tearing the goddamned house apart." Dawson's voice throbbed with frustrated rage. "I even searched the hot tub. Page taunted me. I really believed him when he said it was somewhere in plain sight."

"But you've run out of time, haven't you?" Jack said. "Even if the cops don't find you, your offshore business associates will. How far do you think you'll get?"

"All I have to do is get off this damned mountain." Dawson's cheek twitched nervously. "Once I'm out of Mirror Springs, I'll be in the clear. I have a new ID. All I have to do is disappear for a while."

"The cops will catch you before you get off this mountain," Elizabeth said.

"I don't think so." Dawson smiled coldly. "But just in case, I'm going to have a hostage with me. Insurance, you understand. I've always been a big believer in insurance."

Elizabeth sucked in her breath. "If you think I'm going to go with you—"

"That is exactly what I think." Dawson motioned with the hand that held the flashlight. "Come over here. Quickly."

"What about Soft Focus?" Jack asked. "Are you going to give up on it?"

"One learns to cut one's losses, Fairfax." Dawson made another gesture with the flashlight. "Come here now, Elizabeth. Or I will shoot Fairfax."

He meant it, she thought. Holland would not hesitate to kill again. She walked slowly toward him.

"Quickly, my dear. Fairfax is correct in one regard. Time has run out on me." When she was no more than a step away from him, he took the gun off Jack and aimed it at her instead. "Excellent. Now, then, Fairfax. One move and I will kill her without a second's hesitation and take my chances. Is that clear?"

"Yes," Jack said softly. "It's clear."

"My car is parked on a side road not far from here." Dawson kept the gun trained on Elizabeth, but he did not take his gaze off Jack as he issued instructions. "Move. Slowly, Elizabeth."

She did not budge. "You're going to kill Jack as soon as I start toward the car, aren't you?"

He smiled approvingly. "You really are an intelligent woman, my dear. Under other circumstances we might have done very well together."

"Not for long," she said.

"No, not for long. Now, move, or you will have to watch him die, and somehow I do not think you would like that."

She looked at Jack. He was still crouched beside the body, a good two yards from the gun that Page had dropped.

"Jack?"

"It's okay, Elizabeth. Do what you have to do." Jack paused for a heartbeat. "But do it quick, okay?"

"Right." She turned as if to walk back around the deck.

Dawson continued to point the gun at her head, but his attention was on Jack.

The handle of the cooking fork that she had swiped off the grill and shoved under her sleeve a moment earlier was in her fingers. She pulled the implement free of her sleeve.

She felt Dawson's weight shift. He took the gun off her and started to swing the barrel toward Jack.

There was no time to aim the fork. She plunged it wildly toward Dawson. She felt the tines tear through the fabric of his trousers, felt the sickening resistance of flesh and muscle.

Holland convulsed in pain and fury. He screamed.

"Bitch."

The pistol roared, deafening her. Light sparked. Dawson's flashlight hit the deck and rolled. She felt rather than saw the collision as Jack slammed into Dawson. The two men struck the deck with enough force to send a shudder through the wooden supports.

Elizabeth scrambled madly out of the way. She tripped and reeled back against the railing. She swung around.

A bloody apparition rose from the shadows of the hot tub. Tyler Page sat up slowly. He swept out a hand, groping blindly. His fingers closed around the gun. He seized it and pointed it toward the struggling men. His arm shook wildly.

"You stole her away from me," he gasped in a quivering voice. "She betrayed me with you."

"*Jack*," Elizabeth yelled. "Get out of the way."

Jack glanced up, saw Page, and assessed the situation in a single glance. He rolled free of Holland and threw himself headlong out of range.

"Don't do it," he yelled. "It's okay, he's—"

But it was too late. There was another crash and a flash of light, and then Holland went utterly limp on the deck.

"Angel Face," Tyler whispered. "My beautiful Angel Face."

He fell back and lay still once more.

A stark silence descended.

"Elizabeth?"

"I'm okay." She stared at Tyler Page. "I thought he was dead."

"No, unconscious. Holland's bullet got him on the side of the head." Jack went down beside Dawson and felt for a pulse. "Holland's still alive, too. Got your cell phone?"

"Yes." Grateful for the distraction, she pulled the little phone out of her coat pocket and concentrated hard on punching in the emergency number.

It seemed an eternity before the emergency operator came on the line and Elizabeth gave her the details of the situation.

When she finished the call, she saw that Jack had moved back to the hot tub. As she watched, he bent down to scoop up the silvery container that had fallen on the deck.

She walked slowly toward him. In the distance she heard the first keening wail of a siren.

"What are you doing with that cocktail shaker?"

"It's not a cocktail shaker." He aimed the flashlight at the object. "It's a sort of high-tech thermos. Designed in the Excalibur lab specifically to transport Soft Focus."

She stared at it, suddenly riveted. "It's empty. Do you think Page threw the crystal into the woods to spite Holland?"

"Next to *Fast Company,* the development of the crystal was Page's only major accomplishment in life. I don't think he would have destroyed it." Jack gazed thoughtfully into the hot tub. "He told Holland that it was right in front of his eyes. Maybe he was telling the truth."

Jack went to the control panel and flipped a switch. The underwater lights came on inside the tub.

Elizabeth peered over the edge. "You think he tossed it in there? But Holland said he looked in the tub." The submerged lighting provided a clear view of the interior. There was nothing under the water except the benches.

"Holland was no high-tech wizard. Gillian probably told him they were going to steal a crystal, so he naturally assumed that Soft Focus would look like a chunk of quartz." Jack upended the thermos and unscrewed a small section. "And it does. Sort of. When it's not in a state of suspension, that is."

Elizabeth suddenly understood. "Of course. It's a new type of colloidal crystal, isn't it? Page transported it in the thermos because the particles are suspended in a liquid."

"Only under certain conditions. Soft Focus has several unique properties."

The sirens were closer now. Elizabeth glanced out across the valley. She caught a glimpse of flashing lights on Loop Road.

"You've got maybe ten minutes at most," she said. "Once they're here this whole house will become a crime scene. They won't let you tear the place up to search for Soft Focus."

"If I'm right, I won't need ten minutes."

Jack had the bottom of the container off now. A small plastic envelope fell into his hand. He opened it and tossed the contents into the hot tub.

"What's that?" Elizabeth demanded.

"The catalyst. Unlike true colloidal crystals, Soft Focus needs this stuff to make the particles clump together in a semisolid form. It won't take long. If Page dumped the specimen into this tub, it will take shape fast."

Elizabeth watched intently. At first she saw nothing. Then she caught a glint of what looked like a shard of blue-green glass on one of the benches.

"There it is." Satisfaction laced Jack's voice. He rolled up the sleeve of his shirt. "Just another couple of minutes and we'll have the whole damn thing."

The chunk of crystal grew swiftly beneath the water as the tiny particles floating invisibly in the pool reacted to the attractive force induced by the catalyst.

The sirens were very loud now. The first car had turned into the access road that led to the house.

"That looks about right." Jack plunged his bare arm into the water and scooped the crystal off the bench.

He held it cradled in his palm for a moment and aimed the flashlight beam into its heart.

Elizabeth caught her breath. It was like looking into the depths of an impossibly brilliant diamond. Soft Focus glowed with blue-green fire. It pulsed and sparkled and glittered.

"It's spectacular," she whispered.

"And it's ours."

The sirens cut off abruptly. Car doors slammed. Footsteps sounded on the rear deck.

Jack closed his fingers around Soft Focus and dropped it very casually into his pocket.

"If the question should arise," he said, "the crystal Page took was a mock-up, a decoy version of the actual crystal. Luckily, the real one is safe in the Excalibur labs."

"You think that story will work?"

"Like I said, a good CEO can talk his way through anything."

Chapter Twenty-Seven

Tyler Page was a tragic figure in the hospital bed. His head was swathed in bandages. An IV line hung from a nearby stand, the contents dripping into his veins. His bent glasses sat askew on his nose. He looked up at Jack with sad resignation.

"I know it's too late to apologize, Mr. Fairfax. Nevertheless, I would like to tell you how sorry I am about this entire affair. I don't know what came over me."

Elizabeth saw the derisive look in Jack's eyes and quickly moved closer to the bed. "Jack understands, Dr. Page. You were a victim of passion. For a time you lost your bearings. These things happen."

Jack raised his eyes to the ceiling.

Tyler switched his glum gaze to Elizabeth. "She was so beautiful. Beautiful women like her never notice men like me. But she did. She made me feel brilliant and important and dashing. When I was with her I was Bogart and Mitchum and Grant, all rolled into one."

"Gillian used you," Jack said bluntly.

Elizabeth frowned at him from the other side of the bed. "There's no need to belabor the point."

"I know she used me," Tyler said. "But by the time I understood that she had convinced me to steal Soft Focus for her own purposes, not so that we could run off to a tropical island together, it was too late. The whole thing became a nightmare. I couldn't see any way out."

"Did you ever think of picking up the phone and giving me a call?" Jack asked without any evidence of sympathy.

"Jack," Elizabeth said quietly. She infused her tone with a strong note of warning, but she got the distinct impression that he was not paying attention.

"I felt helpless," Tyler explained. "Trapped in her web. Do you know, when Chief Gresham told me that Gillian was dead, I felt a terrible sense of relief. It was as if the scales had fallen away from my eyes. I was finally free of her clutches. Looking back, I can see what a coward I was."

"You are certainly no coward," Elizabeth said firmly. "You stood up to Dawson Holland, even though he tried to murder you. That was a very brave thing to do. Incredibly heroic, in fact."

Jack raised his brows but said nothing.

Tyler looked at her with fragile hope. "Do you really think so, Ms. Cabot?"

"Yes, and so does everyone else." Elizabeth pinned Jack with a bristling expression. "Isn't that right, Jack?"

"Yeah, sure," Jack said. Then his mouth curved slightly. "As a matter of fact, it was. Defying Dawson Holland took balls, Tyler."

Tyler blushed. "Thank you, sir. Is Mr. Holland . . . ?"

"Dead?" Jack nodded. "An hour ago. In surgery."

"I see." Tyler looked as if he was trying to square his shoulders against the pillows. "I suppose I shall have to stand trial for that, as well."

"Don't think so," Jack said easily. "Gresham is convinced that it was a pretty clear-cut case of self-defense. Holland was trying to kill us, remember."

Elizabeth met Jack's eyes across the white-sheeted bed. Neither of them had seen any reason to point out to Gresham that Jack had already subdued Holland when Tyler surfaced briefly from his unconscious state and fired the fatal shot. Details, Jack had said. Unimportant details.

"The chief is not happy with any of us," Jack continued, "but no one is going to jail."

Tyler blinked owlishly. "But surely I must pay for my crime."

"Excalibur is not pressing charges," Elizabeth said.

Tyler blinked again. "I don't understand. I stole the result of a valuable research project. I'm a thief."

"Excalibur has decided to overlook the incident," Jack said smoothly. "Especially in light of the fact that the item you took was merely a mock-up of the original, which has been in safekeeping at Excalibur the entire time."

Tyler's mouth dropped open. "But—"

"New security measure that was installed last month," Jack said. "Milo and I were the only ones who knew about it."

"But—"

"I ought to know, don't you think?" Jack gave him a cool look, heavy with meaning. "I *am* the CEO of the company."

Tyler brightened as understanding dawned. "I'm very glad to hear that, sir. That was . . . extremely clever and far-sighted of you, Mr. Fairfax."

"Yes, it was, wasn't it?"

"I can't tell you how delighted I am to know that there will be no long-term ill effects on Excalibur from my actions. It's a fine company. The Ingersolls have always treated me well. I shall miss them."

"Not for long," Jack said. "You're expected to report back for work in the lab as soon as you're released from the hospital."

Tyler stared at him. "You want me to return to Excalibur?" Elizabeth smiled. "The company needs you, Dr. Page. You're the only one who truly understood the theoretical work that Patricia Ingersoll did on colloidal crystals. The firm would be lost without you."

"Lost." Tyler looked dazed. "Without me."

"Absolutely." Elizabeth looked at Jack. "Isn't that right?"

"Damn right," Jack said. "Absolutely lost."

"I hadn't realized—" Tyler broke off, a look of wonder in his eyes. "Nobody's ever been lost without me before, you see."

*The tension in Excalibur's executive suite was so thick, Eliza*beth was amazed that she could breathe the air. She glanced around at the anxious faces of the other members of the Excalibur board of directors. The various Ingersolls were scattered about the office. Some slumped in chairs. Some gulped coffee. Some paced. All had gone from a state of euphoric excitement to one of deep despair.

Elizabeth couldn't blame them. The presentation to Grady Veltran and his people had begun three hours ago. Thus far no one had emerged from the lab to give a report. With every passing moment, disaster seemed more imminent.

"Something's gone wrong." Angela came to a halt in front of the window. "If Soft Focus had worked as Page promised it would, we'd have heard something by now. We might as well face the facts. We're ruined."

"Everything Patricia worked for all those years," Milo's uncle, Ivo, muttered. "Down the drain."

Angela looked grim. "I knew we shouldn't have let Jack concentrate all of our resources on a single project. I told you it was a mistake. I told all of you. Remember?"

Milo's aunt glared. "It's not as if we had any choice," Dolores retorted. "This company was going under. Jack was our only hope."

Elizabeth turned away from the window. "Calm down, everyone. If there had been a problem in the lab, I'm sure the Veltran people would have left by now. They're still here. I can see the limos in the parking lot. That means there's still hope."

"It's over," Ivo moaned. "Nothing left but liquidation. We should have done it months ago."

The door opened before Elizabeth could respond. Everyone turned to watch Milo walk somberly into the room. Jack was a pace behind him. Both men were stone-faced.

Milo came to a halt and faced his relatives. For a second he showed no emotion whatsoever.

Then he broke into a huge, boyish grin. He let out a whoop that rattled the windows and punched the air with his fist. "*Yes*. The sucker worked. Just like Tyler Page said it would. The demonstration went perfectly. Tell 'em, Jack."

Jack met Elizabeth's eyes across the room. His smile was slow and satisfied. Not unlike the way he smiled when he made love to her, she thought.

"Well?" she prompted.

"We were delayed getting back here because Grady Veltran insisted on signing a preliminary licensing agreement before we even got out of the lab," Jack said. "We had to wait until the lawyers could get everyone's signature."

"Hot damn." Ivo shot to his feet. "Hot damn. You did it."

"Jack did it." Milo grinned and pounded Jack on the back. "He pulled it off."

"*We* did it." Jack clapped his shoulder. "You were cool during the demo, Milo. Nerves of steel."

Milo could not seem to stop grinning.

"I don't believe it," Angela whispered, hope and relief lighting her eyes. "It worked?"

"Perfectly." After a quick glance at Jack, who was leaning very casually, arms folded, against the edge of his desk, Milo cleared his throat.

Elizabeth watched the younger man assume a cloak of composure that bore a startling resemblance to Jack's own enigmatic air of executive cool. She hid a smile. Milo was learning fast. Then again, he was taking lessons from a master.

"Aunt Patricia's theories concerning the fundamental nature of colloidal crystals were right," Milo said. "Tyler Page was right when he said he could make them work. Hell, we're *all* right." He nodded toward Jack. "Thanks to you and the Aurora Fund, Excalibur is set to be a major player in the next generation of light-based computer technology."

Elizabeth went to a cupboard, opened it, and removed the two silver buckets she had placed there nearly three hours earlier. Each held a bottle of champagne. The ice in each bucket had long since melted.

"I think this calls for a celebration," she said. She looked at Jack and Milo. "Will you two gentlemen do the honors?"

"Oh, wow," Milo said, cool slipping away as quickly as it had come. "Champagne."

"Great idea." Jack straightened from the desk and walked across the room to pick up one of the bottles. He looked at Elizabeth as he went to work on the cork. "I take it you never had any doubts?"

She smiled. "None at all."

"What a coincidence," he said softly. "Neither did I."

She looked into his eyes and saw the intense happiness there. She knew that he saw the same expression mirrored in hers. Both of them knew that it had nothing to do with Soft Focus.

The cork came out of the bottle with a very satisfactory pop. It hit the ceiling. Everyone laughed with delight.

Milo held up a brimming glass. "Here's to Soft Focus. And while we're doing toasts, I'd like to be the first to propose another. 'To Jack and Elizabeth. May they live happily ever after.' "

Chapter Twenty-Eight

She was late.

She saw him waiting for her the moment she walked into the Pacific Rim Club restaurant. He was seated in the exact same booth in which he had waited for her on the day after their ill-fated first night together. Not a coincidence, she thought. She smiled to herself.

Hugo, the maître d', hurried over to greet her. "Ah, you're here, Miss Cabot. Mr. Fairfax has already arrived."

"So I see."

Hugo escorted her to the booth. Elizabeth sensed several heads turn en route. She caught glimpses of smiles and knew that she was not the only one who was experiencing a mild case of déjà vu. This was the first time that she had met Jack for lunch here since their spectacular scene.

She saw the gleam of amusement in his eyes and knew that he was enjoying watching her walk the elegant gauntlet. When she reached the table, he got to his feet and brushed her mouth in an unmistakably possessive kiss.

"You're late," he said.

She ignored him to smile at Hugo. "Thank you."

"Of course, Miss Cabot." Hugo beamed. "Please allow me to offer my sincerest congratulations on your engagement. We look forward to holding the reception here on Friday."

"We're both looking forward to the party, too," Elizabeth said.

Hugo smiled again and retreated.

Elizabeth refused to acknowledge any of the sidelong looks from the other diners. She set her purse down on the cushion and slipped into the booth. Jack sat down across from her.

"You're probably wondering why I called this meeting," he said.

She glanced meaningfully around the room. "I assumed it was to make a point."

He grinned. "Okay, I admit I couldn't resist replaying this particular scene in front of this particular audience. I wanted to get it right."

"You're doing very well so far. At least I haven't poured ice water over you."

"Things are definitely looking up," he agreed.

She helped herself to a bread stick. "By the way, we got an engagement present from Vicky."

"No kidding? What did she send?"

"An autographed poster of *Fast Company*. I'm going to get it framed for my office."

"I saw Page this morning. He was excited. Seems that the film has been picked up for foreign distribution and is going to be available on video. It'll never make any money, of course, but at least it's out there." Jack leaned back in the booth and fixed her with a steady gaze. "Want to order first, or shall we get right down to business?"

"You're starting to scare me, Jack." She reached for the menu. "What's this all about?"

"While we were in Mirror Springs you offered me a business proposition."

"You never got back to me on the offer, as I recall."

"I've been doing a lot of thinking."

She slowly lowered the menu. "Are you serious? You want to go to work for the Aurora Fund?"

"Not exactly. But something you said at the time you made your offer stuck with me."

"What was that?"

"You pointed out that the goals of the Fund and the goals of Fairfax Consulting are very similar. You search out small companies that need venture capital. I specialize in turning around small companies that are in serious trouble. Why not join forces and offer a package deal?"

She smiled. "Sounds like a winning combination to me. But I've got to say, I'm a little surprised. I thought that the idea of taking orders from me was more than you could handle."

"It is." He sat forward and clasped his hands on the table. He looked directly into her eyes. "I love you more than I have ever loved anyone else in my life, but I don't intend to work for you. Nothing personal. It's just that I don't take orders well. However, I have another arrangement in mind."

"I knew it. There's a catch."

"Not a catch, an alternative. I'm proposing a joint venture. Fairfax Consulting and the Aurora Fund will maintain their individual business identities, but they will form a partnership to handle certain selected projects."

"Hmm." The muted buzzing of her cell phone interrupted her contemplation of his suggestion. She opened her purse, reached inside, and withdrew the small instrument. "This is Elizabeth."

"Lizzie?" Merrick's ever-cheerful voice boomed in her ear. "I've been trying to get hold of you all week. Did you get a chance to take a look at my business plan?"

She stifled a small groan. "I did glance at it, but I've been a little busy lately, Merrick. What with the arrangements for the engagement party and all, I haven't—"

"I know, I know. Congratulations, by the way. But getting back to my plan. This is the big one, Lizzie. I can feel it in my bones."

"As I said, I haven't gone through the plan in detail, Merrick." She saw a glint appear in Jack's eyes. She had not discussed Merrick's business plan with him, and she was pretty sure that he could guess why she had not done so. His obvious disapproval irritated her, so she spoke rashly. "But I trust your instincts. I'll have the funds transferred into your account immediately."

"Hey, Lizzie, that's terrific." Merrick's enthusiasm was, as usual, contagious. "Fantastic. You won't regret it. Things are going to work this time. You'll see."

"Give me that phone." Jack reached across the table and deftly removed it from her fingers.

She glared at him. "What do you think you're doing?"

He paid no attention to her fuming. "Merrick? Jack Fairfax here. Yeah, yeah, I know how lucky I am. Now, about your business plan. The Aurora Fund and Fairfax Consulting are setting up a joint venture. If you take the funding, you also take the consulting."

Elizabeth felt her jaw drop. She tried to grab the phone out of his hand. "Jack, wait, we haven't really discussed this yet."

He held the phone out of reach and continued to speak to Merrick. "I'll be working with Elizabeth, not for her. No, we haven't signed the papers yet."

"We haven't even talked about the details." Elizabeth stood up and tried again to swipe the phone away from him. "For all you know, I've changed my mind."

Jack angled his head to indicate the three business executives seated in the booth across the aisle. She glanced at them and saw that they were watching her with keen expectation.

"I agree," Jack said. "A good matchup of skills and market niches. Thanks, I thought it was a pretty good idea myself."

Blushing furiously, Elizabeth subsided back into her seat with ill grace. She tapped one red nail pointedly on the table as Jack concluded the call.

"It's a deal," he said finally. "I'll be in touch."

He handed the phone back to Elizabeth. "There you go, our first joint-venture client."

She glowered at him. "That was a little premature, don't you think? Something tells me that if that's an example of the way you do business, this joint venture of ours is not going to be as easy and smooth as you seem to believe."

"Are you reneging on your offer?"

"My original offer," she reminded him very evenly, "involved you working for the Aurora Fund. Not a joint venture."

"You're just ticked because I won't agree to an organizational chart that has me taking orders from you."

She started to argue, hesitated, and then reluctantly succumbed to the laughter that was fizzing inside. "Dang. It was such a lovely fantasy."

He grinned. "You want a good fantasy? Wait until tonight. I bought a book on massage. And if that doesn't work, I think I can come up with something else that will entertain you. What's more, it won't be a fantasy, either. Guaranteed."

She felt herself grow warm in the glow of love that she saw in his eyes. This was the real thing, she thought. This was the love that would last a lifetime. She knew that as surely as she knew that the sun would rise.

"What are you thinking?" he asked.

"Just that we lucked out."

"We sure did." He smiled. "We got the happy ending."

After Dark

Chapter One

*If it had not been horribly obvious that Chester Brady was al-*ready dead, Lydia Smith might have strangled him herself.

Her first assumption when she rounded the corner into the shadowy Dead City Tomb wing of Shrimpton's House of Ancient Horrors was that Chester was pulling another scam. It had to be some bizarre con tactic designed to steal her new client prospect right out from under her nose before she could get his name on a contract.

It was so typical of the little sneak. And after all she'd done for him.

She came to a halt and stared at the leg and arm hanging limply over the side of the ancient sarcophagus. Maybe it was just a weird gag this time. After all, Chester's sense of humor did lean toward childish pranks.

But there was something a little too realistic about the way he was slumped in the not-quite-human-shaped coffin.

"Maybe he just fainted or something," she said, without much hope.

"Don't think so." Emmett London glided around her and walked forward to gaze down into the green quartz burial box. "He's very dead. You'd better call the authorities."

She took another cautious step forward and saw the blood. It had drained from Chester's throat into the bottom of the coffin.

The reality of what she was staring at hit her with a numbing jolt. She could not believe it. *Not Chester.* He was a thief and a con artist, the kind of shady character who gave a bad name to all legitimate antiquities dealers and respectable para-archaeologists, but he was a friend too. Sort of.

She swallowed heavily. "An ambulance?"

Emmett looked at her. Something about his gaze made her uncomfortable. Maybe it was the eerie gold-green hue. It was a little too close to the color of her pet dust-bunny's second pair of eyes, the ones it used for hunting.

"There's no rush on the ambulance," Emmett said. "I'd start with the police if I were you."

Easy for him to say, Lydia thought. The problem was that the first person the cops would want to talk to would probably be her. Everyone on Ruin Row knew that she'd had a furious argument with Chester last month because the little creep had snaffled off her first potential client.

Oh, God, Chester was dead—genuinely *dead*. It was difficult to grasp the concept. This wasn't another one of his convenient disappearing acts designed to keep him one step ahead of an enraged client. This time his death was for real.

She suddenly felt light-headed. This could not be happening.

Deep breaths, she thought. Take some deep breaths. She would not fall apart. She would not lose it. She was not going to crack under stress the way everyone expected her to do.

With an effort she pulled herself together.

She glanced up from Chester's body and found Emmett London watching her. His expression was oddly thoughtful, even mildly curious in a detached sort of way. It was as if he was waiting to see how she would react, as if her response to the sight of a dead body in a sarcophagus was merely an interesting academic puzzle.

Unconsciously, her gaze went to his wrist. She had caught a glimpse of his watch a few minutes ago. The dial was set in an amber face. No big deal, she thought. Amber accessories were fashionable. A lot of people wore amber simply because it was stylish. But some people wore it because amber was the medium that powerful para-resonators used to focus their psychic talents.

Another shiver went through her.

"Yes, of course, the police," she whispered. "There's a phone in my office. If you'll excuse me, Mr. London, I'll go call them."

"I'll wait here," Emmett said.

So calm and unruffled, she thought. Maybe stumbling across dead bodies was routine for him.

"I'm really very sorry about this." She didn't know what else to say.

Emmett regarded her with that unwavering expression of polite interest. "Did you kill him?"

The shock of the question left her momentarily speechless.

"*No,*" she finally gasped. "No, I most certainly did not kill Chester."

"Then it's not your fault, is it? There's no need to apologize."

She got the distinct impression that he would not have been especially troubled if she *had* admitted to murdering poor Chester. She wondered uneasily what that said about him.

She turned away to walk back along the gloom-filled display gallery to her office. Her glance fell on Chester's foot propped on the edge of the green sarcophagus. The foot was encased in a boot made of some sort of cheap imitation lizard skin.

Chester had always been a flashy dresser, Lydia reflected. To her surprise, she felt a pang of wholly unexpected sadness. True, he had been a sleazy, opportunistic hustler. But he was only one of many who eked out a living on the fringes of the booming antiquities trade here in Cadence. The eerie green quartz ruins of the long-vanished alien civilization that had once flourished here on Harmony provided a variety of profit niches for industrious entrepreneurs. Chester had not been the worst of the lot who worked in the shadow of the Dead City wall.

He had been a nuisance, but he had been colorful. She was going to miss him.

*At five o'clock that afternoon, Melanie Toft stood in the door*way of Lydia's tiny office, her dark eyes alight with curiosity. "What did they say? Are you in the clear?"

"Not entirely." Exhausted by the hours of police questioning, Lydia sagged back into the depths of her chair. "Detective Martinez said they think Chester was murdered sometime between midnight and three A.M. I was home in bed at the time."

Melanie made a tut-tutting sound. "Alone, I suppose?"

Melanie was never loath to bring up the subject of sex. Six months ago she had terminated her third, or maybe it was her fourth, Marriage of Convenience. She made no secret about the fact that she was open to the notion of a fifth.

On the basis of her considerable experience, Melanie had appointed herself Lydia's personal sex advisor. Not that she had any great need of the expertise, Lydia thought. Her sex life, never what anyone would term lively, had become downright moribund in the past year.

Lydia absently fingered the amber stones in her bracelet. "How does a person verify that she was innocently asleep in her own bed when someone got murdered?"

Melanie folded her arms and leaned against the door frame. "It would certainly be a whole lot easier to prove if you had not been alone in said bed. I've been warning you for months about the dangers of not having a more active social life. Now you see the risks of being celibate for extended periods of time."

"Right. A person never knows when she's going to need a good alibi for murder."

Concern replaced some of the fascinated interest on Melanie's face. "Lydia, are you—you know—okay?"

It was starting already, Lydia thought. "Don't worry, you don't have to call the folks in the white coats yet. I'm not going to have a nervous break-down in front of you. Thought I'd save it until I get home tonight."

"Sorry. It's just that you told me that the para-rez shrinks had advised you to avoid stressful situations."

"What makes you think I've had a stressful day? All I've done so far is find a dead body in the Tomb Gallery, spend a few hours being grilled by the cops, and probably lose my shot at signing up a private client who could have single-handedly elevated my financial status into the next tax bracket."

"I see your point. Nothing stressful about a day like that. Not in the least." Melanie straightened away from the door frame and moved into the office. She sat down in one of the two chairs in front of the desk. "Just a walk in the park."

A new worry descended on Lydia. She could not afford to lose this job. "I wonder what Shrimpton will say when he gets back from vacation to-morrow and finds out what happened."

"Are you kidding? Shrimp will probably give you a raise." Melanie chuckled. "What better publicity for Shrimpton's House of Ancient Horrors than the discovery of a murder victim in one of the exhibits?"

Lydia groaned. "That's the sad part, isn't it? If this makes the evening papers, there will probably be a line of people around the block tomorrow morning."

"Uh-huh." Melanie's expression turned serious again. "I thought the po-lice questioning was strictly routine. Are you really a suspect?"

"Beats me. I'm still sitting here behind my desk, which means no one's arrested me so far. I take that as a positive sign." Lydia drummed her fingers on the arm of her chair. "But the cops knew about my flaming row with Chester in the Surreal Lounge last month."

Melanie frowned. "Not good."

"No. Fortunately, Detective Martinez also seems to be aware of the fact that Chester had a lot of disgruntled clients and more than a few enemies on Ruin Row. It'll take her a while to sort out all the possible suspects. It's going to be a long list."

Melanie shrugged. "I doubt the police will spend too much time on the case. Chester Brady wasn't exactly a high-profile victim or an upstanding member of the community. He had several brushes with the law, and his name was compost with the Society of Para-archaeologists."

"True. I imagine the only people at his funeral will be the folks he ripped off. They'll attend just to make sure he's actually dead."

"Probably hold a celebration at the nearest bar afterward."

"Probably." Lydia sighed. "I don't think there will be any family at the graveside, either. Chester once told me that he had no close relatives. He was always saying that was one of the things he and I had in common."

Melanie snorted softly. "You and Chester Brady had nothing at all in common. He was a classic loser, always looking for the big score and always screwing it up whenever he came close to getting it."

"I know." Not so very different from her at all, Lydia thought glumly. But she refrained from saying that aloud. "It's weird, but I think I'm going to miss him."

Melanie rolled her eyes. "I don't see how you can summon up any sympathy for the little jerk after the way he stole your first client away from you last month."

"He just looked so pathetic lying there in that sarcophagus, Mel. The blood and everything." Lydia shuddered. "It was awful. You know, Chester was pond scum, but I'm surprised that he actually made someone mad enough to murder him."

"Among his other glowing qualities, Brady was a thief. That tends to irritate folks."

"There is that," Lydia conceded. "And as a parting gift to me, on his way to the afterlife he managed to sabotage the sweet deal I had going this morning."

"Think you've lost the client who came to interview you today?"

"For sure. The poor guy had to spend an hour with the cops because of what happened. He was polite about it, but I got the impression that Mr. London is not accustomed to tolerating that kind of inconvenience. He's a rich, successful businessman from Resonance City. When he phoned earlier he made it clear he prefers to keep a very low profile. He wanted all sorts of assurances about discretion and confidentiality. Thanks to me, he'll probably wind up in the evening papers."

"Not real discreet or confidential," Melanie agreed.

"Considering the circumstances, he was amazingly civil about the whole thing." Lydia propped her chin on her hands. "He didn't say anything rude, but I know I'll never see him again."

"Hmm."

Lydia cocked a brow. "What's that supposed to mean?"

"Nothing, really. It just occurred to me to wonder why a rich, successful businessman who likes to keep a low profile would contact a para-archaeologist who worked in a place like Shrimpton's House of Ancient Horrors."

"When he could have had his pick of university consultants from the Society of Para-archaeologists?" Lydia asked grimly. "Okay, I'll admit I sort of wondered about that, too. But I didn't want to push my good luck, so I refrained from posing such delicate questions."

Melanie leaned across the desk to pat her arm. "Hang in there, pal. There will be other clients."

"Not like this one. This one had money, and I had plans." Lydia held up her thumb and forefinger spaced an inch apart. "I was this close to giving my landlord notice that I would not be renewing my lease on that large closet he calls an apartment."

"Bummer."

"Yeah. But maybe it's all for the best."

"What makes you say that?" Melanie asked.

Lydia thought about the too casual way London had asked her if she had murdered Chester. "Something makes me think that working for Emmett London might have been almost as stressful as finding dead bodies in the Tomb Gallery."

Chapter Two

An hour later Lydia emerged from the stairwell on the fifth floor of the Dead City View Apartments.

She was gaining stamina, she thought as she walked down the dark hall to her front door. She wasn't panting nearly as much after the five flights of stairs now as she had in the first week after the elevator had stopped functioning. Better than a gym workout, and much cheaper.

It was important to stay positive.

She slid the amber key into the lock, gave it a small pulse of psychic energy, and opened the front door.

Her pet dust-bunny, Fuzz, drifted toward her across the floor. If she had not been anticipating his greeting, she would not have seen him until he appeared at her feet. None of his six paws made any sound on the tile floor of the postage-stamp-size foyer. Fuzz's daylight eyes were open, glowing a brilliant, innocent blue against his dull, nondescript fur. He was fully fluffed, making it impossible to see his ears or his paws. He looked like something that had just rolled out from under the bed.

"Hey, Fuzz, you are not gonna believe the day I had." Lydia scooped him up and plopped him on her shoulder. "Oomph! Been into the pretzels again?"

The sturdy weight of the little beast always surprised her. One tended to forget that the scruffy, unprepossessing exterior of a dust-bunny concealed the sleek muscles and sinews of a small but serious predator.

"Chester Brady got himself murdered in my new sarcophagus. The one I told you I got for Shrimp's museum super cheap from the University Museum because they had two hundred extra ones in the basement. Plus they owed me, on account of I found a couple of dozen of their best examples in the first place."

Fuzz rumbled cheerfully and settled into a more comfortable position on her shoulder.

"I know, I know, you never did like Chester, did you? You were in good company. Still, it's strange to think that he's gone."

Several months ago she had stopped worrying about whether or not her one-sided conversations with Fuzz were an indication of deteriorating mental and psychic health. She'd had more pressing matters to occupy her attention. Chief among them had been finding a job and stabilizing her personal finances after the disaster.

Besides, as far as everyone else was concerned, she had cracked up big time after her Lost Weekend. Given the diagnosis she had gotten from the shrinks following the incident, talking out loud to a pet seemed pretty close to normal.

The disaster in the Dead City six months ago had not only destroyed her career at the university and wreaked havoc on her personal finances, it had also left phrases like "psychic dissonance" and "para-trauma" sprinkled liberally about in her medical records.

The doctors had recommended that she avoid excessive stress. Unfortunately, that was easier said than done when one was trying to forge a new career on the ruins of one that had crashed and burned.

For all their pompous-sounding pronouncements, Lydia knew that the rez-shrinks didn't have a clue about the true state of her mental and psychic health. Neither did she, for that matter. She remembered almost nothing about the forty-eight hours that had passed after she fell into the illusion trap.

The doctors said she had repressed the memories. They claimed that, given her high-rez psychic profile, it was probably better that way.

The paranormal ability to resonate with amber and use it to focus psychic energy had begun to appear in the human population shortly after the colonists came through the Curtain to settle the planet of Harmony. At first the talent was little more than a curiosity. It was only gradually that the true potential of the phenomenon became apparent.

Today, almost two hundred years after the discovery of Harmonic amber, it was routinely used for everything from switching on car engines to running dishwashers. Any child over the age of four could generate enough psychic energy to "rez" untuned amber. Few people, however, could summon enough psi power to do more than use it to drive cars or operate a computer. But there were exceptions.

In some people the ability to para-resonate took odd, extremely powerful twists. Lydia was one of those people. In technical terms, she was an ephemeral-energy para-resonator. The common term was "trap tangler." For some unknown reason she could use tuned amber to resonate with the dangerous psychic illusion traps that had been left behind by the long-vanished Harmonics. Being able to de-rez the nightmarish snares practically guaranteed that a person would end up in the field of para-archaeology. The alternative career path was dealing stolen antiquities.

Until six months ago, she had been advancing quickly through the hierarchy of the academic world. It had been only a matter of time before she made full professor in the Department of Para-archaeology.

And then came the disaster.

Her only clear recollection of what she privately called her Lost Weekend was that of coming to in a Dead City catacomb and discovering that not only was she alone but she had somehow lost her amber. Without it she faced the nearly impossible task of finding her way to one of the exits.

But Fuzz found her. She had never figured out how he got out of the apartment, let alone prowled the Dead City until he discovered her. But he had. He had saved her life.

She was not the first strong para-archaeologist to lose control and be overwhelmed by the alien nightmares enmeshed in the traps, but she was one of the few who had not wound up in an institution after the ordeal.

Lydia removed Fuzz from her shoulder and dumped him on the bed while she changed clothes. If it weren't for his bright blue eyes he could have been mistaken for a large ball of lint sitting on the quilt.

"Bad news on the client front today, Fuzz. Looks like we won't be moving into that spiffy new apartment at the end of the month after all. And I may have to cut back your pretzel ration."

Fuzz rumbled again. He watched without much interest as she kicked off her low-heeled shoes and climbed out of her business suit.

She pulled on a pair of well-worn jeans and an oversized white shirt, then resettled Fuzz on her shoulder.

Barefoot, she padded into her pint-size kitchen, poured herself a glass of wine from the twist-cap jug she kept in the refrigerator, and fixed a plate with a couple of crackers and some cheese. She removed the lid from the pretzel jar and grabbed a handful of munchies for Fuzz.

When that was done, she carried the makeshift hors d'oeuvres and the wine out onto the minuscule deck. Sinking into one of the loungers, she fed a pretzel to Fuzz, propped her feet on the railing, and settled back to watch the sun go down behind the great green quartz wall that surrounded the Dead City.

Her small apartment was overpriced, considering its size, the outdated kitchen, and the bad section of town in which it was located, but it had two important features. The first was that it was within walking distance of Shrimpton's House of Ancient Horrors, which meant she did not have to buy a car. The second, and in some ways more important, feature was that it was located in the Old Quarter, near the western wall of the Dead City. From her balcony she had a tiny sliver of a view of the ruins of the Dead City of Old Cadence.

It seemed to her that the ancient, mysterious metropolis was at its most hauntingly magnificent when it was silhouetted against the light of the dying sun. She contemplated the narrow wedge of the wall that she could see from the balcony and watched the last of the daylight illuminate the emerald glow of the stone. The nearly indestructible green quartz had been the Harmonics' favorite building material. The four dead cities that had been discovered thus far—Old Frequency, Old Resonance, Old Crystal, and Old Cadence—had all been constructed of the stuff.

Aboveground the architecture of the various alien buildings as-sumed a dazzling variety of fanciful shapes and sizes. No one knew how the Harmonics had actually used any of the structures that were being painstakingly uncovered by the archaeological teams contracted to the university.

The only thing para-archaeologists could be sure of was that whatever had gone on aboveground in the eerie ruins, it was nothing compared to what had gone on underground. By several estimates, less than twenty per-cent of the catacombs had been explored. Illusion traps and energy ghosts made the work slow and fraught with danger.

She had told the doctors that she had no memories at all of what had happened during the forty-eight hours she had spent in the glowing green catacombs, but that was not entirely true. Sometimes, when she sat on her deck like this and watched night descend on the Dead City, fleeting images came to hover at the farthest corners of her mind. The wraiths always stayed just out of sight, disappearing whenever she tried to draw them into the light of day.

A part of her was more than content, even eager, to leave them in the shadows. But her intuition warned her that if she did not eventually find a way to expose them, the phantoms would haunt her until the end of her days.

She sipped her wine, gazed at the green wall, and felt the familiar little shivers go down her spine.

The knock on her door startled her so profoundly that wine sloshed over the edge of her glass.

Fuzz rumbled in annoyance.

"Could be Driffield." Lydia sucked the drops off her fingers as she got to her feet. "Maybe he got my last letter threatening to call a lawyer and decided he'd better do something about the elevator. Naw, I can't see him climbing five flights of steps to tell me he's going to get it fixed."

With Fuzz on her shoulder, she went back into the apartment and crossed the miniature living room. When she reached the door she stood on tiptoe to peer through the peephole.

Emmett London stood in the hall. He did not appear to be breathing hard after the five-story climb.

For a few seconds she just stared, unable to believe her eyes. Emmett gazed calmly back. He was not exactly smiling, but there was a trace of amusement in his expression. He was obviously aware that he was being observed.

She noticed that he had picked up the evening edition of the *Cadence Star*, which had been left on her doorstep, and held it absently in one hand. She could read the headline of the lead story: MUSEUM ASSISTANT QUESTIONED IN MURDER.

She wondered if London had stopped by to tell her just how much he disliked being connected to a murder investigation.

Taking a deep dreath, she summoned up enough bravado to open the door.

"Mr. London." She gave him her best professional smile. "What a surprise. I wasn't expecting you."

"I was in the neighborhood," he said dryly.

Not bloody likely, she thought. Hers was not the sort of neighborhood that attracted upscale businessmen who were inclined to worry about getting mugged.

On the other hand, something told her that Emmett didn't fret too much about street crime. He looked quite capable of taking care of himself.

Fuzz rumbled. It wasn't a warning. The dust-bunny sounded inquisitive.

"I see." Lydia looked at the newspaper in Emmett's hand. "It really wasn't necessary to go out of your way to tell me that you've changed your mind about hiring me as a consultant. I already assumed I wouldn't get the job."

"Did you?"

"You, uh, indicated that you were real big on discretion. I sort of figured that what with the dead body and the cops and the evening headlines, you might conclude that discretion wasn't my strong point."

"Apparently not." He glanced back along the shabby hallway and then looked at her. "I would prefer not to continue this conversation out here in the hall. May I come in?"

"Huh?" At first she thought she had misunderstood. "You want to come inside?"

"If you don't mind."

She flushed and hurriedly stepped back. "Oh, sure, sure. Please, come on in."

"Thank you."

When he moved into the foyer, he made no more noise than Fuzz did. That was where the resemblance ended, Lydia decided. Emmett London did not in the least resemble a dust-bunny blowing across the floor. There was nothing haphazard, fluffy, or scruffy about him.

He looked like someone who made his own rules. The expression in his uncompromising eyes and the severe lines of his face told her that he also lived by those rules. An ominous sign, she thought. In her experience, people who adhered to a rigid code were not particularly flexible.

Emmett studied Fuzz with a thoughtful expression as Lydia closed the door. "I assume he bites?"

"Don't be ridiculous. Fuzz is perfectly harmless."

"Is he?"

"As long as all you can see are his daylight eyes, there's nothing to be concerned about. The only time you have to worry about a dust-bunny is when he stops looking like a wad of dryer lint."

Emmett raised his brows. "They say that by the time you see the teeth it's too late."

"Yes, well—as I said, there's no need to be alarmed. Fuzz won't bite."

"I'll take your word for it."

The conversation was deteriorating, Lydia thought. She needed a distraction. "I just poured myself some wine. Will you join me?"

"Yes, thank you."

She relaxed slightly. Maybe he wasn't here to tell her that he was annoyed with her for getting him involved with the cops. Surely he wouldn't accept an offer of hospitality and then inform her that he was going to sue her and Shrimpton's House of Ancient Horrors.

Then again, maybe he would do exactly that.

"When I heard your knock, I thought you were my landlord." She went into the kitchen, yanked open the refrigerator, and removed the jug of wine. "I've been after him to get the elevator fixed. It isn't working—but I expect you noticed."

Emmett came to stand in the doorway. "I noticed."

"Driffield is a lousy landlord." She poured the wine into a glass. "I'm trying to get enough cash together to move soon. In the meantime, he and I are locked in an ongoing war. So far he's winning. I've given him so much trouble lately that I have a hunch he's looking for an excuse to evict me."

"I understand."

Oh, sure. She seriously doubted that anyone had ever tried to evict Emmett London, but she decided it would probably not be politic to say so.

"Enough about me," she said smoothly. "It's a dull subject. Let's go out onto the balcony. I've got a view of the ruins."

He followed her outside and carefully lowered himself into the other lounger.

It was amazing how much smaller her treasured balcony seemed with him occupying such a large portion of the limited space. It wasn't that he was an especially big man, she thought. He probably qualified as medium on most counts. Medium height, medium build. It was just that what there was of him was awfully concentrated.

She had a feeling that with Emmett, like Fuzz, by the time you saw the teeth it was too late.

In spite of having spent nearly half an hour with him this morning, she knew little more about him than she had when he'd called her office and made the appointment. He had told her only that he was a business consultant from Resonance City who collected antiquities.

"We didn't have a chance to finish our conversation this morning," Emmett said.

Lydia thought about Chester's body in the sarcophagus and sighed. "No."

"I'll come straight to the point. I need a good P-A and I think you'll do."

She stared at him. Apparently he wasn't going to sue her, after all. "You still want to hire me? In spite of the fact that I got you into the evening papers?"

"I'm not in the papers." He sampled the wine. "Detective Martinez very kindly refrained from giving my name to the press."

She whistled softly. "Lucky you."

"Luck had nothing to do with it."

She relaxed slightly. "Well, if it makes you feel any better, I'm really very good at what I do."

"I'm glad to hear that." His smile lacked all trace of true humor. "It's not like I've got a lot of choice."

That gave her pause. She recalled Melanie's question that afternoon. Why hadn't he gone to the Society or to a classy museum to find a para-archaeologist?

She cleared her throat. "I don't want to talk myself out of a job, Mr. London, but you do seem to be, for want of a better phrase, financially comfortable."

He shrugged. "I'm rich, if that's what you mean."

"Yeah, that's what I mean. Let's be honest here. With your money you could go to the Society of Para-archaeologists and pick a private consultant who has established a reputation with big-time collectors."

"I know," he said simply. "But I need one who isn't too particular."

She chilled. "Too particular about what?"

"About getting involved in the illegal side of the antiquities trade."

Lydia went very still. "Oh, damn. I knew you were too good to be true."

Chapter Three

He had not handled that well. Emmett realized his mistake immediately. Lydia looked as if she had been flash-frozen in her chair. She did not move so much as a single muscle.

The dust-bunny on her shoulder stirred, but since it didn't open its second pair of eyes Emmett figured he was safe for the moment.

Lydia's lagoon-blue eyes gleamed with anger, however. It was probably just his imagination or maybe a trick of the evening light, but he could have sworn that her red-gold hair had turned an even more fiery shade. Unlike the dust-bunny, she did look dangerous.

"Perhaps I should explain," he said gently.

"Don't bother. I get the picture." She narrowed her eyes. "You're under the impression that I'm a thief? That I deal in illicit antiquities?"

Obviously a bit of diplomacy was required at this juncture, Emmett decided.

"I think you have connections in the underground market here in Cadence," he said deliberately. "I need those contacts, and I'm willing to pay well for them."

She slammed down her wineglass. "I am not a ruin rat. I'm a respectable member of the Society of Para-archaeologists. Okay, so I haven't worked on any licensed excavation teams lately, but I am in good standing with the Society. I've got enough academic credentials to paper a wall, and I've worked with some of the most noted experts in Cadence. How dare you imply—"

"My mistake." He held up one hand to silence her. "I apologize."

She was clearly not mollified. "If you want to hire a thief, Mr. London, I suggest you go elsewhere."

"I don't want to hire a thief, Miss Smith. I want to find one. Preferably with as little publicity as possible. To do that, I figured I'd need someone who knew the underground side of the antiquities business."

"I see." Her voice was as brittle as glass. "What made you think that I could help you?"

"I did a little research."

"You mean you went looking for a P-A who was not employed by a legitimate excavation team?"

He shrugged and took a sip of the truly awful wine. He congratulated himself on not wincing.

Lydia's smile was getting colder by the second. "Did you work on the assumption that any P-A who could not get respectable employment on a team or in a museum must be involved in the illegal trade?"

"It seemed like a reasonable theory. I regret any misunderstandings."

"*Misunderstandings?*" She leaned forward slightly. "Calling me a thief comes under the heading of *insults,* not misunderstandings."

"If it makes any difference, I'm not especially concerned with your professional ethics."

"It makes a difference, all right," she said ominously. "A big difference."

"Be fair, Miss Smith. No one expects to find a legitimate para-archaeologist working at a place like Shrimpton's House of Ancient Horrors." He paused. "And then there was that business with the body in the sarcophagus this morning."

"I knew you were going to hold that against me." She flung out a hand in disgust. "One lousy body and you leap to the conclusion that I'm up to my ears in the illegal trade."

"It wasn't finding the body that made me think you might have some contacts in the business, it was the fact that you seemed well acquainted with the victim. I'm told that, among other things, Chester Brady was a ruin rat."

Her mouth opened, closed, and then opened again. "Oh." After a moment she settled wearily back into her chair. "I suppose that could lead a person to some inaccurate conclusions."

"I appreciate your cutting me some slack on that point." He took another cautious swallow of wine and pondered the razor-thin view of the Old Wall. "So how did you come to know Brady?"

Lydia slanted him a meditative glance. Out of the corner of his eye he studied her expressive, intelligent face. He got the feeling that she was debating just how much to tell him. He would no doubt get the highly edited version of the story, he thought. She had no reason to confide in him.

Not that he didn't already know a good deal about her. In the past twenty-four hours he had made it a point to learn a lot. He was aware of the two days she'd spent trapped underground in the Dead City six months ago. His people in Resonance had briefed him on her medical reports—reports that were supposed to be private and confidential but that were extraordinarily easy to come by if you had money and connections. He had plenty of both.

This morning when he'd walked into her office and seen the gutsy determination in her eyes, he'd immediately dismissed the opinions of the para-rez psychiatrists. Whatever else she was, Lydia was not weak or delicate. He knew another fighter when he saw one.

The little rush of pure sexual awareness that went through him in that first moment was a warning. He had chosen to ignore it. That, he reflected, might not have been one of his smarter decisions. But he knew himself well enough to realize that he was not going to change his mind.

"I met Chester a few years ago," Lydia said after a while. "He was a strong ephemeral-energy para-resonator."

"A tangler?"

"Yes. But he came from nothing. No family, no proper schooling. He never went to the university. Never studied archaeology the way most good tanglers do. He was never allowed into the Society."

"That's not exactly a mark against him. Everyone knows the Society of Para-archaeologists is as arrogant and elitist as they come."

She glowered. "I agree that the Society is inclined to be a bit stiff-necked, academically speaking. But it's because of their high standards and strict admission requirements that tanglers haven't got the same disreputable public image as those ghost-hunters in the Guilds."

"The Guilds have standards," he made himself say in a neutral tone.

"Hah. What the Guilds have are bosses who run things the way gangster bosses run their gangs, and everyone knows it. In this town, the Guild boss is Mercer Wyatt and I can assure you that whatever standards he imposes have nothing to do with academic qualifications or credentials."

Emmett contemplated the bright flash of anger that lit her eyes. "It's no secret that there's a lot of professional rivalry between hunters and tanglers, but you seem to have taken it to an extreme."

"Whatever else you can say about the members of the Society, we're respected professionals, not members of an organization that is only one step above an underworld mob."

"I believe that we were discussing Chester Brady."

Lydia blinked a few times, scowled, and then subsided back into her chair. "Yeah, Poor Chester."

"You said he never gained admission to the Society?"

"He preferred to work the, uh, fringes of the antiquities trade."

"Meaning he was a thief?"

"Well, yes. But I sort of liked him anyway. At least, when I wasn't mad as hell at him. He really was an incredible tangler, you know. Very few could resonate with the ephemeral energy in the illusion traps the way he could. I once saw him de-rez a whole series of vicious little traps in one of the catacombs." She broke off abruptly and dabbed surreptitiously at the corner of her eye with the sleeve of her shirt.

"How did you become friends?"

"He runs—ran—a little shop in the Old Quarter near the east wall. Sort of a combination pawnshop and antiquities gallery. Small-time stuff. Anyhow, a couple of years ago he ripped off a little tomb vase from the lab where I was working. I traced it to his shop. Confronted him. We got to talking, and one thing led to another."

"You bonded with a small-time thief? Just like that?" Emmett said in surprise.

Her jaw tightened. "I got my tomb vase back first. As a gesture of thanks for not handing him over to the authorities, Chester did a small favor for me. As time went on, he did other favors."

"What kind of favors?"

She turned her glass between her fingers. "He knew everyone involved in Dead City work, legal and illegal. He knew who could be trusted and who would rip you off without a second thought. He also knew who was hiding a major find and who'd just secured funding from questionable sources. There's a lot of competition among the excavation teams, you see. Inside information is useful."

"There's always a lot of competition when there's a lot of money at stake."

"It's not only the money. Careers are made and broken out there on the sites."

"So good old Chester clued you in on the players in the business?"

"Something like that."

Emmett looked at her. "What did you do for him in return?"

"I . . . talked to him. And once I listed him as a consulting source in a paper I published in the *Journal of Para-archaeology*." She smiled sadly. "Chester really got a kick out of that."

"You said you talked to him." Emmett paused. "What did you talk about?"

"Lots of things. Chester spent years underground. Illegally, of course, but he sure knew a lot of stuff. Sometimes we talked about how it felt to go into para-resonate mode with the really old illusion traps. The kind that can suck you into a nightmare before you know what hit you."

"I see."

"Chester was a loner, but even loners get lonely occasionally. And tanglers need to talk to other tanglers sometimes. The Society provides more than just decent career opportunities for ephemeral-energy para-resonators. It functions as a club. A place where you can meet and talk to other people, share experiences."

"But Brady wasn't a member of the club."

She shook her head. "No. So he talked to me instead."

"In other words, Brady was an outcast tangler who sometimes pined for company, and you provided it?"

"That about sums it up."

"Any idea who might have wanted to kill him?"

"No. But there was always someone around who was unhappy with Chester." She made a face. "Including me. I've been struggling to get a private consulting business up and running. Last month he lured away my first important client. I was furious with him for a while. But it was hard to stay mad at him."

"I see."

Lydia straightened in her seat. "I think it's time you told me exactly why you wanted to hire me, Mr. London."

He leaned back in his chair and propped his feet up on the railing. "Recently a family heirloom was taken from my private collection. I have reason to believe that the thief brought it here to Cadence and sold it on the underground market. I want it back."

"You want me to help you trace it?"

"Yes."

"It's a Harmonic artifact, I assume?"

"No. As a matter of fact, it's not an antiquity from the ruins. This particular artifact came through the Curtain with my ancestors."

Her eyes widened. "You're looking for something pre-colonial? An object from Earth?"

"Yes." The barely suppressed excitement in her voice amused him. "It's not nearly as old as anything from the Dead Cities here on Harmony, of course. But it is, obviously, extremely valuable."

"Naturally." Enthusiasm lit her face. "Anything from the Old World is worth a fortune to collectors. So little remains."

"Yes."

Everyone knew that after the mysterious gate between worlds known as the Curtain closed forever, the settlers on Harmony had found themselves stranded. Lacking replacement parts, the equipment the colonists had brought with them had ultimately failed. Everything that could be used had been stripped. Many valuable artifacts had been lost during the violent, tumultuous period known as the Era of Discord. Most of the rest had been discarded, lost, or destroyed in the two hundred years that had passed since colonization.

"What was it?" Lydia demanded eagerly. "One of the computers? An agricultural tool of some kind?"

"It's a box," Emmett said.

Her face fell. "A box?"

"A very special box. Hand-carved from some sort of golden-brown wood and trimmed with gold and silver metals. It's called a cabinet of curiosities. It contains dozens and dozens of small secret drawers. My great-grandmother claimed that no one in the family had ever found and unlocked all of them."

Lydia frowned. "I don't understand. It sounds like a work of art, not a piece of Old Earth equipment or a mechanical device."

"It is a work of art. Handmade by an Old World craftsman some four hundred years before the Curtain opened. One of my Earth-side ancestors had the wood especially treated to preserve it indefinitely."

"But that's not possible." Lydia's voice gentled, although she did not trouble to hide the disappointment in her eyes. "You know as well as I do that the settlers brought no art with them. Space on the transports was too limited. And the Curtain closed before trade between the two worlds could be established. Perhaps it's something one of your ancestors made after arriving here on Harmony."

"No," Emmett said. "The cabinet of curiosities is from Old Earth."

"But how did your ancestors get it here?"

Emmett glanced at her. "I'm told that my several-times-great-grandfather had no choice. He married just before he came through the Curtain, and his new wife insisted on bringing the cabinet with her. Apparently she was a strong-willed woman. Somehow, she convinced my ancestor to smuggle it on board the transport."

Lydia looked politely doubtful. "I see."

"You don't believe me?" he asked skeptically.

"Every family has a few quaint legends concerning its Old World history."

"You think I'm looking for a colonial-era box that one of my forebears crafted right here on Harmony, don't you?"

She gave him a breezy, reassuring smile. "Don't worry. It really doesn't matter what I think about the provenance of your missing artifact. I don't have to believe that it came through the Curtain in order to find it for you."

"True, but there's a small problem with that approach."

"What problem?"

"If you really think that I'm semidelusional or just overly sentimental about an old family antique, you probably won't be sufficiently careful."

"Why do I need to be careful?"

"Because there are collectors who do believe that the box dates from pre-Curtain Earth. Some of them would no doubt kill to get their hands on it."

Chapter Four

"A small chest, you say." Bartholomew Greeley *folded his* hands on top of the locked glass case. His broad, ruddy features assumed a meditative expression. "Made of a yellowish wood. With a number of tiny hidden drawers."

"That's how my client described it." Lydia glanced at her watch. She had only twenty minutes left on her lunch hour. "Apparently it's been in his family for several generations. Between you and me, he's convinced it's an Old World antique."

Greeley looked pained. "Highly unlikely."

"Yeah, I know. Probably a nice heirloom-quality piece made right here on Harmony less than a hundred years ago but with a history that has been, shall we say, embellished by a long series of grandfathers and grandmothers." Lydia nodded. "You know how families are when it comes to that kind of thing."

"Indeed." Bartholomew's eyes gleamed. "But if the particular family in question actually believes the item is of Old World manufacture—" He let the sentence trail off suggestively.

Lydia got the point. "Rest assured, my client is convinced that the cabinet came from Earth, and he is prepared to pay well to get it back."

"How well?" Bartholomew asked bluntly.

"He has instructed me to put out the word that he will top any offer from a private collector."

"What about an offer from a museum?"

"My client says he can prove ownership of the cabinet and will go to court to get it back if necessary. No curator will touch it if he or she thinks the museum will lose it in a legal battle. What with the initial expense plus legal costs, it wouldn't be worth the price."

"True. Not unless the artifact in question actually is a work of art from the home world."

"As you said, highly unlikely. The thing to keep in mind is that my client *believes* it's from Earth. That means there will probably be some other collectors who can be persuaded to believe it too."

"Hmm." Bartholomew pursed his lips. "So you need concern yourself only with the private market."

"Not just the private collector market, Bart." Lydia gave him a meaningful look. "A very special segment of that market."

He did not pretend to misunderstand. "The segment that does not ask too many questions."

"Right. We both know that you would never get involved in questionable transactions, of course."

"Absolutely not. I have my reputation to consider."

"Naturally." Lydia was proud of the fact that she did not even blink at that statement. "But a dealer in your position sometimes hears things. I just want you to know that my client is prepared to compensate you for any information that leads to the recovery of his antique box."

"Indeed." Bartholomew glanced around the cluttered interior of Greeley's Antiques with an air of satisfaction. "You're quite right, of course. A dealer in my position occasionally picks up rumors."

Lydia followed his gaze. The display cabinets were crammed with odd bits and pieces of rusty metal and warped, faded plastic. She recognized some of the items in the cases, including what looked like the remains of an Old World weather forecasting instrument and the hilt of a knife. They were typical of the kind of basic tools the settlers had brought through the Curtain or crafted shortly after their arrival on Harmony.

A torn, badly stained shirt with a round colonial-style collar was displayed in one of the glass-topped counters. Next to it was a pair of boots that looked as old as the shirt. Neither the shirt nor the boots bore any traces of artistic adornment. The colonists had tended to be an austere lot. They'd become even more focused on the basics of survival after the Curtain had closed.

She took a step closer to the case that held the shirt and boots, widening her eyes at the neatly penned description and price.

"You're selling these as genuine first-generation apparel?" she asked politely.

"Both the shirt and the boots have been authenticated," Bartholomew said smoothly. "Excellent examples of early colonial-era work. There is every reason to believe that they were crafted within the first decade after the closing of the Curtain."

"I'd say it's a lot more likely that they were made last year by a forger who didn't do enough research."

Bartholomew scowled. "No offense, Lydia, but you're an expert in Harmonic antiquities, not colonial antiques."

"Give me some credit, Bart." Lydia eyed him. "Just because I specialize in ruin work doesn't mean I don't know a fake human antique when I see one. I was trained to recognize all kinds of frauds."

Bartholomew's wide face reddened in outrage. "What makes you think that shirt is not first generation?"

"The color. That particular shade of green wasn't used in the early colonial era. It appeared about forty years after the Curtain closed."

Bartholomew sighed. "Thank you for your opinion."

Lydia chuckled. "Hey, don't go changing the price on my account. Like you said, I'm no colonial-antiques expert."

"Quite true," Bartholomew said a little too readily. "And I won't be changing the price."

She took another look at her watch. Fifteen minutes left until she had to be back at Shrimpton's House of Ancient Horrors. There had been time for visits to only two antique galleries on her lunch hour today. She had deliberately chosen to start with Greeley's Antiques and Hickman's Colonial Artifacts because both proprietors dealt in Old Earth and first-generation artifacts and because neither gallery owner was overburdened with scruples.

"I've got to get back to the office," Lydia said. "We've been swamped at Shrimpton's today. You will let me know right away if you hear anything, won't you?"

"You have my word on it, my dear." Bartholomew looked at her. "Speaking of your job at Shrimpton's little museum, mind if I ask a question?"

"I didn't murder poor Chester."

Bartholomew gave her a limpid glance. "Good heavens, Lydia, I wasn't about to suggest that you did."

"Why not? Everyone else has felt free to suggest exactly that."

Bartholomew leaned forward and rested his elbows on the counter. "The thing is, why was he found in that tacky little establishment where you work?"

"Haven't got a clue." Lydia turned to walk toward the front door. "But I'll tell you one thing. If I had killed Chester, I wouldn't have left his body just down the hall from my own office. A little too obvious."

Bartholomew looked thoughtful. "I suppose that's true. But it does raise another interesting question."

"I know." Lydia opened the door. "What was Chester doing in Shrimpton's in the first place?"

"What do the cops think?"

"They think he went there to steal something. Granted, we're not a front-rank museum, but we do have some interesting items in the collection, especially in the Tomb Gallery. I wouldn't put it past Chester to lift a couple of vases or some tomb mirrors."

"I wouldn't put anything past Chester. But why was he murdered, do you think?"

Lydia shook her head. "Who knows? Detective Martinez believes that one of his truly annoyed clients followed him and killed him in the museum."

"Poor Chester. He never got that big break he was always looking for, did he?"

"No," Lydia said quietly, "he didn't."

She stepped out onto the sidewalk and closed the door behind herself. She was satisfied with what she had accomplished. Both Greeley and Hickman operated in the gray area between the world of respectable galleries and the illegal underground of the antiques business. By tonight, the news that she was looking for the cabinet of curiosities would have reached every dealer in Cadence.

She shot another glance at her watch and smiled to herself. So what if she was a suspect in a murder investigation? Things were looking up. Counting travel time to and from Ruin Row, she was about to post her first billable hour to Emmett London's account.

Her first job as a private consultant was off to a nice start. She could only hope that she wasn't successful too soon. The less time it took to track down the London family heirloom, the less she could charge Emmett for her services. She pursed her lips. Maybe she should have done a fixed-price contract.

Emmett emerged from the crowded bar and walked down the cracked sidewalk. The weak streetlamps in this section of the Old Quarter made only small inroads in the dark valleys of the night, and the light fog didn't help. It created impenetrable pockets of shadow in the unlit doorways of the looming buildings. It was a little like moving through a Dead City catacomb, Emmett thought, but without the green glow and the eerie, alien quality.

He crossed the silent street, automatically adjusting his balance so that his boot heels did not echo on the pavement.

He walked deliberately back to where he had parked the Slider, but he did not hurry. He was in no great rush to return to his hotel. He needed to think, and it was easier to do that out here in the shadows.

Things were becoming complicated, he reflected. Hiring Lydia Smith had not been part of the original plan. But with Brady dead, the only thing he could do was improvise.

The prickle of awareness at the top of his spine interrupted his thoughts. It got his immediate and complete attention.

The telltale whiff of synch-smoke told him that the watcher was somewhere in the shadows to his left. He continued along the sidewalk without pause, but he took his hands out of his pockets.

A figure stirred in an unlit doorway.

"Mr. Emmett London?"

Well, that was a first, Emmett thought. Small-time thugs who preyed on late-night bar crawlers rarely addressed their intended victims by name, let alone in a polite, damn near deferential tone.

Which meant that the young man in the shadows of the doorway was probably not a garden-variety street thief.

Emmett came to a halt and waited.

The man stepped out of the shadows into the pale glow of the street-lamp. He was thin and lanky, and he had the trademark ghost-hunter slouch down cold. He also had the wardrobe. He was dressed in khakis, boots, and a supple black leather jacket with the collar pulled up around his ears in a rakish manner. His long hair was tied back at his nape with a black leather thong. He wore his amber in a belt buckle the size of a car.

The size of one's amber wasn't important. It took only a small chunk of the stuff to focus psi power and convert it into a usable energy field. But try telling that to the flashy dressers.

"Didn't mean to alarm you, sir. My name is Renny. I'm just the messenger."

"That can be a high-risk profession."

"That sounds like something the boss would say," Renny replied.

"Who's your boss?"

Renny scowled. "I'm a guildman. My boss is Mercer Wyatt."

"Really?" Emmett smiled slightly. "You take orders from Wyatt?"

Renny flushed. "Well, not directly, of course. Not yet, at any rate. But I'm movin' up fast in the Guild. One of these days I'm gonna take orders from the big man himself. Meanwhile, I get 'em through Bonner."

"And what exactly did Bonner tell you to tell me?"

Renny drew himself up as if preparing to recite from memory. "Mr. Wyatt requests your presence at dinner. His place."

"Let me be sure I've got this straight. This is an invitation."

"Yeah, right."

"So why didn't Wyatt just pick up the phone and call me at my hotel?"

Renny looked slightly taken aback by that suggestion. "With all due respect, sir, Mr. Wyatt is real big on tradition, y'know? He likes to do things in the old ways."

"You mean he likes to run things the way they were run in the days following the Era of Discord. Somebody ought to tell him that times have changed."

Renny's brow furrowed deeply. "Just because the Resonance City Guild decided to turn itself into some kinda wimpy business corporation doesn't mean the other Guilds got to do things that way. Here in Cadence, we're into tradition."

"Well. Benny—"

"Renny."

"Excuse me. Renny. Tell you what. Go ahead and honor your traditions. In the meantime, not only is the Resonance Guild making money hand over fist, but one of the vice presidents is getting ready to run for a seat on the Federation Council."

Renny's mouth dropped open. "The Council? Are you serious? A guild-man is running for public office?"

"He's mounting a campaign, and the latest polls show he's probably going to get elected. You know why? The voters think he's had a lot of good, solid business experience because of his executive position in the Guild."

"Well, shit." Renny shook his head. "If that don't beat all. How the hell did they do it?"

Emmett shrugged. "Let's just say that the last boss of the Resonance Guild decided he didn't like being regarded as the CEO of a racketeering mob. He decided to upgrade the Guild image. You know, mainstream the organization."

Renny's face scrunched up into a puzzled frown. "Mainstream?"

"Never mind. Look, it's getting late. You've delivered your message, so why don't we just say good night?"

"Wait—you haven't accepted Mr. Wyatt's invitation."

"I'll go back to my hotel and think about it. If I decide I can fit it into my busy social schedule, I'll give him a call." Emmett started to move on. "You know, on the phone?"

Renny looked alarmed. "Mr. Wyatt will be real disappointed if you don't have dinner with him, sir."

"Good old Mercer. He always was the sentimental type."

Renny cleared his throat. "One more thing. I'm supposed to tell you that if you accept Mr. Wyatt's invitation, he might be able to help you out with your business here in Cadence."

Emmitt stopped and looked back over his shoulder. "Is that a fact?"

"Yes, sir."

Emmett considered that for a moment while Renny twitched uneasily. Striking a bargain with Mercer Wyatt definitely came under the heading of risky business. But if he got some assistance from the Guild out of the deal, it just might be worth it.

"Tell Wyatt I'll call him in the morning," Emmett said.

Renny blinked a couple of times. "You mean you ain't gonna accept right now?"

"No. I want to think about this for a while." Emmett turned away again.

"Mr. Wyatt's not gonna like being told he's gotta wait," Renny called out behind him.

"I warned you that being a messenger was a high-risk job," Emmett said. He walked off into the fog.

Chapter Five

Lydia was not sure what it was that awakened her. It could have been Fuzz shifting his weight at the foot of the bed. She lay unmoving and opened all of her senses.

The unmistakable aura of psi energy vibrated in the air around her.

"Damn."

She knew this prickling sensation all too well.

"Fuzz. Don't move."

The dust-bunny made a low rumbling sound, not a purr but a hissing growl. Lydia sat up cautiously, searching the shadows swiftly for what she knew had to be there.

The bedroom was not very dark. After the Lost Weekend incident, she had altered more than one routine. These days she left the light on in the adjoining bathroom all night long. In addition, she slept with the curtains open to allow the reflected glow of the streetlamps and some moonlight into the bedroom. There had been other changes, too. She wore one of her personalized amber bracelets to bed and kept half a dozen others scattered around the apartment.

Forty-eight hours in the catacombs had left their mark.

She saw Fuzz's eyes first—his second pair, the ones he used for hunting. They glowed a fiery gold in the dimly lit room. Fuzz was seriously concerned. That meant that she was not overreacting.

She swept the rest of the bedroom, seeking the telltale glow.

Nothing.

The whisper of energy shimmered again in the air. Lydia concentrated. No doubt about it, a ghost had invaded her bedroom. But it had not yet materialized.

"Just a tingle. A small one, Fuzz."

Of course it was a small ghost, she thought, desperately trying to reassure herself and the dust-bunny at the same time. Here in the Old Quarter, psi energy leaked freely out of unseen cracks in the Dead City. Nevertheless, even a strong ghost-hunter could summon only a small manifestation of dissonance energy outside the catacombs.

But the conclusion was obvious. If there was a ghost in the vicinity, there was a ghost-hunter somewhere nearby. Unstable Dissonance Energy Manifestations did not appear on their own outside the catacombs. And the only folks who could manipulate energy ghosts were ghost-hunters.

A shadow moved on the balcony outside her window. Lydia turned her head quickly, but she caught only a fleeting glimpse of a figure.

"Pervert!" she shouted.

The shadow disappeared from sight.

She longed to give chase, but she had to deal with the ghost first. Even small UDEMs could do a considerable amount of damage.

She eased aside the bedclothes, got to her feet, and scooped Fuzz off the quilt. The dust-bunny did not relax in her arms. His hunting eyes were twin flames in the shadows. His small body trembled. Lydia caught a glimpse of fang. He was staring at the space above her pillow.

The ghost began to materialize. Acid-green energy pulsed erratically. Lydia edged back toward the door. Fuzz hissed.

"Take it easy. There's nothing either of us can do except stay out of its way until it vaporizes. It really is pretty small. I doubt it will last more than a few minutes."

She did not turn her back on the ghost as she retreated into the hall. The green glow of the coalescing form grew steadily more intense.

"That bastard out on my balcony probably thinks this is very funny. If I find out who it is, I'm going to turn him in to the cops. Summoning ghosts outside the Dead City is illegal, and everyone knows it."

But the vow was a waste of breath. Even if she managed to discover which of the neighborhood toughs had pulled this vicious trick on her tonight, the police were unlikely to get involved. At most, someone would contact the Guild authorities and report the incident. The Guild might or might not take action.

Fuzz growled again. His hunting eyes gleamed more fiercely.

In the air above her bed, the green ball of energy started to move. There was an audible crackle as it floated closer to the wall. Lydia grew more uneasy. There was no sign that the ghost was weakening. More disturbing was the fact that it did not seem to be moving randomly now.

Fuzz stared, unblinking, at the pulsating energy ball over the bed. Lydia knew that there was nothing either of them could do about the ghost except stay out of its way and hope that it did no serious damage. Only a dissonance-energy para-resonator—a ghost-hunter—could summon one; only a hunter could de-rez it.

The small, pulsing green specter was almost touching the wall over the bed now. Lydia watched in frustration.

Then she smelled scorched paint.

"My wall!" Lydia whirled and ran down the hall, barely avoiding a collision with the small end table she had put there because there was no other space for it.

She dashed into the kitchen, tossed Fuzz onto the counter, flung open the door under the sink, and grabbed the household fire extinguisher, then raced back toward her bedroom.

Fuzz gamely tumbled down from the counter and scampered after her.

"It can't last much longer," she told him. "It just *can't*. Not here, outside the wall."

The smell of burning paint reached her before she got back to the bedroom doorway. She rounded the corner just in time to see the eerie green glow wink out of existence.

"It's gone." She breathed a sigh of relief. "Told you it couldn't last, Fuzz."

The odor of charred paint was unpleasantly strong. Lydia groped for the light switch, flipped it. And then groaned when she saw the scorch marks the ghost had left on the formerly pristine white surface of the wall.

With the immediate danger past, she whirled and went to the window. She was just in time to see a figure garbed in dark clothing vanish up a rope ladder that dangled from the roof. As she watched, outraged, the ladder was pulled up and out of sight. She yanked open the window and leaned out.

"Little punk! If I ever get my hands on you—"

But the jerk was gone, and she knew the odds of learning his identity were virtually zip.

That was when the full implications of the situation hit her. She had given her landlord so much trouble lately that he would probably seize upon any excuse to terminate her lease. Fire and smoke damage no doubt came under the heading of "willful destruction of property by tenant" or some other vague clause in the contract.

"If Driffield finds out about this, we're fried, Fuzz."

Emmett glanced at the amber face of his watch as he got out of the Slider. It was barely seven o'clock. The morning sun had not yet penetrated the blanket of fog that had crawled in from the river late last night.

He walked across the small, cramped parking lot of the Dead City View Apartments, let himself in through the broken security gate, and started up the stairwell.

He had called twice before leaving the hotel, but Lydia had not answered her phone. Probably in the shower, he thought. He had considered waiting until she got to work before he talked to her, but in the end he'd decided it would be better if he spoke to her outside Shrimpton's museum.

He was halfway down the dingy corridor to her door before the obvious explanation for Lydia's failure to answer her phone this morning occurred to him. Maybe she had spent the night somewhere other than her own apartment.

For some obscure reason, that possibility irritated him. She was *his* consultant. He had first claim on the hours that she did not spend at Shrimpton's House of Ancient Horrors.

He started to lean on the doorbell, recalled that it did not function, and knocked instead. The door opened with unexpected speed. He caught a whiff of fresh paint.

"Stop by to see the damage you caused, you little thug?" Lydia jerked the door wide. "If you think I won't go to the cops just because you're a kid, you—" She broke off, her eyes widening in shock. "Mr. London."

He studied her with deep interest. Clearly, she had not yet dressed for her job at Shrimpton's. She wore an old denim shirt and a pair of well-worn, faded jeans. Her fiery hair was held back off her face with a wide blue band. The style underscored the intriguing angles of her face. There was a paintbrush in her left hand.

The dust-bunny was perched on her shoulder, looking like a dirty cotton ball. Blue eyes blinked innocently at him.

"Little thug?" Emmett repeated politely.

A deep red blush crept up Lydia's throat into her cheeks. "Sorry about the greeting," she said gruffly. "I, uh, was expecting someone else."

He glanced at the paintbrush. "Does this mean you won't be going to your office at the museum today?"

"I wish." She wrinkled her nose. "Unfortunately, I've got less than two hours to finish repainting my bedroom wall, get changed, and get to work. Look, I know you're here because you want an update on how my search for your heirloom is going, but I really don't have time to talk right now."

"I can see that. Mind if I ask why you didn't wait until the weekend to undertake a major household-remodeling project?"

"I don't have much choice. One of the neighborhood ghost-hunter wanna-bes paid me a visit last night. Pulled a particularly nasty prank."

Emmett moved into the small foyer without waiting for an invitation. "What kind of prank?"

"He managed to summon a small ghost. It materialized in my bedroom. I don't know if he meant to do damage or if the UDEM just got away from him. Whatever, my wall looks like someone tried to use it for a barbecue grill. If my landlord finds out about the damage, he'll probably try to use it as an excuse to cancel my lease."

"I'll give you a hand," Emmett said.

"I beg your pardon?"

Her astonishment amused him for some reason. "I can paint a wall."

"Oh." She glanced uncertainly down the hall. "It's very nice of you to offer to help, but—"

He removed the brush from her hand. "Let me have that." He started down the hall.

"Wait." She hurried after him. "You'll ruin that spiffy jacket. It looks like it cost a fortune. I can't afford to replace it for you."

"Don't worry about the jacket." He came to a halt in the bedroom doorway and studied the scene.

He had invited himself inside because he needed to see the evidence of ghost damage. Neighborhood punk or not, the fact that his new consultant had received a "visitation" within twenty-four hours of going to work for him set off several alarm bells.

Even though he was here to examine the wall, the first thing he noticed was the unmade bed. There was something very intimate about the sight of the tangled white sheets and rumpled quilt. Lydia had slept here last night. Alone, from all indications. He felt the same whisper of sexual awareness that he had experienced the other morning at Shrimpton's when he had interviewed her. The sensation was stronger this time. He wondered how much of a complication it would prove to be.

Lydia came up behind him in the doorway. He forced his attention back to the matter at hand.

The bed had been pushed away from the wall. A sheet spread out on the floor served as a makeshift tarp. A bucket of white paint sat on the sheet. Rags were piled in a heap.

Emmett looked at the smoky traces on the wall. Three wavy lines. A chill settled in his gut.

"We've got a problem," he said.

"I know I've got a problem. His name is Driffield. But as you can see, I'm almost half finished with that wall. If you'll just get out of my way—"

Emmett shook his head a single time, his gaze still on the marks that had been burned into the paint. "Your landlord is not your biggest issue right now."

"What are you talking about?"

He did not answer right away. Hell, maybe he was wrong, he thought. Maybe he was letting his imagination run riot. It was just barely possible the marks were merely random.

He walked slowly into the room, examining the singed paint. The more closely he looked, the more he knew that his first reaction had been the right one. The marks were not the haphazard scorching of a small out-of-control ghost. Admittedly it was sloppy work, but he could make out the design. The three wavy lines were unmistakable.

"Your neighborhood punk didn't do this," Emmett said.

"Don't bet on it. We've got some strong young budding ghost-hunters around here. Future hoodlums, all of 'em. And all itching to join the Guild."

"I don't care how strong they are. Those burn marks are deliberate. They aren't random scorches. Whoever summoned the ghost had it under full control. No untrained dissonance-energy para-rez could have managed that degree of accuracy with a wild ghost."

She eyed him uneasily. "Do you really think so?"

"Yeah," Emmett said very quietly. "I really think so. We need to talk."

She studied him for a long moment. "You think this has something to do with your missing cabinet, don't you?"

"Yes."

She hesitated. "Okay, we'll talk. But the conversation will have to take place some other time. Right now I've got to get this wall painted, and then I have to get to work."

She snatched the paintbrush back out of his hand, stepped around him, and started toward the wall.

His first impulse was to grab the brush again, but he resisted the temptation. Maybe he'd been wrong about her relationship with Chester Brady. Maybe he'd been wrong about some other things as well. He was still winging it, he reminded himself. Still playing it by ear. So much depended on hitting the right notes.

"I'll take you to dinner tonight," he said. "We'll talk then."

She frowned. "What is this? Has something changed since yesterday?"

He glanced at the design that had been etched into her wall. "Maybe. Maybe not."

She gave him a steely look. "I'd better remind you that we have a contract, Mr. London."

"I'm aware of that, Miss Smith. Like I said, I'll fill you in this evening. In the meantime, don't make any further inquiries concerning my cabinet."

Alarm flashed in her eyes. "Why not?"

"There isn't time to go into it now."

"Wait just one damn minute here." Her voice heated swiftly. "I've got plans to talk to three more antique shop owners today."

"Forget them."

"But—"

He turned to face her. "That is a direct order, Miss Smith. I don't want you making any more inquiries on my behalf concerning the cabinet until we've discussed the matter tonight. Is that understood?"

Most people backed down when he used that tone. Lydia's jaw tightened, but she did not give so much as an inch.

"No," she said, "it is not understood."

"Let's get something clear here. I'm the client. I'm telling you that I will not pay you another cent if you continue talking to dealers about the cabinet."

"But we have a contract," she protested.

"Paint your wall, Miss Smith. I'll pick you up tonight at seven."

Chapter Six

"So who's this guy you're going out with tonight?" Zane Hoyt helped himself to a can of Curtain Cola from Lydia's small refrigerator. "Someone you met at the museum?"

"Sort of. He's a new client." Lydia peered into the hall mirror and adjusted the gold hoop in her ear. "It's a business meeting, not a date."

"Sounds boring."

Whatever else Emmett London was, Lydia thought, he was definitely not boring. She met Zane's gaze in the mirror and smiled.

Zane had just turned thirteen. Dark-haired and dark-eyed, he was slim, energetic, and hitting the awkward stage when he badly needed a man's firm hand on his shoulder. Unfortunately, there was no adult male in the picture. His father, a ghost-hunter, had been killed years ago in the catacombs. His mother had died in a drunk-driving accident shortly thereafter. Zane was being raised by his aunt, Olinda Hoyt. They lived downstairs on the third floor.

The majority of Lydia's so-called friends and colleagues at the University had disappeared after the Lost Weekend incident. Zane and Olinda had befriended Lydia at a time when she had found herself badly in need of friends. She was deeply grateful.

"The important thing is that Mr. London is going to pay me big bucks to help him find a lost family heirloom," Lydia said.

"Huh. Still sounds boring." Zane paused hopefully. "Unless we're talking about something from the catacombs?"

"Nope. It's an Old Earth antique."

"Why do you want to mess around with Old Earth stuff? I thought you wanted to get back underground."

"I do. But before I can attract that kind of business, I need to establish my reputation as a private consultant. That means I'll take any business I can get."

"I guess." Zane took a swallow of cola and wrinkled his nose. "So is it okay for me to study here tonight with Fuzz while you're out?"

"Sure." Anything to encourage his educational efforts, Lydia thought. "Fuzz enjoys the company."

Zane was a budding dissonance-energy para-rez. Unless he was forcibly prodded into a different path, his career prospects were all too obvious. It was almost a given that he would join the Guild when he turned eighteen and become a ghost-hunter. To make matters worse, he was thrilled with the image of himself in leather and khaki.

Lydia was doing her utmost to discourage him. At best, ghost-hunters were little more than high-priced bodyguards, in her opinion. Bodyguards, furthermore, who could not be depended upon in a crunch, as she had discovered at her own expense six months ago. At worst, they were gangsters.

Zane was too bright to waste his life in a dead-end muscle job. She might not be able to keep him from doing some ghost-hunting on the side, but she was determined that he get a college degree and study a respectable profession.

She sat down in the chair across from him. "Zane, before Mr. London gets here, I want to ask you a question. This is real serious, okay? So please don't tease me."

He gave her a quizzical look. "Something wrong?"

"Maybe. Last night someone summoned a ghost and sent it into my bedroom to frighten me. Today, at work, I got a weird phone call about it. I think it must have been someone from the neighborhood. Any idea who it was?"

Zane sputtered on a mouthful of cola. "Are you kidding? None of the guys I hang with are strong enough yet to actually summon a ghost."

"How about one of the older boys? Derrick or Rich?"

Zane took another swig of his soda while he pondered that. "Jeez, I dunno, Lyd. I don't think so. Maybe it's someone new in the area."

"I was afraid you'd say that," Lydia muttered.

"A lot of the guys would probably *tell* you they could do it, but don't believe 'em. They like to flash a lot of amber around, but I've never actually seen any of 'em do much except maybe get a couple of flickers going." Zane eyed her closely. "You sure that wasn't what you saw? Some flickers?"

"Positive." Lydia knew that Zane and his buddies used the word "flickers" to describe the tiny, harmless scraps of energy that were too small to be classified as real ghosts. They lasted, on average, for only a few seconds before winking out of existence. They were too little and too weak to be manipulated. Even the youngest and weakest hunters could summon flickers by the time they reached puberty.

"You're sure it was a real ghost?" Zane looked doubtful.

"Trust me on this, Zane. If there's one thing I can recognize on sight, it's a real ghost."

"Yeah, sure," he said much too quickly. "I believe you, Lyd."

But she caught the flash of concern in his gaze and knew what he was thinking. Zane was her friend and loyal defender, but deep down he, too, was worried that she had been badly damaged by whatever she had experienced during her Lost Weekend in the catacombs.

Until she got back underground and faced a few traps, she could not prove to herself or anyone else that she wasn't going to crack under pressure.

The knock on the front door interrupted her before she could grill Zane further.

"That will be my hot date." She started to get to her feet.

But Zane leaped off the sofa and charged toward the door. "I'll get it."

He opened the door with a flourish. There was a moment of acute silence while man and boy regarded each other.

"Hello," Emmett said. "I'm here to pick up Lydia."

Zane grinned. "Hi. I'm a friend of Lydia's. Zane. Zane Hoyt."

"Nice to meet you, Zane. I'm Emmett London." Emmett glanced at the large chunk of amber that hung around Zane's neck. "Nice necklace."

"Thanks. I'm a dissonance-energy para-rez. Gonna join the Guild and become a ghost-hunter when I turn eighteen."

"That right?" Emmett asked politely.

Lydia frowned. "You're only thirteen, Zane. You'll probably change your mind about what you want to do a thousand times before you turn eighteen."

"No way," Zane said with absolute conviction. He grimaced at Emmett. "Lydia's not real keen on ghost-hunting. She had a bad experience a few months ago, you see, and she blames—"

"That's enough, Zane," Lydia cut in swiftly. "I'm sure Mr. London has dinner reservations. We'd better be on our way."

"Yeah, sure," Zane said. He looked at Emmett with a proprietary gleam in his eyes. "Lyd's ready to go, Mr. London. She looks real nice, doesn't she?"

Emmett swept Lydia with a considering expression. His eyes gleamed, too. Lydia was pretty sure she saw amusement in that amber-colored gaze, but she thought she also saw something else, something that might have been masculine appreciation. She grew unaccountably warm.

She wasn't blushing. She could not possibly be blushing. This was business, after all.

Maybe she should have worn a business suit instead of the little aqua dinner dress. She had bought it just before the disaster in the catacombs, right after she and Ryan Kelso had started dating. But Ryan had eased himself out of her life in the weeks following her Lost Weekend, and she'd never had an opportunity to wear the dress.

When she had taken the frock out of the back of the closet where it had been hanging unworn for more than six months, it had seemed discreet enough for a business dinner. The long sleeves and the high neckline gave the garment an almost prim look. At least, that's what she had told herself. Suddenly she was not so sure.

"Yes," Emmett said, "she looks very nice."

Nice? What did "nice" mean? She wondered. She eyed his slouchy, unconstructed black linen jacket, black T-shirt, and black trousers. Definitely not nice, she decided. Dangerous, sexy, intriguing, but not nice.

She cleared her throat. "We'd better be on our way. Zane, you can do your homework here and keep Fuzz company until it's time for you to go back to your place. But no watching the rez-screen. Understood?"

Zane made a face. "Jeez, Lyd, I don't have enough homework to fill up the whole evening."

"If, by some bizarre chance, you happen to finish your schoolwork early, you can read a book until it's time to go home," she said heartlessly.

Zane groaned. "Okay, okay. No rez-screen." He paused speculatively. "How about ice cream?"

Lydia grinned. "Sure. As long as you leave some for me."

"No problem." Zane waved her through the door with a gallant motion of his hand. "Have a good time."

Lydia grasped the strap of her purse tightly and moved out into the hall. When Zane closed the door very loudly behind her, she was suddenly conscious of being alone with Emmett. Without a word, she walked beside him to the stairwell.

"Known Zane long?" Emmett asked as they started down to the fourth floor.

"I met him and his aunt right after I moved into this apartment complex. He and Olinda were very kind to me at a time when I, well, when I needed friends."

"Olinda is the aunt?"

"Yes." Lydia stepped into the elevator. "She's okay. A good-hearted soul. Runs the Quartz Café down the street. But I'm afraid she's got plans for Zane, and they don't include a college education."

"What kind of plans?"

"Olinda makes no secret of the fact that she can't wait until Zane is old enough to join the Guild and train as a ghost-hunter. A good one can make excellent money, you know."

"So I'm told."

Lydia grimaced. "Unfortunately, Zane shows every sign of becoming a very powerful dissonance-energy para-rez."

"In other words, good old Aunt Olinda thinks Zane's going to become an asset to the family's cash flow as soon as she gets him into the Guild."

"Exactly." Lydia glanced at him. "Don't get me wrong. I'm very fond of Olinda, but she and I are engaged in an undeclared war. I'm fighting to make sure Zane goes to college before he even thinks about becoming a ghost-hunter. Olinda wants him to join the Guild the day he turns eighteen."

"I get the picture."

"I'm doing my best to discourage his fantasies about ghost-hunting, but I'm not making much headway. Young boys are so impressionable. All that macho hunter stuff really appeals to them, especially at Zane's age."

Emmett slanted her an enigmatic look as they exited the stairwell and walked out into the parking lot.

"Being a dissonance-energy para-rez isn't something you can ignore.

Sooner or later Zane will have to come to terms with that side of his nature. He won't be able to pretend his talent doesn't exist, no matter how much he tries."

His calm logic irritated her. "Zane's a bright kid. He could be a doctor or a professor or an artist. I'm not saying he can't exercise his talents on the side. But I don't want him to become just another high-priced, overrated bodyguard."

"I realize the profession doesn't rank very high with you, but bodyguards occasionally have their uses."

"Huh. That's a matter of opinion."

He stopped beside a dark gray Slider and reached out to open the passenger door for her. "If you were going to continue as my consultant, you might need one."

She paused, one high-heel-shod foot inside the car. "What are you talking about?"

"I'm afraid I'm going to have to fire you."

Outrage and disbelief swept through her. "You're taking me out to dinner to tell me that you want out of our contract?"

"That pretty much sums it up. Those burn marks on your wall have changed everything, Lydia. There's some stuff I haven't told you about this job."

Chapter Seven

He'd chosen the restaurant with the help of the concierge at his hotel.

"The kind of place where the university crowd hangs out; you know, the professors, not the students."

"Don't worry, I know the perfect restaurant, sir. A charming little bistro. It's called Counterpoint. Specializes in New Wave cuisine. Excellent wine list. Very popular with the university crowd."

Lydia said nothing as she followed the maitre d' to a table near the window. Emmett knew that she was fuming. But beneath the simmering anger, he caught the glint of recognition in her expression. He made a mental note to tip the concierge. The guy had nailed it with the restaurant.

Emmett's gaze swept the room, assessing the polished wooden floors, the intimately lit tables, and the waiters dressed in black and white. In recent years he had finally grasped the concept of casual chic. He knew it when he saw it—and Counterpoint was definitely it. The sort of place that served a lot of pasta and did terribly clever, artistic things with miniature vegetables.

Lydia managed to contain herself until after the waiter had taken the order. Then she folded her arms on the table and narrowed her eyes at him over the candle flame.

"Okay, talk," she said. "What's all this about firing me?"

He had given a lot of thought to the problem of how much to tell her. In the end he had decided it would be best to go with at least a measure of the truth. He couldn't think of any other way to convince her that she did not want the job.

"I told you that I came to Cadence to search for a family heirloom that had been stolen from my collection," he said.

Her fingertips did a quick staccato on the table. "Are you going to tell me that your story about the missing cabinet of curiosities wasn't for real?"

"It's for real, all right. What I didn't get around to mentioning was that the person who took it was my nephew, Quinn."

That information made her blink a couple of times. "Your nephew?"

"My sister's kid. He's . . .." Emmett paused, thinking. "Eighteen as of last month."

"I don't understand. He stole a family heirloom?"

"I doubt if he looks at it quite that way."

"What other way is there to look at it?"

"Technically, what he actually did was pawn it. He dropped a copy of the receipt into the mail to me. Just in case, he said."

"Just in case of what?"

"I'd better start at the beginning. A few months ago Quinn took up with a new friend, a young lady named Sylvia. My sister and her husband did not approve. The long and short of it is that Sylvia came here to Cadence, apparently looking for work. Quinn followed."

Lydia frowned. "What kind of work?"

"Don't know. Quinn told me that she's a fairly strong ephemeral-energy para-rez and she dreams of working in the field of para-archaeology. But she's untrained and uncertified. Unfortunately, her resources are quite limited. No family to speak of. When Quinn met her, she was barely keeping herself off the streets by working as a waitress."

"Okay, so she came here to Cadence, and Quinn followed. With your cabinet."

"Right. And now he's disappeared. No one's heard from him for nearly two weeks. My sister is getting frantic. Her husband is concerned."

Lydia studied him. "So you agreed to come look for him?"

"Yes. As near as I can tell, he sold the cabinet to a dealer in the Old Quarter and used the money to get a hotel room. But he only spent two nights at the hotel, and then he just vanished."

Lydia looked thoughtful. "What about the dealer who bought the cabinet? Have you talked to him?"

"I went to his shop, but he wasn't there. Neither was the cabinet."

She stared at him, understanding dawning in her eyes. "Are you talking about Chester? Was he the dealer who bought the cabinet from Quinn?"

"Yes." He watched her face. "His shop was closed when I arrived. I went in anyway, to have a look around."

You broke into his shop?

"I didn't want to waste any time."

"Good grief!"

He reached into the inside pocket of his jacket. "I didn't find the cabinet or any clue to who might have bought it off Brady, but I did find this."

He removed the photo he had found on the wall behind Brady's shop counter and placed it on the table in front of Lydia.

The picture showed a woman with brilliant red hair seated in a booth in what looked like a seedy nightclub. She was smiling ruefully into the camera. Next to her sat an oily little man with slicked-back hair and a cheap, flashy sport coat. The man was grinning from ear to ear.

Lydia glanced down at the photo and then looked up swiftly, her eyes darkening. "That's a picture of Chester and me at the Surreal Lounge. We were celebrating my last birthday. He was always asking someone to take pictures of the two of us together there. It was his home away from home."

"When I couldn't locate Brady, I decided to look for you instead." Emmett picked up the picture and tucked it back into his jacket. "You weren't hard to find. But right after I located you, Brady turned up dead in that sarcophagus."

Anger flushed her cheeks. "My God, it was all a sham, right from the start, wasn't it? You came looking for me because you thought I was involved with Chester. You pretended to be a genuine client, but all along you thought I could give you a lead on your missing cabinet and your missing nephew."

"I didn't have much else to go on," he said quietly.

"I knew it."

"Knew what?"

Her hand tightened into a small fist on the white tablecloth. "You really were too good to be true."

He shrugged and said nothing.

"What made you decide to end the charade tonight?" she demanded fiercely.

"The scorch marks that ghost burned into your bedroom wall."

Confusion defused some of her outrage. "What in the world does that have to do—"

She broke off as the waiter returned to the table with the appetizers. Emmett looked at the dish that was set in front of him. The menu had listed it as Prawns in Three-Part Harmony.

None of the three perfectly cooked prawns sitting atop the bed of thin-sliced radishes appeared to be singing, in three-part harmony or otherwise, but he decided not to make an issue of it. New Wave cuisine was a state of mind, he reminded himself.

Lydia leaned forward impatiently as soon as the waiter had vanished. "All right, explain yourself, London. What did you mean about my scorched wall changing things?"

"The mark that ghost left on your wall was not a random design, Lydia. If you looked at it closely, you could make out three wavy lines. It was a sloppy job. The hunter obviously didn't have complete control of the ghost, but I'm sure about the lines."

"So?"

"I think someone may have tried to leave you a message."

She looked wary now. "You're saying that you recognized these three wavy lines?"

"Yeah." He took a bite of one of the prawns. "I've seen them before."

"Where?" Her voice was very tight.

He put down his fork, opened his jacket, and removed the scrap of notepaper he had found on Quinn's desk. Without a word he handed it to Lydia.

She snapped it out of his fingers and glanced at the three wavy lines. She raised her eyes. "I don't get it."

"I found that mark on a pad of paper next to the phone in Quinn's room. I think he made the notation after taking a phone call from Sylvia. He disappeared a few hours after he got that call."

"Do you know what the lines signify?"

"No. I'm looking into it. But the fact that someone used a ghost to burn them into your wall tells me they're probably important. And possibly dangerous."

Absently she tapped the piece of paper on the tablecloth. "It also tells you that I probably don't know what happened to your cabinet or to Quinn after all, right?"

He shrugged. "It did strike me that if someone had risked warning you off with an illegal manifestation, you might be in danger because you'd started asking questions. And if you had to ask questions, you probably don't know where my cabinet or my nephew is."

"Guess that explains the phone call I got at work this morning," she said reluctantly.

"What call?"

"I thought it was a crank call." She moved one hand in a dismissive gesture. "It was a man's voice. A young man, I think. I didn't recognize it. All he said was, 'No more questions.' Then he hung up."

"Damn it, why the hell didn't you tell me?"

She glared at him. "I just finished explaining that I thought it was a crank call. It didn't make any sense. I didn't connect it to my inquiries about your missing cabinet."

"The hell you didn't. You're too smart not to have figured out the connection."

Annoyance strained her voice. "Okay, okay, I admit the possibility crossed my mind. But I was afraid that if you thought I might be in danger, you'd fire me."

"That's exactly what I'm going to do. It's pretty clear now that I miscalculated. You weren't involved in this until I involved you."

"You think you can un-involve me by reneging on our contract? Is that it?"

"I want you out of this, Lydia." He was prepared for the stubborn anger that blazed in her face. What surprised him was the flash of something else. Desperation?

"Even if you're right, it's too late," she said quickly. "I've talked to some dealers. The word is out that I'm looking for the cabinet."

"Tomorrow morning you can put the word out that your new client fired you and you are no longer looking for his heirloom."

"What makes you think that will work? The word is already out in the antiquities community. I can't cancel it just like that. If someone knows anything about the cabinet, I'll be contacted, whether or not you fire me."

"Tell your contacts to get in touch with me."

"The ones who are most likely to know anything useful won't want to talk directly to you." She leaned forward, determination vibrating around her in an almost palpable energy field. "I know this crowd. They trust me, but they don't trust outsiders. You need me, London."

"Not badly enough to put you at risk."

"You didn't mind putting me at risk when you thought I might be in cahoots with Chester."

"That was different," he muttered.

"It was a very small ghost."

"Even the weak ones can cause a very unpleasant reaction. They can freeze you, knock you unconscious for as long as fifteen or twenty minutes."

"Fainting or temporary paralysis are common, transient side effects of direct contact with a weak UDEM," she said primly. "Permanent damage is rare."

"You sound like you're quoting from a textbook or an emergency room pamphlet. Do you know what it really *feels* like?"

"Yes." Her eyes were cool. "I know what it really feels like. It feels like all of your psychic senses have been rezzed to the breaking point. Everything is too bright, too hot, too cold, too dark, too loud. Sensation overwhelms you and you pass out. Unless, of course, you're a very strong ghost-hunter, in which case I understand you have some limited immunity."

He drew a deep breath. "Okay, so you do know what it feels like."

"Let's get something straight here. I spent most of the past four years of my working life in the Dead City. No para-archaeologist, regardless of how effective the team's hunters are, can spend that much time in the field without brushing up against a few small ghosts."

He was not going to get far with logic and reason, he realized. Might as well cut to the chase. "You don't seem to get the picture here, Miss Smith. I'm firing you."

"You're the one who doesn't get it, Mr. London. You can't fire me. We've got a contract."

"Don't worry. I'll compensate you for your time."

"There's more than money involved now. If what you say is true, it's possible that poor Chester was killed because of your cabinet—" She broke off abruptly.

He realized she was looking at someone who was approaching the table.

"Hope I'm not interrupting anything, Lydia. Saw you from across the room and had to say hello."

The voice was easy, refined, masculine. The kind of voice that projected well, Emmett thought. The voice of a man accustomed to the lecture hall. An educated voice.

"Hello, Ryan." Lydia forced a chilly smile. "It's been a while, hasn't it? This is Emmett London. Emmett, this is Professor Ryan Kelso. He's head of the Department of Para-archaeology at the university." She paused delicately. "A former colleague."

And formerly something more than a colleague, Emmett thought. He didn't consider himself the intuitive type, but even he couldn't miss the undercurrents swirling around the small table. A disturbing tendril of possessiveness uncoiled deep inside him. Probably not a good thing. He could have done without the added complications.

He took his time getting to his feet, absorbing the salient points of Ryan Kelso in a single glance. Tall, athletically fit, dark hair, gray eyes. Chiseled features.

Ryan looked every inch the fashionable academic in a brown turtleneck, a tweed jacket, and a pair of trousers that rode low on his hips. He wore amber in a chunky wristband on his left arm.

Emmett shook hands briefly. "Kelso."

"A pleasure, London."

Ryan gave Emmett a quick, assessing survey and then switched his attention back to Lydia. "What's this about finding a murder victim in that peculiar little place where you work? Saw something about it in the papers."

"His name was Chester Brady," Lydia said stiffly. "I doubt if you knew him."

"Can't say that I did." Ryan's mouth curved with amused disdain. "The papers implied that he was a ruin rat who had probably been killed by one of his criminal associates. What was he doing at Shrimpton's? Trying to steal one of your acquisitions?"

"Chester was a friend of mine. A very strong trap tangler," Lydia said in a steely voice. "One of the most powerful I've ever met. Who knows? If he'd had access to a decent education, he would have been a first-rate para-archaeologist. Probably could have been chairman of the department at the university by now."

Ryan dismissed that with a chuckle. Then his eyes softened with concern. "It must have been very traumatic for you, finding the body and all. I mean, the shock of that coming on top of what happened six months ago—"

"Not everyone thinks I'm fragile," Lydia said with conviction. "Believe it or not, the detective in charge of the case put me on her list of suspects. Apparently she believes I'm fully capable of handling the stress of murdering an old pal and stuffing his body into a sarcophagus."

"Uh—" Ryan floundered briefly, clearly unable to figure out where to go with that.

"I have to tell you, it was almost flattering in a way," Lydia continued.

She was on a roll. Emmett was amused. Nevertheless, it was time to intervene.

"Cops always question the people who find the victim," London said easily. "Naturally they talked to Lydia. They also talked to me. I was with her when she discovered the body. But the detective in charge made it clear that she's not seriously interested in either of us. We both have alibis."

"Some of us have better alibis than others," Lydia murmured.

Emmett ignored that. He kept his attention on Ryan. "Apparently Brady had a lot of disgruntled friends, clients, and associates. The police think one of them did him in."

"Makes sense." Ryan seized the opportunity to change the subject. "Anyway, it's great to see you looking so well, Lydia."

"Amazing, isn't it? I managed not to go stark-staring bonkers after all. At least, not yet. But never fear, there's always hope. I might still go over the edge one of these days."

Ryan had the grace to turn red. "You can't blame your friends for worrying about you."

"If my so-called *friends* had been genuinely worried about me, they would have seen to it that I got my old job back after the doctors turned me loose," she said much too sweetly.

She was not going to let up, Emmett realized. He wondered how Ryan had ever come to the conclusion that she was too delicate to continue in her archaeological work.

Kelso managed an expression of polite confusion. "I'm not sure what you're implying, Lydia. The decision to, uh, release you from your university contract—"

"You mean fire me."

"The decision was made by the administration," Ryan said quickly. "You know that. It wasn't a departmental decision."

"Give me a break." She made a small but unmistakably disgusted sound. "We both know the administration takes the recommendation of the department heads. Why don't you just be honest about the whole thing? You figured I was a candidate for the funny farm, and that's what you told the academic council."

"Lydia, we were all devastated by what happened to you."

"But not devastated enough to let me come back to the department."

"As chairman of the department, I have a grave responsibility. I couldn't take the risk of sending you out with the team after what happened. I had to keep your best interests in mind."

"If you were really that nervous about my para-psych profile, you wouldn't have had to send me back out into the Dead City right away. You could have let me work in the labs for a while until everyone was convinced that I wasn't going to freak under stress."

Ryan's frown of earnest concern darkened into annoyance. He glanced hastily around the restaurant, clearly uncomfortable, searching for an excuse to get himself out of what had become an awkward situation.

"Policy is policy," he said stiffly. "What you've got to remember, Lydia, is that your para-psychological health is the most important element in the equation. You went through a brutal experience. Got to allow yourself plenty of time to recover."

"I'm fully recovered, Ryan."

"Tell you what," he said a little too heartily. "Give yourself another six months and then reapply to the department. I'll make sure your application gets special consideration."

"Gee, thanks, Ryan. But six months from now I won't need my old job. I expect to have my own full-time consulting business up and running."

He looked slightly disconcerted. "You're going private?"

"That's right. I'm already working at it part-time."

"I hadn't realized—"

"Two months ago I registered as a private consultant in para-archaeology with the Society." Her eyes gleamed. "Mr. London here is my first client. Isn't that right, Emmett?"

He had to hand it to her, Emmett thought. She had backed him rather neatly into this corner.

"Lydia and I signed a contract two days ago," he said.

"I see." Ryan frowned at Emmett and then looked at Lydia. "What about your job at Shrimpton's?"

"As soon as I build my private business into a full-time enterprise, I will, of course, resign my position at Shrimpton's. In the meantime, I need the money. I was pretty well wiped out financially after losing my job at the university, you know."

"I see." Ryan started edging back. "Well, that's great. Just great. Say, the department occasionally uses private consultants and outside experts. Maybe we'll have occasion to call on you one of these days."

"I will, of course, be happy to consider contracts with the university," she said with grand aplomb, "but bear in mind that the private sector commands very high fees. Just ask Emmett."

Emmett managed not to choke on the swallow of wine he had just taken. He shot her a warning look across the top of the candles. *Don't push your luck, lady.*

"Worth every penny," he said aloud, with what he thought was commendable gallantry under the circumstances.

Lydia rewarded him with a triumphant smile that outshone the candles.

Ryan studied him with wary curiosity. "What do you collect, Mr. London?"

Emmett saw Lydia's mouth open. But he'd had enough of her reckless conversation. Beneath the table, he brought his shoe down on the toe of one of her sexy little black evening sandals with enough force to get her attention. Her eyes widened, but she closed her mouth.

Emmett looked at Ryan. "I'm into tomb mirrors."

"Tomb mirrors." If the amused condescension in Ryan's voice had been any thicker, it would have dripped onto the table. "Well, that's very interesting."

"Got a room full of 'em at home in Resonance City," Emmett continued expansively. "Had the walls lined with real mirrors, put the tomb mirrors on little stands in front and then lit the whole gallery with green lights. Really impresses guests."

Across the table, Emmett caught Lydia's attention and knew that she was torn between irritation and laughter. She knew even better than he did that tomb mirrors were among the most common and least valuable Har-

monic artifacts. They were also among the most commonly faked. Repro-
ductions and frauds abounded in the shops near the Dead Cities. Only
novices and the most unsophisticated private collectors bothered to acquire
them.

"Green lights?" Ryan looked pained. "How original."

"Cost a bundle, but I'm pleased with the effect," Emmett said. "The
lights and the wall mirrors give the gallery a real weird feel, know what I
mean?"

"I can imagine," Ryan murmured dryly.

Lydia smiled blandly. "Sounds like you've achieved exactly the sort of
creepy effect that we strive for at Shrimpton's, Emmett."

" 'Creepy'—that's the word." Emmett looked at Ryan. "I need a few
more pieces to fill out the collection, though. That's why I'm here in Cadence. Lydia thinks she can turn up some choice mirrors for me."

"I'm sure she will." Ryan glanced over his shoulder. "If you'll excuse me,
I'd better get back to my companion. Nice to meet you, London."

"Sure," Emmett said.

Ryan turned to Lydia. "It's great to see you getting out again, Lydia."

He leaned down with the obvious intention of giving her the sort of casual peck on the cheek that constituted a friendly farewell between old
friends, but he missed his target. At the last possible instant, Lydia, acting
as though she was entirely unaware of his intent, reached out to pick up her
fork, and her elbow somehow connected with his groin.

"Umph." Ryan took a hasty step back, started to put a hand gingerly on
his crotch, then apparently thought better of it and took some shallow
breaths instead.

"Oh, sorry." Lydia paused with the fork in midair. "Didn't realize you
were standing quite so close. It was terrific seeing you again too, Ryan. Give
my regards to everyone at the lab."

"Right." He backed away from the table. "Catch you later, Lydia. Good
luck with the consulting work."

Turning on his heel, he moved quickly off through the maze of small tables. Emmett watched him go and decided that Ryan had the air of a man
making a strategic retreat. Or maybe it was more of a desperate flight to safety.

Chapter Eight

Silence descended on them. Emmett looked at Lydia. She met his eyes. A moment of perfect comprehension, he thought.

The waiter returned with the entrees. When he was gone, Lydia refocused her attention on her food.

"He thinks I lost my para-rez pitch because of something that happened to me six months ago," she said after a while.

"I got that impression."

"I had a bad experience in the Dead City."

"I know," Emmett said quietly.

"You do?" She looked up quickly, frowning. "I hadn't realized—" Then she grimaced. "Yes, I suppose you would know."

"I called one of my people back in Resonance City. Had him take a quick look into your background."

"I see."

"The report said you were surprised by an illusion trap. It overwhelmed you, and you disappeared into the catacombs before anyone else on the team realized what had happened. There was a search, but you had vanished. Two days later you walked out on your own."

She shrugged. "So they say. To be honest, I can't remember anything about the forty-eight hours I spent underground. The para-rez shrinks said it's probably better that way."

"What do you think happened?"

She hesitated. "I may have gotten caught in a trap. I'm good, but no tangler is perfect. But there's another possibility."

"What's that?"

"I could have gotten badly fried by a really powerful ghost. That would also account for two full days of amnesia."

He frowned. "Couldn't have been a ghost. You were with a university excavation team. The report said you had two fully qualified ghost-hunters."

She cocked a brow. "You read the official report of the inquiry council, didn't you?"

"Yes."

"It's supposed to be confidential, you know."

"I know."

She let that go. "You're right. There were two hunters with us. They claim they accompanied me to the entrance to the tomb chamber. They told the committee that while they were dealing with a couple of small ghosts at the entrance, I disappeared into one of the antechambers. That was the last they saw of me."

Emmett waited.

"They said I didn't follow standard safety procedures." Her mouth tightened. "They implied I behaved recklessly."

Emmett nodded. The two hunters swore that, in her eagerness to explore the newly discovered antechamber, Lydia had gone ahead without waiting for them or any of the other members of the team. The conclusion of the report had been blunt: she had gotten herself into trouble.

He watched her twirl pasta around the tines of her fork. "Must have been an illusion trap. If it had been a real monster ghost the two hunters would have detected traces of energy in the vicinity."

"So they say." She ate some pasta.

"Are you telling me that you don't believe the hunters' version of events?" Emmett asked very neutrally.

She put down her fork. "I'm saying I don't know what happened. I've got no clear memories of what occurred in that antechamber. I've been forced to take the word of the others who were on the team that day."

"No *clear* memories?" Emmett watched her closely. "A moment ago you said that you couldn't remember *anything* about the forty-eight hours you spent in the catacombs."

She said nothing for a time, just looked at him. In the light of the candle her face was shrouded in mystery. He thought about what it must have been like to lose forty-eight hours out of your life and then wake up in the endless green night of an alien catacomb without amber. A lot of people who got lost underground never returned. Those who did find their way out were usually so psychically traumatized that they wound up in para-rez wards for a long time.

For a few seconds he thought Lydia was not going to respond to his question. Then she appeared to come to some inner decision.

"I've never told anyone else, but lately I think I've been getting little bits of memory." She gazed into the heart of the candle flame. "The only problem is, I can't make them out. It's like catching a glimpse of a ghost, the old-fashioned, horror-story kind—a shade or a phantom, not a UDEM."

"Have you gone back to the doctors?"

Her mouth twisted. "The last thing I need is another note in my parapsych file telling the world that I'm showing increasing signs of post-paratraumatic stress. I've already lost one good job because of the shrinks' report."

"And because the chairman of your former department was not willing to give you a chance to prove the doctors were wrong," Emmett reminded her.

"Ryan and I used to be colleagues. He got promoted to chair of the department one month after my Lost Weekend. That's when he apparently decided that I'm too fragile to do my job."

"I see."

"I can't really blame him. Everyone in the department is convinced that no tangler can go through what I did and come out of it with all parafaculties intact. No one wants to work on a team with someone who's—" She broke off to twirl her fingers in a circle. "You know, unreliable. A team member who loses her nerve or her edge in the Dead City puts everyone else in danger."

Emmett thought about how he had found her repainting her bedroom wall that morning to remove scorch marks left by a ghost. Whoever had summoned the UDEM must have known about her terrifying experience six months ago, he reflected. Most people could be expected to panic at the sight of a wild ghost, no matter how small, in their own homes. Anyone who had spent forty-eight hours alone in the catacombs would be especially vulnerable to that kind of small-scale terror.

Before this was over, he thought, he would very much like to get his hands on the hunter who had cold-bloodedly attempted to frighten her.

"If it makes any difference," he said, "I don't think you're delicate or fragile or inclined to fracture under stress. In my opinion, you are one very gutsy lady."

"Hey, that's great." She smiled with iron-willed intent. "I'm so glad you think I can do my job. Because we've got a contract and I'm not going to let you fire me."

He groaned. "So we're back to that, are we?"

"Sorry." She took another bite of pasta. "But it is the subject that is uppermost in my mind tonight."

"Lydia, you're missing the point here. I'm the reason someone sent that ghost to your bedroom last night. Don't you get it? If you continue to work with me, there may be other incidents. Someone is trying to make it plain that he or she doesn't want you to help me search for the cabinet."

"True. I wonder why not?"

He shrugged. "It's obvious. Whoever is behind this is afraid that the cabinet will lead me to Quinn. From now on, I have to go on the assumption that someone doesn't want me to find him."

She tapped one glossy green-and-gold-tinted nail against her plate. "If there is someone out there who feels that strongly about it, your nephew may be in serious danger."

"Yes. Until now, I've assumed he was just a lovestruck kid with rampaging hormones chasing after a girlfriend. But after what happened in your bedroom last night—"

"You need me, Emmett." She aimed the fork at him. "Admit it. You need all the help you can get."

"Maybe. But I don't want to be responsible for putting you in danger."

"That didn't worry you when you believed that I was working with Chester."

"That's different."

"No, it's not. Nothing has changed except that you no longer think I know the whereabouts of your cabinet. Look, I'm an adult and I'm a professional. I can make my own decisions."

"Lydia—"

"I won't let you push me out of this, Emmett. I need this job and you need me. I'm going to continue looking for your cabinet, regardless of what you choose to do."

"There's a word for that kind of threat."

"Yeah. Blackmail. You can't stop me. If there is any real danger involved, it will be safer for both of us if we work together. We should share information."

He studied her for a long moment. He knew beyond a shadow of a doubt that she meant every word. She would continue to search for the cabinet, with or without his permission. He should have known that it was not going to be easy to fire her.

"All right," he said after a while. "Okay. You win."

She felt triumphant.

"But as you said," he continued evenly, "it will be safer if we work to-gether."

"Right. No problem. I'll keep you informed—"

"You should be reasonably safe during the days while you're at the mu-seum," he said, talking straight over the top of her eager promise. "There's obviously a renegade ghost-hunter involved in this somewhere, but he isn't likely to try to terrorize you when there are witnesses around."

She quirked a brow. "No?"

"I doubt it. Too much chance of getting caught. Hunters have to work at close range, you know that. Even a strong, well-trained, very experienced one can't summon a ghost and manipulate it from more than half a city block away, even when he's working near the Old Wall. And I don't think we're dealing with a well-trained one here."

"You sound like an authority on the subject," she said coolly.

"Use your head. You know as well as I do that it's illegal to summon ghosts outside the Dead City. Any renegade hunter doing so risks drawing the attention of the Guild authorities. They tend to frown on that kind of thing."

"Especially if there's no profit in it for the Guild," Lydia shot back. "But what if he's not a renegade? What if he's working for the Guild?"

"You really don't hold ghost-hunters in high esteem, do you?"

"Let's just say that I don't think the Guild is above allowing its members to get involved in a few personal financial adventures on the side, provided, of course, that they cut the Guild in for a percentage."

"Are all para-archaeologists here in Cadence that cynical about the Guild?"

"No." She dunked a chunk of bread into the olive oil. "A few of my for-mer colleagues think hunters are sort of sexy, believe it or not. They've ac-tually had affairs with some of them. My friend Melanie Toft at Shrimpton's told me that she once dated a hunter for several weeks."

For a few seconds he thought she must be teasing him. Then he real-ized she was serious. "I take it the idea of having an affair with a hunter doesn't appeal to you?"

She blew that off with a wave of her hand and bit down on the bread. "Forget my personal opinions on the subject. We've got more important things to worry about."

"All right. As I said, I'm not too concerned about the days, provided you're willing to follow some reasonable precautions. It's the nights that are a problem."

"So?"

"So," he said deliberately, "if you insist on carrying out the terms of our contract, as of tonight you've got a roommate."

She gaped at him in stunned silence. Maybe it hadn't occurred to her that he could play tough too, he thought. Damned if he would let her blackmail him without paying a price.

Not a very big price, of course. Her dumbfounded expression was no doubt as much satisfaction as he would get.

Chapter Nine

"Don't you think you're overreacting here, London?"

"No." Emmett reached into the backseat of the Slider to retrieve his small duffel bag.

On the way back to Lydia's apartment, he had stopped off at his hotel long enough to collect the things he figured he would need tonight. A razor, a change of clothes, and the other small paraphernalia a man required for an overnight stay in a lady's home.

He would pick up the rest of his stuff in the morning when he checked out of the hotel. Assuming he did check out. There was, he assured himself, always the possibility that Lydia would lose her enthusiasm for this consulting job after she discovered what it was really like to give up her sofa and share her bathroom. Her apartment, after all, was very small.

"Well, if you're going to be stubborn about it—"

"I am," he assured her. "Stubbornness is one of my most distinctive personality traits."

"I believe it." She threw him a pointed look and jerked the door handle.

He popped open his own door and got out of the car. Automatically, he

examined the small, ill-lit parking lot. It was crowded tonight. Tenants' vehicles, the majority displaying worn paint and battered fenders, loomed in
the shadows. A large refuse container occupied one of the spaces near the
side wall. It was filled to overflowing. Empty cardboard boxes that had apparently not fit into the bin were stacked beside it.

There was an air of resignation about the Dead City View Apartments. It was as if everyone inside had abandoned all hope of upward
mobility.

Everyone except Lydia. It didn't take much to figure out why she was
reluctant to let go of him as a client. It wasn't just the money. He'd offered
to buy his way out of the contract. He was certain that she had her own
agenda, no doubt aimed at getting herself back underground and working
in the catacombs. He was her ticket out of Shrimpton's House of Ancient
Horrors.

He walked beside her to the door with the broken security lock. "I assume you've mentioned this to your landlord?"

"In the same letter in which I mentioned the broken elevator and several other problems," she assured him.

They started up the first flight of stairs.

"I'll get the lock repaired first thing tomorrow," he said.

She glanced at him in surprise as they turned up the second flight. "It's
not your problem."

"It is now. You could say I've got a vested interest in security in this
building."

She looked as if she wanted to object, but in the end she did not comment. Probably wanted to save her breath for the long climb to the fifth
floor, he thought.

He didn't blame her. On the third landing he glanced at her. "How long
has the elevator been out?"

"Couple of months. It was never what you'd call reliable, even before that."

"No wonder you're in such good shape."

"Thanks. I guess." She gave him a strange look. "Staying with me means
you're going to have to climb these stairs on a regular basis. I wouldn't count
on Driffield getting the elevator fixed anytime soon."

"You're not going to scare me off that easily," he replied.

She groaned. "I was afraid of that."

They made it to the fifth floor side by side, then headed down the dark
corridor.

"Maybe I'll see about getting some new bulbs for the overhead lights in this hall too," Emmett said.

"What are you, Mr. Fixit?"

"I've always sort of enjoyed fixing things—" Emmett broke off as he caught the telltale trace of ghost energy.

"Ah, shit." He dropped the duffel. "Give me your key."

"What?" She had her apartment key out, but she made no move to hand it over. "What's wrong?"

"Give it to me." He snapped the key out of her hand and started forward. "Stay here."

He did not wait to see if she would obey orders. It was probably a fifty-fifty proposition at best. He got the feeling she did not take direction well.

But there was no time to enforce the directive. Unstable dissonance energy shimmered in the vicinity. The odds that it was seeping out of Lydia's apartment were much too good.

He made the door, shoved the key into the lock, rezzed it with a small pulse of psi power, and twisted the knob.

A poisonous green glow spilled through the opening.

He slammed the door wide and saw the ghost.

The garbage-lid-size ball of green throbbed in the corner. In the eerie glare Emmett could see the two figures against the wall. Zane was curled into a hard, tight ball. Fuzz's hunting eyes gleamed from the shelter of his arm. Small white fangs glistened. Neither could move. The leading edge of the ghost's energy spasms was only inches from Zane's arm as he struggled to protect Fuzz.

Emmett concentrated briefly. Sought and found the violent energy pattern of the UDEM. It was uncomplicated and weak. The work of an untrained, inexperienced amateur. That did not mean it could not do some unpleasant damage if it touched Zane or Fuzz.

He resonated for a few seconds with the wildfire energy that was the essence of a ghost. When he was fully tuned to it, he sent out the dissonant psychic waves that would disrupt and destroy the harmonic resonance pattern. The amber in his watch warmed slightly.

The ghost flared, winked out, and disappeared as though it had never existed.

In the sudden darkness Zane and Fuzz were no more than shadows in the corner.

"Zane?"

"He's in the bedroom," Zane whispered, his voice strained and hoarse.

He lurched to his feet. "He's got a knife, Mr. London. He said he'd gut Fuzz if I even—"

"Get out of here. Take Fuzz. Go."

Zane did not argue. Clutching the dust-bunny, he ran toward the open door. Fuzz's amber hunting eyes blazed in the darkness.

"Zane," Lydia shouted from the doorway, "what happened? Are you all right?"

"Sure, Lyd."

Metal scraped. The sound emanated from the bedroom, echoing loudly in the dark hall. Emmett remembered the window. It was five stories above the ground, but only a short distance from the roof.

It was a risk, but if the intruder was sufficiently agile and sufficiently bold, he might figure that he could wriggle out the window and scramble up to the roof.

The front door was the only other way out of the apartment.

Emmett went down the hall, listening carefully.

Another scrape, followed by a dull thud. The intruder had gotten the window open.

Emmett flattened his body against the wall beside the doorway and gathered himself to go in low and fast.

"Emmett." Lydia's slender figure materialized at the other end of the hall, blocking some of the light. "What do you think you're doing? For God's sake, get out of there. Zane says he's got a knife."

Without warning fresh ghost energy sizzled in the hallway, inches away from Emmett. A poisonous green glow announced the new UDEM. Smaller this time, Emmett noted. The intruder was weakening. Or maybe he was distracted with the task of trying to escape.

"Look out," Lydia shouted.

Zane bounced up and down behind her. "Holy shit, another ghost! Watch this, Lydia."

Emmett concentrated briefly and then swatted the new ghost with a pulse of psi energy.

"Man, that is so dissonant," Zane crowed. The fear that had underscored his words a moment earlier had been replaced with excitement. "Did you see what Mr. London did?"

Emmett did not hang around to catch Lydia's response. This far from the ruins, it was harder to conjure a ghost than it was to banish one. The use of so much psychic energy drained the body's resources quickly.

The intruder had wasted a lot of his strength on the task of summoning the second UDEM, strength that he should have saved for crawling through the window. There would never be a better opportunity to take him.

Emmett shot through the doorway into the bedroom.

The ghost-hunter had one leg through the open window. The dark outline of his body was clearly visible against the night sky. He scrabbled wildly, trying to find leverage.

Emmett seized one booted foot and yanked hard. The hunter tumbled back into the room and landed on the carpet with a heavy thump.

The man stared up at him through the eyeholes in his stocking mask. Moonlight gleamed on the knife in his hand. Emmett circled warily, watching for an opening. The hunter rolled once and surged to his feet.

He made no move to close with Emmett.

"Stay back, you sonofabitch," he warned. He shifted toward the door of the bedroom. "Just stay outta my way and nobody will get hurt."

He was tightly wound, Emmett thought. Not in full control. Maybe having two of his ghosts neutralized in quick succession had made him nervous.

"What are you doing here?" Emmett moved toward him, staying just out of range of the knife. "What the hell is this all about?"

"None of your business." The hunter made a short, brutal, slashing motion with the knife. "Get back, damn it."

"Talk to me," Emmett said quietly. "Or you'll end up talking to the cops and to the Guild."

The hunter laughed, a harsh bark of sound. "The cops can't hurt me, and the Guild can't touch me."

He was at the doorway now. He eased through it, into the hall, never taking his eyes off Emmett.

"You were the one who summoned the ghost here last night weren't you?" Emmett kept his voice casual, almost conversational. "Why the warning to Lydia?"

"Shut *up*. I'm not answering any of your stupid questions." He risked a hasty glance over his shoulder, apparently checking to see that the path was clear.

When he turned back, Emmett had a ghost waiting for him. A big one.

Green energy pulsed in front of the intruder, filling the room with the strange light that was the hallmark of a dangerously intricate ghost.

"Oh, *shit*! No one said anything about this." The hunter whirled and fled down the short hallway.

He collided with the small table there, staggered, righted himself, and dashed into the foyer. He was clearly in the grip of panic. He did not even bother trying to neutralize Emmett's ghost.

The problem with ghosts was that although they could be maneuvered, it was impossible to make them move quickly. The hunter could easily outrun the UDEM Emmett had summoned.

In the meantime, it was blocking Emmett's path. He zapped the energy pattern. The ghost winked out, enabling him to plunge through the doorway and out into the hall.

Ahead of him the intruder pounded toward the stairwell. Emmett gave chase.

"Let him go, Emmett," Lydia called. "I saw the knife in his hand."

It was not the knife that worried him, Emmett thought. It was the fact that the intruder was already at the stairwell, about to disappear down it.

A robust middle-aged woman built like a monument to the colonial settlers hauled herself out of the stairwell just as the hunter reached it. A T-shirt emblazoned with the message DISSONANCE HAPPENS in sequined letters heralded her ample bosom. In the weak light of the dimly lit hallway, Emmett saw the other man's start of panicky surprise. And then the unmistakable hesitation.

It hadn't taken the hunter long to realize that he had just been handed a potential hostage, Emmett thought.

"Get down," Emmett shouted to the woman. "Hit the deck. Now!"

To his great relief, the newcomer assessed the situation with commendable speed and came to the correct conclusion. There was an audible thud as she dropped to the floor like a block of marble.

The ghost-hunter started to reach down for a fistful of the woman's jacket, belatedly realized he could not possibly haul her to her feet, and abandoned the hostage idea.

He whirled and leaped into the stairwell. The echo of his boots rang loudly as he plummeted downward.

Emmett had to vault the prone woman to reach the opening.

"What the hell's going on here?" She sat up warily. "Who are you?"

"Later." Emmett gripped the railing to control his swift descent.

The sound of the hunter's footfalls was already receding into the distance. He would never catch him now, and he dared not risk another ghost. There was no telling who else might enter the stairwell from one of the

other floors. A brush with a UDEM would not endear him to the neighbors.
And then there were the awkward legalities to be considered.

He was on the second landing when he heard his quarry slam through
the broken security door.

I'm going to lose him, Emmett thought.

The intruder was fast. He moved with the speed and agility of a young,
athletic male. But he had not yet learned to marshal and control his psychic
energies. He had freaked at the sight of the large ghost that Emmett had conjured. He obviously lacked the kind of practical experience that came only with
extensive work in the field. Which put him in his late teens.

About the same age as Quinn.

Emmett glanced over the railing in time to see the masked figure dash
out into the parking lot. When he reached the ground floor he heard the
whine of a highly revved mag-rez engine and knew that he had lost whatever small chance he'd had. A long, six-inch-wide band of bright light appeared suddenly in the darkness, the distinctive glowing tube that marked
the front grill of a Coaster.

The vehicle's passenger door slammed shut. The Coaster glided forward
between the rows of parked cars, heading straight for Emmett.

He threw himself into the dark space between an ancient Lyre and a
small Float. The Coaster howled as it went past, a hungry beast that had
been denied its intended prey.

It did not turn back. Emmett stood between the Lyre and the Float and
watched the car roar out of the small lot and into the street. A few seconds
later it disappeared around the corner.

He was still standing there, thinking, when Lydia, followed by Zane,
dashed out of the stairwell to join him.

"My God!" Lydia stared at the empty street. Then she swung around to
face him. "Are you all right?"

"Yeah." Emmett drew a deep breath, exhaled slowly. "Yeah, I'm okay."

It was not as though he could have kept it a secret for much longer, anyway, he thought. Lydia was smart. Sooner or later she would have figured
out that he was a ghost-hunter.

Chapter Ten

*"No need to let it get you down." Olinda Hoyt clapped Em-*mett on the shoulder. "Hell, even if you'd caught him, he'd have been out on bail by morning."

Emmett managed, barely, not to stagger beneath the blow. Olinda was no dainty pigeon. Years of wielding commercial-weight pots and pans and waiting on customers in her café had endowed her with a respectable layer of muscle.

The sequined DISSONANCE HAPPENS T-shirt Emmett had glimpsed earlier when she had emerged from the stairwell glowed even more brightly in the lights of the living room. Tight jeans cinched with a glittering rhinestone-studded belt sheathed her full-figured thighs. She wore a pair of running shoes decorated with neon-pink shoelaces. Her long gray hair was tied back in a ponytail.

Definitely not a woman who would go unnoticed in a crowd, Emmett thought.

He nodded absently in response to her observation. "Yeah, probably."

"Man, that was one amazing ghost you threw at him, Mr. London," Zane observed for what must have been the hundredth time. "You shoulda seen it, Aunt Olinda. It was huge. It filled the whole doorway—and we're not even inside the Dead City."

"Sorry I missed it." Olinda winked broadly. "But don't worry, Zane, my boy, one of these days you'll be summoning ghosts that size yerself."

"Made the other guy's ghost look like nothing," Zane crowed.

Emmett saw Lydia's jaw tighten as she set a cup of tea down in front of Zane, but she made no comment on the battle of the ghosts.

"You're sure you're all right?" she asked Zane again. "That man didn't hurt you?"

"Heck, no. I'm fine." Zane ignored the tea. He could not seem to take his eyes off Emmett.

Emmett stifled a groan at the unabashed hero worship in Zane's gaze. Lydia was not going to like this turn of events.

"Let's go through this from the beginning," he said quietly. "Tell me exactly what happened, Zane."

"Sure. Like I said, I'd finished my homework and was just getting ready to go downstairs. I opened the door and there was this guy in the hall. All I could see was his eyes, on accounta the mask. Fuzz didn't like him one bit. He started growling right off."

Emmett crouched down in front of him. "What did he say? Did he ask for Lydia by name? Do you think he knew who lived here or was he just looking for an empty apartment to burglarize?"

"I dunno. At first he seemed as surprised to see me as I was to see him. Guess he'd figured there was no one home. But before I could ask him what he wanted, he summoned the ghost. I tried—" Zane stopped suddenly. "But I couldn't do anything, y'know?"

"It's okay, Zane." Emmett put his hand on the thin shoulder. "A man's got to work with what he's got. You don't have the strength or training yet to neutralize a ghost. So you did something more important. You kept your head. You didn't panic. And you probably saved Fuzz's life."

Zane looked up quickly. "Fuzz wanted to attack him, but I knew that if I let him go, the guy would fry him with that ghost. And I was pretty sure a UDEM that big would kill something as small as Fuzz."

"Emmett's right." Lydia stroked Fuzz's ratty gray fur. "You saved Fuzz. If you hadn't been here, I'm sure he would have gone for the burglar, and that would have been the end of him."

Zane looked at the dust-bunny perched on Lydia's knee. "The sucker used the ghost to pin me and Fuzz in the corner. Then he started tearing the place apart. I figured he was looking for stuff he could sell, y'know? But he didn't pay any attention to your rez-screen."

"Not surprising," Lydia remarked. "It's at least eight years old. I got it at a rummage sale a few months ago. I can see why a burglar would pass it up."

Olinda snorted. "I told you I could get you a deal on a nice new model not more than a few months old at most."

"And I told you I'll pass," Lydia said. "I prefer to purchase appliances that did not fall off the back of a truck. That way I've got a shot at the warranty."

"Yeah, sure. Whatever. I just don't see why you gotta deprive yerself of some of life's little pleasures just because you don't like the notion of not knowing exactly where they came from, is all."

Emmett silenced them both with a look and turned back to Zane. "You don't have any idea what the burglar might have been looking for? He didn't say anything at all while he was tossing the place?"

"Not really." Zane bit his lip, thinking hard. "He swore a lot. He was kinda nervous, y'know? I guess that guy in the Coaster was waiting for him to hurry up and finish."

"I think you're right." Emmett glanced at Olinda. "You didn't see anything?"

"No." She shook her head. "First I knew somethin' was wrong was when I closed up the café and hiked up those damned stairs to see why Zane here hadn't come back down. Thought maybe he'd gone to sleep in front of the rez-screen. At the top of the stairs I saw the guy with the knife and heard you yell to get down. That's all I know about the situation."

"All right." Emmett got to his feet. "There's no point going over this again tonight. We all need some sleep."

"You gonna call the cops?" Olinda asked in a very neutral tone of voice.

Emmett turned toward Lydia. "We can call them, but I doubt that it will do any good. No one was hurt and nothing was stolen. They probably won't even bother to send out an officer to take a report."

"Huh. Not to this neighborhood, that's for sure," Olinda muttered. "Now, if this apartment complex was up on Ruin View Hill, they'd have someone out quicker 'n a man can say he's gotta take a leak."

"Thank you for that insightful observation," Lydia said. "Let's not forget that we do have a clue or two. He used a ghost in the course of an attempted burglary. We know he was a hunter."

"And a young one," Emmett added absently. "With a very limited amount of training."

"You're certain?"

"Reasonably certain." Emmett went to stand at the sliding window that opened onto the balcony. "But those two facts leave us with a very large group of suspects. The cops will be too busy to bother with this, but we've got another option."

There was a short, stark silence behind him. "Are you suggesting that we take this to the Guild?" Lydia asked eventually.

"It's local Guild business when a hunter uses his talents to commit crimes," Emmett reminded her.

"What makes you think we'll get the time of day from those thugs?" she demanded. "No offense, Emmett, but for all we know, the Guild itself is involved in this."

"No way, Lydia." Zane's voice was hot with feeling. "The Guild polices its own. Everyone knows that. Ever since the Era of Discord, the hunters have taken care of any member who went renegade."

"Yes, of course," Lydia said dryly. "How could I forget my history so easily? We all know the Guild deals with its own internal problems. I can't imagine what got into me to even suggest that it wouldn't fall all over itself to help outsiders prove one of its members was a knife-wielding burglar who likes to terrorize people with ghosts."

Emmett ignored the sarcasm in her voice. "I'll talk to the head of the Cadence Guild tomorrow."

"Mercer Wyatt?" She stared at him in disbelief. "You think you can just walk up to his front door and ask to speak to him? You're crazy. And you're also from out of town. That means that even though you're a hunter, you're not a member of the local Guild. What makes you think Wyatt will see you?"

"Professional courtesy."

She blinked. "I beg your pardon?"

He shrugged. "You can come with me if you like."

She looked slightly stunned. But she recovered swiftly. "Sorry. I've got a funeral to attend."

Olinda looked blank. "Anyone I know?"

"Chester Brady."

"Oh, yeah, right. Chester." Olinda shook her head. "Reckon you were the closest thing he had to a friend. Not that that's saying much about Chester's circle of acquaintances."

"I'll go with you," Emmett said. "My meeting with Wyatt isn't until seven o'clock in the evening."

Lydia frowned. "You've already got an appointment with him? At night?"

"I've been invited to dinner," Emmett said.

They all stared at him this time. The only one whose eyes were not opened unnaturally wide was Fuzz.

"Holy shit!" Zane mouthed in awe. "You've been invited to dinner with Mercer Wyatt?"

"I'll be damned," Olinda breathed.

"Exactly," Lydia said. "Better take a very long spoon."

She was in the tomb chamber again. Ancient though it was, it glowed faintly with the mysterious ambient green light emitted by the quartz

walls. She knew the eerie luminescence was dangerous because it
masked the energy of the illusion traps and the ghosts the Old Ones
had set to guard their underground maze.

She could see the dark opening to the antechamber. She went
toward it, just as she always did in this dream; and then she sensed the
presence behind her, just as she always did. She started to turn,
glimpsed the shifting of shadows, felt the cold chill . . .

She woke with a start, shivering. For a moment she could not think where
she was. The disorientation was stronger this time. The chilly sensation was
new, though.

Another cold draft swept across the bed. Then came the muted sound
of the sliding glass door closing out in the living room. Belatedly she recalled
that she and Fuzz were not alone in the apartment tonight. The knowledge
that Emmett was here was as disconcerting as the dream. Maybe more so.
She sat up slowly, aware that the whisper of cold night air and the sound of
the door indicated that Emmett had gone out onto the balcony.

She glanced at the clock. Three A.M. They had gone to bed at one. She
had been adamant about restoring order to her apartment before retiring.
No one had argued. No one had suggested that the task could wait until
morning. Instead, they had all pitched in to help her clean up the mess the
intruder had left in his wake. It was as if everyone understood that it would
have been impossible for her to sleep in the midst of the chaos. It had
taken nearly two hours to get things back into their proper drawers and
cupboards.

Three o'clock in the morning was a weird time to go outside for a breath
of fresh air. She wondered if her new roommate had any other odd habits.

"Fuzz?"

At the foot of the bed Fuzz yawned and opened his daylight eyes. They
gleamed colorlessly in the moonlight.

"Okay, okay, go back to sleep. Sorry I woke you."

She pushed aside the covers and got out of bed. She started toward the
door without thinking and then paused to grab her robe. Sharing the small
living space with Emmett required a few modifications in her own habits,
she thought. She could only hope he didn't get in the way too much.

She slid her feet into a pair of slippers, belted the robe, and padded out
into the front room. The curtains were open. Moonlight spilled across the
sofa, revealing that the makeshift bed was empty.

She looked out at the balcony and saw Emmett. He had pulled on his jeans, but that was all. He leaned negligently against the railing, gazing out at her sliver-size view of the green wall. In the light of the moon his shoulders looked very broad.

She hesitated, struggling briefly against the impulse to take a closer look at his back. What the heck? she thought. This was her apartment, her balcony. If he was going to wander around half naked, he had to expect that she would notice.

She hadn't been getting out a lot lately, after all.

She walked closer to the glass door and peered through the window at sleek lines of moon-sculpted masculine muscle. A man's back, at least this particular man's back, said a lot about him, she decided. There was power, both psychic and physical, in him. And a riveting sensuality.

There was also grace. An easy, unconscious grace, the kind that came from full control, the internal kind. Something about the way he held himself—even now, when he was simply lounging against a rail—spoke volumes about that inner control. She searched her brain for the right description.

"Centered." That was as good a word as any. This was a man who knew his own resources, made his own decisions, his own judgments of others. He had not accepted the experts' verdict on her para-psychological health, as Ryan and her other former colleagues had done. He had not bought the usual assumptions about people who had survived forty-eight hours alone in the catacombs. He didn't think she was too delicate to do her job.

Okay, so Emmett was a ghost-hunter, and a strong one at that. No one was perfect.

She opened the sliding glass door and stepped out onto the balcony.

He did not turn around. "Everything okay?"

She had the uneasy feeling that he had known she was there, watching him through the window, all along.

"Not quite." She joined him at the rail. "I don't think I ever got around to thanking you for what you did for Zane and Fuzz this evening."

"If it makes you feel any better, I doubt that the intruder intended to hurt either of them. He just wanted them out of the way while he went through your place."

"Maybe. But I don't think he would have hesitated to singe them if they had gotten in his path."

Emmett did not deny that. He lifted one shoulder, the movement of muscle and bone fluid in the moonlight.

Take deep breaths, she instructed herself. Lots of deep breaths.

Silence fell. Lydia focused on the dark silhouettes of the nearby buildings. She wondered why Emmett did not seem to feel the chill in the night air.

"You want to know why I didn't tell you, don't you?" he asked eventually.

She knew what he meant. "Why you didn't tell me that you're a dissonance-energy para-rez? I know why. I made my opinions about ghost-hunters fairly obvious right from the start. I don't blame you for keeping quiet about your talent. It was a perfectly reasonable decision for you to make under the circumstances."

"I thought so."

She fiddled with the belt of her robe. "The rest of it, the part about being a businessman from Resonance City. That's all true, isn't it?"

"Yes."

She relaxed. "Mind if I ask why you don't make your living as a ghost-hunter?"

"I did for a while."

"What happened?"

"I quit."

She looked up at the stars. "Okay, I know a dead-end conversational wall when I see one."

There was a short silence.

"You think that those two ghost-hunters who were on your team six months ago are responsible for what happened to you in those catacombs, don't you?" Emmett said.

She gripped the railing. "I told you, I don't know what happened to me six months ago. I can't remember."

"But you blame the hunters."

"They blamed my recklessness. We all agreed to disagree."

He nodded. "I'm not the only one with dead-end conversational walls."

"No, you're not." She turned sideways and studied his unforgiving profile. "So let's change the subject again. You think there's a connection between what happened here tonight and the ghost who appeared in my bedroom last night."

"Sort of obvious, don't you think?"

She tightened her fingers around the rail again. "I've tried to talk myself into believing that the two incidents could be unrelated. But I've got to admit I haven't been able to convince myself."

"The ghost last night was intended as a warning." Emmett gazed out into the night. "Presumably meant to stop you from looking for the cabinet. But why did someone search your apartment tonight? What was he looking for?"

"I haven't got a clue." She contemplated the night for a time. "Maybe we should take this to the police, Emmett."

"The cops can't handle it. Hell, they can't even find the guy who killed your pal Brady. This involves hunters. And hunters stick together. We need the Guild's cooperation. Here in Cadence, that means we need Mercer Wyatt's help."

"But maybe the police could talk to him."

"No," he said. "No cops. Wyatt would view it as an infringement of his own authority. Besides, we don't have much to give the police. The ghost last night and the break-in tonight won't amount to much in their eyes."

"What about the fact that your nephew is missing?"

"There's no evidence of foul play. Quinn is eighteen years old, not a little kid. The cops don't have any reason to look for him. They'd say it's a family matter. And they'd be right. Finding Quinn is my problem, not theirs."

"What about the cabinet of curiosities?"

"Same thing. A family problem. It wasn't exactly stolen, after all. It was pawned. I've got a copy of the receipt. No, we can't go to the cops. At least not until I figure out what the hell we're up against."

Some of her gratitude gave way to irritation in the face of his hard-headed attitude. "What harm can it do to at least talk to them?"

"For starters, it might get my nephew killed."

She stilled. "What do you mean?"

"Bringing the cops into it now will drive everyone involved further underground. Whoever's behind this might decide that the easiest way to deal with the problem is to get rid of whatever it is that's drawing the attention of the authorities."

She sighed. "In other words, your missing nephew."

"Yeah."

"All right. Oddly enough, I can see your point of view. No cops. Not yet."

He turned partway around to face her. "Thanks. I appreciate your co-operation."

"Hey, I'm your high-priced private consultant, remember? A satisfied client is my only goal."

He ignored that. "I wish like hell that I could get you out of this."

"I told you, you can't fire me."

He watched her with somber intensity. "Even if I could, it's too late."

"What's that supposed to mean?"

"After what happened here tonight, we have to assume that for some reason you're in this up to your neck."

Another chill went through her. This one had nothing to do with the temperature. "I sort of came to that very same conclusion myself this evening. It's not always real obvious, but I'm actually pretty smart, you know."

"I know. Looks like we're going to be sharing a bathroom for a while."

She had a sudden thought and found herself grinning.

"What?" he asked.

"Just make sure you stay out of sight if my landlord comes to the door. I'm not supposed to have long-term houseguests. Driffield says it's a violation of the lease to have anyone living in the apartment who's not named in the lease."

"I'll hide under the bed if he shows up."

"You won't fit. Relax. Odds are, he won't make it up all five flights of stairs." She turned away, intending to go back through the door. Then she paused. "I almost forgot. In addition to saving Zane and Fuzz, I wanted to thank you for something else."

"And that is?"

"For not labeling me delicate." She smiled tremulously. "That counts for a lot in my book."

"Even if the compliment comes from a hunter?"

"I thought you said you were a businessman."

He smiled slowly. "That's right."

She took hold of the handle, started to open the door.

"One more thing," Emmett said softly.

She glanced back inquiringly and discovered that he had moved away from the rail. He was standing very close to her now. Almost touching her. Totally blocking the night view. If she moved, she would brush up against his bare chest.

Deep breaths, she reminded herself. More deep breaths.

"What?" she asked. Damn. So much for deep breaths. She was suddenly breathless.

"Given that you're not the delicate type, and all," he began deliberately.

She searched his face. "Yes?"

"Do you think that you're likely to faint if I make a pass?"

She was no longer just breathless, she discovered. She was out of oxygen altogether. "Is this a hypothetical question?"

"No."

His hands closed around her shoulders. A sizzling charge, more shocking in its own way than a jolt of UDEM energy, shot through her. Every nerve resonated in response. She wondered if her hair was standing on end.

Like brushing up against a ghost but without the pain. No pain at all. Just an exquisite sense of excitement. Very high-rez stuff, she concluded. Very high-rez indeed.

He bent his head slightly. His mouth closed over hers in a kiss that held the concentrated essence of everything she had deduced from her intensive study of his back. Control, power, sensuality.

To hell with deep breaths. It had been a long, long time since she'd been involved in anything that could even remotely be described as an intimate relationship. And this was *her* balcony, after all.

She flattened her palms on his chest. The heat of his skin burned nicely. She let her mouth soften beneath his.

He groaned. It was the unmistakable sound of hunger stirring in the depths. It should have made her cautious, but instead it only heightened the thrill. Experimentally, she flexed her fingers, savoring the feel of muscle beneath skin.

He tightened his hold on her immediately, wrapping her in his heat and strength. One of his hands slid down her spine, glided over her buttocks, cupping them.

Her lower body was suddenly tight against his. Even through the layers of his jeans and her bathrobe, she was intensely aware of his erection.

And just as intensely aware of the sudden dampness gathering between her legs. He took one hand off of her long enough to grasp the door handle.

"Inside," he muttered against her mouth. "No room out here."

She did not argue. It *was* a very small balcony.

He got the door open, got her into the living room. She was conscious of movement. Her feet left the floor. And then she felt the tumbled bedding and the cushions of the sofa beneath her. She turned her head into the pillow and caught his scent—heady, utterly male, unique. As exhilarating as the tangled energy in an illusion trap. And no doubt just as dangerous.

His hands left her. She was once again conscious of the coolness of the room.

She opened her eyes and looked up. Emmett loomed over her. His fingers were busy at the fastening of his jeans.

The unmistakable frisson of psi energy sparked invisibly in the vicinity. She glimpsed tiny flickers in the air just behind Emmett. He was causing them, she realized. *Probably wasn't even aware of it.*

The little flashes of green light brought her back to reality with a jolt. From out of nowhere came a sharp memory of Melanie's description of a sexual encounter with a hunter who had recently summoned a ghost. *Using their talent gives them a hard-on like you wouldn't believe. Makes 'em sexy as hell. Something to do with the aftereffects of exercising dissonance energy. The experts think it's linked to their hormones or something.*

Lydia froze. She could not abide the thought that Emmett's eagerness to go to bed with her was just a byproduct of his earlier use of his paranormal talents. It was too depressing to think that *any* woman might do for him right now.

"Time out." She sat up quickly and shoved her fingers through her hair to get it out of her eyes. *Deep breaths.* "This is not smart. This is definitely not smart. Everyone knows that this sort of thing plays havoc with a business relationship."

His hands stopped moving at the waistband of his jeans. For a long moment he said nothing. Behind him, the little green sparklers winked out.

"You're right," he said eventually. "Everyone knows that."

He didn't have to agree with her so readily, she thought, irritated. It wasn't as if there weren't several good counterarguments he could have made.

With an effort of will she summoned what she prayed was a nonchalant nod and managed to struggle up off the sofa. "I realize that this was a unique situation. It's not your fault. I completely understand."

"Good to know," he replied as she gathered her robe more snugly around her and edged toward the hall. "Nothing like an understanding woman, I always say."

"My friend Melanie explained everything to me."

"Terrific. Mind if I ask exactly what she explained?"

"You know, all that stuff about how using your particular type of psi energy affects your, uh, libido."

"Lydia—"

"It's okay. Really." She flapped her hands at him as she backed away. "Every type of psi talent produces certain eccentricities."

"Eccentricities," he repeated in that oddly neutral tone.

"Don't worry. I'm sure you'll be back to normal in the morning."

"You really think so?"

"Melanie said the effects are transitory." She paused to give him a chance to respond, and when he didn't she whirled and fled back to the safety of her own bed. She forgot about the little table until her knee glanced painfully off the corner. She knew she would have a bruise in the morning. More than one kind, she thought, thinking of how close she had come to letting Emmett seduce her.

She could only hope that none of the bruises showed.

Chapter Eleven

*Perpetual Resonance Cemetery had historical significance be-*cause it dated from Settlement days, but it was no longer the most fashionable final address in town. The oldest headstones, the ones that marked the graves of several pioneers, were chipped, scarred, and weather-worn. Graffiti had been liberally spray-painted on some of the markers. Weeds grew with carefree abandon on most of the plots.

The day had dawned sunny and bright, but clouds were moving in from the west. There would be rain by nightfall. A bitter breeze was already rustling the leaves of the trees.

The only fresh flowers in sight were the ones Lydia had picked up on the way to the funeral. Tears burned in her eyes, surprising her, when she bent down to place the bouquet on Chester's grave.

She straightened and fumbled for a hankie. Belatedly she realized she hadn't thought to put one in her shoulder bag before leaving the apartment. But, then, she hadn't planned to cry. Not at Chester's funeral. Chester had been a thief, a liar, and a bloody nuisance.

Oh, God. Bloody. A vision of Chester's body in the sarcophagus appeared in her mind. The tears burned hotter in her eyes and spilled down her cheeks. Whatever else you could say about Chester, he had never killed anyone. No one had had any right to kill him.

Emmett put a large square of white cloth in her hand.

"Thanks." She hurriedly blotted her eyes. "He wasn't a very nice person, you know."

"I know."

"When you don't have any family of your own, you sometimes hook up with odd people." She blew her nose, realized what she had done, and hastily stuffed the hankie into her bag. "I'll wash it and return it."

"No rush."

She looked around, eager to change the subject. Things had been somewhat strained since they had bumped into each other coming and going from the bathroom that morning.

After she had gone to bed for the second time last night, she thought long and hard about how to handle the situation between them. She concluded that by morning Emmett would have recovered from the aftereffects of using his para-rez talent and would no doubt be embarrassed by his psi-driven pass last night.

Aware that he would probably regret everything, she had determined to pretend that nothing had happened. Unfortunately, as far as she could tell, her strict avoidance of any reference to the steamy kiss had done nothing to improve his mood. He had been grim and taciturn all morning.

"Olinda was right about one thing," she said as they turned to walk back to the car. "We were the only ones who came to the funeral."

"Not quite," Emmett said, looking past her toward the parking lot.

Startled, she followed his gaze to where the familiar figure of Detective Alice Martinez lounged against the fender of a nondescript blue Harp.

"Great," Lydia muttered. "Just what I needed to brighten my day. I wonder what she's doing here. She didn't even know Chester when he was alive."

"Might as well say hello, since we all seem to be in the same neighborhood."

Emmett took Lydia's arm and steered her toward the Harp. Martinez watched their approach through a pair of wraparound dark glasses that concealed her expression.

"Good morning, Detective." Lydia refused to be intimidated by the shades. "Nice of the department to send a representative to the funeral. I didn't know the police had a budget that allowed them to provide professional mourners."

"Take it easy, Lydia," Emmett said. "I'm sure Detective Martinez is here in an official capacity. Isn't that right, Detective?"

"Hello, Miss Smith." Alice nodded at Emmett. "Mr. London. As a matter of fact, I'm here on my own time today."

"Working on the old theory that murderers often show up at their victims' funerals?" Emmett asked casually.

"You never know," Alice said.

"Emmett and I were the only ones who showed up today."

"Couldn't help but notice that," Alice said.

"I assume this means that you're no further along in solving this case than you were on the day of the murder. You're still looking at the same two suspects. Emmett and me."

"Not exactly," Alice said. "Mr. London is not on my list. He never was. His alibi checked out. Yours, of course, is a little harder to verify. Something about being home in bed, wasn't it? Alone. That kind of story is always hard to substantiate."

"Hard to disprove, too," Lydia shot back.

Emmett interrupted. "Taunting the investigating officer is not generally considered to be a sign of good citizenship and willingness to cooperate with the investigation, Lydia."

Lydia felt herself turn red. "I happen to think Detective Martinez is wasting her time here. What kind of murderer would be dumb enough to show up at the funeral?"

Alice straightened away from the fender and opened the door of the Harp. "You'd be surprised how often the old theories prove to be true. Worth a shot, at any rate."

"Have you turned up any clues at all?" Lydia demanded.

"Nothing you'd call real useful," Alice said. "There was one small item of minor interest, however."

"What was that?"

"We went to Brady's apartment and his shop to take a look around," Alice said. "But someone else had been there first, looking for something, I think. The place was a shambles."

Lydia felt Emmett go very still beside her. She stared at Alice. "Why would anyone have searched Chester's place?"

"No idea," Alice said. "Don't suppose you could shed any light on the subject?"

"Chester didn't hang out with a lot of sterling citizens," Lydia said.

"Present company excepted, of course," Emmett inserted softly.

Lydia glanced at him quickly, realized he meant her. She noticed that Alice was watching the byplay very closely.

"Chester was a ruin rat," Lydia said. "Once in a while he came across some moderately valuable artifacts. Whoever went through his things was probably someone who had heard about his death and decided to see what he could find before the cops got there."

"Or it could have been the killer." Alice got behind the wheel. "Making certain there was no evidence to point back to him." She started to close the door.

"Wait a second." Lydia stepped closer to the Harp. "What did you mean about being here on your own time?"

Alice turned her head to look out over the forlorn cemetery. Sunlight glanced off her shades. For a moment Lydia thought she would not answer.

"My boss tells me I've got to learn to prioritize," Alice said.

"And Chester Brady's death doesn't rank very high on your boss's list of high-profile investigations, does it?" Lydia said acidly.

"No. In fact as of Monday, the Brady murder officially goes on the back burner. The department doesn't have the time or the manpower to spend on it. Too many other cases need attention. But I had the morning off, so I figured it wouldn't hurt to attend the funeral. Like I said, you never know."

It occurred to Lydia that maybe she could learn to like this woman after all. "Speaking as a concerned citizen, thanks."

Alice nodded once and rezzed the Harp's ignition.

Lydia watched the car move off down the narrow road that led away from the cemetery. Then she turned to Emmett.

"Whew, that was close," she said.

"What do you mean?"

Lydia frowned. "You heard Martinez. They know someone searched Chester's shop and apartment. You told me you went through his things looking for a lead on your cabinet, remember? That's how you found that photo that led you to me."

"Someone else must have gone in after me." Emmett looked thoughtful. "I left everything exactly the way I found it, except for the photo."

"Are you sure?"

"Of course I'm sure."

Lydia nibbled on her lower lip. "That means that someone else—"

"Uh-huh. Maybe the same someone else who tore your place apart last night."

Lydia shivered and looked out at the deserted cemetery. "Too bad the old cop theory about the killer attending the funeral didn't work this time."

Emmett removed his sunglasses from the pocket of his jacket and put them on. He took Lydia's arm again and walked toward the Slider.

"I'm not so sure the theory failed," he said quietly.

"What do you mean?"

"If you look up at that stand of trees on the hillside above the cemetery, you can see sunlight reflecting off something. Metal, maybe. Or glass."

"Are you serious?" Squinting against the glare, she studied the trees for a few seconds. "I don't see anything." She started to turn back. Light winked at the edge of her vision. "There. Yes. I caught it. Could be anything."

"Anything including the lenses of a pair of field glasses."

"A bird-watcher? Kids playing in the woods?"

Emmett said nothing. He opened the door of the Slider.

"Okay, okay." Lydia got into the car. "It could have been someone watching the funeral with a pair of field glasses. But why?"

"Maybe because he knew Martinez was here and didn't want to take the risk of being seen. Or—" Emmett closed the door and walked around the front of the Slider.

"Or what?" Lydia prompted the instant he got behind the wheel.

"Or maybe he was there for the same reason Martinez was."

"He wanted to see who showed up at the funeral?"

"Yeah."

"Kind of gives you the creeps, doesn't it?" Emmett did not reply. He rezzed the ignition. Flash-rock melted. The big engine whined hungrily.

He swung the Slider out of the small dirt lot and drove toward the narrow road. Lydia sank back into her seat and took one last look at the sad little cemetery.

She thought about the very abbreviated graveside service the funeral home had arranged. The check she had written to cover the cost of Chester's funeral had taken her account dangerously low. She hoped she wouldn't have to cut back Fuzz's pretzel ration.

Then she thought about how she was the only one who had attended the funeral for personal reasons. Emmett and Alice didn't count. They both had other agendas.

She shouldn't have been surprised by how pathetically lonely the short service had seemed. It was only to be expected. That was the way it was when you didn't have any close family or friends.

Memories of something Chester had once said to her over a couple of glasses of cheap wine at the Surreal Lounge returned. *You and me, Lydia, we got something in common. We're both alone in the world. Got to stick together.*

She wondered how many people would have turned up today if it had been her funeral. Mentally she started to tick off potential mourners. Olinda and Zane would probably have attended. Ryan? No, he wouldn't have bothered to come. A couple of others from the para-archaeology department might have shown up, though. Melanie Toft? Maybe. They had worked together for several months now.

Emmett glanced down at her hand on the seat. "What are you doing?"

"What?" Briefly distracted from her reverie, she looked at him. "I was just thinking about something."

"You were counting."

"Counting?"

"On your fingers," he said.

She looked down at her left hand where it rested on the seat beside her thigh and was embarrassed to see that she had extended her first three fingers.

"Math was never my strong suit," she said. Very deliberately she splayed all five fingers on the car seat.

Emmett, thank heaven, did not push it. She did not want to have to tell him that she had been trying to figure out how many people might show up at her funeral. The last thing she wanted to do was give the client any reason to believe the rumors that she was not mentally stable.

Nevertheless, for the first time in several months she thought she detected a hint of the dull gray mist that had obscured her world for a while after her Lost Weekend. She knew from experience that it was better not to examine the fog too closely. Better to focus on something else.

"I think Detective Martinez may actually be sincere about wanting to find Chester's killer," she said. "But it doesn't sound like she's going to get much support from her superiors."

"Priorities," Emmett said. "Everyone has them, including cops."

"Yeah, right. Priorities. You know, Emmett, I don't think Detective Martinez is going to find Chester's killer."

Emmett said nothing.

Surreptitiously she fished his limp handkerchief out of her pocket and mopped up a few more ridiculous, totally unwarranted tears.

Chapter Twelve

Shortly after five that afternoon, Emmett eased the Slider into a loading zone on the street a short distance from the entrance to Shrimpton's House of Ancient Horrors. He got out, leaned against the fender, and folded his arms. Waiting for Lydia.

After the small funeral that morning he had dropped her off at Shrimpton's and told her that he would pick her up after work. He had spent the rest of the day plotting a new strategy for finding Quinn. At least that's what he had told himself he was doing.

He had been reasonably successful in focusing his attention on the mess he had come to Cadence to resolve. The problem was that Lydia was part of that mess, and every time he thought about her things got a lot messier.

Her words from last night reverberated dissonantly in his brain, disrupting the rest of his orderly thoughts. *Every type of psi talent produces certain eccentricities. . . . Don't worry. I'm sure you'll be back to normal in the morning.*

Damn. Did she really think the passion that had resonated between them was the result of a peculiar para-rez eccentricity that affected only ghost-hunters?

He forced his mind away from that line of thought and studied the outrageous, over-the-top imitation Dead City facade of the structure that housed Shrimpton's. In his opinion, the building itself, with its garish domes, phony spires, and fake arches, qualified as a horror, architecturally speaking. It was supposed to be a replica of a ruin, but the only thing vaguely authentic about it was the green paint on the walls. It lacked the characteristic grace and Harmonic proportions of the aboveground Dead City structures.

As he watched, Lydia walked out through the front gate, spotted the Slider, and hurried toward him.

How the hell had she ended up working in a place like this? he wondered. Then he reflected on what he knew of her personal history. He thought about how and why she had formed a bond with a character like Chester Brady and knew he had already answered his own question. She was alone in the world. When disaster had struck six months ago, she'd had no family and very few resources to cushion the fall.

Ryan Kelso had certainly not rushed to her aid. Emmett found that interesting. He knew from the hastily assembled background report his people had prepared that Lydia and Kelso had worked on the same team together for nearly a year. They had coauthored several papers on Harmonic excavations. Apparently after the Lost Weekend, Kelso had concluded that she would be of no further professional use to him. What was it Martinez had said? *Priorities*.

Sonofabitch.

"Something wrong, Emmett?" Lydia came to a halt in front of him, frowning in concern. "Did you get a ticket for parking in a loading zone?"

"No." He shook off the ambient hostility that he felt toward Kelso, straightened, and opened the door for her. "My record as an upstanding pillar of the community is still clean."

He closed the door behind her and went around to the other side of the Slider. She looked better than she had that morning, he decided. The worrisome shadows had retreated from her eyes. He had the feeling that they were still there, somewhere, but the familiar look of determination had returned. Definitely a fighter.

"How did things go at work?" he asked as he pulled away from the curb.

"Quiet." She made a face. "Shrimp is whining because the little flurry of business we had following Chester's murder has faded. I almost slugged him. Probably would have if Melanie hadn't stopped me."

"Good way to lose a job."

"I know." She fell silent for a while. "I've been thinking about Chester all day."

"What about him?"

"I want his killer found, Emmett."

"Martinez is doing her best."

"Martinez as much as admitted that she's got nothing. I've been thinking about hiring a private detective. How much do you think it would cost?"

"A lot more than you can afford," he said gently. "We've got other problems at the moment, Lydia. Stay focused."

"Yeah. Focused. Maybe it's all connected, Emmett. Maybe when we find your nephew and your cabinet we'll find Chester's killer."

"Maybe," he said cautiously.

"I'd like that." She flexed her hand. "I'd really like that."

He did not want her to start obsessing on that aspect of the case, he thought. According to the reports he had read, she was inclined to take risks in pursuit of a goal.

"With luck I'll get some information out of Wyatt tonight that may give us a lead," he said.

Her head came around very quickly. "Are you nervous about the dinner with Mercer Wyatt?"

"No. But I'm not exactly looking forward to it."

"I don't blame you. I can think of a thousand other things I'd rather do, including go to the dentist."

"What makes you say that?"

"Mercer Wyatt is very powerful in this town. That means he's dangerous."

"All of the heads of the Guilds wield a lot of economic and political influence in their cities."

"Wyatt runs the Cadence Guild as if it were a private fiefdom. Everyone knows it. He's grown enormously wealthy off Guild income. Politicians jump through hoops when he suggests that they do so."

"So he's a man with a lot of clout. Every community has its movers and shakers." He was in no mood for this. "No offense, Lydia, but your anti-hunter paranoia is showing."

Her mouth tightened in an annoyed line. For a couple of seconds he thought she was going to tell him that he was free to fire her after all.

Instead, she said, "I've changed my mind. I'm going with you."

He was so surprised that he nearly missed the turn into the Dead City View Apartments parking lot.

"Not necessary," he said brusquely.

"No, it's okay. You're my client, after all. And this is a sort of business dinner, isn't it?"

He thought about just how complicated this dinner was going to be. "Sort of."

He slid his vehicle into a slot beside an aging Float, de-rezzed the engine and opened the door. Lydia got out on her side. Together they walked toward the security door. Lydia stopped and stared in astonishment.

"It's fixed."

"Zane and I took care of it today while you were at work," Emmett explained. "Unfortunately, I don't know much about elevator repair." He de-rezzed the lock.

"Hey, Lydia. Mr. London." Zane waved to them from the third-floor landing.

"Hi, Zane. Nice job on the security gate."

"Mr. London helped," Zane said proudly. "Guess what?"

"What?" she asked.

"A letter came for you. A guy from Resonance Relay Messenger Service brought it. He wanted someone to sign for it, so I did."

"Wow." She gave him a wry grin. "Probably my invitation to the Restoration Ball. I've been wondering what happened to it. Dang, I just hope it isn't too late for me to get a decent ball gown. The good ones are probably all gone by now."

Zane guffawed. "No, no, this is for real. I'll get it." He whirled and ran off down the hall.

Emmett looked at Lydia as they started up the stairwell. "Restoration Ball?"

She wrinkled her nose. "Big society shindig at the end of the year. Seventy-five years ago it started out as part of the annual festivities staged to celebrate the end of the Era of Discord, but somewhere along the way it became *the* social event here in Cadence. Everyone who matters in local politics and business will be there."

He nodded. "Got it. Do you usually attend?"

She gave him an amused look. "Don't be ridiculous. I was just joking. Of course I don't go to the Restoration Ball. What do I look like? Amberella? Fairy godmothers don't hang out in this neighborhood after dark."

Zane popped into the stairwell waving a brown envelope, saving Emmett from having to respond to what he was pretty sure was one of those awkward rhetorical questions.

"Who's it from?" Lydia asked.

"Don't know." Zane handed it to her. "The return address is one of those box numbers they use at those private mail service operations."

Lydia eyed him as she took the envelope. "Already checked, did you?"

"Sure. We don't get a lot of deliveries from outfits like Resonance Relay. I think the guy was a little nervous about being in this neighborhood. That's why he made me sign for it. He didn't want to have to make a return trip."

"Wimp." Lydia tore open the envelope. A key fell out. It clattered on the step.

"I'll get it." Emmett scooped up the amber-and-steel key.

"Thanks." She opened the single-page letter that she had withdrawn from the envelope. The amusement evaporated from her eyes. "My God, it's from Chester."

"Brady?" Emmett closed his fingers around the key. "When was it written?"

She scanned the note. "His writing is terrible. I don't see a date. Oh, yes, here it is. Last Monday."

Emmett calculated quickly. "The day before he was killed. Wonder why you didn't get it until today?"

Lydia scanned the note quickly. "He says he left instructions for it to be delivered after his funeral."

Emmett propped one shoulder against the stairwell wall. "Let's hear what he has to say."

Lydia took a breath and started to read the note aloud.

Dear Lydia:

If you're reading this letter, it means I've gone back through the Curtain the hard way. You can consider this my last Will and Testament. I know we've had a few run-ins, but that was just business.

I never told you this, but sometimes when we talked about stuff over drinks at the Surreal, I used to pretend that we were out on a real date together. Sometimes I went back to my place and thought about how things could have been if you weren't so nice and I wasn't so screwed up.

I always told you that you're too good for your own good. I still say being honest and loyal and hardworking and all that shit won't get you far. But, got to admit that it was kind of nice to know that there actually are people like you out there in the world—and I'm not saying that just because I made a lot of easy money off folks like you.

Anyhow, what all this is leading up to is that if anything happens to me I want you to have the assets in my retirement plan. It's at the Bank of Rose. Use the key to get into it.

Good-bye, Lydia. And thanks for everything.

Love,
Chester

P.S. I still say you're better off without that son of a bitch Kelso hanging around. You'll see. He's a user, Lydia. I know his kind. Maybe it's because I'm one of them.

Lydia stopped reading suddenly. There was a short pause during which Emmett watched her dig out the handkerchief he had given her at the funeral. Zane looked alarmed when she brushed away the fresh tears. He opened his mouth to say something but subsided when Emmett caught his attention and shook his head.

After a while Lydia stuffed the handkerchief back into her purse and took the key from Emmett.

"Well," she said, "this should be interesting. I wonder what kind of assets Chester would keep in a retirement plan?"

He glanced at his watch. "Too late to find out tonight. The banks are closed."

"Not the Bank of Rose," she assured him. "It never closes."

Chapter Thirteen

The Surreal Lounge was everything one would have expected in a place that had served as Chester Brady's home away from home, Emmett decided an hour and a half later. The atmosphere reeked of second-rate liquor, synch-smoke, and rancid cooking grease. The place was drenched in the perpetual gloom that was the quintessential hallmark of cheap nightclubs.

It was nearly seven o'clock. The regulars had already begun to settle in for the evening. The shabby booths were populated with men whose hair gleamed from too much pomade and women whose dresses fit too snugly. There was a small stage. A sign announced that a musical group calling itself the Earth Tones was scheduled to play at nine. In the meantime, some surprisingly good rez-jazz emanated from a pair of speakers.

Emmett thought about the photo of Lydia sharing a drink with Chester Brady in one of the red vinyl booths.

"Come here a lot?" he asked dryly.

"Couple of times a month for the past two years," she said quite seriously. "The music's good."

"Two years?"

"I told you, that was how long I knew Chester."

"Ah."

He adroitly eased both of them out of the path of a waitress. The woman carried a tray laden with bottles of White Noise beer and a bowl filled with bite-size chunks of something that had been deep-fried beyond recognition.

"Which one is Rose?" Emmett asked Lydia.

"Behind the bar." She led the way through the crowded room with the ease of someone who knew her way around.

Emmett watched her as she moved ahead of him. She made an incongruous picture here in this sordid setting. Her red hair glowed like a cheerful bonfire in the sickly yellow gleam of the table lamps. She had dressed for the dinner with Mercer Wyatt as though she were going to meet with her lawyer or banker. All business in her trim, dark-brown business suit and demure pumps, she looked wildly out of place. But the waitress gave her a friendly nod. Lydia returned the gesture.

"Hi, Becky."

She came to a halt at the far end of the bar. Emmett stopped beside her.

"That's Rose," she said, indicating the huge man with the shaved head pouring whiskey at the other end.

Emmett contemplated the thick neck, mountainous shoulders, and tattoos on biceps that bulged beneath the sleeves of a lime-green T-shirt.

"By any other name," he muttered.

"Rose is really very sweet," Lydia confided.

"I'll bet."

"He's a musical-harmonic para-rez," she said. "Trained as a classical musician. But he prefers rez-jazz."

That explained the excellent sound track playing in the background, Emmett thought. Rose knew music.

"Hey there, Lydia." The big man's face lit up when he spotted her at the end of the bar. "Glad you could drop by. Thought maybe we wouldn't see much of you what with Chester gone and all."

Emmett watched Rose glide toward them. The bartender moved in a soft, easy, coordinated way that belied his size.

"Hi, Rose." Lydia stood on tiptoe and leaned across the bar to brush her lips lightly against Rose's cheek. "Hard to believe Chester's gone, isn't it?"

"To tell you the truth, I'm surprised he lived as long as he did." Rose folded his big arms on the bar. "In the course of his long and varied career, Brady managed to piss off just about everyone who knew him." Rose looked at Emmett. "Who's your friend?"

Emmett put out his hand. "Emmett London. I'm a client of Lydia's."

"Client, huh?"

Rose shook hands firmly but politely, making no attempt to demonstrate his strength with a crushing grip. Emmett concluded that Rose was a man who was comfortable with himself and his size. He thought he understood why Lydia liked him.

"We're on our way to a business dinner," Lydia said.

"No kidding." Rose surveyed her from head to toe. "No offense, Lyd, but brown is not your color."

"I'll remember that next time I go shopping. Rose, we don't have a lot of time. I've got the key to Chester's locker. Mind if I pick up his things?"

"Nope. He once told me you'd be by for them if anything ever happened to him." Rose glanced at the waitress. "Keep an eye on things, Becky. I'll be right back."

Becky raised a hand to indicate she'd heard him.

"This way to the Bank of Rose," Rose said to Lydia.

He unlocked a door behind the bar and led the way into a dark hall. Lydia followed. Emmett trailed after her.

The door was surprisingly heavy. It closed behind the trio with a solid thud. Mag-steel, Emmett thought. It would take a blowtorch or a small bomb to get through it. The walls of the hallway were lined with the same material.

Rose rezzed a switch. The cold light of a fluo-rez tube in the ceiling illuminated the hallway, revealing two rows of mag-steel lockers. All of them were secured with heavy mag-rez locks.

"Looks like a bank vault," Emmett said.

"With twenty-four-hour security." The fluo-rez light gleamed on Rose's bald head as he walked down the aisle between the lockers. "To get in here, you got to get past me or my partner. The Surreal Lounge is open day and night, so there's never a time when there's no one behind the bar. Proud to say the Bank of Rose has never been robbed."

"Or audited or insured or taxed or licensed, either, I'll bet," Emmett concluded.

Rose came to a halt in front of a locker. "Nope. We here at the Bank of Rose don't have much to do with the various regulatory authorities."

"Rose caters to a rather select clientele," Lydia murmured as she reached into her shoulder bag.

"We rent out lockers to folks who prefer not to patronize what you'd call a more traditional bank," Rose explained.

"Probably because most of 'em would get arrested on sight if they went through the front door of a real bank." Lydia held out the key that had come in the brown envelope. "Any idea what Chester kept here?"

"No." Rose took the key from her. "Bank of Rose policy is not to ask any awkward or embarrassing questions. So long as you pay your rent on time, you're a valued customer."

The lock clicked as the key briefly disrupted the pattern of its internal resonance. Rose opened the door. Lydia stepped forward to peer into the small locker.

"Looks like an old duffel bag," she said. She started to reach for it.

"I'll get it," Emmett said.

She got out of his way so that he could haul the small, battered canvas bag out of the locker. It was not very heavy.

Lydia looked at the old bag. "I wonder why he wanted me to get this."

"Not like he had anyone else to leave his stuff to." Rose closed the locker door. "You were the closest thing to a friend that old Chester had. He always told me that the two of you had a lot in common."

Lydia set the duffel bag in front of her on the floor of the Slider. She unzipped it while Emmett got in behind the wheel and rezzed the engine. In the reflected glow of the dashboard she could see a bulging envelope and a small paper sack.

"Maybe you're about to become the lucky owner of a winning lottery ticket," Emmett said.

"I won't hold my breath." Lydia removed the envelope. "Chester was not what anyone would call lucky."

She broke the seal on the envelope and took out the handful of yellowed papers inside. She glanced at the first one. The tide of gloom that had ebbed and flowed around her all day rose once more, swamped her again for a moment.

"What are they?" Emmett asked.

"Chester's applications for membership in the Society of Para-archaeologists. And the rejections the Society sent back to him." She shook her head, amazed. "He always talked about how much he disdained the Society. But according to these, he applied for membership every year for twenty years."

"And got rejected every year?"

"Uh-huh. Poor Chester. Deep down, he must have desperately wanted to become legitimate."

"I doubt if those papers constitute his retirement plan."

"Probably not."

She put the papers back into the envelope and reached into the duffel for the paper sack. She froze the instant she touched it. A thrill of aware-ness sang through her nerves. Psi energy.

"Oh, my," she whispered.

Emmett glanced at her sharply. "What is it?"

"Something old." Very gently she put the paper sack on her lap. "Some-thing very, very old."

"Harmonic artifact?"

"Yes." There was no mistaking the resonance. She was a para-archaeologist, after all. One of the best. "But there's something different. I could swear I'm picking up a trace of trap energy. But that's impossible. No traps have ever been found outside the Dead Cities. No way to anchor them."

"Never say never when it comes to the ancient Harmonics. There's still one hell of a lot that we don't know about them. Be careful, Lydia."

"Hey, I'm the expert here, remember?"

"I remember," he said. "Be careful anyway."

"I'll bet you were a real pain to work with when you ghost-hunted pro-fessionally."

"It was mentioned from time to time," he agreed. "On the plus side, I never lost a single para-archaeologist."

She ignored him, turning the paper sack cautiously in her hands. Then she opened it very carefully and looked inside. In the dim light she could just barely make out a dark, rounded object about the size of her two hands clasped together.

"There's something strange about the resonance," she said. "It's defi-nitely genuine. Very, very old. But the vibrations are different from anything else I've ever sensed from artifacts this old."

"Still catching traces of trap energy?"

"I'm not sure. There's too much else going on here. It feels almost like—" She broke off abruptly. It was never good policy to make a fool of oneself in front of the client.

"Like what?"

"You wouldn't believe me if I told you." Lydia held the paper sack cradled in both hands and tried to get a grip on her runaway imagination. Impossible, she thought. It couldn't be.

But what if?

Her euphoria evaporated as another *what if* occurred to her. What if she really had lost her para-rez pitch, just as Ryan and the others assumed? What if the disaster six months ago was only now producing a delayed reaction? What if she was wrong?

"Lydia? You okay?"

"Yes."

"What's inside the sack?"

Emmett's calm voice brought her out of the downward spiral. She stared through the window of the Slider and saw that they had left the busy city streets behind. They were climbing one of the hills above town, a neighborhood of exclusive estates. Massive gates guarded the long drives that led to the mansions.

"Lydia? Are you going to tell me what's inside the sack?"

"Yes." There was only one way to find out if she held something truly incredible in her hands or if she should check into a nice, quiet para-psych ward first thing tomorrow morning.

Deep breaths.

She took one, steeled herself, and reached into the sack. Another, much stronger shock of tingling excitement went through her when she actually touched the warm, smooth surface.

"It feels like a bottle," she whispered.

Emmett did not take his eyes off the winding road. "What about the trap energy you said you felt?"

"Stop worrying. I know what I'm doing."

He said nothing, but he pulled the Slider over to the side of the road and de-rezzed the engine. He turned in the seat to watch intently as she slowly removed the artifact from the paper sack.

She saw at once that she had been right about the bottle shape.

"What the hell is it?" Emmett asked softly.

"An unguent jar, I think." She studied it more closely, trying to focus on the shimmering surface. "But not like any that I've ever seen."

She stared at the thing she held. In the dim backwash of illumination provided by the dashboard the sealed jar seemed to glow with an inner light of its own. Colors shifted, stirred, and swirled on the surface. She saw shades of reds and golds that had no name. They flowed into strange greens and blues before she could describe them.

She swallowed hard. "Emmett? Please tell me I'm not seeing things. I really don't want to have to go back into therapy."

He gazed fixedly at the jar. "Hell, that's not—It can't be. We need better light."

He reached into the console between the seats and removed a small flashlight. He rezzed it and aimed the beam at the ancient jar.

For a long moment they both just sat and stared at the artifact. In the bright light of the flash, the colors on the surface of the bottle leaped into full, pulsing life. A restless sea of light and darkness surged around the widest portion of the elegantly shaped jar. Each hue seemed to be animated by its own inner energy source. Vast depths of dazzling light and color appeared and disappeared.

"Dreamstone," Emmett said in a voice that held no inflection at all.

"Impossible," Lydia said again.

"You know as well as I do that there's nothing else it could be." He took the jar from her and turned it slightly so that the flashlight beam played across its surface. "Pure worked dreamstone. Damn. Talk about a retirement plan."

Lydia shook her head slowly, unable to believe her eyes or her para-rez senses.

Dreamstone was well named. Small deposits of it were occasionally found, usually embedded in clear quartz in the vicinity of dead volcanoes. Not only was it extremely rare but it had thus far defied any attempt to extract it from the protective quartz. It shattered at the slightest touch, simultaneously appearing to melt and fracture into microscopic shards.

No technology yet devised by the human population on Harmony had been able to handle it without destroying it. For prospectors and mining companies, it was indeed the stuff of dreams. Beautiful to look at when it was found, it evaporated the instant you reached out to touch it.

But the unguent jar in Emmett's hand was firm and solid proof that the ancient Harmonics had discovered how to work dreamstone.

Lydia felt the hair stir on the nape of her neck. "Maybe this is what got Chester killed."

"I'd say that is an excellent possibility." Emmett gave the jar a quarter turn. "Incredible."

"Do you realize what this means?"

"It means that if Chester had lived long enough to sell this to a museum or a private collector, he would have been set for life."

Lydia waved that aside. "The monetary value is beside the point. You can't put a price on it, since nothing else like it has ever been found."

"Trust me, Lydia, you can put a price on anything."

"But the significance of worked dreamstone is absolutely extraordinary. Don't you see? This jar means that it can be done. There must be a way to psychically tune dreamstone so that it can be manipulated like other raw materials. Who knows what properties it has in this form?"

"Good question." He did not look up from his examination of the jar.

"Somewhere in their past, the Harmonics found a way to actually mine the stuff."

"Yes."

She frowned. He did not seem to be as impressed by the full implications of this staggering discovery as she was. Then again, he was a businessman, not an archaeologist. Make that *ghost-hunter-businessman,* she amended silently. Probably took a lot to impress him.

Emmett gave the jar another turn. "I wonder where Brady found it?"

"Who knows? Chester was a ruin rat. He was always exploring illegally on his own. He must have stumbled across this jar on one of his forays into the catacombs."

She watched as Emmett gave the jar another quarter turn, bringing another section into the beam of the flashlight. When she saw the figure of a bird in flight imprisoned forever within the shifting rivers of color, she nearly stopped breathing altogether.

"*Emmett.*"

"I see it," he said.

Now he did sound impressed. As well he should be, she thought. In all the years in which humans had been excavating the ruins of the Harmonics, no one had ever come across any indication that the ancient people had indulged in representational art.

The long-vanished inhabitants of the Dead Cities had left no pictures or drawings of animals, plants, or themselves. There were no seascapes or landscapes, no scenes of what the world had looked like to them or images of how they had seen themselves in their environment—at least none that humans could interpret.

Until now.

Now there was a small bird flying in the depths of a sea of colors flowing across the surface of a little jar that should not exist.

Emmett straightened slowly and clicked off the flashlight. "Looks like your pal Brady made the most significant discovery since Caldwell Frost blundered into the ruins of Old Frequency and decided that someone had made him a god."

"I'm stunned," Lydia whispered. "This is so amazing."

"Anything else in the duffel bag?"

"What? Oh, right, the bag." Lydia peered into the unzipped canvas carryall again and rummaged around. Her hand brushed against another envelope. "There's something."

She withdrew the envelope and opened it. A photo fell out. She held it to the light and saw another picture of herself and Chester in a booth at the Surreal Lounge. There was a familiar volume of the *Journal of Paraarchaeology* propped in front of Chester, who was beaming proudly.

"He did like photos of the two of you together, didn't he?" Emmett said.

"Yes." She got teary again as she examined the photo. "He had several pictures taken of us."

"Must have fed his fantasy that the two of you were a couple."

"Probably." She blinked rapidly to clear her eyes. "This was a special one, though. I had just published a paper in the journal. Coauthored with Ryan, naturally. I had to fight tooth and nail, but I made sure that Chester got credit as a consultant on the project."

"Probably his only brush with legitimacy."

"I hadn't realized until now how important it must have been to him," she whispered.

"You'd better put the jar in your purse until we get home." Emmett handed it to her. "And whatever you do, don't say anything about it in front of Mercer Wyatt and his wife."

"What do you think I am?" she asked as she rewrapped the jar and stashed it inside her purse. "Crazy?"

Emmett's mouth curved slightly as he rezzed the engine and pulled back onto the road. "No, I don't think you're crazy."

Lydia settled into her seat, clutching her purse very tightly. Excitement snapped and sizzled through her again. Euphoria followed in its wake. Worked dreamstone. And a picture of a bird.

"Thanks," she said, feeling very smug. "I appreciate that."

Chapter Fourteen

Midway through the painfully formal dinner, Lydia reached a major conclusion about her hostess. She did not like Tamara Wyatt. More precisely, she did not like the way Tamara looked at Emmett when she thought no one was watching.

The speculative gleam in Tamara's gaze reminded Lydia of the way Fuzz looked when he peered at the pretzel jar. As if he was willing to devote a lot of thought and energy to a consideration of ways and means of removing the lid.

Tamara was sleek and polished, with an indefinable edge of glamour that would set her apart in any room. Her dark hair was bound up in an elegant chignon that accented her aristocratic cheekbones and fine jawline. A fortune in gemstones sparkled at her throat. She wore amber set in gold in her ears. The deep decolletage of her gown stopped just short of being indiscreet.

Lydia had realized when they had arrived an hour and a half earlier that Emmett had met both the Wyatts previously. Mercer and Emmett had greeted each other with polite civility. But something else had been going on between Tamara and Emmett just beneath the surface.

It had taken her a little longer than it should have to recognize the resonance patterns between these two, Lydia thought. She excused herself for the delay. After all, she had been seriously distracted this evening. Approximately one-third of her attention was focused on the bizarre experience of being entertained by the head of the Cadence Guild. The remainder was consumed with speculation about the extraordinary little jar Chester had bequeathed to her. It was all she could do not to excuse herself every five minutes to run down the hall to check the elegant armoire where the butler had placed her purse.

Calm down, she told herself as a white-gloved waiter removed the plate in front of her. If the jar wasn't safe here in Mercer Wyatt's mansion, it wasn't safe anywhere. The only other place she'd seen with so much security was the University of Cadence Museum.

"So, Lydia, you're in the private consulting business?" Mercer asked with seemingly polite interest.

Tamara smiled. "Rather young to have left university work, aren't you? Most consultants tend to be older. More experienced."

Lydia pulled herself away from concerns about her purse. She ignored Tamara and studied Mercer instead.

Mercer Wyatt had to be at least forty years older than his wife. Silver-haired, with hawklike features, he was a man who was clearly accustomed to the accoutrements of money and power. He wore his amber on his hands in the form of large, heavy rings. As head of the Guild, he would necessarily have to be a very powerful dissonance-energy para-rez, she thought.

"It's not routine for a para-archaeologist my age to go into the private sector," Lydia said, "but it's not unheard of."

Conversation to this point had consisted of the sort of superficial patter she had learned to tolerate at faculty teas. Lydia had a feeling that the real talking would be done after dinner.

"Some people don't fit into the academic bureaucracy very well," Emmett said casually. "Just as some can't tolerate the corporate environment. Lydia has what you'd call an entrepreneurial spirit."

Tamara gave Lydia a polished smile. "How did Emmett find you?"

"I'm listed with the Society of Para-archaeologists as a consultant, and I advertise in the *Journal of Para-archaeology*," Lydia said smoothly.

"That's hardly a guarantee of honesty and integrity, is it?" Tamara said. "There are so many frauds and scam artists in the antiquities trade."

"Very true," Lydia murmured. "But on the whole, I'd have to say that one's odds of getting a dishonest P-A from the Society's lists are considerably lower than the odds of getting a dishonest hunter from the Guild hall."

Tamara's eyes darkened with anger. "The Guild maintains the strictest standards."

"Uh-huh." Lydia spooned up a bite of the fruit ice that had been served for dessert. "Is that why I've had at least two break-ins recently by ghost-hunters?"

Mercer pinned Emmett with a cold glare. "What the devil is she talking about?"

Emmett shrugged. "You heard her. She's had some unfortunate experiences with hunters recently. Kind of soured her view of the profession, I'm afraid."

Mercer turned back to Lydia. "Kindly explain yourself."

Lydia put down her spoon. "As the head of the Guild here in Cadence, you must be aware that there are some ghost-hunters running around the city committing illegal acts. What's more, they are summoning ghosts to aid in the commission of those crimes. My apartment has been vandalized twice."

Mercer's jaw clenched. He flicked a quick look at Emmett and then went back to Lydia. "Are you absolutely certain ghost-hunters were involved?"

"I saw the ghosts they summoned," she said very steadily. "Ask Emmett. He chased off one of the hunters. Would have caught him if the little sneak hadn't had an accomplice waiting for him in the parking lot."

Mercer's piercing gaze swung back to Emmett. "Is this true?"

"All true," Emmett said easily. "I assume you can assure us that the intruders were not working for the Guild?"

"Of course they weren't working for the Guild." Mercer flung down his napkin and stood abruptly. "I assure you, I will have my people look into the matter. The Guild polices its own."

"How convenient," Lydia said politely.

Mercer glowered at her.

Lydia turned toward Tamara. "So, what's it like being the wife of the head of the Cadence Guild? What do you do besides go to the Restoration Ball every year?"

"I manage to keep busy," Tamara said coolly.

Mercer studied her with obvious pride. "Tamara is an executive in her own right. Thanks to her, the Guild has established a very active foundation that funds several Cadence charities. She oversees the administration of the Foundation."

Tamara's expression warmed noticeably under the praise. "I don't do it all alone, of course. I am extremely fortunate to have Denver Galbraith-

Thorndyke as my chief administrator. I'm sure you're aware of the Galbraith-Thorndyke family's long history here in Cadence?"

"As in the Galbraith-Thorndykes who pretty much dominate the social scene?" Lydia was impressed in spite of herself. "Give tons of money to charity? Patrons of the University Museum, sit on all the important boards, et cetera, et cetera? Of course I've heard of them. I didn't know they were connected to the Guild."

Mercer chuckled. "They weren't—until Tamara approached them and asked young Denver to take over the job of administering the Guild Foundation."

"Nice move, Tamara," Emmett congratulated her.

"Thank you," Tamara murmured. "I see it as a major first step toward elevating the image of the Guild in the community."

"Indeed," Mercer said briskly. "A brilliant first step, if I do say so myself. Young Denver is a lawyer. He has connections with all of the movers and shakers in town."

"So how come he went to work for the Guild?" Lydia asked bluntly.

Tamara looked annoyed, but Mercer merely chuckled.

"Usual story," he said easily. "Young scion of a rich and socially prominent family longs to prove himself to his father. Denver did not want to join the family law firm. Didn't want to go to work for good old Dad, I suppose. He wanted to stand on his own two feet. Tamara offered him the Foundation job and he grabbed it."

"He's very committed," Tamara said.

Mercer turned to Emmett. "You and I need to talk privately. Tamara, please take Lydia into the salon for tea. We will join you later."

"Of course, my dear." Tamara rose gracefully from her chair and began to usher Lydia out of the room.

Lydia glanced at Emmett. He inclined his head a bare half inch. She had no problem at all reading his message. She hesitated and then decided that he was right. They might learn more separately than they could together. Without a word she followed Tamara out of the dining room.

They walked down a hall paneled in a dark, richly grained wood that had been polished until it glowed. Tamara led the way through double doors set with squares of beveled glass into a room done in yellow and maroon.

A frisson of awareness sparkled across Lydia's nerves. She turned and saw the cabinet filled with ancient Harmonic artifacts. So many of them grouped in close proximity produced more than enough resonance energy to reach her here on the other side of the salon. Automatically she went toward the cabinet and came to a halt in front of it.

"A magnificent collection," she murmured.

"My husband started it years ago, long before we were married." Tamara picked up the pot that had been placed on a small round table. "Tea?"

"Thank you, yes." Lydia studied an oddly shaped green quartz panel that had probably formed a portion of a tomb chamber door. "You and your husband were married a year ago, weren't you? I seem to recall seeing something about it in the papers. You're not from Cadence, are you?"

"No. I was living in Resonance City when I met Mercer." Tamara walked forward, a cup and saucer in one hand. "He attended a meeting of the Guild Council there. We were introduced at a reception."

"I see."

"The reception was held to announce the engagement of the head of the Resonance Guild," Tamara clarified softly.

An icy sensation swept through Lydia. She watched her fingers to make certain that they did not tremble when she took the cup and saucer from Tamara. It wouldn't do to spill rez-tea on what was no doubt a fabulously expensive carpet. The Guild would probably send her a bill that she would not be able to pay.

"No kidding." Lydia sipped tea. It was, as everything else had been at dinner, excellent. "Whom did the Resonance Guild boss marry?"

Tamara looked amused. "He was engaged to marry me. But things did not work out. We ended the engagement soon after the reception. I moved here to Cadence a short time later."

"I see." Stop right now, Lydia told herself. Just because you see an accident waiting to happen doesn't mean you have to help it along.

But she couldn't stop. She had to know for certain.

"So, who was this Guild boss you were going to marry back in Resonance?"

"Emmett, of course," Tamara said sweetly. "He was the head of the Resonance Guild for six years until he resigned ten months ago."

Mercer lowered himself into the plum-colored leather of the massive reading chair. He raised his brandy glass to his mouth and studied Emmett above the rim. "I will get right to the point. I had two reasons for asking you to come here tonight. One of those reasons is that I wish to offer you a bargain, son."

"I'm not your son." Emmett rested an arm along the top of the mantel. "And I sure as hell won't agree to any deal until I know all of the terms."

Mercer exhaled deeply. "I'll level with you, Emmett. I need your help. And I think I can help you in return."

"Why do you need me? You've got a Guild full of people you can call on for help."

Mercer shook his head. "Not for this. Let me explain. I haven't yet made any official public announcement, but I intend to step down sometime during the coming year. Only the members of my personal staff are aware of my decision. They have all been sworn to secrecy."

This was the last thing he had expected to hear tonight, Emmett thought. Mercer Wyatt had held the Cadence Guild in an iron grip for more than three decades. It was widely assumed that he would die at the helm.

"You're going to retire?" Emmett said warily.

"I've been running this show for a long time. Until recently the Guild was always the most important thing in my life. My first wife was a wonderful woman, but I never took the time to know her. After her death I was left with two children. I let someone else raise them. They're both grown now, and I've got three grandkids, but I hardly know any of them."

"Let me guess. You've finally decided to stop and smell the roses, is that it?"

"You find that amusing?"

"Let's just say it's unanticipated. What the hell brought on the sudden change? Get a health scare from your doctor?"

"Nothing like that. I got a new wife."

"Oh, yeah, right. Must have slipped my mind."

"I am in love for the first time in my life, Emmett," Mercer said very seriously. "My marriage to Tamara is a Marriage of Convenience at the moment, as you know, but we plan to convert it into a Covenant Marriage."

Emmett stared at him. "You want more children?"

"There are other reasons for entering a Covenant Marriage besides the desire to have children," Mercer reminded him.

Emmett grunted. "True love? Give me a break. Aren't you a little old for that kind of romantic nonsense, Mercer?"

"You are not a romantic man, Emmett."

"Neither were you, last time I checked. Terminating a Covenant Marriage is a legal and financial nightmare." He did not add what they both knew, which was that adultery was one of the very few legally accepted reasons for dissolving a Covenant Marriage. "What's the point of getting into one if you don't want kids?"

Mercer stretched out his legs and gazed into the fire. "Obviously you do not understand, so we'll drop the subject. The bottom line here is my intention to step down."

"No offense, Mercer, but I find it a little tough to grasp the concept."

"Why? I'm forty years older than Tamara. I don't know how long I'll have with her. I intend to enjoy every minute of whatever time I have left, however. I've got money, I've got my health, and I've got a beautiful woman at my side. I'd be a fool to continue to devote myself to the Guild."

Emmett contemplated him for a while. "Does Tamara know of your decision?"

"She knows."

"Huh." He shrugged. "So what does this have to do with me?"

"I want your help. And I'm willing to bargain for it. I know why you are here in Cadence. My people told me about your missing nephew. I may be able to assist you."

Tonight was turning out to be one big surprise after another, Emmett thought. There was nothing he could do but go with the flow. "Before we talk about doing any kind of deal, you'd better tell me what you want from me."

Mercer nodded slowly and sipped his brandy. After a moment he set the glass aside. He propped his elbows on the arms of the heavy chair and steepled his fingers.

"As I said, I am preparing to step down. But I intend to do so in an orderly manner, one that will leave the Guild on the right course for the future."

"In other words," Emmett said, "you want to handpick your successor."

"Precisely. I have worked for years to create a strong organization that can take care of its own. To a large extent, I have achieved my goals. All members in good standing can be assured of an excellent pay scale and a safety net of benefits for themselves and their families."

"So long as they follow orders, don't ask any questions, and don't cross you," Emmett said.

"I have always rewarded loyalty well."

"And crushed anyone who stood up to you or questioned your decisions. You're a real old-fashioned kind of guy, Mercer."

"I will admit that in the past you and I have differed on the subject of how an organization such as the Guild should be run."

"You could say that. Your approach is about seventy years out of date."

"It is true that I have honored tradition during my tenure as chief of the Cadence Guild."

Emmett grunted again. Hard to argue that one.

"It may interest you to know, however," Mercer continued, "that I have concluded it is time for the Cadence Guild to change."

"I'll believe that when I see it."

"I intend for Cadence to follow the lead of the Resonance Guild," Mercer said steadily. "I want to see it restructured and modernized along the same lines."

Emmett searched his face. "You're serious, aren't you?"

"Entirely serious. But sudden shifts cannot be effected overnight. Furthermore, they must be accompanied by strong leadership. I shall begin the process of change this year, with Tamara's help."

"You mean her Guild Foundation work?"

"It's a start, and she is very committed to her charities. Her Foundation will go far toward helping to change the image of the Guild here in Cadence. But the task of restructuring the organization itself cannot be completed in the few months during which I will remain as head of it. Therefore, I must make arrangements to, as you say, handpick my successor."

A sudden dark suspicion sparked. Emmett folded his arms across his chest and leaned one shoulder against the mantel. "Got someone in mind for the job?"

"Yes, of course." Mercer smiled humorlessly. "You."

Emmett exhaled slowly. "I hate to have to be the one to tell you this, Mercer, but I think you may have accidentally gotten fried the last time you summoned a ghost."

"I realize my proposal is coming as something of a shock. But surely you can see why I want you to consider it. That's all I'm asking at the moment. There's no rush. We've got a year to make plans. Plenty of time to work out the details."

"There's nothing to work out. I'm giving you my answer right now. I don't want the job. I've gone into the private sector, Mercer. I'm just a businessman these days."

Mercer unlocked his hands and leaned forward. His fierce eyes glowed with energy and determination. "Listen to me, son—"

"I am not your son," Emmett repeated through his teeth.

"Sorry. Slip of the tongue."

The hell it was, Emmett thought. They were both aware of the gossip and rumors that had circulated for years. He had no intention of going down that road tonight. Not with Mercer Wyatt.

"As I was saying," Mercer continued, "I want to leave the Guild in good hands. Hands that can steer it on a new, modern course. You are the best possible person to do that."

"No."

"You're the one who single-handedly restructured the Resonance Guild when you took charge. You're the one who established the new ways, turned it into a business, made it respectable. I want you to do the same for the Cadence Guild."

"In case you haven't heard, I'm out of Guild politics. I'm a business consultant now."

"That is precisely what I want," Mercer said seriously. "A business consultant who is uniquely qualified to help transform the Cadence Guild into a respected business enterprise."

"Forget it, Mercer. I don't want any part of your plan. I wish you luck with it, but I don't want to be involved."

"I see." Mercer sat back in his chair. He did not look defeated; he looked more like a man who was content to bide his time. "We'll leave that for the moment, then. Let's move on to other matters."

Emmett came away from the mantel. He walked to the window and looked out over the lights of the city below. "Do you really know something about my nephew, Mercer? Or was that just a lure to get me here tonight so that you could try to talk me into taking over the Guild?"

"I'll be honest with you. I have no direct knowledge of young Quinn's whereabouts. But my sources tell me that he followed a young woman here to Cadence. True?"

"Yes."

"The young lady apparently disappeared, and your nephew, who, I understand, is a dissonance-energy para-rez, vanished shortly thereafter, according to my information."

Emmett looked out at the brooding, moonlit ruins of the Dead City. "Your information is good."

"There are some advantages to having been in my position as head of the Cadence Guild for so long," Mercer said dryly. "I've had plenty of time to set up reliable information networks both inside and outside the organization."

Emmett turned slowly to face him. "What do you know?"

"I know that Quinn's lady friend is not the first young person to disappear here in Cadence in recent weeks," Mercer went on. "No one has taken much notice of the fact because none of the missing persons was underage and none appears to have had much in the way of concerned family."

"Until now."

"Until now," Mercer agreed. "In addition, there has been no indication of foul play."

"How many have turned up missing?"

"I can't be certain. You'd be amazed at how many young people disappear every year. Had no idea myself until I started looking into it. Most of them wind up on the streets or in Curtain cults. Some go to another city. No one seems to notice."

"Why did you suddenly decide to take notice?"

"Because when I heard that you were in town looking for your nephew, I made a few inquiries. I learned that some of the young people who have disappeared in recent weeks have been dissonance-energy para-rezes. Untrained ghost-hunters who were in the process of applying to the Guild. They never appeared for basic training and indoctrination. My first assumption was that someone had enticed them into a gang or cult or an unlicensed excavation team. The Guild takes a dim view of outsiders using ghost-hunters for illegal purposes."

"Bad for the public image," Emmett said dryly.

"Yes. This sort of thing has occurred occasionally in the past. It's been relatively easy to put a stop to it. But this time there are complications."

"Tried going to the police?" Emmett suggested mildly.

Mercer gave him a disgusted look. "Of course not. If I did that, the media would get wind of it in no time. I won't have the papers running headlines declaring that the Guild can no longer police itself. Not on my watch, by God."

"Right." Mainstreaming the Cadence Guild was not going to be easy, Emmett thought. Not with attitudes like this at the top.

"As I was saying," Mercer continued, "I have concluded that you and I might be able to work together."

"You mean you're willing to give me access to the resources of the Guild to help me look for Quinn?"

Mercer closed his eyes briefly. When he opened them there was a bleak rage in his gaze. "I only wish it were that simple. I am sorry to tell you that the resources of the Guild cannot be relied upon at the moment."

Emmett watched him for a long time as the full implications of that statement sank in. "Maybe you'd better explain."

"I have reason to believe that there is a traitor in my organization," Mercer said wearily. "Someone close to me."

Emmett said nothing. He knew what it must have cost Mercer to acknowledge such a thing.

"I had to go outside my own Guild just to discover what little information I managed to learn about the situation involving your nephew," Mercer said. "Someone I trust is plotting against me, Emmett."

"Every Guild chief has enemies. Fact of life."

"Of course. And I have dealt with many in the past. But this is different. More insidious. I have been unable to isolate the traitor. It could be anyone on my administrative staff. *Anyone.*"

"Someone who knows about your plans for the future of the Cadence Guild and doesn't like them?"

"I believe so. But it may be more than that. It may be personal. I simply don't know at this point. I only know I can no longer trust my staff."

"What does that have to do with luring young, untrained hunters off the street?"

"It has occurred to me that this traitor, whoever he is, may be trying to create his own private army of hunters who will take orders directly from him and who will be loyal only to him."

"Set up a rival organization? Hell, Mercer, that's a little over the top, isn't it?"

"Think about it," Mercer insisted. "If this bastard wishes to go against me, he will need a power base. That means he will need his own trained ghost-hunters. What better way to do that than to grab young ones who have not yet been indoctrinated into the Guild?"

Emmett whistled soundlessly. "Are you sure you're not sliding into paranoia here, Mercer?"

"I'm being careful. There's a difference."

There was a difference, Emmett reflected, but it was not always easy to see it when you were a Guild boss.

Mercer Wyatt was not a stupid man, he reminded himself, even if he was seriously lovestruck at the moment. Wyatt was smart, powerful, and, above all, he was a survivor. If his instincts told him he had a traitor on his staff, chances were good that he was right.

Emmett studied the pattern of the carpet beneath his feet for a while. Then he looked up. "What all this boils down to is you want me to get rid of your so-called traitor for you."

"I won't deny that I need your assistance in this unpleasant affair, since I can no longer trust my personal staff. The way I see it, our interests are aligned, son. You want to find your nephew. I want the person who may have caused him to disappear."

Emmett ignored the *son* reference this time. He had other priorities now. He contemplated the city lights for several long seconds while he weighed the pros and cons of getting more closely involved with Mercer Wyatt.

The truth was, he had very little choice. Quinn's safety came first.

"What information can you give me?" he said at last.

"Not much, I admit. As I said, I had to go outside the Guild to get even that. On your own, you will no doubt stumble onto the few facts I've got. But at least I can save you some time. And time may be of the essence here."

Emmett looked at him over his shoulder. "I'm listening."

Mercer leaned forward in his chair, his expression intense. "The day your nephew disappeared, he paid a visit to a youth shelter in the Old Quarter near the east wall."

"What's the name of the place?" Emmett asked swiftly.

"It's called the Transverse Wave. It was founded years ago by the Anderson Ames Trust. It's a place to start looking, Emmett, but I want your word that you will be discreet."

"Why the hell do you care if I'm discreet?"

Mercer sighed. "Two years ago Anderson Ames died. When the lawyers finally unraveled the trust, which took several months, it was discovered to be nearly bankrupt. The Transverse Wave Youth Shelter was in danger of closing last year, but at the last minute new funding was found for it. Just in time to enable it to remain open."

"Oh, shit." He had the whole picture now, Emmett realized. "You're going to tell me that the Guild Foundation stepped in and is now supporting the Transverse Wave, aren't you? The reason you want me to be discreet is because the shelter is one of Tamara's new pet charity projects."

Mercer narrowed his eyes. He suddenly looked like the ruthless specter-cat that he was. "Tamara knows nothing of my suspicions. I want this mess cleaned up without any publicity that might embarrass her or the Guild Foundation. Is that understood?"

Chapter Fifteen

Lydia clutched her purse very tightly on her knees and smiled blandly through the window at the guard as Emmett drove out through the front gates of the Wyatt mansion.

Silence welled up inside the car. It thickened rapidly.

"If I had to rate the evening on a scale of faculty social events at the university, I would have to say it scored a two," she said finally.

"That high?" Emmett asked.

"Somewhat less tolerable than the monthly sherry hour but not quite as bad as the weekly coffee hour in the Department of Para-archaeology."

"Personally, I'm giving it a one," Emmett said.

She glanced at him. "You mean it was worse than your engagement party where your fiancée decided she was in love with Mercer Wyatt instead of you?"

"So you heard about that, huh?" Emmett downshifted for a curve. "Sounds like you and Tamara got friendly in the salon."

"Actually, the subject of your engagement came up right at the beginning, and conversation sort of fizzled after that. I spent a lot of time admiring the Wyatt collection of Harmonic antiquities. Fortunately, I can talk about relics for hours on end. By the time you came out of the library with Mercer, Tamara was half asleep from boredom."

"Tamara has a short attention span if the subject is not one of great personal interest to her. Take our engagement, for example."

"Something tells me she can be very focused if the subject *is* one of great personal interest to her." Lydia paused. "She wears amber. Is it for real or just for looks?"

"It's for real. She's a strong dissonance-energy para-rez."

"I see." It figured, Lydia thought. Statistically speaking, most ghost-hunters were male, but she had worked with more than one female hunter in the catacombs. "Well, if she was engaged to you, I'd say she must have been extremely interested. Probably liked the thought of becoming the wife of the Resonance Guild boss."

A cold smile came and went at the corners of Emmett's mouth. "You did pick up a lot of trivia over tea."

She whipped around in the seat, anger sweeping away her control. *"Why didn't you tell me?"*

"Couple of reasons." He sounded far too casual. "First, given your general opinion of ghost-hunters, I didn't see any reason to bring up Guild politics. Second, I didn't think it had any direct bearing on the situation."

She stared at him. "I don't believe this. You're an ex-Guild boss and you don't think it has any *bearing* on our business arrangements?"

"Does whatever happened to you during those forty-eight hours you spent underground six months ago have any bearing on them?"

"That's entirely different."

"Each of us has a past. Neither of us can change it. But we've both moved on. I'm no longer in the Guild."

"The heck you aren't. Once a guildman, always a guildman."

"Some people say that once a tangler's been badly fried in a trap, she's never the same again."

"Stop trying to pretend there's a parallel here," she shot back.

"What do you want to do, Lydia? Do you want out of the contract?"

"No, damn it, you're not going to get rid of me that easily."

"Then we have to find a way to work together."

"How can we do that when you keep springing these surprises on me?" she demanded furiously.

"Just because we have a contract doesn't mean we have to tell each other every damn personal thing that ever happened to us, does it?"

"The fact that you're a Guild boss is not exactly a private, personal matter."

"I'm an ex-Guild boss."

"How come I never heard of you?"

"Can you name the heads of the Frequency or Crystal City Guilds?"

"Well . . . no." She frowned. "I admit, I've never paid much attention to Guild politics outside of Cadence. I had heard something to the effect that the Resonance Guild had instituted some changes, but—"

"But you were skeptical, so you didn't take any notice. Is that it?"

"It wasn't that so much as that I didn't think those changes would have any influence on the Cadence Guild. At least not while Mercer Wyatt is in charge."

"If it makes you feel any better, you probably wouldn't have remembered my name, even if you had followed the news." Emmett guided the Slider through an intersection. "I kept a low profile while I held the position."

"I see."

There was another brittle silence. Lydia fumed. She had a contract with a Guild boss. Make that ex-Guild boss.

A freelance consultant had to be flexible, she thought. She was no longer safely ensconced in academia, with its rigid hierarchy and social rules, both written and unwritten. If she was going to establish herself as a private consultant, she would have to take a few risks.

"Why did you decide to step down?" she asked gruffly.

"I ran the Resonance Guild for six years. It took me that long to get it restructured organizationally. When I was finished, I wanted out of the job. So I turned down the board's offer to renew my contract, and I made sure they appointed Daniel instead."

"Who's Daniel?"

"My younger brother."

"So you handpicked your successor?"

"Daniel and I think alike when it comes to Guild politics. He'll keep the organization moving forward in the new direction. In a few more years no one will even remember the old days. The Resonance Guild will be just one more major corporation in the city."

Lydia hesitated, but morbid curiosity got the better of her. "When did you tell Tamara that you were planning to step down?"

"A few days before our engagement party. Since she did not immediately give me back my ring, I assumed she understood and supported my decision."

"Probably thought she could talk you into changing your mind."

"We had a few conversations on the subject," Emmett admitted. "I didn't change my mind."

He eased the Slider into the parking lot of Lydia's apartment complex.

"In the six years I spent reorganizing the Resonance Guild, Tamara was my one major miscalculation."

"No kidding."

He brought the car to a halt and shut off the engine. For a moment he just sat there behind the wheel, saying nothing. Lydia got the feeling that he was thinking. Hard.

"You figure I should have known right from the start that it was the idea of being married to the head of the Guild, not me personally, that she loved?" he asked neutrally.

"Hey, don't feel bad." Lydia gripped the handle and opened the door. "I wasn't any smarter about Ryan. He was only interested in me as long as I was moving up in the para-archaeology department and could write papers that got our names in print."

"You wrote the papers?" Emmett inquired.

"Ryan's a good P-A, but he's not as good as I am," she said evenly. "After my Lost Weekend, it was obvious that I was not going to be real useful to him as a coauthor, at least not for a long time. But it all worked out very nicely. He got promoted, based on our last paper together. Now, as head of the department, he gets his name on every paper that is published by the people under him. They do all the research, he gets the credit. Pretty neat, huh?"

She got out of the car, keeping her arms wrapped tightly around her purse. Emmett climbed out from the driver's seat, closed and locked the door, and came around the vehicle to join her. Together they walked toward the stairwell.

"I could have clued you in on Ryan Kelso if I'd been around when you were dating him," Emmett offered.

"I could have told you that Tamara is a shrewd, ambitious woman who won't let anyone or anything get in her way. She's into power. It attracts her."

Emmett de-rezzed the security door. "You can tell that after spending one evening in her company?"

She cleared her throat and strove for an academic tone. "In parapsychological terms, she no doubt connects sex with power and vice versa."

"In other words, when I resigned as head of the Guild, I no longer looked quite as sexy. Is that it?"

Lydia hugged her purse as they started up the stairwell. "Power is always interesting, but it comes in two different forms, the personal, internal kind and the kind that depends on the trappings."

"The trappings?"

"You know—office, position, social standing. That sort of thing. Some people are only attracted to that type of power. I'd say Tamara is in that crowd."

"You may be right." Emmett climbed the stairs beside her. "I know she sure as hell lost interest in me after she found out that I intended to become a business consultant."

"Live and learn," Lydia said.

"So do we still have a contract?"

"Yes," Lydia said, "we still have a contract." They reached the fifth floor together in silence and turned to walk along the corridor to her front door.

Lydia looked down at the purse she had clutched to her bosom. "I've got to find a safe place for this until I decide what to do with it."

"Why don't you put it in a real bank safe-deposit vault tomorrow morning?"

"Good idea. But I can't leave it there indefinitely. This is an incredible find, Emmett. It needs to be properly studied."

He gave her a wicked, knowing grin. "Hey, I've got an idea. You can turn that dreamstone jar over to the university and let Ryan Kelso and his staff write it up for the *Journal of Para-archaeology*."

"Over my dead body," she muttered. Then she thought about Chester and winced. "Guess that wasn't really a good metaphor under the circumstances."

His grin vanished. "Guess not."

"I can't think clearly about the problem of what to do with the jar tonight. I do believe I've had a little too much high-rez input this evening. My nerves aren't accustomed to so much excitement."

"Excitement?"

"Yeah, you know, excitement. This artifact, dinner with the head of the Cadence Guild, the discovery that my first consulting client is the ex-CEO of the Resonance Guild. It takes its toll, you know."

"I see," he said. "Excitement."

"I live a quiet life, for the most part, these days. Oh, now and again I come across dead bodies. And there are the occasional moments of hilarity when I get the odd ghost burning holes in my bedroom wall. But that's about it."

"Sounds quiet, all right." He inserted the key into the lock.

She gave him a sharp glance. "By the way, I almost forgot to ask—did you learn anything useful about your nephew from Wyatt?"

"Maybe."

"That's all you can say? Maybe?"

"He gave me a possible lead," Emmett said casually as he opened the door. "I'll check it out tomorrow."

Lydia stepped into the foyer. "And just what did Boss Wyatt want in exchange for this so-called lead?"

"Has anyone ever told you that you have an extremely cynical streak in your nature?"

"What I've got is a good working understanding of how Guild politics work."

He looked at her, saying nothing.

"At least I know how they work here in Cadence," she amended. "Mercer Wyatt doesn't do anything for anyone out of the goodness of his heart."

Emmett shrugged. He reached down to pick up Fuzz, who was drifting around at his feet. "We made a deal."

Lydia froze. "What kind of deal?"

"It doesn't concern you," he said quietly. "It's Guild business."

"Damn it, don't you dare pull that 'Guild business' routine with me. I'm your consultant in this thing, remember? I have a right to know what's going on."

"My arrangement with Wyatt falls outside the terms of our contract."

"I'm not buying that. Not for one minute."

"That's your problem." He went into the kitchen and took the lid off the pretzel jar. "Because that's all I'm selling."

She opened her mouth to continue the argument, but the blinking light on the telephone answering machine caught her attention.

She crossed the room and pushed the button. *"This is Bartholomew Greeley of Greeley's Antiques calling about the item we discussed when you visited my shop. I have received word regarding its present whereabouts. I am told that the collector who bought it will be willing to sell for the right price. I will be happy to act as a go-between and to accept the finder's fee you mentioned. Please meet me at my shop tomorrow morning. I will open early to conduct the negotiations. Shall we say ten-ish?"*

Triumph flashed through Lydia. "Sounds like I've found your cabinet for you, Emmett."

Emmett glanced at the answering machine. Then he gave her a level look. "If that's true, then your job is done, isn't it? That will simplify things. Tomorrow we'll collect the cabinet and I'll give you your check. Our contract will be legally terminated and you'll be out of this."

Her triumph evaporated in a heartbeat. He was right. Once the cabinet of curiosities was back in his hands, their contract would be fulfilled. There was nothing she could do about it.

Why the hell did she want to do anything about it, anyway? He was an ex-Guild boss, for crying out loud. He did social dinners with Mercer Wyatt. Worse yet, he did deals with Mercer Wyatt. His ex-fiancée was married to the boss of the Cadence Guild. Things couldn't get much messier.

Yes, sir, she wanted this contract to end just as quickly as possible. With the fees Emmett would pay her she could move into a new apartment. With his name on her list of satisfied clients, she would be off to a stunning start in her new career as a consultant. Life was looking up.

So why wasn't she thrilled?

She flashed him a brilliant smile. "Looks like I'll be getting my sofa back tomorrow night."

Chapter Sixteen

The sound of the bedroom door being stealthily opened brought him out of his brooding thoughts. His first reaction was a small rush of relief. He had been sinking deeper and deeper into the morass of possibilities, angles, problems, and risks since he had stretched out on the sofa and turned off the light.

His contemplation of how to juggle the search for Quinn with his bargain with Wyatt had been continually interrupted by the memory of Lydia's flashing smile when she agreed that their contract would be terminated tomorrow. *Looks like I'll be getting my sofa back . . .*

She didn't have to be quite so thrilled at the prospect of getting him off her sofa. Hell, she was welcome to it. The damn thing sagged in all the wrong places. It was lumpy and it was too short.

He caught the faint thump of a bare toe striking a wooden table leg in the hall. The small sound was followed by a stifled groan and a muffled curse. He moved one arm from behind his head and glanced at the fluo-rez-lit face of his watch. Two in the morning. Apparently Lydia had not had any more luck getting to sleep than he had.

All the plans and contingency schemes he had been crafting receded in the face of the more immediate question that had just arisen. Why was Lydia coming down the hall?

He was keenly aware that the question was not the only thing that had arisen. The knowledge that she was up and moving toward him had been enough to give him an erection.

He wondered if she was still angry. Then he wondered if it had occurred to her, as it had to him, that they had no logical reason to see each other again after they retrieved the cabinet tomorrow. Did she even give a damn? She had looked extremely pleased by Bartholomew Greeley's call. Just delighted at the news that their contract was about to end.

He lay unmoving, conscious that his blood was heating up with what had to be really stupid anticipation. What the hell did he think was going to happen now? Was he really dumb enough to believe that she might be coming out here to join him on the sofa?

More likely she was headed for the kitchen. Only logical destination under the circumstances. She couldn't sleep, so she was going to get herself a nice glass of warm milk. Or something.

He saw the pale outline of her white robe as she tiptoed around the corner, the shadowy blob that was Fuzz perched on her shoulder.

He held his breath and willed Lydia to come toward the sofa.

She headed for the kitchen.

He exhaled deeply and watched her disappear through the doorway. A few seconds later he heard the refrigerator door open. Light glowed briefly from the opening to the kitchen and then disappeared again. There was a soft clink. Lydia had removed a glass from the cupboard. Then he heard the lid of the pretzel jar.

Well, hell. Did she really expect him to sleep through all that racket?

He eased the covers aside and got to his feet. Halfway to the kitchen he remembered that he was wearing only his briefs. He glanced down and noticed that they did not provide much in the way of camouflage for his aroused body. Suppressing a groan, he reached into his open carryall and snagged his jeans. He yanked them on quickly.

"Didn't mean to wake you," Lydia said from the kitchen doorway.

He kept his back to her as he struggled carefully with the zipper. "I wasn't asleep."

At last he managed to get the pants fastened and turned to face her. She looked so good that it was all he could do not to take a bite.

She had a glass in one hand, a couple of pretzels in the other. She fed one of the pretzels to Fuzz.

"Mind if I have one?" Emmett asked, disgusted by his inability to come up with a more stimulating conversational gambit.

"Help yourself."

His arm brushed against the sleeve of her robe as he went into the kitchen. It was as though he'd touched a live wire and sent a jolt of raw energy straight to his already over-rezzed body.

He yanked the lid off the pretzel jar and started to reach inside.

"I don't think you want one of those," Lydia said. "Fuzz has probably drooled on them. Get one out of the bag in the oven. That's where I keep mine. Fuzz isn't strong enough to open the door."

Emmett replaced the lid and jerked the oven open. He gazed at the bag of pretzels inside. "Ever accidentally turn this thing on while the bag was in here?"

"Once," she admitted. "I keep a fire extinguisher under the sink now."

He helped himself to a handful and closed the oven door.

He could tell that she was still pissed. All because he hadn't told her the details of his deal with Mercer Wyatt.

What did he have to lose? he wondered. She probably couldn't get much more ticked off. It was Guild business, but maybe she had a right to know some of it.

"Okay, I'll tell you about my deal with Wyatt," he said around a mouthful of pretzel.

She lifted her chin. "Don't bother. You made it perfectly clear that you don't consider it any of my affair."

"It isn't. But the cold-shoulder treatment is working."

"I'm amazed. A Guild boss who's susceptible to the cold shoulder?"

"Ex-Guild boss." He crunched another pretzel. "In a nutshell, Mercer found out that Quinn disappeared shortly after visiting a youth shelter in the Old Quarter. A place called the Transverse Wave."

She looked thoughtful. "I know it. It's been around for several years. They offer social services to street kids."

"Wyatt thinks there's some connection. A couple of other young, untrained dissonance-energy para-rezes have disappeared too. They'd also had some contact with the shelter. He wants me to find out what's going on. But he wants it done discreetly."

She tipped her head to one side. "Why discreetly?"

"Because, as of a few months ago, the Cadence Guild Foundation began funding the shelter."

"Ah."

"Right. Ah." He shoved another pretzel into his mouth.

"Could be real embarrassing for the Guild if it turns out something illegal is going on at the shelter."

"In particular, it could be very awkward for Tamara." Emmett hesitated. "Mercer's in love with her. He wants to protect her."

"Hard to picture Mercer Wyatt in love with anyone except the power he exercises as a Guild boss."

"People change."

"Some do. Some don't."

"Little cynic. There's more. Wyatt thinks he's got a traitor on his administrative staff. He believes that person is responsible for whatever is going on at the shelter."

"Uh-oh. I think I know where this is going."

"In exchange for the lead on Quinn, I agreed to try to uncover the traitor on Wyatt's staff."

She blew out a deep breath. "I see. So now you're a spy for the Cadence Guild boss."

He said nothing, just munched.

"Okay, okay, I don't blame you," Lydia said.

That surprised him. "You don't?"

"No. In your shoes, I'd have made the same bargain. After all, your primary responsibility is to find your nephew. And it does sound as though Wyatt may have given you a solid lead. No one gets anything for nothing in this life. And that goes double where the Guild is concerned."

"That's kind of how I viewed it." He swallowed the last of his pretzel. "Sorry I got edgy earlier."

"You're probably not accustomed to having to explain yourself."

He looked at her. "It wasn't that. I didn't want to go into the details because I know how you feel about Wyatt and the local Guild."

"I admit I wouldn't trust Mercer Wyatt any farther than I could throw him. But—"

"But what?"

She smiled wryly. "But you're not Mercer Wyatt."

Something eased deep inside him. "Does that mean you do trust me?"

She lifted one shoulder in a small shrug. "A lot further than I would Wyatt."

Okay, so she wasn't declaring her undying faith in him. At least he wasn't in the same category as Wyatt.

"Tomorrow, after we pick up the cabinet, I'll check out the youth center," he said.

"Sounds like a plan. I wish you luck, Emmett. I hope your nephew is okay."

He waited a beat or two. "Something I think you should know before we terminate our contract."

"What's that?"

"I want to correct a slight misconception you have about ghost-hunters."

She watched him from the shadows. "If this is another lecture on Guild politics—"

"It's got nothing to do with politics."

"No?"

He leaned back against the refrigerator and folded his arms. "It's about that little eccentricity problem you mentioned last night. I don't know where you got your information, but you've been misinformed."

"Melanie." She cleared her throat. "Melanie Toft mentioned the eccentricity thing. She seemed very sure of her facts."

"Summoning a ghost or neutralizing one does generate a buzz," he said very deliberately. "But the point I want to make here is that the effect is short-lived."

"How short?"

"Half hour, max."

She considered that. "Come to think of it, I don't believe Melanie mentioned the time factor."

"Yeah, well, I just wanted to make it clear that the effect wouldn't last anywhere near long enough to account for what happened between us last night."

"I see," she whispered.

He unfolded his arms and took one step toward her. Given the small confines of the kitchen, that was enough to put him directly in front of her. The warm scent of her sent a thrill of hunger through him. He knew she sensed it, but she made no move to dodge him. Fuzz eyed Emmett for a few seconds and then tumbled off Lydia's shoulder and disappeared in the direction of the pretzel jar.

"And it sure as hell wouldn't account for this." Emmett pulled her into his arms and covered her mouth with his own.

For a couple of what he decided were some of the worst seconds of his life he thought she was going to push him away.

Then he felt her soften against him, and suddenly everything was all right. Better than all right. Very, very good.

Her arms went around his neck, her fingers slid into his hair. Her lips parted. He could taste her now. Need roared through him. A euphoric excitement followed. He was pretty sure that he could summon a dozen, hell, a *hundred* ghosts right now—but he was otherwise occupied.

Long periods of abstinence were probably not good for a man his age, he thought. A man his age was not supposed to be engaging in occasional flings. A man his age was supposed to be married. A man his age was supposed to have a wife in his bed. He was supposed to be getting sex so regularly that it became routine, maybe even a little dull, like eating breakfast.

Breakfast had never tasted so good.

Lydia was warm and she smelled of night things, female things. Things that were unique and astonishing and mysterious, things that he had never inhaled before in his entire life and that he was pretty sure he would never forget.

He moved his hand down over the full curve of her hip and closed his fingers around her thigh. She stirred against him. Her toe touched his foot. He eased her back against the counter, kissed her throat.

He reached between their bodies, found the sash of her robe, and untied it. She cupped his face in her hands.

"No, Emmett."

He stilled. Then he raised his head to look down at her. "No?"

She smiled wistfully. "I really don't think this is a good idea. Technically speaking, we're still involved in a business contract."

"That ends tomorrow morning."

"I know. But until then we're business associates."

Anger and frustration uncoiled deep within him. "What the hell is this? You want me. I want you. Where's the problem?"

"The problem," she said steadily, "is that we don't know each other very well. The problem is that you're a client. The problem is that I don't want a one-night stand."

"Why don't you be honest about it? The real problem is that I'm ex-Guild, isn't it?"

"No."

"The hell it isn't." He released her abruptly, pushed himself away from the counter. "You're so damned biased against anyone connected to the Guild that you can't even let yourself have a normal physical relationship with a hunter."

"Don't you dare blame this on me." She retied the sash of her robe with short, violent motions. "Just because I'm not into flings with men I hardly know doesn't mean I'm not normal, damn it."

"Shit." He shoved his fingers through his hair. "I didn't mean to imply you weren't normal."

"Yes, you did. That is exactly what you said. Bad enough that my former colleagues think I've lost my para-harmonic pitch. I don't need to be told that I'm not *normal* in other ways as well. If you'll excuse me, I've had enough. I'm going back to bed."

He watched helplessly as she whirled and stomped out of the kitchen. Then he looked down at Fuzz, who was gazing at him from the countertop.

"Ever had the feeling that you just screwed up big-time?" Emmett asked.

Chapter Seventeen

Lydia awoke to the ringing of the bedside phone. Her hand smacked the table, groped briefly, found the instrument.

She managed to get the receiver to her ear in time to hear Emmett answer on the living room extension.

"London," he growled.

Horrified, Lydia sat straight up in bed. "Hello? Hello?"

"Excuse me," Ryan Kelso said brusquely. "I believe I have the wrong number."

"Ryan?" Lydia said quickly. "Wait."

"Is that you, Lydia?" He sounded confused now.

"It's me. Emmett, I've got it. You can hang up now."

"Sorry," Emmett said easily. "I'll get breakfast started while you two talk. Take your time. I haven't even had my shower yet."

There was a click as he hung up the phone. A short, stark silence ensued during which Lydia knew that Ryan was absorbing the implications of Emmett's having answered the phone in her apartment at this hour of the morning. With a supreme effort of will she resisted the urge to storm into the other room and scream at Emmett.

She composed herself and swiftly considered the possibilities. Maybe Ryan was calling to tell her that the department had decided to give her back her job. Maybe he was calling with the offer of a private consulting contract with the university. Maybe her new career was finally about to take off.

"Sorry," she said crisply. "Someone else picked up the phone by mistake."

"The man who answered, he was the one who was with you the other night at the Counterpoint, wasn't he?"

There was a note of disapproval in Ryan's voice now. It irritated Lydia. As if he had a right to comment on the situation.

"Mr. London is my guest."

A shadow loomed. She looked across the room and saw Mr. London filling her doorway. He was wearing only the jeans he'd had on last night. She waved him off. He did not budge.

"What was it you wanted, Ryan?" she asked.

He cleared his throat. When he spoke this time, his tone was a bit too affable. "As a matter of fact, I was calling to suggest that we get together for lunch."

"Lunch?"

"Seeing you the other night made me realize how long it's been since we had a chance to sit down and talk," he said quickly. "Got a lot of news to catch up on."

"I see." She couldn't decide if he was hinting at a business discussion or just being friendly. "When did you want to do this lunch?"

"How about today?" Ryan said.

Lydia thought about the dreamstone jar that she had to get safely stored in a bank vault this morning and the cabinet of curiosities that she and Emmett were going to retrieve from Bartholomew Greeley. And then there was her job at the museum. She would be going in late today. She probably ought to work through lunch.

"I'm pretty tightly scheduled today, Ryan. How about tomorrow?"

"Damn it, Lydia, I've got to talk to you." He sounded both annoyed and urgent. "Today. As soon as possible. I could come to your apartment."

Ryan was definitely anxious about something. She tried to ignore Emmett, who had propped one shoulder against the doorjamb and was watching her with deep interest.

"What's this all about, Ryan?" she asked.

"It involves a professional matter," he said stiffly.

She tried to conceal her eagerness. "Are you saying you want me to consult for the department?"

There was a slight but meaningful pause. "Not exactly."

Her enthusiasm waned abruptly. "Ryan, I've got a busy day ahead. I don't have time for games."

"Wait, don't hang up, Lydia. This is important. Maybe the most important thing that's ever come along. I don't want to discuss it on the phone. But trust me, we're talking about a major Harmonic find."

Lydia tightened her grip on the phone. "What kind of find?"

"We can't talk about it now. I've got to see you." Ryan hesitated. "There's a rumor. I can't say any more about it, but I can tell you this much. If it's for real, it could remake your career for you."

Lydia felt her confidence return in a rush. Ryan needed her. That meant she was in control here. She had to play her cards carefully.

"Tell you what, Ryan, I'll give you a call later in the day when I've got my schedule nailed down for the week."

"Lydia, wait, don't hang up. Damn it, *don't hang up*. Both of our futures are riding on this."

"I'll call you later, Ryan." Very gently she replaced the phone. She looked at Emmett.

"What?" he said.

"I have a nasty feeling that Ryan may have heard some rumors about my bequest from Chester."

"You think he knows you've got the jar?"

"No, but I got the impression that he thinks I may know something about it."

"That's bad enough." He came away from the door, walked to the bed, and tossed her robe to her. "Rise and shine, my little sex goddess. We're going to be standing at the door of the bank when it opens. I want that jar in a safe-deposit box before we do anything else."

Lydia clutched the robe and met his gaze. " 'Sex goddess'?"

"You prefer the term 'sex kitten'?"

"No, that's okay. 'Sex goddess' will do."

The Cadence City Bank opened promptly at nine. By nine-twenty Lydia had filled out all the paperwork required for a safe-deposit box. The clerk showed her and Emmett into the hushed solitude of the vault room and left them alone.

Lydia removed the dreamstone jar from the paper sack for one last look before she sealed it safely away in the safe-deposit box.

"I still can't quite believe this is real." She studied the small streams of ever-changing colors that encircled the jar like tiny alien seas. "Solid as a rock and yet it's pure dreamstone. How is it possible? By rights it should have melted and splintered into a gazillion different molecules."

"I don't know if it's all that unexpected," Emmett said.

"Unexpected? The ability to work dreamstone is unheard of."

"Think about it." Emmett studied the jar in her hands. "We humans have only been here a couple of hundred years, but we've already developed ways of resonating psychically with rez-amber. We use the stuff every day to do everything from turning on the rez-screen to cooking dinner and hunting ghosts. The Harmonics probably evolved on this planet."

"We don't know that for certain," Lydia said quickly. "They may have come through the Curtain thousands of years ago, the same way we did two centuries ago. The experts say there's no telling how many times the Curtain has opened and closed in the past or which planets it linked when it was open."

Emmett shrugged. "Whatever. Any way you look at it, the Harmonics could have been here for thousands of years, right?"

"Right."

"Plenty of time to get psychically tuned to the basic harmonic frequencies of the planet. Who knows what they could do with rez-amber? Hell, we still can't even figure out how they created ghosts or the illusion traps. Some of us can manipulate them, but no one has come up with a way to create a ghost or a trap from scratch."

"True."

Lydia looked at the jar she held. She could feel the weight of the centuries and the echoes of a creativity that was not quite human but that nevertheless resonated on a very human frequency. "Maybe they discovered or invented something even better than rez-amber to help them focus their psi talents."

"Wouldn't be surprised. Given a couple of thousand more years here, we'll probably come up with something more efficient, too." Emmett glanced at his watch. "It's almost nine-thirty. Greeley will be waiting for us."

"Yes." She could come back here later to look at her fabulous jar, Lydia reminded herself. She started to rewrap it in the paper sack. Midway through the process she paused.

"What's wrong?" Emmett asked.

"I'm not sure." She removed the jar from the sack again and hefted it in her bare hands. She sent out a gentle psychic probe. Her amber bracelet grew warm against her skin. Cautiously, she felt for the harmonic pulse of the energy that emanated from the jar.

The amber grew warmer. A small chill went through her. "Oh, jeez."

Emmett moved closer, intent on her face. "What are you picking up? The age of the thing?"

"No. Something else. Remember, last night I told you it felt strange? Almost like a bit of illusion trap energy. I thought it was just something unique to dreamstone. But now I'm not so sure."

He glanced at the jar, and then his eyes lifted swiftly to meet hers. She saw that he understood the implications of what she had just said.

"Not ghost energy," he said with absolute certainty. "I'd sense it more clearly than you would."

"No," she whispered. "Illusion energy."

"Illusion traps are very rare outside the catacombs."

She nodded mutely. He was right. Even so, she could not help looking around the vault room. She studied every corner intently, amplifying and focusing her para-resonating senses through the amber bracelet. She saw no pools of darkness in the corners. There were no inexplicable shadows under the table or near the ceiling.

Of course there weren't any illusion snares in here, she thought. They were standing in the middle of the Cadence City Bank, for crying out loud.

But the amber in her bracelet was very warm against her skin. Traces of energy shimmered in the room.

She looked down at the jar. Then she looked at Emmett.

"Something to do with worked dreamstone, maybe?" Emmett asked. "Some property that we don't know about because no human has been able to manipulate the stuff?"

She held the artifact up to the light. "There's a lid, I think. It really should be removed in a lab. I don't want to risk damaging the jar."

"It's lasted this long," Emmett reminded her. "It can't be too fragile."

"I'll give it a try."

She set the jar on the table and very gingerly pried at the tightly closed lid. To her surprise it came off easily. She found herself looking down into the dark—very dark—interior of the little artifact.

"Hmm."

She picked up the jar and angled it so that light from the overhead fixture shafted into the interior. It could not penetrate the darkness. There was no gleam or sparkle from the dreamstone inside the jar. Just thick, impenetrable, black mist.

There were two possibilities, she thought. She was either losing it, pararez-wise, just as Ryan and the others suspected, or she was holding a jar filled with an illusion trap.

"Uh-oh," she said.

"The real thing?" Emmett asked quietly.

"Yeah. Not much of it. Just enough to fit inside this jar."

He hadn't questioned her judgment, she thought. He'd accepted her verdict even though he had every right to doubt it.

He watched as she very carefully set the jar back down on the table. "What do you think?"

"I don't know. Like everyone else, I've never seen much of this stuff outside the Dead City. The very fact that it exists inside this jar may mean that this trap is different from the others I've worked with. It must be anchored somehow to the dreamstone. Only one way to find out." He looked at her over the top of the jar. "Go for it."

"Might be better if you stepped into the other room. Just in case."

"Not a chance. I'm staying right here."

"Suit yourself."

She took another breath and concentrated on sending psi energy through the amber on her wrist. The stones warmed quickly again. The unmistakable pulse of resonating energy vibrated through her. Weak, but steady and clear.

"It's such a small trap," she whispered. "It's only giving off a trickle of energy."

"Even a trickle can cause some very unpleasant effects," Emmett warned.

She said nothing. They had both worked in the catacombs. They knew what the ancient Harmonic snares could do. Alien dreams. Alien nightmares.

She channeled psi energy steadily through the amber while she gazed down into the palpable night inside the jar. After a few seconds she saw something stir in the depths. The dark itself appeared to be condensing and coalescing. It was reacting to the pulses of energy she was forcing through it. If she screwed up at this stage, she could all too easily spring the trap.

If she triggered the illusion trap, she would have only about one second to realize she was in trouble. There would be no time to do anything about it. The darkness would snap back along the psi-frequencies that she herself had provided it. The stuff would swamp her mind before she could react.

If it was sufficiently powerful, the snare would not only plunge her into a disorienting illusion that her human mind could not accept for long but it would use her own psi energy to trap anyone else who had the misfortune to be standing nearby. Emmett, for example.

How long the nightmare would last or what form it would take was anyone's guess. Given the size of the trap, one could only hope that the dream it produced would be correspondingly limited and short-lived.

But she knew that even if it lasted for only a few minutes, it would take days to recover.

Using her para-rez senses, she edged deeper into the little patch of darkness. She sifted through the cloaking ephemeral energy until she caught the telltale echo of resonance. She fine-tuned her probe, found the hidden design inside the masking pattern, and fed energy into it, dampening the wave motion.

Slowly, carefully, she began to adjust the resonance frequency of the trap. It grew weaker, flattened.

The darkness inside the jar winked out abruptly.

Lydia released the breath she had not realized she was holding. She looked up and saw Emmett grinning at her.

"Nice work," he said.

It was then that the elation ripped through her. This was the first time she'd had a chance to work illusion trap energy since the Lost Weekend. The first time she'd been able to prove to herself that she still had her harmonic pitch. She hadn't lost her edge.

She tried to stay cool, tried not to let her bubbling excitement show. "It's been a while," she said offhandedly. "I was afraid I might be a little rusty."

"Rusty, hell. Screw the whole damn University of Cadence Department of Para-archaeology and the ghost they rode in on. You haven't lost your touch."

She gave up trying to squelch the delight and relief that were surging within her. With a small shriek, she flung herself into Emmett's arms. They closed swiftly around her.

"I'm okay," she whispered into the fabric of his jacket. "I really am okay. I can still handle the stuff." She was laughing now.

He hoisted her off her feet and laughed with her. "You can say that again." He slid her back down the length of his body and kissed her hard.

For a moment she clung to him, savoring the triumphant, congratulatory embrace. She knew then that there was no one, no one else at all, with whom she would rather have celebrated that moment.

When the initial blast of euphoria finally began to subside, she became conscious of the fact that she was kissing Emmett in the middle of a bank vault. Reality returned with a jolt. Slowly, reluctantly, she stepped back, flushed and breathless. She was supposed to be a professional, she thought. Professionals didn't behave this way.

Emmett seemed unaware of her chagrin. He glanced at the jar on the table. "Anything else inside besides the de-rezzed trap?"

Lydia hurried back to the table. She picked up the jar and angled it once more toward the light. "I don't see anything. No, wait—there is something. It looks like a piece of paper."

"Paper?"

"Yes." She lowered the jar and tipped it upside down.

They both stared at the slip of paper that fell into her palm. It was ordinary, everyday paper. It certainly was not thousand-year-old paper. No one had ever found anything that resembled paper in the ruins.

"Chester," Lydia whispered. "He could have de-rezzed the trap, stuck the paper inside the jar, and then reset the snare."

She put down the jar and carefully unfolded the paper. A familiar scrawl sloped across the page. There were three lines of jumbled letters and numbers. They were followed by a short message:

Dear Lydia:

Hell of a retirement plan, isn't it? Just wish I was there with you to enjoy it. I promised you that one day I'd surprise all those bastards up at the university. The really big news is that I think there's more where this came from. The bad news is that some other ruin rats are already excavating the site illegally. But it's going to take them weeks, if not months, to get all the dreamstone out. From what I could tell, every damn corridor in that catacomb branch is crawling with illusion traps and ghosts. I've never seen anything in the underground city that was this well guarded. Whatever you do, don't go in alone. You'll need a ghost-hunter to help you, and even then it will be dangerous. Whoever you choose, make sure you can trust him or her with your life. There's enough dreamstone involved to make your best friend contemplate murder.

The coordinates above are in code. Sorry. Had to do it this way. I can't be sure that someone else besides you won't find this jar first or that whoever it is won't get past the little trap inside. Nasty little bugger, wasn't it? It's anchored to the dreamstone. Amazing.

You'll need a key to the code. I didn't want to leave it in here with the coordinates for obvious reasons. But don't worry, I'll make sure you get it.

Be careful when you go after the rest of the dreamstone. The other ruin rats at the site are real SOBs. I don't think they'd hesitate to cut your throat if they caught you.

Love,
Chester

"My God!" Lydia whispered. "There's a whole site full of this stuff."

Emmett studied the three lines of letters and numbers Chester had written. "He says he'll make sure you get the key to those coordinates."

Lydia's jaw dropped for a few seconds as lightning struck. "Emmett, maybe that's what Chester was doing in the museum the night he was killed. Maybe he came there to leave the key in my office. The killer must have followed him, murdered him, and taken the key."

"Okay, I'll buy that. But getting the key didn't do the bastard any good, because the coordinates were hidden inside the jar." Emmett glanced at his watch. "Let's go. We've got an appointment with Greeley."

Chapter Eighteen

The morning fog off the river had thickened since she and Emmett set out for the bank an hour ago. It was so dense now that Lydia could not see to the end of the block. The shops along Ruin Row were still dark. By mutual agreement and long-standing tradition, they did not open until eleven. Behind the low buildings the massive green walls of the Dead City loomed in the mist.

She rubbed her arms briskly against the chill as she got out of the Slider. She noticed that Emmett had put on his black leather jacket. She reached back into the vehicle for her coat before she joined him on the sidewalk. Together they walked toward the front door of Greeley's Antiques.

Emmett glanced at the amber face of his watch. "Not quite ten."

"Ruin Row doesn't really get humming until noon. But I'm sure Greeley will be in his shop."

They walked to the front door. The shop was unlit inside. Lydia tried the door. It was locked.

"I was certain he'd be here early." She cupped her hands on the glass and peered into the dingy interior. "I'll bet he's in his back room. Try knocking."

Emmett made an easy fist and rapped loudly. Lydia watched closely, but no one emerged from the gloom behind the front counter. She stepped back from the window.

"He's getting a little hard of hearing," she said. "Let's try the rear door."

She led the way to the corner and turned down the narrow service alley that ran behind the shops. Here the fog seemed even heavier, and the close confines heightened the gloom. The fleeting traces of stray energy leaking from the Old Wall made her feel edgy. Emmett followed close behind.

A frisson of awareness wafted through her. Para-rez energy. Her own amber was still at skin temperature.

"Emmett? Is that you?"

"Sorry," he said absently. "Just checking."

She glared at him over her shoulder. "Checking for what?"

"Dissonance energy. Thought I caught a trace."

"Hold it right there." She stopped, spun around, and shoved her hands into the pockets of her jacket. "Are you telling me that there's a ghost-hunter working somewhere near here?"

"Not at the moment. If there was one here, he's either gone or he's stopped working."

She contemplated the fog-filled alley uneasily. "A lot of kids hang out in this part of town. They like to play with the energy that leaks through the Dead City walls. Young dissonance para-rezes like Zane come here to practice summoning flickers."

Emmett nodded. "It's the same way near the walls of Old Resonance. Maybe I picked up the traces of some would-be junior hunter."

He did not sound convinced, Lydia thought. But who was she to argue?

She turned around, pulled up the collar of her coat, and started walking again. When she reached the rear entrance of Greeley's Antiques, she came to a halt and knocked forcefully on the door.

No answer.

"Damn," she said. "He said he'd be here around ten. Looks like we'll have to wait in the car. I don't think he'll be very late. Greeley's got a short list of priorities. Money is right at the top."

Emmett studied the closed door for a few seconds, saying nothing. Then he pulled a pair of gloves out of the pockets of his jacket.

Lydia suddenly felt very cold. She cleared her throat. "Speaking as your consultant, I really can't recommend breaking into Greeley's Antiques. No point in it. Bartholomew wouldn't have left anything as valuable as your cabinet in his back room overnight. Trust me on this, Emmett."

"I believe you." He reached for the doorknob with his gloved hand. "About the cabinet. But I'm still getting traces of rez energy. Don't you feel it?"

She frowned. "No. I felt your energy when you used it a minute ago, but I'm not picking up anything now."

"Probably because you're a tangler. These are hunter vibes."

She hunched deeper into her coat. Most people could pick up faint traces of psi energy when someone in the vicinity was actively working with amber. But the average individual was far more sensitive to others who had similar paranormal talents. Ghost-hunters could more easily detect the energy trail left by another hunter. Ephemeral-energy para-rezes such as herself were more likely to be aware of another tangler working nearby.

But even the most powerful para-energy trace dissipated quickly after the user had stopped resonating through amber. If Emmett was picking up a hint of dissonance energy, it meant that the hunter had worked somewhere close by and sometime in the past few minutes.

Lydia watched Emmett twist the doorknob. It turned easily in his fingers. Too easily.

"I don't think the fact that the back door is unlocked is a good sign, Emmett."

"Funny you should say that. I was coming to the same conclusion." He pushed the door open wide and gazed into the back room of Greeley's Antiques.

Lydia stood on tiptoe so that she could see over his shoulder. At first she could make out nothing except the shadowy shapes of cartons and some green quartz vases.

Then she saw the body sprawled on the floor.

"Oh, my God, Emmett!"

Bartholomew Greeley lay facedown in a pool of rapidly drying blood. His throat had been slit.

"Oh, God!" Lydia exclaimed again. It was hard to catch her breath. Her fingers shook so hard she had to cram them back into her pockets. "Just like Chester."

"There is a pattern here, isn't there?" Emmett contemplated the scene. His intent, focused awareness was clear.

"What is it?" Lydia demanded. "What are you picking up?"

"A hunter worked amber in this room. Not long ago. Probably summoned a ghost to stun Greeley before he cut his throat. Whoever he was, he must have been in a hurry."

"Why do you say that?"

"He singed something. Can't you smell it?"

Lydia inhaled cautiously, caught a whiff of charred packing-crate filler. "Yes."

Emmett glanced at her. "You okay?"

"Yes." That was a flat-out lie, she thought. Her stomach was roiling. The sheer cold-blooded brutality of the scene was making her nauseous.

"Don't get sick here," Emmett warned.

"I'm not going to throw up."

He gave her a doubtful look. Then he stepped into the death room, blocking her view.

"Wait! What are you doing?" She glanced urgently back down the alley. "This is a crime scene."

"I know. I just want to take a quick look around before we leave."

An ominous feeling settled on her. "Leave?"

"Yeah." He edged cautiously through the gloom, avoiding the blood.

"What about the police? You're the one who insisted we call them when we found Chester, remember?"

"There wasn't any choice then. This time around, though, we've got an option. We'll call from a pay phone after we're out of the area."

She realized where he was going with this. The unpleasant sensation in her stomach worsened.

"Anonymously, I take it?" she said dryly.

Emmett leaned down to examine the floor near the body. She thought she saw him pick something up, but she could not see what it was.

"Under the circumstances," he said, getting to his feet. "I think anonymity is our best bet. Detective Martinez hasn't had any breaks in the Brady case. I got the feeling that she's hungry for one. If she finds out that you've turned up yet again as the first person on the scene of a second murder—" He let the sentence trail off meaningfully.

"She's going to move me up into first place on her list of suspects, isn't she?"

"Probably."

Lydia thought about that. "I'm not the only person who's turned up twice at a recent murder scene."

"You don't need to remind me." He straightened and moved toward a desk littered with papers. "I skated the first time, but something tells me Martinez won't let me off the hook so easily again."

"Especially since you've been keeping company with me," Lydia said glumly.

"Uh-huh." He riffled through the papers gingerly with his gloved fingers.

"There's no hard evidence to tie either of us to the murders. Surely Martinez will acknowledge that. She's got nothing solid to use against either of us."

Emmett left the desk and walked to the door. Without a word he opened his hand as he came back through the opening.

Lydia stared at the rez-amber bracelet in his palm. Six good-quality stones, each with her initials inscribed on it, set in inexpensive imitation gold. Another wave of sick dread rose up inside her.

"That's one of my bracelets," she whispered.

"I was afraid of that." He dropped the amber into her hand and then took her arm, leading her quickly away from Greeley's back door. "What do you want to bet the ghost-hunter who tossed your apartment took it?"

"And planted it at the scene of this murder?"

"I doubt if it was the same guy. He was just a kid."

"Kids can kill."

"But usually not as efficiently as that." Emmett glanced back over his shoulder. "The kid in your apartment was probably working for someone else."

"Someone tried to tie me to Greeley's murder." She was shivering so hard now that she almost dropped the bracelet. "I can't believe it. Why would anyone do that?"

"Probably to make sure you'd be very busy for the next few days. Too busy to pay attention to little things like a priceless dreamstone jar or my cabinet of curiosities."

She tried to think logically. It wasn't easy. "There's another reason why he might have left my bracelet near Greeley's body. If Martinez gets called in on this murder, she's going to find that charred paper on the desk. She'll suspect a ghost-hunter was involved."

"Yes."

"And she knows that you and I have been working together lately."

"Yes."

She glanced at him. "Tying me to the murder scene is a good way of implicating you too."

"The thought did cross my mind."

"Oh, damn."

"My sentiments exactly," Emmett said.

Ten minutes later Lydia sat tensely in the passenger seat of the Slider and watched Emmett hang up the pay phone. He left the booth and walked back to the car, his face hard.

He glanced at her as he got in behind the wheel and rezzed the ignition. "You sure you're not going to throw up?"

"Pretty sure. What did you tell the cops?"

"I reported an unlocked back door at Greeley's Antiques. Anonymously." He eased the Slider away from the curb. "Suggested it looked like a burglary-in-progress. They'll send a car to take a look."

She forced herself to think. "Maybe that's what it was, Emmett. Maybe

Greeley surprised the killer when he opened early to get ready for us. If I hadn't agreed to meet with him this morning—"

"Stop right here. You had nothing to do with this. It was Greeley's idea to do the deal for the cabinet before he opened the shop, remember?"

"Well, yes, but—"

"But nothing. He set up the schedule." Emmett slowed for a corner. "And he may have invited the killer inside."

"What are you talking about?" she said in disbelief.

"Let's go someplace where we can get coffee. I need to think."

Chapter Nineteen

The Amber Sky Café was one of those comfortable places where you could sit in a booth and huddle over a cup of rez-tea and a jelly doughnut for at least an hour before the waitress started to glare. Emmett did a quick survey and spotted a quiet booth at the back.

He studied Lydia's face as she ordered tea. She seemed to be holding up well, but he was worried about her. The strain showed on her face. She was amazingly resilient, but the shocks were coming fast and hard. A lot of people he knew would be in screaming hysterics by now. He wondered how much she could take. Everyone had a breaking point, even intrepid para-archaeologists who could de-rez Harmonic illusion traps while standing in the middle of a downtown bank.

To make matters worse, he didn't think she trusted him completely. She probably couldn't bring herself to trust anyone with Guild connections.

They sat in silence until their refreshments arrived. Lydia picked up the steaming cup of tea. She ignored the doughnuts.

"Tell me why you think Greeley may have known the killer," she said steadily.

He thought back to the grisly scene at Greeley's Antiques.

"It looked like the killer went through Greeley's desk in a hurry," he said. "The papers were scattered and mixed up on top. Two of the drawers were half open."

"What do you think he was looking for?"

"No way to be certain, but several sheets had been torn from the desk calendar. Yesterday's and today's pages were missing. So were two or three on either side."

"You think the killer was concerned that whatever was written on one of the pages had left an imprint on the next one?"

"It's a possibility." Emmett paused. "I wonder if Greeley tried to set up an auction in order to drive up the price of my cabinet?"

"Wouldn't put it past him." She drummed her fingers on the table. "If he did, it's entirely possible that he made a note about the auction on his desk calendar. He was very methodical. He could have written the killer's name and phone number on today's date."

"As well as our names and your phone number."

She shuddered visibly. "Whoever killed him knew that we were due to arrive at ten. He must have contacted Greeley yesterday. Arranged the whole thing. Oh, God, Emmett, that means—"

"It was a setup."

Lydia pondered for a while. "I can see someone murdering poor Chester for the key to the dreamstone coordinates. I can even envision someone killing Greeley for the cabinet. It's not exactly priceless, but it is extremely valuable. But what's the link between the two?"

"You," Emmett said. "And me. And the dreamstone."

"And a supposed traitor inside the Cadence Guild," she added.

"What do you mean, 'supposed'?" he asked.

"It's possible we've been suckered into some illegal antiquities operation run by Mercer Wyatt," she said coolly.

Emmett felt his jaw tighten. Her dislike and distrust of all things related to the Guild was not news. He would not let himself get drawn into an argument on the subject of hunter ethics.

"If the Guild was involved in this," he said in his most reasonable tone, "Mercer Wyatt would not have invited me to dinner. He would not have told me that Quinn had been seen at the Transverse Wave. He would not have made a deal with me."

"You can't be sure of that. Who knows what Wyatt's real agenda is? He told you he wanted you to help him squash some rival who's supposedly training young ghost-hunters without Guild approval. But what if he lied to you? What if he's trying to set you up for murder?"

"Believe me, the last thing Wyatt wants to do is get me arrested for murder. He needs me. And not just to help him get rid of a renegade ghost-hunter."

She sat back against the plastic seat. Her gaze turned very cool. "You didn't tell me everything about your bargain with Wyatt, did you?"

Anger roared through him. He leaned across the table, pinning her without touching her. "I told you the truth about the arrangement I made with Mercer Wyatt."

"What didn't you tell me?"

"Damn it, the rest of it has nothing to do with this."

"Tell me."

He sat back slowly. With an effort of will he brought himself under control. "Wyatt told me that he's planning to retire in a year."

She made a soft, disgusted sound. "That's good news, I suppose. I, for one, won't miss him. But what has that got to do with you?"

"He claims he has some big plan to restructure the Cadence Guild along the same lines as the Resonance Guild before he steps down."

"Really . . . and he wants you to do a little business consulting for him, is that it? Help him modernize things?"

Emmett hesitated. "He wants a little more than just some consulting."

"Damn. He wants to handpick his own successor, doesn't he? And he wants you for the job."

Her stunned outrage aroused the anger he thought he had suppressed a moment ago. He tossed a meaningful glance to the side to remind her that they were not alone in the restaurant.

"You might want to keep your voice down. We've got enough problems on our hands without starting wild rumors about internal Guild politics. Mercer Wyatt wouldn't like it."

"I don't care what Mercer Wyatt likes or doesn't like."

"More to the point," he said softly, "I wouldn't like it."

"Are you, by any chance, trying to intimidate me?"

"Yes."

She gave him a ferocious glare. But when she spoke, her voice was barely above a whisper. "What did you tell Wyatt when he informed you he wanted you to take over the Guild?"

Emmett picked up his tea. "I told him I didn't want the job."

"You think that's going to stop him from trying to make you take it?"

"I can handle Mercer Wyatt." He set his cup down a little harder than necessary. "Look, the future of the Cadence Guild is not the main issue here. In case you've forgotten, we're trying to keep ourselves from getting arrested for murder."

"Must have slipped my mind," she said into her tea mug.

"I have a hunch that Detective Martinez is one of those real dogged types. If she gets wind of Greeley's murder and makes a connection to the Brady case, you can bet she'll come around asking questions. We need to get our stories straight."

Lydia sighed. "What kind of stories are we going to tell her?"

"The truth, insofar as we can."

"Sounds tricky."

"It's always safer to stick as close to the truth as possible. Less chance to screw up that way."

"You've had a lot of experience in this kind of thing?"

He said nothing, just looked at her.

She flushed. "Sorry. I'm a little tense today."

"I'm not exactly at my best, either." He rested his elbows on the table. "Here's how it goes: We were together all last night and this morning. First at your place, then at the bank. We had tea here, and I dropped you off at Shrimpton's. We simply don't mention the few minutes we spent at Greeley's Antiques. We should be covered. Plenty of witnesses. Kelso's call earlier, and the people at the bank will back us up. I'll leave a good tip here so the waitress will remember us. The missing time in between we'll attribute to traffic congestion."

"What if someone on Ruin Row saw us?"

"I doubt if anyone noticed us in the fog. None of the other shops were open. We should be in the clear."

"You think so?" Lydia looked worried. "Your story is going to raise some questions in other people's minds."

"Such as?"

"Such as, why were you at my apartment last night and why were you still there this morning? Why are we sitting here in a café together when I should be at work? You know—questions like those."

"Fortunately, those questions have a real easy and obvious answer."

"They certainly do. For crying out loud, Emmett, everyone will think we're having an affair."

"Better they think you're sleeping with me than have them conclude that you're murdering your associates in the antiquities field."

She paled. "Point taken."

"You and I are each other's alibis."

"Great. My alibi is that I'm sleeping with my first major client. Heck of a way to launch my new career as a private consultant. Can't wait to see what type of high-class clientele I attract after this gets out."

The message slips on her phone were an ominous sign. Lydia sat down very gingerly at her desk and reached for the sticky little papers. She flipped through them quickly. Two calls from Ryan and a message from a woman who wanted to schedule a tour of Shrimpton's for her seven-year-old son's birthday party. The good news was that there were no messages from Detective Alice Martinez.

Lydia allowed herself to relax ever so slightly.

Her life had certainly undergone some major alterations lately. Who would have thought that there would come a day when she would be hanging out with a past and possibly future Guild boss and ducking phone calls from the cops?

She stared at the bookcase on the other side of the office and thought about the blood on the floor of Greeley's back room.

Melanie opened the office door and put her head around the edge. "Well, well, well. I see you finally decided to come to work."

Lydia started. "I had a breakfast meeting with my client. The time got away from me."

Melanie glanced over her shoulder, apparently checking the hallway, and then bustled into the small room. "Thought I saw you get out of London's car a few minutes ago. Breakfast meeting, huh?"

"Yes." Lydia got up and went over to the hot plate that sat on top of the bookcase. She didn't really want any more tea, but she needed to do something, anything, while she endured the inevitable inquisition.

"So, how is the consulting project going?" Melanie asked a little too brightly.

"We're making progress." Lydia spooned tea leaves into a pot.

"I just wondered," Melanie said.

"What did you wonder, Melanie?"

"Why Mr. London gave you a lift to work. Usually you walk."

If she couldn't handle Melanie, Lydia thought, she wouldn't have a snowball's chance in a very warm place of handling Detective Alice Martinez. *Think of this conversation as a good chance to practice your story.*

She put down the pot, turned around, and leaned back against the bookcase. She braced her hands on the wooden shelving behind her and smiled at Melanie.

"Mr. London very kindly offered to drop me off here after our breakfast meeting."

"That was nice of him."

"Yes, it was."

"Don't imagine too many high-end clients could be bothered to chauffeur their consultants around. Just think of all the trouble he went to. He had to get up early, leave his hotel, drive to the Old Quarter to pick you up, drive you to the café, drop you off here—"

Lydia took the plunge. "Mr. London is staying with me while we work on his project."

Melanie's face lit up with horrified fascination. "Omigod, you're sleeping with him, aren't you? You're having an affair with your new client. I knew it. I knew it the minute I saw you get out of that Slider this morning."

Lydia was saved from having to respond by the sight of the six-and-a-half-foot-tall skeletal shadow that darkened the glass panel of the office door. A bony hand lifted to knock.

"Come in, Mr. Shrimpton," Lydia called. The more, the merrier. Martinez would probably show up any minute now.

The door opened. Winchell Shrimpton looked at her with his undertaker's gaze. "You're here."

"Sorry I was a little late getting in to work this morning. I had some personal business. Don't worry, I'm going to make up for it by working through lunch."

Shrimpton inclined his skull-head in a glum gesture. "Don't suppose it makes much difference. As you may have noticed, business has fallen off again. Customers are not exactly thronging the galleries anymore."

Shrimpton's chronic pessimism was more irritating than usual this morning. The last thing she wanted to do was listen to her boss whine about the fall-off of business. It wasn't as if she didn't have her own problems, Lydia thought. It was all she could do not to yell at him. *You want something to whine about? Try walking into a murder scene first thing in the morning. Try finding out that the killer left one of your personalized amber bracelets next to the body. Try worrying about whether you're going to be arrested at any mo-*

ment. Try wondering if the man who is sleeping on your sofa and using your shower is scheduled to become the next boss of the Cadence Guild.

Lydia pulled herself up short and gave herself a mental shake. It was not Shrimpton's fault that he not only looked as if he had just walked out of a crypt but had a personality to go with his looks. The man had given her a job when she desperately needed one. That counted for a lot in her book. Besides, as a boss, he literally and figuratively towered over a lot of the egotistical academics she'd worked with at the university.

"Don't worry, Mr. Shrimpton," she said, struggling for a note of professional good cheer. "The spring holidays are coming. Things always pick up during school vacations. Kids love this place."

Shrimpton did not brighten noticeably, but his cadaverous features realigned themselves into a thoughtful expression.

"It was the body in the sarcophagus in the Tomb Gallery that caused business to pick up for a day or two," he said. "I wonder if there's any way we could arrange for another little *incident.*"

Lydia felt her jaw unhinge.

Melanie bounced with excitement. "What a great idea, boss! You know, if a second body turned up here at the museum, we could probably get a good legend started."

Shrimpton looked at her hopefully. "What sort of legend?"

"Something along the lines of an ancient Harmonic curse would probably work best." Melanie tapped her finger against her cheek. "People love that sort of thing, you know. Maybe we could mount an ad campaign based on the Curse of the Harmonic Sarcophagus."

Shrimpton nodded. "I like it. It has possibilities."

Lydia dropped her head into her hands.

Chapter Twenty

The damp fog had driven off the usual denizens of the tiny park, but Emmett and Zane had to weave a path through a maze of discarded bottles of Night Vibe wine and Acid-Aura beer.

"The Transverse Wave?" Zane looked away from Fuzz, who was investigating the grass around a tree. "Yeah, sure, I know it. A lot of street kids hang there. They've got free food and video games and a neat gym. I used to go there sometimes after school until Lydia found out."

Emmett shoved his hands into the pockets of his leather jacket. "Lydia doesn't approve of the place?"

"Nah." Zane rolled his eyes. "She convinced Aunt Olinda it wasn't a good *environment* for me."

"Ah."

"She said it was a place for kids who didn't have a home. She said I've got one."

"Guess there is some logic to that."

"Maybe. Aunt Olinda bought it, at any rate."

Emmett watched Fuzz tumble toward them across the scraggly lawn. "Is it open twenty-four hours a day?"

"Used to be. But a few months ago they started closing it at midnight. Someone said the lady who runs the place claimed there were new legal problems and restrictions on all-night shelters."

"Think you could describe the interior of the place to me?"

"Sure." Zane squinted up at him. "How come you want to know about the Wave?"

"I'm thinking of dropping in to take a look around."

"Lydia probably won't like that."

"Probably not."

They headed back to the Slider, leaned against the fender, and watched Fuzz bob happily around the empty bottles.

"Lydia thinks I should go to college," Zane said after a while.

Emmett nodded. "Doesn't surprise me."

"I don't want to go to college. I want to join the Guild."

"No reason you can't do both."

Zane snorted. "College is a waste of time for a ghost-hunter."

"Lot of hunters lose interest in full-time ghost-hunting after they've done it for a while. Or they get fried one too many times and decide to call it quits. If they haven't trained for anything else, they have a tough time finding another job."

"I can't imagine ever getting tired of hunting."

"It's okay once in a while. But it's not exactly the most intellectually challenging occupation in the world."

Zane gave another snort. "Who cares about intellectual stuff?"

"Being good at ghost-hunting is sort of like being good at crossing a busy street in the middle of the block. If you're fast you don't get clipped too often. Sure, it's kind of exciting for a while, but do you really want to spend your whole life doing it?"

Zane glowered. "It's not like that at all."

"It's no different from being able to de-rez illusion traps the way Lydia does. She's good at it and she could probably make a living doing nothing but springing traps, but she'd get bored if that was all she did."

"I won't get bored ghost-hunting," Zane vowed.

Emmett shrugged. "Maybe not."

"Did you go to college?"

"Yeah. I zapped ghosts in the Resonance catacombs on the side. Did it full-time for a while after I graduated. But I got tired of seeing the para-archaeologists get all the credit for the discoveries."

Zane scowled. "What do you mean?"

"No one gives the hunters any credit when a new catacomb is excavated. We're just hired muscle as far as most people are concerned. It's the P-As who get their pictures in the papers and write the articles in the journals."

"That's not fair."

"I know," Emmett said. "But that's how it works."

"Please come in, Mr. London." Denver Galbraith-Thorndyke rose from behind the broad desk. He pushed his glasses up higher on his nose and motioned Emmett to a chair. "I got a call from Mr. Wyatt telling me to expect you."

"I won't take too much of your time." Emmett surveyed the plush offices of the Guild Foundation. Tamara had certainly pulled out all the stops in her goal to start reshaping the Guild's image. The rich paneling, expensive carpets, and deeply polished wood furnishings had obviously been chosen by a designer who had been instructed to project Expensive Good Taste.

Denver Galbraith-Thorndyke fit in naturally with his surroundings. The years of private schooling and social connections were evident. But there was an earnest, determined quality about him also. Mercer had gauged him correctly, Emmett thought. This was a young man out to prove himself. He wanted to make it on his own. Tamara had offered him the means of doing just that.

"I understand that you're interested in the details of our contributions to the Transverse Wave Youth Shelter." Denver adjusted his gold-rimmed glasses again and opened a thick file. "I don't know exactly what it is you want, but I've got a full financial summary here, if that will help."

"I'd like to see it." Emmett reached across the desk to take the report. He glanced through it quickly. "I assume any prospective charity is well researched before you authorize funding?"

"Of course. I verify all of the relevant facts personally. Background checks on the individuals associated with the organization are always performed, as are financial checks. The objective is to assure ourselves that the institution is legitimate. There are a lot of scam artists out there, you know."

"I know." Emmett scanned the financial data in front of him. "I see that the Transverse Wave was in financial trouble when the Foundation began funding it."

"Yes." Denver leaned back in his chair. "When the founder died, the finances were in chaos. We almost didn't go through with the project because of that. But historically the shelter has had a good reputation for getting kids off the street, and Mrs. Wyatt was determined to fund a project that was oriented toward street youth. We decided we could work with Miss Vickers to get the Wave back on its feet. We've been quite successful."

Emmett looked up. "Miss Vickers?"

"She's the person responsible for the day-to-day operation of the shelter. She went to work for it shortly before Ames died. A very dedicated woman."

Lydia gazed down into the sarcophagus where Chester's body had been found. The janitorial staff had done an excellent job. The bloodstains were gone. But, after all, the translucent green quartz the Harmonics had used to construct their cities and the catacombs and much of what went into them was not only virtually indestructible, it cleaned up easily. If humans ever learned how to duplicate the para-resonating process used to create the stuff, Lydia thought, it would probably sell well to home builders and remodelers. It would be perfect for use in bathrooms and kitchens, assuming your interior designer liked green.

She turned slowly on her heel and surveyed the dimly lit gallery.

What had Chester been doing here the night he died? Detective Martinez and everyone else assumed that he had come to steal one of the artifacts. On its good days Shrimpton's House of Ancient Horrors was only a third-rate museum. There was nothing of extraordinary value here, but there were some things, such as the tomb mirrors, that would be of interest to small-time collectors. And Chester had a reputation, after all, of being a *petty* thief.

But if she and Emmett had interpreted Chester's note correctly, he had not come here to steal. He had been attempting to conceal the key to his private code.

It was likely that he had been killed before he accomplished his goal. If that was the case, then his killer had the key and there was no point looking for it.

But what if he had been murdered on his way *out* of the museum? What if he had hidden the key *before* someone slit his throat?

She studied the row of display vaults that lined the gallery. On Shrimpton's orders, the green quartz urns, tomb mirrors, and other objects had been dramatically lit so that they glowed eerily in the shadows.

There were literally hundreds of places in this wing alone in which Chester could have hidden his key. He must have known how difficult if not downright impossible it would be for her to search the entire museum.

"Lydia?"

The sound of Ryan's voice behind her startled her out of her reverie. She turned quickly and saw him walking toward her with an urgent stride.

"Hello, Ryan."

"I left a dozen messages for you," he said without preamble.

"I saw them."

"Why in hell didn't you return my calls?"

"I've been a little busy lately."

"Damn it, I've been trying to get hold of you all day."

"In case you've forgotten, Ryan, I don't work for the department anymore. That means I don't always return phone calls to my former colleagues with my former efficiency. I've got other priorities these days."

"Such as your new so-called client?"

A chill of unease shot through her. "Not so-called," she said evenly. "Mr. London is as real as clients get."

"He answered the phone in your apartment this morning. You're sleeping with him, for God's sake. Do you have any idea who he is?"

"Yes."

He ignored that. "London's a Guild boss from Resonance City. I would have thought that you, of all people, would have a few problems with the idea of having an affair with a guy like that."

"He's an ex-Guild boss."

"You know what they say, once in the Guild, always in the Guild."

"My client is my problem, not yours."

"That's not true." Ryan's voice softened. "We're friends, Lydia. Colleagues. I have a responsibility to warn you about London. He's using you."

"Consider me warned. Look, I haven't got time for this. Let's cut to the chase here. What do you want?"

"Damn it, I'm trying to do you a favor."

"The last time you did me a favor, I lost my job."

"Work with me on this and I might be able to get you back into the department."

She had been right, she thought. Only one thing could explain Ryan's persistence today. He must have heard something about the dreamstone.

"What's going on, Ryan?"

"I need to talk to you." He glanced around, apparently assuring himself that the gallery was still empty. "Something big has come up."

It might be smart to find out just how much he knew about the dreamstone. She folded her arms and propped one hip on the corner of the green sarcophagus. "Tell me about it."

"We can't talk here."

"Why not? The museum closed a few minutes ago. We're alone."

He shoved his fingers through his hair and glanced back over his shoulder again. The tension in him was palpable.

He turned back to her and took a step closer. When he spoke, it was in a whisper. "I've got a private client of my own."

"Congratulations. What does that have to do with me?"

He watched her closely. "Last night he approached me about a rumor concerning a piece of worked dreamstone."

She went cold inside, but she managed a derisive chuckle. "Sounds like your hotshot private client is an escapee from a para-psych ward. Everyone knows there's no such thing as worked dreamstone."

"My client is serious." Ryan continued to focus on her with unwavering intensity. "He's no fool. He thinks the rumor is solid, and he's asked me to help him check it out."

She grinned. "Easy money. You wrack up a bunch of hours looking for a bogus piece of dreamstone, and then you tell him it doesn't exist and send him the bill."

"He thinks you may know something about it, Lydia."

"Me?" She deliberately widened her eyes, going for stunned innocence. "Why in the world would he connect me to a wild rumor about dreamstone?"

"Because you're working for London, and he thinks London came to Cadence to find the dreamstone."

"Look, Ryan, your client obviously got badly fried somewhere along the line," Lydia said. "Mr. London is not chasing a fantastic rumor. He came here to look for a family heirloom."

"I don't believe you." Ryan moved in closer. "You're not cooperating with me because you want to keep this to yourself. You think you can find the dreamstone on your own."

"Are you crazy? You think I'd be working here at Shrimpton's today if I was on the trail of a piece of dreamstone? Believe me, I'd have quit to spend full time on a project like that. Locating a chunk of worked dreamstone would put me on the cover of the *Journal of Para-archaeology*. I'd have my pick of posts at the university. Heck, they'd probably make me head of the P-A department. Just think, Ryan, I could have *your* job."

Ryan blinked, apparently startled by that possibility. Then he recovered, his handsome features twisting into a grim mask. "My client is an experienced collector who knows all about ruin rumors. He's convinced the dreamstone exists."

"What's the name of this experienced collector?"

"I can't tell you that." Ryan's shoulders stiffened. "He prefers to remain anonymous."

"Yeah, I'll just bet he does. If people find out he's searching for dreamstone, someone may call the guys in white coats to have him taken away."

Ryan clamped his teeth together so fiercely that Lydia heard the click. "Damn it, Lydia, it's in your best interests to work with me on this."

"Yeah? Why?"

"My client has not only agreed to pay me a fortune if I turn up the dreamstone, he's agreed to allow the artifact to be studied and written up by the department."

She pursed her lips. "That means that your name would go on all the journal articles."

"Naturally, I'd make sure you got credit."

"Oh, boy. Just like the old days, huh? I write the article and you get to put your name on it as lead author. Be still, my beating heart."

He drew himself up. "All right. I promise you will be listed as lead author."

"I don't believe that for a moment. You've tried that line before, remember?"

"Lydia, this is no time to indulge in petty quarrels. If my client is right about this dreamstone, you and I are standing on the brink of the most important career moment of our lives."

She studied him for a moment. "You really believe your client is right about the dreamstone, don't you?"

"Like I said, he talks like an experienced collector. I think he knows what he's doing. He sounds much too smart and too savvy to be chasing a fantasy."

"I dunno. Collectors are weird. They wouldn't be collectors if they weren't a little strange."

"But if he's right, there's a fortune at stake here. And not just in cash. This could wipe out your past for you. No one would give a damn about what happened to you six months ago if you show up with dreamstone."

"Okay, convince me. What do you know about this so-called dreamstone?"

"I'm not going to tell you a bloody thing until you've agreed to work with me," he said warily.

"Well, in that case"—she straightened away from the sarcophagus—"looks like this conversation is over. See you around, Ryan."

"*Wait.*" He grabbed her arm in a fierce grip as she made to walk past him. "You're a pro. You know as well as I do that if there's any truth to this rumor, it would be the find of the decade. This is too important to allow personal feelings to get in the way."

"*If* there's any truth to it." She looked pointedly down at his hand on her arm. "Kindly take your hand off me."

"It's London, isn't it?" Ryan shouted furiously. "He *is* after the dream-stone, and you figure you'll do better to stick with him instead of teaming up with me."

"Take your hand off me, Ryan."

"He's Guild. That means he's dangerous."

"Let me go, Ryan."

"Shit, haven't you figured out what's going on here? He's using you."

"What are you talking about?"

"You now damn well what I'm talking about. He's got an agenda."

"Everyone's got an agenda. Including you."

"Whatever London is up to, you can bet it's outside the law."

"I wouldn't go around accusing Emmett London of being a criminal if I were you." She recalled Emmett's words in the café. "He might not like it."

Ryan flushed a dull red. "What is this? Just because he's screwing you, you believe every word he says? I thought you were smarter than that, Lydia."

"My private life is none of your concern, Ryan. Not anymore."

"Pay attention here," he snarled. "The fact that London hired you in the first place should tell you he's got plans that probably aren't going to do you any good."

"What do you mean?"

"You know as well as I do that if his consulting job had been legitimate, he'd have gone through the Society to hire a private P-A. Instead, he chose you. Doesn't that tell you something?"

"I think you've said enough, Ryan."

"He picked you, a tangler working in a place like this because she got so badly fried that she lost her job at the university. You tell me why he'd want a P-A who will probably never work on a reputable excavation team again."

"Shut up, Ryan," Lydia said steadily.

"Have you seen your own para-psych files?" he demanded. "At least two of the shrinks who treated you after you came out of the catacombs recommended that you check into a nice, tranquil para-psych ward for an extended stay."

She clenched her fists. "Those files are supposed to be private."

"Ghost-shit. Everyone in the department knows what's in them. You were diagnosed as suffering from extreme para-dissonance, amnesia, and general psychic trauma. We both know what that means. As far as the experts are concerned, you're liable to crack under the slightest pressure."

"That won't happen."

"For sure you'll never work underground again, at least not with a legit-imate team." He flung out one hand. "Hell, you're lucky to get a job in this two-bit carnival house of horrors."

Rage flooded through her. She felt pain in her palm and realized that her nails were biting into her skin. "If you don't remove your hand, I'm going to yell. Maybe I can get you arrested. How do you think the folks back in the lab would react to that? For that matter, how would your new *client* take it? Something tells me that if he's after dreamstone, he'd prefer a little dis-cretion from his consultant."

Ryan's face mottled with fury. For a few seconds she thought she would have to make good on her threat. But he must have read the determination in her eyes.

With a disgusted oath he dropped his hand. "Listen to me, Lydia. You don't know what you're getting into here. I tell you, London is dangerous. There's something else you should know. He's got enemies who are also dangerous."

That gave her pause. "Enemies?"

"My client tells me that not everyone in the Resonance Guild likes the changes he made in the organization there." Ryan lowered his voice. "What's more, a couple of the people who stood in his way wound up dead in a catacomb. A lot of people think London arranged for their unfortunate accidents."

"That's absurd. If your client told you that, he really is deep-fried. You'll have to excuse me, Ryan." She made a show of glancing at her watch. "I'm going home."

"Damn it, haven't you heard a word I've said? You can't trust London. He's using you."

"Maybe I haven't made my position clear," Lydia said evenly. "As things stand now, I trust London more than I trust you."

"You should have told me that all it took to buy your trust was a good fuck. Hell, I'd have screwed you myself."

She would not let the bastard make her lose her self-control, she vowed silently. She was trembling with anger, but she kept her voice cool.

"You did ask, as I recall," she said very evenly. "Maybe you've forgotten that I declined. I think I had to wash my hair that night."

His hand came up. She watched in disbelief, wondering if he intended to strike her. Energy hummed silently in the gallery. *Not her own.* Her amber was still only skin temperature on her wrist. The invisible vibrations weren't coming from Ryan, either. This was a ghost-hunter frequency.

With a visible effort Ryan lowered his hand. He seemed oblivious to the energy in the air, though. He was too tense, too emotionally involved in the argument to notice it.

"You're in a very serious situation, Lydia. I can help you. Call me when you come to your senses. It's not just my future riding on this. Yours is also on the line."

He turned on his heel and strode off down the gallery. Lydia watched him walk away. Energy continued to vibrate gently, protectively, in the air around her.

She turned slowly and watched Emmett step out of the deep shadows cast by a large green quartz pillar.

"How long were you standing there?" she asked.

"Long enough."

"You heard? About his new client and all the rest?"

"I heard."

"Emmett, this means that someone else really is after the dreamstone. Whoever he is, he thinks that's the reason you're here in Cadence."

"Looks that way." Emmett glanced down the gallery to where Ryan had disappeared. "Thought I was going to have to fry him."

"Fry who? You mean Ryan?" She was briefly distracted by that. "Could you? This far from the Dead City?"

Emmett did not answer. Instead he took her arm. "Let's go. We've got an appointment."

"With whom?"

"Miss Helen Vickers."

"Who's she?"

"The good lady in charge of the day-to-day operations of the Transverse Wave Youth Shelter. I'll give you the rundown on our cover story on the way."

"Hey, I've got an idea. I could be your lawyer and you could be some rich, eccentric guy looking to give away lots of money."

"Too late," Emmett said. "When I called Miss Vickers, I told her that I would be bringing my wife with me. By the way, our last name is Carstairs."

Chapter Twenty-One

As things stand now, I trust London more than I trust you.

Okay, so it fell a little short of a ringing endorsement, Emmett thought as he followed Lydia into the offices of the Transverse Wave Youth Shelter. She could have been a touch more eloquent and maybe a shade more dramatic. *I would trust London with my life, my fortune, and my sacred honor,* would have done nicely. Or maybe, *I would trust London to the ends of the universe.* But he would take what he could get.

Probably should have gone ahead and fried Ryan while he had the chance, though.

The youth shelter's business office was located next door to the main facility. From where he stood, Emmett could see a handful of young people who looked to be in their late teens loitering on the sidewalk in front of the shelter. One of them was idly dribbling a frequency ball.

This section of the Old Quarter of Cadence, situated adjacent to the east wall of the Dead City, had clearly never felt the brush of gentrification. It was a mix of shabby chic, bohemian charm, and genuine urban blight. From the window of the Transverse Wave office, Emmett could see missions catering to the down-and-out hunkering cheek by jowl with pawnshops and seedy taverns. Boarded-up, dilapidated buildings occupied the spaces in between. Panhandlers and prostitutes brushed shoulders on the narrow sidewalks. It was easy to see why Lydia hadn't wanted Zane hanging out in this neighborhood.

Towering above the low, squat structures built by the first human residents of Cadence was the massive green quartz wall of the Dead City. The building that housed the Transverse Wave and its associated offices was one of the oldest in the quarter. It had been constructed in the very shadow of the wall.

Ambient psi energy leaked freely through small, often invisible cracks in the quartz. Emmett ignored the frissons that flickered through his parasenses. He knew Lydia felt them too. The little currents and eddies of energy were part of the atmosphere in the Old Quarters of the ancient cities. Tourists loved the creepy sensations.

He glanced around the dingy, cramped office as the door closed behind him. Two battered metal desks piled high with papers and folders, a couple of file cabinets, a telephone, and some scarred wooden chairs completed the decor. Just the sort of furnishings one would expect to see in the storefront charity run on a shoestring. A narrow hall led to another office and a closed door that looked like a storage closet.

An earnest, somewhat harried-looking woman who appeared to be in her early forties sat behind the front desk. She wore no makeup. Her graying hair was done in a simple, no-nonsense bun. Emmett did not see any amber accessories.

She glanced up expectantly. "Mr. and Mrs. Carstairs?"

Lydia held out her hand. "You must be Miss Vickers. Emmett and I are delighted to meet you."

Emmett was amused by her rich, plummy tones. Her academic accent, he figured.

"Call me Helen." Helen Vickers indicated two of the chairs. "Please sit down. Can I get you some tea?"

Emmett opened his mouth to say no.

"Thank you," Lydia murmured. "That would be very nice."

Emmett glanced at her and decided to follow her lead. "I'd appreciate that."

"I was delighted to get your phone call this afternoon, Mr. Carstairs." Helen got to her feet to pour tea from a pot that sat on the other desk. "May I ask how you heard about the work that we do here at the Transverse Wave Youth Shelter?"

"A friend of ours mentioned your facility," Emmett said easily. "He knew that we were very interested in giving money to an organization that focused on young people."

"That's wonderful." Helen glowed with enthusiasm as she handed them the cups. "You've come to the right place. We here at Transverse Wave have dedicated ourselves to helping young people who have nowhere else to turn."

Lydia sipped tea. "My husband and I have been advised by our accountant to investigate a number of different charities that work with young people before we make our decision. He warned us that there are a number of less than ethical charitable organizations around."

"Unfortunately that is all too true. But we here at the Wave are very proud of the fact that the vast majority of our donations go straight back into the work of the shelter. Only a tiny amount is used for overhead and fundraising. Let me give you a brochure and our latest annual report."

She went to a file cabinet, opened a drawer, and plucked out a folder. She handed it to Emmett.

He opened the annual report and flipped to the organizational information at the back. He studied the list of donors while he listened to Lydia gently question Helen Vickers.

"Can you tell us a little about the history of the Transverse Wave, Helen?" Lydia asked. "We understand it's been in existence for a number of years."

"Over thirty years," Helen assured her. "It was established by Anderson Ames, a wealthy industrialist who came from an impoverished background. He knew the perils of the street firsthand and wanted to set up a foundation that would help young people avoid them."

"Is Mr. Ames still involved in the work of the shelter?" Lydia asked innocently.

"I'm sorry to say that he died two years ago," Helen said. "He had hoped that the shelter would go on without him, but the lawyers discovered irregularities in the trust's finances. Things looked bleak until—"

The front door opened at that moment. A tall, well-built man dressed in gray sweats and a pair of sports shoes strode into the office. He carried a frequency ball under one arm. A film of perspiration gleamed on his forehead.

Helen Vickers smiled. "This is Bob Matthews. He volunteers as our recreational director. Bob, meet Mr. and Mrs. Carstairs. They're considering a donation to the shelter."

"Hey, that's great!" Bob grabbed Emmett's hand and pumped it enthusiastically. "If there's one thing we need more of around here, it's donors. Always glad to meet one."

Emmett nodded and retrieved his hand. "It looks like you do good work."

Bob chuckled. "We try. Mind if I give you my sales pitch for some new gym equipment?"

"Another time, Bob," Helen said firmly. "Mr. and Mrs. Carstairs are just gathering information today."

"Got it." Bob held up a hand. "Helen knows me too well. I tend to get a little carried away when it comes to getting stuff for my kids."

"How long have you been volunteering at the shelter?" Emmett asked.

"Let's see, what is it now, Helen? Six? Eight months?"

"Eight, I think." Helen smiled. "And I don't know what we'd do without you." She looked at Emmett. "Bob has really rezzed up our athletic program. Physical activity is so important for the kids. It helps work off some of their frustration and anger."

"I understand." Lydia rose, cup in hand, and sauntered toward a large calendar that hung on the wall near the closet.

Emmett knew she was up to something.

"Looks like you have a very active schedule here at the shelter," Lydia said, surveying the little squares around each date of the calendar.

Helen glowed. "Thanks in large part to Bob."

Bob grinned. "Don't you believe it. I do what I can, but Helen is the one who keeps this place running day in and day out. Now, if you'll excuse me, I just stopped to pick up some keys from my office. Sorry to interrupt."

"No problem," Emmett said.

Bob went down the hall to the small office, opened the door, and disappeared inside.

Lydia looked at Emmett. "Did you have any more questions, *dear*?"

"Just one." He closed the annual report and glanced at Helen. "I see the Guild is listed as one of your major donors."

"It is indeed," Helen said. "And I can tell you in all honesty that if it weren't for the Cadence Guild stepping in last year when we were going through a bad patch financially, the shelter would have had to close its doors. We have Mercer Wyatt's new wife to thank for our continued existence. A very gracious and caring lady."

"Really?" Lydia mused.

"Indeed, just as we were staring financial disaster in the face, the new Mrs. Wyatt launched the Cadence Guild Foundation. We were one of the first charities chosen to receive grants. The Guild money was a godsend."

"All right, let's have it," Lydia said twenty minutes later as she got in on the passenger side of the Slider. "What are you thinking about the Guild's involvement in the Transverse Wave Shelter?"

"I don't know what to think yet," Emmett said. "I'm still gathering data. I called my office in Resonance City this morning. I'm having someone there do what the administrators of the Cadence Guild Foundation did."

"Look into the shelter's background?"

"Right." He eased the Slider away from the curb. "A duplication of effort, but I couldn't ask for the Foundation's report without raising questions that I'm not prepared to answer yet."

"Speaking of the Guild Foundation, doesn't Tamara Wyatt's interest in social responsibility strike you as a little hard to swallow?"

"No. Tamara was always very big on enhancing the Guild's social image."

"I see."

He smiled slightly. "I realize you don't view that as an achievable goal. There are, however, some of us who think the Guilds can take their place in society as respectable businesses."

"Next thing you know, some Guild boss will be running for mayor."

"Maybe we should get back to the subject at hand," Emmett said.

"Maybe we should." She hesitated, wondering how far she could go. She decided to take the plunge. "Level with me, Emmett. All personal issues aside, do you think Tamara is involved in this?"

He kept his attention on the narrow, crowded street. "It's not beyond the realm of possibility. Wyatt told me that he started making plans to retire shortly after he and Tamara got married."

"Must have come as a shock to Tamara."

"I think it would be safe to assume that she was probably not thrilled."

"Possibly even stunned," Lydia said dryly. "Just think about it. First she dumps you because she finds out that you're planning to resign your position as head of the Resonance Guild and she won't get to be Mrs. Guild Boss if she goes through with the marriage. Then she sweeps the Cadence Guild boss off his feet, marries him, and he promptly announces that he intends to retire too. What's a girl gonna do?"

"An interesting question," Emmett said. "But knowing Tamara, I wouldn't be surprised to find out that she came up with an idea or two."

"I still don't see what you saw in her."

"Funny, I still can't figure out what you saw in Kelso," Emmett retaliated. "What were you doing back there at the shelter when you were looking at the calendar on the office wall?"

"I thought I caught a trace of rez energy."

He frowned. "The office is right next to the Old Wall. There's stray rez energy leaking all over the place around here."

"If I'm not mistaken, this was illusion trap energy," she said softly.

That got his attention. "Are you sure?"

"No. It was faint." She looked out the window toward the towering green quartz walls.

He thought about the little snare she had discovered in the dreamstone jar. "See anything suspicious in the office when you looked around?"

"No, nothing. It must have been a stray leak. Could have come up through the foundation and the floorboards, I suppose. Some of the experts, including Ryan, think that we haven't mapped more than twenty percent of the catacombs here in Cadence, let alone cleared them of traps. They extend for miles underground."

"Speaking of the professor," Emmett said, "I think we'd better see if we can identify his client."

"Probably just some private collector who heard rumors about dreamstone. Happens all the time."

"How often do private collectors follow dreamstone rumors that lead to you?"

She winced. "Okay, I see what you mean. Whoever approached Ryan not only knows that I'm involved in this, he's linked you to it too."

"Which means that he may be a hell of a lot more than just a private collector who heard some rumors."

"I agree. And I have an idea how we can find out about Ryan and his new client."

"How?"

"I worked at the university for quite a while. I know a lot of people on the staff. A few of them owe me. I'll make some calls when we get back to my place."

*Emmett went into the kitchen and opened the box that con-*tained the pizza he had picked up on the way back to the apartment. He listened to Lydia's end of the phone call as he took two plates out of the cupboard.

"No, I am not spying on Ryan. For God's sake, Sid, you think I'm jealous because he's dating Suzanne? That's ridiculous. This is a professional inquiry."

There was a short pause. Emmett took the lid off the pretzel jar. Fuzz tumbled through the doorway and looked up at him with wide blue eyes.

"Why do I want to know if he's got any after-work appointments this week?" Lydia said. "I'll tell you why. I think Kelso is trying to steal a client out from under me."

Emmett fed a pretzel to Fuzz.

"No, I don't want you to do anything that could cost you your job, Sid. I just want to know if Ryan has anything on his calendar this week that looks like a non-academic meeting."

Emmett picked up the plates of pizza and went to lounge in the kitchen doorway. On the other side of the small room, Lydia was ensconced on the sofa, feet propped on the coffee table.

"Am I calling in a favor? Guess you could say that. You're right, you do owe me. If I hadn't covered for you and Lorraine that afternoon . . . well, I don't think we need to go into that, do we?"

There was another short pause. Then Lydia grinned. She gave Emmett a thumbs-up signal.

"Thanks, Sid," she said. "I appreciate it. I really can't afford to lose this new client. That's okay, take your time. I'll be at this number all evening."

She hung up the phone and looked at Emmett. "Mission accomplished."

"Who's Sid?" Emmett crossed the room and sat down on the sofa. He put both plates on the table. "And why does he owe you?"

"Sid's a lab tech." She reached for a slice of pizza. "A year ago he and Ryan's secretary, Lorraine, had a mad, passionate affair. They got a little carried away one afternoon. I walked into Ryan's office and found them on top of the desk."

"I take it they were not reading the minutes of the last departmental meeting?"

"Nope. I covered for them. Stalled Ryan out in the hall with some dumb questions until they had a chance to get dressed and Lorraine could take her place at her own desk."

"What would Kelso have done if he'd found them screwing on his desk?"

"Probably fired them both."

"Kelso's a real stickler for appropriate behavior in the office?"

She smiled slowly. "Not exactly. Ryan was sleeping with Lorraine himself at the time. Everyone knew it. He'd have been furious if he'd discovered that she was two-timing him with a lowly lab tech."

"And here I thought academics were a dull, staid lot. Talk about your shattered illusions."

"We have our moments."

He munched pizza while he pondered the details of the conversation he had overheard.

"About that story you used with your friend Sid," he said after a while.

She licked up a long thread of melted cheese that dangled from her slice of pizza. "The one about my being worried that Ryan was trying to steal my client away from me?"

"I believe your exact words were that you were afraid Kelso was trying to steal your client out from under you."

"So?"

"I'd just like to clarify one point."

"What point?"

"Assuming you were referring to me, let me assure you that I have no intention of being stolen out from under you. In fact, I can't imagine any-place I'd rather be than under you. Unless maybe on top of you."

She paused in mid-chew. Her eyes widened. Then she swallowed convulsively. "Uh—"

"Sooner or later we're going to have to talk about it, you know."

"What? Talk about what?" she demanded.

"You. Me. Us."

"There's nothing to talk about. We have a business association. Nothing more."

"I thought it was men who were supposed to have a hard time with re-lationship discussions." He shrugged. "It can wait, if that's the way you want to handle it. But you can't avoid the subject forever."

"Wanna bet?" She started to reach for another slice of pizza.

The phone rang. She dropped the pizza and grabbed the receiver.

"This is Lydia. Yeah, hi, Sid. What have you got?"

Emmett watched the intense concentration gather on her intelligent face as she listened to her friend. He wondered if she knew how incredibly sexy she was when she became so utterly focused.

She waved her hand wildly. It dawned on him that she was signaling for paper and pen. He saw both on the end table, scooped them up, and handed them to her.

Lydia went very still, pen poised over the paper. Then she frowned. "Is that all you've got, Sid? Yeah, yeah, I know. It's better than nothing. Didn't Lorraine have any idea of who called?"

Whatever Sid had to say was apparently not entirely satisfying. Lydia tossed the pen down. "If that's all you've got, it's all you've got. Do me a favor, don't mention this to anyone around the lab, okay? I still entertain a few vague hopes of getting my old job back one of these days. What's that? Right. We'll have drinks after work sometime soon."

She dropped the phone into its cradle and looked at Emmett with a combination of triumph and frustration.

"What did you get?" he asked.

"Sid says he checked with Lorraine. There's nothing on Ryan's schedule that's not routine. But she told him that late yesterday afternoon she answered a call in the office. The man didn't identify himself to her, just asked to speak with Ryan. When he finished the call, Ryan seemed very excited. He came out into the office and asked her for my new phone number."

"Did she give it to him?"

"Yes. Lorraine, figuring there was some hot-and-heavy gossip going down, listened in on Ryan's next call, which was to me. But I wasn't home. Today Ryan was out of the office most of the day. He called in once or twice asking if I had called. When she told him no, he seemed well and truly pissed."

"Pissed, huh?"

"Yeah. I often have that effect on men."

"I'll keep that in mind."

"At any rate," Lydia continued, "she took another call for Ryan just as she was getting ready to leave the office today. It was the same man who had called yesterday. She recognized the voice. She was just about to tell him that Ryan wasn't there when Ryan stormed back into the office."

"Fresh from having just been to see you at Shrimpton's," Emmett observed.

"No doubt. Made exceedingly curious by this exciting turn of events, Lorraine delayed her departure from the office long enough to listen at Ryan's door while he took the call. She heard him agree to meet the caller later tonight. Apparently Ryan was less than thrilled about the location of the rendezvous, however. Lorraine told Sid that Ryan tried to argue about it, but in the end he agreed to meet there."

Emmett glanced at the blank pad of paper. "I assume Lorraine did not get the name of the meeting place?"

"Unfortunately, no." She picked up the pen and irritably tapped the point against the paper. "But I've got an idea."

Emmett helped himself to another slice of pizza. "You want to stake out Kelso's place and see where he goes tonight."

She looked at him. "How did you guess?"

"It just came to me in a blinding flash of the obvious."

Her brows rose. "You mean you were thinking the same thing."

"Right. A case of great minds resonating together, I guess."

Chapter Twenty-Two

Somewhere around ten-thirty Lydia tried to stretch in the close confines of the Slider's front seat. "If Ryan doesn't do anything exciting soon, I'm going to have to knock on his front door and ask to use the bathroom."

"I tried to talk you out of coming with me tonight," Emmett said with no sign of sympathy.

"Just because you don't mind using the bushes in the park—" She broke off abruptly as the front door of Ryan's condo opened. "There he is."

She leaned forward, excitement bubbling inside her. She could see Ryan very clearly in the streetlights as he walked to his Coaster, parked at the curb.

"There he goes," she whispered.

There was no need to keep her voice pitched low. The Slider's front seat afforded ample privacy, parked halfway down the block in the shadow of a large tree. There was no way Ryan could see, let alone hear, her. But the sheer drama of following Ryan to his mysterious appointment had gotten to her. She realized that the rush was not unlike what she experienced when she tangled with an illusion trap.

"I see him," Emmett said.

She heard the edge in his voice and knew that she was not the only one who was feeling the adrenaline.

"I wonder if we made poor career choices somewhere along the line," she said. "Maybe we should have become private investigators or something."

He glanced at her with amusement as he rezzed the ignition. "I'm told the work is not usually this interesting. Most private investigators spend their time getting evidence of adultery to be used in Covenant Marriage dissolution cases."

"Depressing. Guess I'll stick with my job at Shrimpton's."

Emmett waited until Ryan pulled away from the curb, then eased the Slider out from the dark shadows beneath the tree. Lydia listened to the soft, hungry whine of the engine and willed Ryan not to look in his rearview mirror.

Kelso drove at a slow, cautious pace, as though he was not particularly eager to get to his destination.

"Probably doesn't want to have to explain to his client that he failed to get me to cooperate," Lydia said. "I hope the guy fires him on the spot tonight. Serve him right."

"I detect a degree of personal animosity, possibly even vengeance, in your tone," Emmett said.

"Yeah."

Ryan cruised sedately along the broad avenues of the university district, past elegantly maintained lawns and harmonically proportioned homes and condominiums.

When he left the neighborhood he turned left and started toward the Old Quarter.

"Well, well, well," Lydia said.

"My sentiments exactly."

A few minutes later Ryan reached the Quarter and drove even more slowly into the maze of narrow streets that bordered the east wall of the Dead City. Some areas of the neighborhood, those that catered to tourists, were reasonably well lit. But the rest of the Quarter existed in a pervasive gloom.

A block away from the main drag, the tiny, twisted lanes and alleys depended on the weak, erratic glow that spilled from the windows of the area's taverns and clubs.

"Be careful," Lydia said. "It would be easy to lose him here. Some of these alleys aren't even on the city maps."

"I won't lose him," Emmett promised softly.

There was a new quality in his voice. The edge was still present, but now there was something else, something almost feral. She studied him covertly. His expression was unreadable in the shadows, but she sensed the predatory anticipation in him.

A small shiver went through her. Energy leaking from the Dead City, she thought. They were very near the wall.

But she knew that what she felt had nothing to do with stray frissons of ambient psi energy in the area. Her senses were rezzed, and they were vibrating in response to the core of power that resonated deep within Emmett, power that was at once very male and very dangerous. It was as though he was readying himself for hand-to-hand combat. But that made no sense, she thought. They were only here to observe Ryan's meeting with his client. Why was Emmett radiating such intense energy?

She opened her mouth to ask him if something was wrong. But at that moment she saw Ryan's car pull over and park at the curb. She peered through the windshield and saw the dim glow of a tavern sign.

"Good grief," she muttered. "I think he's headed for the Green Wall Tavern. No wonder he tried to talk his client out of meeting him here."

"Not an upscale, trendy kind of place, I take it?"

"It's a bottom-of-the-barrel dive. Makes you wonder what kind of lowlife Ryan is working for. He's got a lot of nerve bad-mouthing you for being involved with the Guild when *his* client schedules meetings in a joint like the Green Wall."

"Nice to know I'm a step up," Emmet said humbly.

Lydia was grateful for the dark shadows of the front seat. She knew she had gone very red.

She watched Ryan climb out of the Coaster, lock it carefully, and then glance around uneasily.

"He doesn't like the looks of the neighborhood," Emmett remarked as he angled the Slider into a space at the curb.

"I don't blame him."

Ryan started down the sidewalk toward the Green Wall Tavern. He glanced back at the Coaster several times.

"He's afraid that when he returns, he's going to find his windows smashed and his car stripped," Lydia said. It belatedly occurred to her that the Slider made an even more tempting target for street vandals than Ryan's Coaster. "And the same thing might happen to your car, Emmett. Maybe we should park somewhere else."

"Don't worry about the Slider." He cracked the door and got out. "I don't think we'll have any trouble."

Unconvinced, Lydia scrambled out of her side and looked at him over the top of the vehicle. "This is one of the worst sections of the Old Quarter in Cadence."

"The car will be okay." Emmett came around the front of the Slider and took her arm. "I've got insurance."

"Even so, if we come back here and find the Slider's been stripped we'll be stuck." She peered worriedly back over her shoulder, much as Ryan had done a moment ago.

She caught a glint of green.

She stopped in her tracks and turned fully around to stare at the parked car. There was a very faint but unmistakable acid-green glow hovering around the license plate of the Slider.

Emmett stopped beside her and glanced casually back at the glowing license plate. "I told you, I have insurance."

"Whew! You can say that again. No car prowler with an eighth of a brain would touch the car of a ghost-hunter strong enough to leave a small ghost hanging around. How did you do that?"

"No big deal. There's plenty of stray psi energy around here. More than enough for me to anchor a little of it to the car for a while."

If Emmett could summon even a tiny ghost and leave it attached to his car while he was halfway down the street, she mused, he was much more powerful than she had guessed.

Not that the news should have come as a major surprise, she thought. Weak ghost-hunters probably did not rise to the top in the Guild's hierarchy. All the same . . .

"Sheesh," she muttered.

"Come on." He took her arm again and tugged her away from the glowing license plate. "We don't want to lose Kelso."

There would be time enough later to sweat out the implications of doing business with a hunter who could set a ghost to guard his car in a bad neighborhood, Lydia thought. She forced herself back to the problem of Ryan's anonymous client.

"We can't follow Ryan into the tavern," she said. "He'll see us."

"So what? We just want to identify his client. Once we see who it is he's meeting, it won't matter if he spots us."

His logic made sense, but it did nothing to quiet her growing unease. On the other hand, she reminded herself, she was in no position to argue. Following Ryan had been her idea.

Mute, she allowed Emmett to guide her into the synch-smoke-and-gloom-filled interior of the Green Wall. She saw at once that the place was several rungs lower on the tavern evolutionary scale than the Surreal Lounge. Whereas the Surreal exuded a kind of cheerful seediness, the Green Wall was a rough-and-ready, serious drinking place—the clientele had no doubt been asked to leave the premises of other, more upwardly mobile establishments.

Her fears of being seen by Ryan faded swiftly. In places like this, people tended to avoid eye contact. Besides, Ryan was bound to be more nervous than anyone else here. The last thing he was likely to do was look for someone he might recognize.

Emmett found a small booth on the side, and Lydia slipped into the corner. A waitress appeared to take their orders. Emmett sent her away with a request for two beers.

Lydia leaned forward. "Do you see Ryan?"

"He's at the bar. Alone."

"Any chance that he spotted us when we came in?"

Emmett shook his head. "He's got his head down, nursing a beer. I don't think he wants to be seen here any more than we want him to see us."

"Hmm. Maybe his big-time client stood him up." That possibility amused her. "He won't like that. Ryan's used to people worrying about keeping *him* waiting."

The beers arrived a few minutes later. Lydia peered cautiously toward the bar. She managed to catch a glimpse of Ryan, who looked as if he wished he was invisible. He was definitely not having a good time, she thought.

"Looks like he's been stood up, all right," Emmett said thoughtfully. "Interesting."

There was another small break in the crowd. Lydia saw the bartender move down the bar to where Ryan was hunched over his beer. The man must have said something, because Ryan's head came up swiftly.

"We've got a problem." Emmett was on his feet. "Stay here. Whatever you do, don't go back to the car alone. Got that?"

"I've got absolutely no intention of leaving without you. What's going on? Where are you going?"

"The bartender just handed Kelso a note. I don't think it was a thank-you from the mystery client. I'll be right back."

He turned and started toward the bar. Lydia gave him a minute, during which a sense of impending disaster settled on her. Emmett was walking into trouble. She knew it as surely as she knew her own name.

She put down the beer, grabbed her purse, and slid out of the booth. Plunging through the crowd, she made her way toward the bar, arriving just in time to see Ryan slinking uncomfortably toward the dark hallway marked REST ROOMS. Emmett was hard on his heels, gliding through the throng like a shark through the water.

Both men disappeared into the shadowy passageway. Panic wafted through her. Something was going very wrong here.

Clutching her purse tightly, she pushed her way through the tangle of people gathered around the bar. The synch-smoke was so thick she had to wave her hand in front of her face to clear the air.

She paused in mid-wave when she saw the huge man with hot, bleary eyes looming in front of her. He wore badly stained ghost-hunter khakis and leathers. His hair had even more grease on it than his clothes did. The smell of alcohol on his breath was so strong she was tempted to stop breathing.

"Hey, there, you're a cute little thing." He gave her what was no doubt meant to be a devilishly sexy grin, but it fell short and landed somewhere in the vicinity of a drunken leer. "You all alone, honey?"

"No," she said coldly. "I'm with someone. Please let me pass."

"Who is he?" The man swayed slightly as he surveyed the crowd behind her. "Point him out. I'll bet I can convince him to let you go home with me."

"I doubt it. Get out of my way."

"The name's Durant. I'm a hunter."

"No kidding." She tried to step around him, but he slid back in front of her.

"You ever had yerself a good time with a hunter, cute thing?" He winked broadly. "We're a little extra-special. Know what I mean?"

"Odd you should bring that up. I just happen to be here with a hunter tonight, and he's not going to be real happy if he finds out you're putting the make on me. Now get out of my way."

"Don't you worry, cute thing. I'll invite him out back and fry his brains for him. He won't have much to say for a while after I get finished with him."

"I was under the impression that the Guild frowned on hunter duels," Lydia said icily.

"Nah. It just don't like 'em to get into the papers, that's all." Durant stretched out a massive hand. "Why don't you and me have us a drink? When your ex-boyfriend shows up, I'll take care of him."

"You want a drink, Durant?" She grabbed a glass off a passing tray. "Here, have one on me."

She dashed the contents of the glass straight into his face. The smell of cheap Green Ruin whiskey made her wince. Durant howled and staggered backward, wiping off the dripping liquid.

"Well, *shit*." Durant blinked several times, then smiled with delight. "I always wanted me a high-spirited-type female."

Seizing her chance, Lydia hurried past him and plunged into the rest-room hallway.

"Hey, come back here, cute thing." Durant lumbered into pursuit. "Don't go runnin' off like that. I do believe you're the woman I've been lookin' for since the day I turned thirteen. *I love you, darlin'*."

The evening was deteriorating rapidly. Lydia wrinkled her nose when she caught a whiff of the odors that seeped beneath the rest-room doors. She kept going, searching for the rear exit.

She turned a corner and saw the door to the alley. There was no sign of either Ryan or Emmett, but she caught a glimpse of a faint green glow coming through the opening. Ghost light.

Bad sign, she thought.

"Come back here, cute thing," Durant shouted euphorically. "I wanna marry you. I want you to have my babies, darlin'."

She stepped through the open doorway into the rank alley. Psi energy crackled in the air. She spun around, searching for the source of the ghost light. She froze when she saw the tableau illuminated in the eerie green glow.

Two ghost-hunters were closing in on Ryan, who had flattened himself against the back wall of the tavern. The assailants were each manipulating moderate-sized ghosts. They were using the green energy manifestations to pin Ryan. In the acid light his face was a mask of fear.

Lydia realized the hunters must have been waiting for him. They had trapped him, and now they were manipulating the ghosts closer. The slow, inefficient way in which the energy danced in the darkness told her that the assailants were young and inexperienced in the handling of psi energy.

But their intentions were clear. They were going to fry Ryan.

The glowing balls of dissonance energy had to be at least eighteen inches across. Serious-sized ghosts, considering that the young specter-cats were working outside the Dead City. The youths might be clumsy, but they were strong para-rezes.

Neither ghost alone would have been enough to do more than knock Ryan unconscious, maybe give him a few hours of amnesia. But together the pair could kill him or, at the very least, scramble his brains, perhaps permanently.

"Well, shit." Durant floundered to a halt behind Lydia and peered out into the alley. "What the hell's goin' on out here? We got us a little hunter duel?"

Lydia ignored him. She was too busy trying to locate Emmett in the darkness.

She saw the ghost he conjured first. Without warning, green fire burst into a sheet of blazing energy that was larger than the two smaller ghosts combined.

Emmett stepped out of the shadows of the Dead City wall on the other side of the alley. Around him, the night shimmered and danced with resonating energy. The ghost he had summoned floated toward the two hunters who had pinned Ryan.

"Well, shit," Durant said again, this time in a tone of near-reverent awe. "I don't believe the size of that ghost. And we're not even inside the wall. Whoever he is, he's gonna fry the lot of 'em."

The two young hunters who were closing in on Ryan must have sensed the large UDEM floating toward them. They whirled quickly.

"What the hell?" The first hunter stared, stunned at the advancing ghost. "There's the other guy. Get him."

"He's too strong. He's gonna fry us."

"We can take him."

They just might be able to do it, Lydia thought, horrified.

"Stop it!" she shouted. "I'm calling the police. This is illegal!"

No one paid any attention to her. The two ghosts the youths had been manipulating toward Ryan reversed course and veered to intercept the energy field that Emmett had summoned. The three shimmering balls of raw energy collided. Green sparks showered the night. Acid-green light flared high, crackling dangerously in the air.

Lydia closed her eyes to keep from being temporarily blinded by the bright flash. When she opened them a second later, fearing the worst, she saw Emmett's face starkly etched in the trailing edge of the eerie glow. She was certain that some of the backwash must have caught him, but he seemed unaffected. He kept moving forward. So did his ghost.

The two smaller ghosts winked out.

"He got mine." The second of the two assailants sounded terrified now. He whirled and ran.

The other youth did not respond. He was already fleeing into the night.

Emmett's ghost disappeared too. But another one, considerably smaller, snapped into existence just in front of one of the running youths.

"I'll be damned," Durant sounded deeply impressed. "Haven't seen anything that quick in years. Bushwhacked the little sonofabitch."

Lydia held her breath as the fleeing youth blundered straight into the energy field. It blinked out of existence as quickly as it had appeared, but she knew it had caught the young man. He stiffened and then crumpled to the pavement. He did not move.

Emmett went to stand beside the fallen youth.

"Is he . . . ?" Lydia took a step toward the pair and halted. "Emmett, is he okay?"

"He'll be fine. He just caught some of the de-rez backwash. He'll be out for a while."

"Thank goodness." She glanced at Ryan, who was still slumped against the wall, looking dazed. When she turned back she saw that Emmett was swiftly going through the hunter's pockets.

"What are we going to do with him?" Lydia asked.

"Nothing." Emmett fished a wallet out of the youth's back pocket, flipped it open. "I just want to see who he is."

"Well, shit," Durant said.

Emmett looked up from the open wallet. For the first time he seemed to notice the big man standing in the open doorway.

"Who's that?" he asked Lydia.

Lydia looked at Durant, who was staring openmouthed at Emmett. "That's Durant. He says he's in love with me. He wants me to marry him and have his babies."

"Is that so?" Emmett gave Durant a speculative look.

Durant gulped and managed to close his mouth. "No. *No.* Big misunderstanding." He flapped his hands in a warding-off gesture. "Just a passing acquaintance, that's all."

"He mentioned something about dueling you for my hand," Lydia said.

"Yeah?" Emmett watched Durant very steadily.

"She's got it all wrong," Durant yelped. He staggered backward, then turned clumsily and disappeared into the darkness of the tavern hall.

"It's exactly like they tell you in all the women's magazines," Lydia said. "Men these days just can't seem to commit."

Chapter Twenty-Three

Ryan sprawled on the sofa in his living room and gulped brandy from the large glass he held in a hand that still shook. "Look, I'd tell you if I knew anything useful. But the truth is, we did everything over the phone until tonight."

Kelso was not the only one still feeling the aftereffects of the ghost-storm in the alley, Emmett thought. There was a price to be paid for using the intensive level of psi energy he had needed to deal with the two young ghost-hunters tonight. And just to make things interesting, he'd been clumsy enough to get caught in the backwash. He'd been here before. He knew what to expect.

Right now he was in the restless stage, his senses still rezzed, the adrenaline not yet flushed from his system. Lydia's friend Melanie had been right about one aspect of hunter physiology, he reflected dourly. In spite of the more immediate issues that logic told him had to be dealt with tonight, he was very horny. It wasn't something he couldn't control, and he knew the sense of urgency would fade soon. Nevertheless, he would have given anything to be alone with Lydia right now.

Not any woman, just Lydia.

Oh, brother. He was in big trouble.

He watched her out of the corner of his eye, yearning and need twisting through him. She was not paying any attention. She was too busy zeroing in on the hapless Ryan.

"You mean to tell me that you didn't sign a formal contract with your client, Ryan?" Her voice was laced with supercilious disapproval.

She was gloating, Emmett thought. On the surface she was projecting concern and a perfectly appropriate degree of professional dismay, but underneath she was definitely gloating. Kelso had screwed up badly, and she was not going to let him forget it. Served the bastard right, Emmett thought. But they did have more pressing concerns at the moment.

"The guy sounded legitimate," Ryan said defensively.

"You mean he mentioned worked dreamstone and you got all rezzed-up," Lydia retorted. "Honestly, Ryan, what were you thinking? Dreamstone, of all things."

Ryan slumped deeper into his brandy, momentarily, at least, a beaten man.

Lydia tut-tutted and moved in for the kill. "And everyone assumes that *my* brains got fried."

Serious gloating, Emmett thought. But she did look sexy as hell.

Damn, this was stupid. Even if he did have her alone in a bedroom, she would probably kick him out. She would assume that his erection was caused by the energy burn.

She would be right, but only partially so. He did want her—badly—but what he was feeling tonight was not the usual short-lived generalized sexual desire that resulted from a major burn. This was a lot stronger, more potent, and it was focused only on her. He didn't want just sex tonight, he wanted sex with Lydia.

He wondered if she could grasp the significance of the distinction. He certainly did. It left him reeling.

He took a deep breath and clamped down on his hormones. In an hour or so, when the last of the burn effects wore off, he would forget all about sex with Lydia or anyone else. The only thing on his mind would be sleep. He would need a bed far more than he would need to get laid. Until then he just had to tough it out and concentrate on the problem of Ryan Kelso.

He studied the spines of the volumes on the bookcase as he listened to Ryan ramble on about the evening's events. He'd seen many of the same titles in Lydia's bookcases, both the one in her apartment and the one in her office. They included Caldwell Frost's infamous *Dawn in a Dead City,* Arriola's *Theory and Practice of Para-archaeology,* and several years' worth of the *Journal of Para-archaeology.* But whereas the books on Lydia's shelves were arranged in a jumbled clutter that gave you the feeling she actually read them, Kelso's library was painfully neat.

Emmett turned slowly to survey the room. The old-fashioned leather furniture, the carved oak desk, and the dark carpet with its intricate, harmonically proportioned design all said, "I Am An Academic Honcho" in capital letters. The place looked as if it was ready to be photographed for a feature on scholarly rooms for *Harmonic Architecture Review.* What the hell had Lydia ever seen in this jerk?

He made himself concentrate on the problem at hand. Turning away from the bookcase, he looked at Ryan. He was pretty sure that Kelso was telling the truth, or at least as much of it as he knew. Ryan was washed out—still scared and still in shock. He knew he'd had one hell of a close call.

"Someone may have tried to kill you tonight," Emmett said flatly. "At the very least, those two hunters intended to fry you into a short-term coma. Your so-called client lured you to the Green Wall Tavern. Therefore, we have to assume he's the one who wanted you burned."

Ryan scowled into his brandy. "What are you saying?"

"I'm saying that you must know something."

"But I don't," Ryan whispered. "I swear it. All I know is a man calls me on the phone, claims to be a collector, talks like he knows the field, says he's heard a rumor of worked dreamstone and that you're in town looking for it, London. He says you've hired Lydia to help you find it."

"That's it?" Emmett asked.

"That's it. You don't fry a man because of a rumor of dreamstone. Hell, there've been wild stories about the stuff since it was first discovered. Collectors have chased the tales for years."

Emmett began to pace in an effort to work off the last of the adrenaline. "Tell me exactly what your client said this afternoon when you informed him that Lydia would not cooperate with you."

Ryan shrugged weakly. "He said he wanted to discuss some other angles we could take to locate the dreamstone. He told me to meet him at the Tavern at eleven. When I got there the bartender gave me that note telling me that the client wanted to rendezvous in the alley."

"You didn't find that just a little suspicious?" Lydia asked archly.

Ryan winced. "The guy made it clear from the beginning that he wanted to maintain a very low profile. I thought he was just trying to avoid being seen in the bar."

"A meeting in a back alley in the Old Quarter is low profile, all right," Lydia murmured.

Ryan's jaw tensed. "So call me stupid."

"Only if you insist," Lydia said cheerfully.

Emmett groaned. "Entertaining though it may be, we don't have time for the sniping. We need to get Ryan out of town. The last commuter flight to Resonance City leaves in less than an hour."

"What?" Ryan straightened abruptly, his face working. "I'm not going anywhere."

"You are if you know what's good for you." Emmett glanced at his watch. The yellow-gold disk was clouded from the intense burn. He must remember to replace it with fresh, tuned amber as soon as possible. So many details. "You've got five minutes to throw some clothes into a bag. Then we've got to get you to the airport."

"But—"

"Someone will meet you at the gate in Resonance," Emmett said.

Ryan looked truculent. "Who's going to meet me?"

"A couple of hunters from the Resonance Guild."

"Thanks, but no thanks." Ryan slammed his brandy glass down on the table. "No offense, but I'm not real keen on meeting any more ghost-hunters tonight."

Emmett held his attention. "Whoever tried to fry you tonight will probably try again. Maybe real soon. You need bodyguards. Under normal circumstances, I'd call Mercer Wyatt and arrange for protection here in Cadence, but I don't think that's a good idea right now. The local Guild is having some problems."

Lydia sniffed. "You can say that again."

Emmett ignored her. "If you don't get on that plane, Kelso, you're going to have to look over your shoulder every minute until this thing is finished."

"What about Lydia?" Ryan demanded. "If I'm in danger, so is she."

Emmett glanced at Lydia.

"Don't even think about it," she said crisply.

He looked back at Ryan. "I'll take care of Lydia."

"Yeah? And who's going to take care of you? The next time they may use three hunters instead of two. Everyone has his limits."

"I'm in a slightly more advantageous position than you are," Emmett said quietly. "For one thing, I'm a lot harder to fry. For another, if someone does succeed in burning me, he'll have a lot more to worry about than if he burns you."

"What do you mean?" Ryan's chin came up with arrogant disdain. "I'm a full professor at the university. I'm the head of the Department of Para-archaeology, damn it. If anything happened to me, the cops would be all over the case in a minute."

Emmett smiled humorlessly. "Maybe. But if anything happens to me while I'm in Cadence, it isn't only the cops who will be all over this thing. Mercer Wyatt would have to explain the situation to the head of the Resonance Guild. He wouldn't like that."

Lydia gave him a sharp, searching look, but she said nothing.

Ryan blinked in a befuddled fashion. Then comprehension settled in his eyes. "I see. This is a Guild matter."

"Yes."

"That does complicate things, doesn't it?" Ryan got to his feet with weary resignation. "I'd better pack." Shoulders slumped, he turned and walked out into the hall.

Lydia waited until he had disappeared. Then she switched her gaze back to Emmett. "Are you sure you're all right?"

"I'm fine. Just got to replace some amber, that's all."

"Replace it?" she said, concern echoing in her voice. "You melted amber?"

He shrugged. "Happens sometimes."

"Not to most people," she said brusquely. "My God, Emmett, if you used so much energy that you actually de-rezzed your amber, you must be half dead on your feet."

"I'll be okay. For a while, at any rate. Long enough to get Kelso to the airport." He rubbed the back of his neck. "When we get back to your place, though, I'm going to need some sleep."

"I can imagine," she said, then lowered her voice. "What did you find in that young hunter's wallet? Anything useful?"

"He wasn't carrying any ID."

"Oh, damn. I was hoping we'd be able to trace him."

"He was probably ordered to make certain he didn't carry anything that could be traced," Emmett said. "But he was a young man. Not well trained and probably not accustomed to thinking things through. He made one small mistake."

"What was that?"

"He'd removed his ID from his wallet, all right, but he forget his gym locker key. I left it where it was. With luck he won't realize that someone looked at it."

Lydia's eyes lit up with eagerness. "What gym does he use?"

"The key was stamped 'Transverse Wave Youth Shelter.' "

An hour later Lydia parked the Slider in the apartment complex lot, de-rezzed the key, and looked at Emmett with growing concern.

He was sprawled in the passenger seat, head against the padded headrest. He kept telling her he was okay, but she no longer believed him.

As soon as they had put Ryan on board the last flight to Resonance City,

Emmett had made a phone call to arrange for someone to meet the plane on the other end. He had talked to the person he reached for a few more minutes and then he had hung up. Standing outside the privacy booth, she was unable to hear the details of the conversation.

By the time he rejoined her, she was too concerned about him to ask any questions. She knew that he was in bad shape. When she took his arm on the way out of the terminal, he did not protest. Halfway back to the car, he started to lean heavily on her. She asked him for the Slider's keys so she could drive them home. He didn't argue.

"Emmett?" She put her hand on his shoulder and shook him gently. "Wake up. We're here."

He stirred but seemed disoriented. "Need some sleep."

She wondered if she ought to call someone for advice on how to handle post-meltdown syndrome. The truth was, she could not think of anyone who might know what to do. Melting amber was a very rare event, primarily because so few people possessed enough psi talent to do it. And those who were capable of it probably did not talk too much about the aftermath, especially if they were macho hunters who didn't like admitting to weakness of any kind.

Melting amber was just an expression. The stuff didn't actually melt under too much psi energy, but it did get "fogged." It lost the fine-tuned quality that made it able to focus accurately.

Lydia reached out, caught Emmett's face between her hands, and forced him to look at her. "Listen to me. Do you need a doctor?"

He shook his head once. She got the impression he was annoyed, maybe even disgusted.

"Need sleep." His voice had thickened.

His hand moved. She realized he was groping for the door handle.

"Hang on." She opened her own door and jumped out of the car. "I'll come around to your side and help you."

By the time she reached him, Emmett had managed to get his door open, but the bleak, barely-hanging-in-there look on his face told her that he did not think he could haul himself out of the front seat.

"I'll just sleep it off here," he said weakly.

"You want to spend the night in your car? In this part of town? Don't be ridiculous. It's not safe."

"Can't make it up the damn stairs."

"Wait here," Lydia said. "I'll get Zane and Olinda. We'll get you up the stairs."

Emmett did not protest. He was evidently beyond making the effort. Lydia hurried to the stairwell and took the steps two at a time to the third floor. She was breathless by the time she reached 3A.

Zane opened the door on the second knock. He was dressed in his pajamas. Behind him, the front room of the apartment was lit by the glow of the rez-screen.

Lydia said the first words that came into her head. "Shouldn't you be in bed?"

"I was in bed. I sleep in the living room, remember?"

This was no time to point out that it was far too late for him to be watching the rez-screen. "I need some help, Zane."

His face scrunched in alarm. "What's wrong? Is it Fuzz? Another ghost?"

"No, it's Emmett. He got into a brawl with some other ghost-hunters tonight. He melted amber and now he's exhausted. I need to get him up the stairs. Is Olinda home?"

"He melted amber?" Zane's eyes widened. "Holy shit!"

Olinda loomed in the hallway. Her robust figure was sheathed in an aging chenille robe. "Must be one hell of a hunter. Where is he?"

"Downstairs in the car." Lydia stepped back. "Can you give me a hand?"

"You bet. Can't wait to see this." Zane dashed through the doorway and pelted wildly toward the stairs.

Olinda followed more sedately. She closed the door behind her and joined Lydia in the hall. "I've heard these guys who can melt amber have to crash for a few hours afterward."

Lydia went swiftly back toward the stairwell. "He keeps saying he needs to sleep."

"Doesn't sound like he'll be much fun for a while." Olinda winked. "Maybe you shoulda picked one who wasn't quite as strong as London. I hear that the aftereffects of a normal-range amber burn are kinda interesting in ghost-hunters."

Chapter Twenty-Four

The hidden chamber glowed with resonating green light. Strange shadows appeared and disappeared on the walls. She sensed that some were doorways, but whenever she tried to approach one of the shifting dark patches, it vanished before she could walk through it.

Panic tightened her throat. She knew she must not let it overwhelm her. There had to be a way out of the chamber.

She went cautiously toward what appeared to be another darkened opening in the green quartz wall. She put out a hand, half expecting that this doorway would dissolve, just as the others had.

But instead of the wall, her fingers touched only air. Hardly daring to breathe, she went through the doorway into the antechamber.

She sensed illusion energy and halted. She searched the deep shadows and saw nothing. But she knew the trap was here, somewhere. She could feel it.

Then she saw the small dreamstone chest in the center of the room. She went slowly toward it, reached down, lifted the lid, and saw the photograph inside. Chester grinned at her from the picture.

Lydia awoke with a start. Fuzz was in her lap, his front paws braced on her chest. All four of his eyes were open.

"What's wrong?" she whispered.

She gazed wildly around the small living room, searching the shadows. But things appeared normal, or at least as normal as they could when you had a ghost-hunter sleeping on the sofa.

Emmett was stretched out on the cushions, still sound asleep, his head turned away from her.

Fuzz took his paws off her chest, closed his hunting eyes, and curled up again on her lap. He closed his daylight eyes too. The all-clear sign.

She stroked his fluffy gray fur absently. She had probably alarmed him when she was in the throes of her dream. Perhaps she had moved or muttered something.

After a while she picked Fuzz up and nestled him into the corner of the big chair. He did not open his eyes, merely shifted and made himself comfortable again.

She got to her feet and padded to the sofa. She reached down and pulled the blankets up higher around Emmett's shoulders. He did not stir.

She went to the window, pushed her hands into the deep sleeves of her robe, and looked out at her sliver-thin view of the Dead City. The images of the dream wafted through her head.

After a while she turned and walked toward the hall that led to her bedroom. In the nick of time she remembered the little table and avoided it.

When she reached her room she went to the dresser and looked down at the photo she had left there. The light from the partially open bathroom door angled across it. She could see Chester grinning at her, just as he had in the dream. She glanced at the copy of the *Journal of Para-archaeology* in his hand. He had been so proud to be listed as a consultant.

She went back out into the living room and settled once more into the depths of the big chair. Stretching out her legs, she propped her slippered feet on the footstool and pulled the lapels of her robe more snugly around her.

For a long time she just sat there, thinking and gazing out into the night.

Emmett awoke with a vague sense of disorientation. Then the memory of the burn-fest in the alley washed through him. He raised his wrist, opened his eyes, and stared at the face of the watch. Five o'clock in the morning. He calculated that he'd had three hours of solid after-burn sleep. Not exactly a good night's rest, but sufficient time for his body to recover from the heavy expenditure of psi energy.

He sensed another presence in the small room and turned his head. Lydia was curled deep into the wing chair near the window, her head pillowed in the corner and her legs tucked beneath the folds of her robe. From the crook of her arm, blue eyes blinked at him.

He pushed aside the covers and sat up cautiously. Glancing down, he discovered that someone, presumably Lydia, had removed his shirt. The thought that she had undressed him was an intriguing one. Then he realized that he was still wearing his trousers. Either she hadn't been able to get them off or the prospect of doing so had not appealed to her. He consoled himself with the possibility that she might simply have lost her nerve.

The blanket fell aside as he got to his feet. He had no memory of pulling it up over himself. He went down the hall to the ever-lit bathroom.

Inside the small room he turned on the faucet and leaned over the sink to splash cold water on his face. When he caught sight of himself in the mirror, he winced.

He went back out into the living room. Lydia had not moved, but Fuzz was gone from beneath her arm. Emmett glanced into the kitchen and saw the dust-bunny on the counter near the pretzel jar. Fuzz didn't appear to need any help getting at the pretzels.

He went back to the sofa, sat down amid the tumbled blankets, and propped his elbows on his thighs. He linked his fingers loosely together and looked at Lydia. Why the hell had she slept in that chair? Did she think she needed to stand guard over him? Was she afraid he was going to go berserk because of the amber burn? Another little hunter eccentricity? Maybe she was worried that he would tear up the place.

He noticed that she was awake now, watching him from the depths of the chair.

"How do you feel?" she asked. Her voice was soft and husky.

"Almost back to normal."

"You gave me a bit of a scare last night. I've never seen a ghost-hunter in that condition."

He ran one hand over his face, felt the rough stubble of his beard. He needed to shave. Soon.

"Speaking personally," he said, "I try to avoid it."

"I can understand that. You still don't look in great shape. Maybe you should go back to sleep."

"I'm okay, damn it."

"You don't have to bite my head off. It's not my fault you look like you just spent the night getting into a brawl behind a sleazy tavern."

He started to answer that and then thought better of it. "Why did you sleep in that chair?"

"I wanted to keep an eye on you. Zane and Olinda seemed to think you would be okay, but I wasn't so sure."

"Shit. I'm not an invalid, you know. The burn-and-crash syndrome is absolutely normal. At least, it is after you've used as much energy as I did last night."

She yawned. "You're welcome."

This was not going well. He was getting edgy again. It seemed to happen a lot around Lydia. He tried to distract himself.

"Thanks for getting me up here," he mumbled. "You were right. Spending the night downstairs in the parking lot was probably not one of my brighter ideas."

"No problem. Zane and Olinda helped."

"Uh-huh." He had a vague memory of everyone dragging, hauling, and pushing him up five flights of stairs. Talk about looking like an invalid. No wonder she had slept in the chair. Probably thought he needed a night nurse.

"Too bad the elevator is out." Great. Now he was rambling.

"You can say that again. Driffield's gonna pay one of these days." She pulled her robe closer around her throat and started to rise. "Well, since it doesn't look like either one of us is going to go back to sleep, I may as well take a shower and get dressed."

He stood up at the same time she did and blocked her path to the bedroom. She came to a halt directly in front of him and searched his face.

"Are you sure you're all right?" she asked.

"No. I am not all right." He cupped her face in his hands. "But I'm not going to go crazy and rip up your apartment."

"I never thought you'd do anything of the kind," she said defensively.

"Sure you did. It was written all over your face. You've been nervous about me right from the start. And every time some little quirk related to hunter physiology comes up, you freak out again. That's what happened last night, isn't it?"

"I don't believe this." She stared at him with gathering outrage. "You're upset because I spent the night here so that I could watch over you?"

"I am not upset," he said through his teeth. "But I am pissed as hell. Damn it, I'm not sick. I'm not going to lose it and wreak havoc in your living room. You didn't have to keep a vigil over me as if I was some unpredictable wild beast."

Temper flared, and then, without warning, her expression softened. "Take it easy. Calm down. You're not quite yourself yet. Why don't you go take your shower first? I'll have a nice hot cup of rez-tea waiting when you come out."

Her soothing tone nearly sent him over the edge. "I don't want any damned tea."

Her gentle concern evaporated. "Why are you so irritable this morning?

I was *worried* about you last night. You scared the daylights out of me when you collapsed on my sofa."

"I didn't collapse. I fell asleep. Big difference."

"You collapsed."

"I fell asleep. But guess what?"

"What?"

"I'm wide awake now." He pulled her close and crushed her mouth beneath his.

For an instant he thought she was going to explode with outrage. She sucked in her breath, her fingers curled into his shoulder.

And then she was kissing him back. *Fiercely*. Everything within him leaped into high rez. Urgency swept through him. He felt her respond to it. Her arms tightened around him as she fought him for the embrace.

They were definitely on the same frequency, he decided. He wasn't quite sure how the dissonance of their mutual hostility had metamorphosed so abruptly into near-violent sexual resonance, but he sure as hell was not going to take time to analyze it right now.

He yanked open her robe. She fumbled with the fastening of his trousers, got them unzipped. He felt himself surge forward into her waiting hands and groaned aloud. When her fingers tightened around him he wanted to shout.

He turned slightly, taking her with him, stepped back and half-fell, half-sank deep into the big, overstuffed chair. She tumbled down on top of him, warm and soft and scented with desire. Her robe fluttered over the arms of the chair as she settled astride him and closed her thighs around his.

He reached down and found the hot, wet place between her legs. She gasped when he dampened his fingers in her heat, breathed deeply when he stroked her clitoris. Her head tipped back. Her hair spilled down her back.

He gripped the wonderfully rounded flesh of her buttocks and thrust himself deep into her snug, tight body.

"*Emmett*."

He felt her fingers digging into his shoulders as he pushed himself to the hilt. She started to move on him, swift, urgent, excited motions. He found the swollen little bud once more, inserted his finger under it, just inside the already tautly stretched passage.

"Yes." Her breath was warm in his ear. "*Yes*."

He stroked into her, oblivious of everything now except the driving sense of need that consumed him. He felt her shudder, felt her convulse along the entire length of him. Her delicate harmonic shivers established a resonance as irresistible as the pull of gravity.

His release burned through him, hotter than melting amber. He pumped himself dry and then collapsed in exhaustion for the second time.

He surfaced a long while later. Lydia was still astride him, her face buried in the curve of his neck. Her body was damp, and he could smell his own scent on her. A raw, elemental sense of possessiveness surged through him. He wrapped his fingers around her upper thighs.

"I'd like to reiterate my main point," she mumbled.

"What was that? I think I forgot."

"I did not sleep out here because I thought you might go berserk and tear up my living room."

"You're sure?"

"I'm sure." She paused. "But if that's what you really want to do, be my guest."

"Thanks. Some other time, maybe."

"Whatever." She raised her head and looked down at him. In the pale dawn light her throat and cheeks were flushed. Her mouth and eyes were soft. She smiled.

He felt his body stir again. He tightened his hands on her thighs. "On second thought, maybe I will go berserk and tear up your apartment after all."

*He put the water on for the rez-tea while Lydia sliced glisten-*ing oranges into two bowls. It occurred to him that he was already starting to feel much too comfortable in the cramped apartment.

He was going to have to come up with an excuse to hang around after he cleared up this mess involving Quinn. He wasn't sure yet what was happening between Lydia and himself, but whatever it was, he didn't want to walk away from it. Not yet.

"What do we do next?" Lydia asked as she sat down beside him at the counter.

Optimism soared. They were apparently on the same frequency again this morning. Life was good.

"Funny you should mention that," he said. "I've been thinking."

"Me, too." She spooned up a mouthful of orange. "Everything points to the Transverse Wave Youth Shelter, right?"

"Right." So much for being on the same frequency. Emmett squelched his brief flash of optimism and refocused his attention.

"The Cadence Guild started funding the shelter earlier this year." Lydia looked at him as she blotted orange juice from her lips. "And we know that Tamara Wyatt was the driving force behind the Guild's new civic consciousness. Mercer Wyatt believes he's got a traitor, close to him. Maybe that traitor is even closer than he thinks."

"I know where you're going here, but it doesn't work."

"Emmett, I understand that you and Tamara have a past. You were in love with her. Maybe you still are—"

"No."

"Denial is no way to deal with these kinds of issues."

"I am not in denial. I'm telling you that I no longer have any strong feelings for Tamara."

"Right. She dumped you for another man. Of course you've got some strong feelings about her."

"Can we stick to the subject?" he asked evenly.

She looked as if she was going to argue. But she must have seen something in his face that changed her mind. She cleared her throat instead.

"Okay, fine," she said briskly. "I believe we were considering the possibility that Tamara is involved in whatever is going on at the shelter."

"Don't think so," Emmett said.

She glared at him. "Why do you keep insisting she's innocent? We've already decided that everything that's happened is connected. Chester's piece of dreamstone, his death, the missing youths, and Greeley's murder."

"I know."

"The common link is the shelter."

"Lydia—"

"There is one other fact that you can't ignore. Everything that's happened has taken place in the past few months. After Tamara's marriage to Wyatt. After she directed the Guild to set up a charitable foundation and start funding the Transverse Wave Youth Shelter. It all points to Tamara. Admit it."

He couldn't deny her logic. He pondered the problem for a few seconds, trying to find words for what until now had been only an instinctive reaction to the facts.

"Whatever is going on at the shelter, I agree that it's probably connected to the dreamstone," he said at last.

"So?"

"Think about it. Dreamstone is potentially extremely valuable both as an archaeological discovery and in the private collectors' market."

"Right. Whoever gets his hands on it can use it to establish an instant, brilliant reputation in the academic world. But in order to do so, he would have to turn it over to a museum."

"If someone who wasn't connected to the university wanted to capitalize on the discovery of dreamstone to become a celebrity, he or she would have to go public. That would mean holding press conferences. Giving interviews."

"Hmm."

"On the other hand, if the discoverer was planning to turn a huge profit on the dreamstone, he would have a good incentive to keep the find secret until he could do deals in the private market. That would be especially true if the excavation work was being carried out illegally."

"It's pretty obvious that someone is trying to keep the discovery quiet and that the excavation work is being done illegally. So what? How does that make Tamara innocent?"

"Everything about this operation points to someone who wants to keep it secret," Emmett said. "If Tamara was involved in this, she would be far more interested in the publicity than the money."

"Hmm," Lydia said again.

"As Mercer Wyatt's wife, she's already got access to all the money she could ever want."

"Some people never have enough money."

"What Tamara craves," he said patiently, "is social status and the power that comes with it. She wants to rub elbows with the right people. She wants to sit on the boards of charitable foundations, give fund-raisers for the arts, get invited to the homes of the movers and shakers. Believe me, if she got her hands on dreamstone, she would go public with it in a big way."

Lydia tapped her spoon on the edge of the bowl that held the oranges. "I guess you know her better than I do."

"Yeah." He shook cereal out of the box into his bowl. "I do."

She gave him a quick, unreadable glance, but she did not pursue the subject of his relationship with Tamara. "Okay, so we rule out Tamara based on your gut feeling that her motives don't fit the secrecy scenario we've uncovered. And it doesn't look like Ryan is directly involved, either."

"Someone tried to use him to find out how much you know about the missing piece of dreamstone, though," Emmett said. "Whoever is behind this knows we're getting close."

Lydia put down her spoon. "Last night I did a lot of thinking. Among other things, it occurred to me that whoever lured Ryan to the Green Wall Tavern may have had something else in mind besides getting rid of him."

He grunted and concentrated on eating cereal.

"Emmett?"

"Yeah?"

"Did you hear me?"

"Of course I heard you."

"Last night you made a big point of telling Ryan that you were safe because of your Guild connections."

"Uh-huh."

"But if you had been killed in that alley, the Cadence Guild authorities could have claimed that it was just the tragic consequences of your going to the aid of a mugging victim. One of those wrong-place-at-the-wrong-time crimes. Everyone's sorry, but it's nobody's fault."

"Wyatt would still have to explain to the Resonance Guild why the mugging was carried out by a couple of hunters," Emmett said.

"That's just the point. Those two youths probably aren't members of the Guild. You said yourself they were untrained. If and when they're caught, Mercer Wyatt can deny all responsibility."

He shrugged. "That doesn't mean the Resonance Guild wouldn't raise hell. A couple of young, strong dissonance-energy para-rezes like those two should have been under the control of the Guild."

"So the Resonance Guild makes a fuss. Big deal. Wyatt promises to investigate and find the bad guys. And that's the end of it."

He smiled briefly, without any amusement. "Take it from me, Lydia, Guild politics aren't that simple."

"You're deliberately missing my point here," she said very steadily. "I think someone hoped you would follow Ryan last night."

He picked up his rez-tea. "You're telling me that you think someone tried to set me up last night, aren't you?"

"Yes."

He took a swallow of tea and said nothing. There wasn't anything to say. He was pretty sure she was right. He'd been sure of it since he'd followed Ryan out into the alley.

"Well?" Lydia said aggressively.

"I can take care of myself, Lydia."

"Damn it, it *was* a setup. *I knew it.*"

She came off the stool with so much speed that her elbow hit the rez-teacup and sent it flying. She ignored it to grab him by the lapels. Since he was not wearing a shirt, she got two fistfuls of T-shirt instead.

"Take it easy, honey," he said soothingly.

"I'm right, aren't I? Someone tried to kill you last night."

"It's okay."

"No, it is not okay. In case it has escaped your notice, we are in big trouble here. We've got to do something. Maybe we should contact Detective Martinez."

"And get ourselves arrested on suspicion of murder? That's not going to do a whole hell of a lot of good."

"Well, what do you suggest, Mr. Ex-Guild Boss?"

He was silent for a moment. Then he said softly, "I suggest I go ahead with the plans I've already made."

"What plans? Why don't I know about these plans?"

"I haven't had much of a chance to discuss them with you," he said, deliberately vague.

"You mean you didn't intend to involve me in them, don't you?"

"Lydia—"

"Never mind. Tell me what you're going to do."

He shrugged. "I'm going to take a look around the offices of the Transverse Wave Youth Shelter tonight. See if I can turn up anything that will give us an idea of who is using the facility to recruit young para-talents off the street to excavate a cache of dreamstone."

"I'll come with you."

"No, you will not."

"You're going to need me, Emmett."

"Give me one good reason why I can't handle it alone."

She smiled coolly. "I told you that I thought I sensed illusion trap energy somewhere in the vicinity of the shelter's office, remember?"

He watched her, wary now. "We agreed that it wasn't unusual to pick up traces of energy leaks that close to the Old Wall."

"What if it wasn't just some leaked energy I sensed? What if it was emanating from a trap set to protect a cache of dreamstone or a small hole-in-the-wall gate that someone found and wants to keep secret?"

"Everyone knows you tanglers are inclined to be over-imaginative," he said.

"Everyone knows you stubborn, arrogant ghost-hunters think you can handle anything with a dose of dissonance energy, but it ain't so. I'm coming with you, Emmett. We're in this together."

She was right, he thought. They were in this together.

Chapter Twenty-Five

Melanie Toft put her head around the corner of the office door. "Thought this was your day off. What are you doing here?"

"I just came in to take care of some paperwork." Lydia turned away from the bookcase and smiled. "Don't worry, I'm not going to stay long."

"I should hope not. I've told you over and over again, you mustn't give Shrimp the idea that just because you're a genuine professional para-archaeologist, you should put in unpaid overtime."

"I promise I'll be out of here in less than ten minutes."

"Good." Melanie eyed her more closely. "Is there anything wrong?"

"No, Melanie, nothing's wrong."

"Look, I know you've been under a strain for the past several days, what with Chester's death and all. If you need more than just your regular day off, don't be afraid to say so. Shrimp won't mind."

"Don't worry." She picked up a pen and then threw it down, very hard, onto the desk. "I'm not going to crack up under the strain."

Melanie looked instantly abashed. "I never meant—"

"I know, I know. It's okay." Lydia pulled herself together and forced a smile. "Don't worry about me, Melanie. I'm fine." Sheesh, now she sounded like Emmett last night when he tried to tell her he was okay after nearly getting killed.

"All right." Melanie looked dubious. "But just remember, you don't have to prove anything to me or to Shrimp. If you want some time off, just speak up."

"Thanks."

Lydia waited until the door had closed behind Melanie. Then she turned back to the bookcase. She gazed thoughtfully at her volumes of the *Journal of Para-archaeology*.

She removed the photograph that Chester had stashed in the duffel bag alongside the dreamstone jar and looked at it again. Chester grinned proudly from the photo, his hand firmly clasped around the issue of the *Journal of Para-archaeology* that contained the article listing him as a contributing consultant.

Fragments of her dream floated through her mind. Along with it came the question she had been asking herself yesterday when Ryan interrupted her.

What if Chester had been on his way *out* of Shrimpton's the night he was killed?

She took a step forward and trailed her fingertip along the spines of the journal volumes. She paused at the one that contained the article naming Chester as a consulting contributor.

She pulled the volume off the shelf and opened it slowly to the familiar page. The title of the article blazed up at her. "An Assessment of Variations Found in the Para-Resonance Frequencies of Ephemeral-Energy Sources."

A slip of paper fluttered to the floor. She bent down, plucked it up, and stared at it. Chester's handwriting was unmistakable. There was a series of numbers. Beneath each number was a letter.

An hour later, Lydia opened the sheet of paper containing the coordinates and spread it out on the kitchen counter. She put Chester's key down beside it. Then she unfurled the university's official archaeological site map of the Dead City.

"The code is simple enough," she said. "Chester used our birthdays, phone numbers, and the date of the issue of the *Journal* in which my article appeared. I recognized them immediately. After that it was just a matter of connecting the dots."

Emmett watched as she penciled in the coordinates on the map. Her gathering excitement fairly shimmered in the air around her. She wanted desperately to get back underground, he realized. She wanted to prove to herself that she could still handle the catacombs.

"If Brady's information is solid," he said, "it indicates an unmapped hole-in-the-wall gate into the catacombs beneath the shelter."

She nodded, concentrating intently on her task. "There are dozens of them, of course. The university authorities seal them whenever they find them, but the ruin rats discover new ones all the time."

"Same story in Old Resonance."

She put down the pencil and looked up, her face flushed with antici-pation. "Somewhere along the line, someone must have discovered this par-ticular hole-in-the-wall gate. For all we know, it's been found and lost many times over the years. But this time someone discovered the dreamstone down there, somewhere in one of the catacombs."

Emmett thought about it. "At the same time, he must have found the passages clogged with ghosts and illusion traps. Probably realized that he needed to put together a team to help him clear the site so that he could ex-cavate."

"But he couldn't put together a legal excavation team because he would have had to report his finds to the university authorities. They would have claimed the dreamstone."

"But it occurred to him that he was sitting on top of a perfect source of unregistered labor. Street kids come and go from the shelter all the time. Some of them are bound to be untrained dissonance and ephemeral-energy para-rezes. Easy to recruit, especially if you promise them a little free train-ing and a share in the profits."

"And if you don't mind risking their young necks," Lydia added grimly. "Excavation work in the unmapped sections of the catacombs is dangerous, even for expert and experienced tanglers and hunters. When I think of a bunch of young people being sent out to clear the tunnels—"

"Cannon fodder," Emmett said softly.

She glanced at him sharply. "What?"

"It's an old Earth term. I came across it once in a book."

"Oh." She let that pass. "Well, one thing's for certain. If someone is using a hole-in-the-wall gate that is accessed via the youth shelter and if he's recruiting kids out of the shelter, then he almost certainly has to be on the staff at the Transverse Wave. It's the only way he could come and go freely."

"Or the only way she could come and go freely," Emmett said quietly.

"True." Lydia agreed. "Hard to believe that anyone could excavate a cat-acomb right under Helen Vickers's feet without her suspecting that some-thing out of the ordinary was going on. She's got to be involved in this."

"I told you, I've got my people in Resonance checking out her back-ground. With any luck we may get some info tomorrow."

"We're talking a couple of murders, basic training for some hunters, and some serious illusion trap work. Hard to believe Vickers is handling all that alone."

Emmett thought about the locker key he had found in the pocket of one of the young hunters. "When did Bob Matthews say he started volunteering at the shelter?"

"A few months ago."

He studied the map while he ran through his options. He wished like hell that there was another way, but he knew there wasn't. He needed to get inside the unmarked catacomb passage, and he needed a good illusion tangler to help him. Lydia was one of the best.

He felt her watching him. He had a hunch she knew exactly what he was thinking.

"Like it or not, the job requires a hunter-tangler team, and you know it," she said.

She was right.

"We'll do it tonight," he said.

She glanced at Fuzz, who was munching a pretzel on the counter. "Don't worry, we'll take backup."

"What do you mean?"

"Fuzz." She plucked the dust-bunny off the counter and stroked his scruffy fur. "His night vision and sense of smell are much better than any human's." She hesitated. "I think of him as my good luck charm."

Chapter Twenty-Six

Lydia stood in the darkened shelter office and looked out at the silent, night-shrouded street. It was two in the morning. The Transverse Wave had been closed since midnight. The doors and windows were locked. There were no street youths hanging around. No one had come or gone from the shelter in two hours. Either the illegal excavation work was not done at night or it was not scheduled for tonight.

The only indication that the neighborhood was not entirely deserted was the pair of drunks Lydia had seen slumped in a doorway as she and Emmett made their way through an alley. The only light in the vicinity was the sickly glow of a tavern sign half a block away.

"Everything okay?" Emmett asked from the shadows behind a metal desk.

She turned quickly, irritated by the query. "I'm fine," she said brusquely. "Just getting the feel of the place. Trying to pick up the illusion trap vibes I sensed the last time we were here."

"Right." There wasn't enough light filtering through the window to show Emmett's expression. His voice was very even. He turned and went down the hall toward Bob Matthews's office.

Lydia followed, fighting the thread of panic that was unfurling deep inside. Not fear of the dark, she thought. At least not yet. This was another kind of fear. Please don't lose faith in me now, she wanted to say to Emmett. You're the only one besides me who thinks I can still do this. Please believe in me.

But she kept silent. Even to voice the plea would be an admission to herself as well as to Emmett that she was anxious about what lay ahead. Ever since she had recovered from her Lost Weekend, she had been desperate to get back underground. Now the moment was upon her, and all she could think about was how she must not screw up.

But what if Ryan and the shrinks and everyone else were right? What if she really had lost some of her ability to tune into the psi frequencies?

Stop it, she told herself. *You de-rezzed that little illusion trap in the dreamstone jar. That was delicate work. If you could handle that, you're okay.*

She reached up to touch Fuzz, who was perched on her shoulder. He did not rumble in response as he usually did when she petted him. She sensed his heightened state of alertness and knew that all four of his eyes were open.

Emmett did not click on the penlight until they reached Matthews's office. Lydia left him to the task of rummaging through the desk drawers. She opened up all of her own senses, physical and paranormal, searching for the invisible traces of ephemeral energy that indicated an illusion trap.

It was never easy sorting out psi sensations this close to the Dead City wall. The overwhelming psychic weight of so much alien antiquity masked frequencies that would have been clearer in another section of town.

She was vaguely aware of Emmett moving around the office, but she concentrated on her job. Quietly she walked back to the door of the interior office and listened. The amber in her bracelet warmed gently against her skin.

Nothing.

As if aware of her tension, Fuzz stirred restlessly. She started to reach up to soothe him and froze. Her amber was heating up.

"There," she whispered.

Emmett paused to watch her intently. He said nothing.

Feathery tendrils of dark psi energy swirled in the invisible currents of the air. Easy to miss amid all the other traces of leaked energy in the vicinity, but she had a fix on the trap now.

"Got it," she said, her self-confidence returning quickly.

Emmett closed the drawer he had been investigating and walked toward her. "A stray leak?"

"Don't think so. A nice, steady frequency. Or at least as steady as ephemeral energy can be." She turned on her heel, orienting herself. "Over there, near that other door."

"The storage closet."

Emmett snapped off the penlight and led the way out of the small office. He walked to the closet door and tried the knob. It did not turn in his hands.

"Guess that would have been a little too easy," Lydia said.

"Guess so." Emmett took out the small metal tool he had used to get them into the front door. His palm closed over the amber in the handle.

"There we go," he said after a moment. "Very sophisticated. Not your ordinary mag-rez lock, even though it looked like one."

Urgency swept through Lydia. "Be careful when you open that door."

In the dim recesses she could not see the arrogant disgust on Emmett's face, but she certainly sensed it. He obviously didn't like having his skills questioned any more than she did.

"Not real likely there's an illusion trap inside the closet," he said coolly. "For one thing, there would be nothing to anchor it."

"Don't forget that jar Chester found. The trap inside was a nasty one. Dreamstone seems to function as an anchor even outside the wall."

"Who would leave a priceless piece of dreamstone in a storage closet?"

Nevertheless, he opened the door with obvious caution. Lydia breathed a little easier when she felt no increase in the intensity of the illusion trap energy.

Emmett opened the door wider and shone the light inside.

Fuzz tensed on Lydia's shoulder; he did not seem to be unduly alarmed, just very alert and watchful. He was in full hunting mode, she thought. So was Emmett.

For that matter, so was she.

Emmett's light revealed several filing cabinets, a couple of cartons of business stationery, and a stack of annual reports.

Lydia moved into the large closet. "Watch out for the shadows. It's easy to conceal a trap in them."

"I've been out of the field for a while, but I'm not a novice at this, Lydia."

"Sorry."

"Forget it. Feel anything?"

She moved slowly, staring intently into the patches of darkness between the filing cabinets. The unique psi-energy waves produced by illusion dark were definitely stronger in here, but whenever Emmett aimed the light beam at a suspicious shadow, it vanished.

She put out a hand and brushed her fingertips along the nearest wall. There was no increase in the resonating frequency. She circled the room, touching each wall in turn. When she came to the east wall, she went still.

Energy pulsed, stronger here. Dark, illusion energy. She stared at the row of file cabinets that lined the wall.

"I think the source is behind one of the cabinets, Emmett."

He did not question her verdict. "All right. Probably one of the lightly loaded ones. No one wants to shove a heavy file cabinet out of the way every time he goes through a door. Open some drawers and see if you can find one that's half empty."

Lydia pulled out the nearest drawer. It was stuffed with files. She grasped the handle of the next one in line and hauled it toward her. The drawer was filled with aging files. Heavy files.

"Here we go," Emmett said softly.

She looked up to see him standing in front of the last file cabinet. He was gazing thoughtfully into what appeared to be an empty drawer.

She hurried toward him. "Illusion shadow?"

He aimed the light inside it. "Doesn't seem so."

She came to a halt and glanced into the darkness of the drawer. "It's okay." She concentrated, felt amber warm on her wrist. "The vibes are coming from the wall behind it."

"Give me a hand."

Fuzz hopped off Lydia's shoulder and perched on the top of the nearest cabinet to supervise.

It came away from the wall with unnerving ease. There was nothing behind it. Just more paneling.

Emmett reached out and traced an almost invisible seam in the cheap wood. Excitement rose again within Lydia, dissolving some of her uneasiness.

"Oh, boy," she said.

"My sentiments exactly," Emmett replied.

He pushed on the section of wall. The door swung inward on well-oiled hinges.

Impenetrable, endless darkness clogged the opening. Emmett played the light across it. The shadows did not disappear. If anything, they seemed to deepen.

"Stand aside," Lydia said softly. "This is where I earn the big bucks."

Emmett stepped back. "Be my guest."

There was no hint of doubt or concern in his voice even though they could both see that the trap was large. She moved forward.

Her natural ability to resonate with the peculiar wavelengths of illusion energy had been honed by academic training and practical experience. All of her senses went into high rez as she readied herself to tackle the task of untangling the trap.

With her paranormal instincts she probed the swirling layers of ephemeral energy that concealed the main resonating frequency of the trap. She looked into it with that part of her that saw beyond the normal spectrum of sensation and viewed colors that had no names, felt harmonic pulses that existed on another plane.

The trap was very ancient. One of the oldest she had ever encountered. It must have been set and de-rezzed any number of times by whoever was using this tunnel entrance, but it did not appear to have lost much of its brute force.

She found the frequency and began to resonate with it, deliberately sending back the vibrations that would dampen the invisible psychic wave motion. This was the most dangerous part. If she made a mistake, the energy pulses would rebound on her, swamping her senses, sucking her into an alien nightmare.

Seconds ticked past, but she lost track of the time. The trap was more complex than she had realized. It resisted her dampening efforts. At the same time it seemed to invite a quick, summary action on her part that would de-rez it instantly. She refused the temptation to rush through the process. More than one trap tangler had been ambushed that way.

Intuition, skill, and a delicate touch were the hallmarks of a good tangler.

She fine-tuned the frequency one more time. And felt the energy of the trap abate.

"Nice work," Emmett said.

The alien darkness was now gone from the tunnel mouth. A flight of glowing green quartz steps descended into the catacombs.

"A hole-in-the-wall gate, all right," Emmett said.

"The wall of the Transverse Wave Youth Shelter must have been built right up against the Dead City wall," Lydia said.

"Some ruin rat probably put up the building years ago to conceal the hidden gate." Emmett started down the stairs. "My guess is that someone else rediscovered it sometime within the past year."

Lydia held out her arm to Fuzz. The dust-bunny scampered up her sleeve to her shoulder, and they followed Emmett down the steps.

When they reached the bottom, Emmett switched off the flashlight. They stood together in silence as their eyes adjusted to the eerie green glow that emanated from the ancient walls. Underground, the green quartz gave off a strange light that had evidently been illuminating the catacombs for millennia.

"Ready?" Emmett drew an amber-rimmed resonating compass out of one pocket.

"Ready."

Euphoria bounced high inside her, a combination of adrenaline and relief. She was back underground. She had her own compass. And she was okay.

The curious ambience of the Harmonic catacombs had not changed. Everything felt normal, from the heaviness of sheer age that seemed to seep from the quartz itself to the dim green glow.

"Screw Ryan and screw the psi-shrinks," she muttered.

"Is that your way of assuring me that you aren't going to crack up?"

"Yep."

"Didn't think you would," he said.

"Thanks."

"Looks like we won't need the compasses," Emmett said after a while.

He was right, Lydia thought. There was enough debris, old and new, in the cleared catacomb tunnel to mark a freeway route. She spotted candy wrappers, empty Curtain Cola bottles, and discarded pizza boxes.

"Very unprofessional," she sniffed.

"They're using kids, remember? Kids eat. A lot."

The passageway was a narrow one, unlike some of the larger branches of the catacombs that Lydia had worked during her career with the university teams. In places there was barely room for her and Emmett to walk side by side. As with all of the mysterious underground tunnels, it was impossible to know why the original builders had designed and built them.

This particular stretch was relatively straightforward in construction. It turned and twisted a couple of times, and there were numerous side branches, but it was easy to stay on the well-beaten, candy-wrapper-strewn path.

"They probably work as many hours of the day as possible," Emmett said. "And they're trying to get the job done as quickly as possible. Every time you reset a trap, you have to have someone untangle it the next time you come through."

"Time-consuming. And dangerous with amateurs involved."

They moved deeper into the glowing green passage. Their soft-soled boots made no sound on the hard quartz. Occasionally Emmett glanced at Fuzz.

"Don't worry," she said. "He'll give us plenty of warning if he senses anyone coming down the corridor."

"If you say so." Emmett studied another bend in the tunnel. "I've never worked with a dust-bunny before."

"Fuzz is now a permanent part of my team. One of these days I'll tell you how he got me out of the catacombs after my Lost Weekend—" She broke off abruptly as she heard Fuzz rumble in her ear. "Uh-oh."

Emmett halted. "I don't hear anything."

"I think Fuzz does. Maybe he senses a ghost."

"I won't argue with him. Both of you stay behind me."

"Damn it, Emmett—"

"I'm the ghost-hunter here, remember? You did your job, let me do mine."

He had a point. Nevertheless, she reached up for Fuzz and settled him on Emmett's shoulder. "Take him. The two of you have something in common."

"Like what?"

She smiled. "By the time you see the teeth it's too late."

Emmett raised his eyebrows but said nothing. He turned and, with Fuzz straining forward eagerly from his shoulder perch, rounded the bend in the tunnel.

Lydia followed, but not too closely. Let the man do his job, she told herself. He let you do yours.

A moment later Emmett's voice drifted back around the corner. "Well, hell!"

Lydia rushed forward. But when she rounded the bend she encountered no ghost light. Instead she saw Emmett standing in front of a large patch of suspicious shadow.

"Can you get rid of it?" he asked urgently.

"Sure." She was getting downright cocky now, she thought. That was not good. She forced herself back into her most professional mode.

She dealt with the trap quickly. When the shadows vanished, she and Emmett stood looking into a small alcove. A lean young man and a woman with long, filthy hair were stretched out on a dirty mattress, sound asleep. They were both clad in stained, ripped clothing that looked as if it had not been washed in a very long time. Next to them were bottles of Curtain Cola and empty sandwich wrappers. A small dreamstone vase stood at the entrance, visible now that the nightmare trap it had anchored had been derezzed.

Emmett started forward.

The young man on the floor stirred and opened his eyes. He sat up slowly and blinked several times in groggy disbelief.

"Uncle Emmett?" His gaze cleared rapidly. Relief transformed his face. "I knew you'd come looking for me."

"You took my cabinet." Emmett reached down to haul the young man to his feet. "What the hell else was I going to do, Quinn?"

Chapter Twenty-Seven

Lydia gave Emmett a withering glare. He got the message. She thought he was being callous.

"For heaven's sake," she snapped, "this is no time to lecture your nephew about that stupid cabinet." She turned to Quinn. "Are you all right?"

Quinn looked slightly baffled by her interference. But he nodded quickly. "Yeah, sure. I'm okay."

"Quinn?" The young woman stirred and sat up slowly. "What's going on? Who are these people?"

"Meet Uncle Emmett, Sylvia. I told you he'd show up sooner or later." Quinn helped her to her feet. "Come on, we're getting out of here."

Lydia glanced around. "Anyone else in here besides you two?"

"No, not at this hour," Quinn exclaimed angrily. "They keep Sylvia and me locked up with traps when they're gone. But the others come and go on a schedule. They're really into the whole thing, y'know? Like to wear little chains with three wavy lines around their necks like scout badges or something. The idiots think they're going to get rich."

"What about guards?" Emmett asked.

"Couple of hunters right now. There was another one when I first got here, but he got fried and wandered off into a tunnel. Never saw him again. They haven't had much luck recruiting anyone else."

"Probably figured they didn't need to leave guards to watch us," Sylvia said, rubbing her arms. "The trap was more than enough to keep us inside that chamber while they were gone." She looked at Lydia. "You must be a very good tangler."

"The best," Emmett said before Lydia could respond. "What about your amber, Quinn?"

"Are you kidding? They take it away from us during rest periods. The main entrance is the only branch of the catacomb that's been pretty well cleared. You can't move ten feet down any of the side passages without amber."

"Where's the dreamstone?" Lydia asked curiously.

"Whenever they dig a piece out, they store it in a chamber located in one of the other passages," Sylvia said. "Except for a couple of places like this one that they use to trap this entrance and the one at the top of the stairs."

Emmett did not like the dangerous professional interest he saw in Lydia's eyes. "Forget the dreamstone. We don't have time to look at it now. We'll come back for it."

"Sure." She looked briefly wistful, but she did not argue.

Emmett turned back to Sylvia and Quinn. "Either of you know of another way out of here besides the stairs that lead up into the shelter office?"

Quinn shook his head. "No. Like I said, the side passages are clogged with traps and ghosts. They haven't bothered to clear any of the other passages, let alone explore them. All they care about is getting the dreamstone out."

Sylvia bit her lip. "They're almost finished. Quinn and I have been working as slowly as possible, but we weren't going to be able to stall much longer."

"Really glad to see you guys." Quinn sounded relieved. "We knew they wouldn't have any more use for us once we finished excavating the site."

Emmett put his hand on Quinn's arm. "You did good, kid. Come on, we're getting you out of here. Lydia, neither of them has amber, so we'll put them between us. I'll take the lead with Fuzz. Got it?"

"Got it." She moved into position behind Sylvia and Quinn. "If Fuzz seems to tense or if he sort of growls, be careful."

"Don't worry, I'll pay attention."

Emmett started back along the corridor, conscious of the weight of the dust-bunny on his shoulder. Ahead of him nothing moved in the dimly glowing quartz hallway. There were no inexplicable shadows or shimmers in the air. Fuzz seemed alert but not alarmed.

Emmett was starting to believe they just might make it out of the catacombs without incident when Fuzz froze. Simultaneously he felt the faint tingle of energy.

"Damn." He slapped his arm out to the side to make sure none of the other three blundered past him. Quinn stumbled, then caught his balance.

"What the . . . ?" Quinn began.

There was no time to respond. Ahead of Emmett the corridor exploded with acid-green energy. The huge ghost flared high and wide, blocking the narrow tunnel.

Sylvia gave a muffled cry. Everyone froze.

Fuzz whined softly. A tremor went through his small body, but all six paws remained firmly planted on Emmett's shirt, facing the pulsing green specter.

"Just what we needed," Lydia said grimly.

"I don't understand," Sylvia whispered. "I thought they'd cleared this corridor. The others come through here all the time."

Emmett figured this wasn't the time to explain that this ghost had been deliberately summoned tonight. The unusual patterns of dissonance told him that it was really two smaller ghosts that had been melded into one.

Two hunters working together at the entrance of the corridor, he thought. But the one he'd singed last night couldn't possibly have recovered this fast. Besides, whoever was controlling this double ghost was no un-trained novice. It took experience and talent to force two dissonant energy fields into one for any length of time.

Another hunter, then. Matthews?

The ghost started to drift down the corridor toward Emmett and the others.

"Uncle Emmett?" Quinn sounded uneasy.

"It's okay, Quinn. It's really a two-in-one. Got to handle it a little differ-ently. Right now it's shielding us from the two hunters who are behind it. We can't see them, but they can't see us either. I'm going to try to take con-trol of the ghost and send it back toward the two guys who summoned it. But if that doesn't work, I'll have to de-rez it. Either way, in the end we'll have to deal with the hunters. They may be armed."

"Right." Quinn eased Sylvia out of the way and moved up to stand next to Emmett. "But without my amber I'm not going to be much help."

"Trust me, at the rate they're using up psi energy, they won't be able to summon more than a couple of flickers by the time we get to them. But we'll have to move fast. As soon as the ghost disappears we take them."

Quinn nodded in understanding. "Hand to hand, huh?"

"Probably."

"Emmett?" Lydia spoke urgently from directly behind him.

"Take care of Sylvia," he ordered softly. "I'll handle the rest."

He probably came off sounding like one of those macho jerk Guild guys she was always complaining about, he thought. But he didn't have time to be diplomatic. Fortunately, she did not argue. He saw her fall back with Sylvia in tow.

He concentrated on the conflicting dissolution patterns in the double ghost. The mingled energy was both its strength and its greatest weakness. There was a lot of power in a ghost this size, but it was inherently unstable. That made it vulnerable to a takeover—*if* he could locate the two main frequencies.

The ghost picked up speed as it moved toward them, but it still wasn't moving fast. No green UDEM had ever been known to shift position at a pace that exceeded a man's moderate walking speed. Furthermore, the bigger the energy field, the more cumbersome it was. But if it backed you into a corner, you were fried meat.

Emmett searched for the frequency patterns. He found the weaker one first. As he had expected, whoever was driving it lacked firm control. The hunter wielding the dominant ghost had already interfered with the wave pattern to a great extent in order to complete the meld.

The ghost floated closer, flaring and pulsing with angry green light, herding Emmett and the others back down the passageway.

Emmett felt the fresh amber in his watch grow warm against the back of his wrist. He poured more psi energy through it.

The ghost slowed, struggling to maintain its internal rhythms, but it did not stop. Emmett knew the precise instant when his watch fogged. He switched his focus to the backup amber he wore on a chain around his neck.

The double ghost was in trouble now. It stopped, pulsing wildly. Emmett recognized the signs of imminent collapse.

"Got it," he said softly. "I'm going to try to reverse it, but if it fails, be ready, Quinn."

"Right."

Working with all the subtlety he could command, Emmett took control of the weakening ghost. He prodded it gently until it began to drift back the way it had come.

There was a shout of alarm from the vicinity of the quartz staircase.

"Shit! He's got it."

Quinn grinned. "You do good work, Uncle Emmett."

"Let's go." Emmett started forward. "Whoever put it together will try to de-rez it as soon as he realizes what's happening."

"I'm right behind you."

"So am I," Lydia said firmly. "And Sylvia's here too."

The woman did have a way of picking the worst possible times to disobey orders, Emmett thought. He opened his mouth to issue fresh instructions.

But at that instant the fading ghost pulsed one last time and winked out. "*Now,* Quinn."

Two figures stood silhouetted in the green glow of the staircase. They were less than ten feet away. As Emmett and Quinn closed on them, they both turned and fled back toward the staircase.

Emmett recognized one of the two young hunters who had attacked Kelso in the alley behind the Green Wall Tavern. The other was Bob Matthews. If either had an illegal mag-rez gun, he was too psi-rezzed to use it.

The two pounded up the staircase, into the gloom of the unlit storage closet.

Emmett dashed through the opening after them. The young hunter had already vanished, fleeing out of the shelter office toward the safety of the street.

But Matthews moved more slowly. Emmett knew that the other man's senses were probably badly jangled from the experience of having had his own ghost turned against him. It *hurt* when that happened. Really hurt.

Emmett caught him, whirled him around, and slammed him up against the nearest file cabinet.

Matthews's face twisted with rage and fear. He made a fist and threw a wild punch. Emmett managed to shift barely enough to avoid taking the blow in the groin. It caught him on his side, however, and sent him reeling backward.

Matthews closed in quickly, carrying both of them to the floor.

"Sonofabitch," Matthews roared, straddling Emmett. He shoved his hand into his jacket. When he pulled it out, a knife gleamed in his fist. "Sonofabitch, we almost had it all, you freaking SOB."

Emmett grabbed Matthews's knife arm at the wrist. Matthews yelled again and dropped the knife, point first, straight toward Emmett's left eye.

Emmett whipped his head to the side, heard the blade clatter to the floor beside his ear.

He jerked hard and forced Matthews off of him. There was a sharp thud. Emmett felt the jolt of the impact and realized that the other man had struck his head against the edge of a cabinet. Matthews slumped and went still.

Two figures dressed in stained rags that reeked of spilled alcohol materialized in the storage closet doorway that connected to the outer office. Emmett gave them a sour glance as he got to his feet.

"Where the hell have you two been?" he asked.

"Sorry we're a little late, boss," Ray Derveni said cheerfully. "We ran into a little trouble outside. The woman set an illusion trap at the front door after you and your lady friend went inside."

"Damnedest thing you ever saw," Harry Adler added. "Didn't think you could set one of those babies above-ground."

Emmett frowned. "How'd you get past it?"

"A kid came runnin' out a minute ago. Guess he didn't know about the trap. Ran straight into it. Got nailed. Once it had been sprung we were able to get around it."

"Emmett," Lydia said urgently, "we've got a problem."

"*Sylvia*," Quinn shouted. "She's got Sylvia."

Emmett swung around. He saw Lydia standing at the top of the staircase next to Quinn. Both were peering through the opening.

"Let her go," Lydia shouted.

Emmett went to where the others were gazing down the green staircase. He saw Helen Vickers at the bottom. She was not alone. She held a magrez gun to Sylvia's head. He wondered how she'd gotten her hands on one.

"Where the hell did she come from?" Emmett muttered.

"She was hiding in the shadows of the staircase," Lydia said quietly. "She grabbed Sylvia while you were dealing with Matthews."

"I'll kill her if anyone comes after me," Helen warned hoarsely. "I swear I will."

"No one will follow you," Lydia promised in a soft, coaxing tone. "You have my word."

"You think I believe that for one minute?" Helen's face was contorted with rage. "You've ruined everything, you stupid bitch. I'm the one who found that dreamstone. I de-rezzed the first traps. It's *mine*."

Emmett watched her move back another pace. Her foot brushed against what looked like a small heap of refuse.

"Please," Quinn said desperately, "let Sylvia go."

"Shut up. I should have gotten rid of you the day you walked through the front door. I thought I could use you if the Guild came around, but you've been nothing but trouble. I should have had one of the others fry you and dump you in the catacombs."

"Helen, be reasonable. You'll get lost in those tunnels," Lydia said. "You don't want to die underground, do you?"

"I won't get lost. There are other ways out of this branch. I've spent months down here. I know my way—"

She broke off on a shattering scream as the little heap of refuse she had nearly stepped on moved. Fuzz thinned himself into the sleek predator he was and scampered up the leg of Helen's trousers in the blink of an eye.

Helen shrieked and batted wildly with her free hand. "What is it? Get it off me! *Get it off!*"

Fuzz reached her throat. His small teeth gleamed just above her jugular.

Helen screamed again. With a convulsive movement she released Sylvia and dropped the gun to claw Fuzz away from her throat.

"Fuzz—" Lydia started down the staircase. *"Jump!"*

Fuzz leaped off Helen's neck and landed on all six paws. He raced toward Lydia, who reached down to scoop him up into her arms.

Sylvia grabbed the gun off the green floor and dashed toward the stairs. Quinn reached for her. She tumbled into his arms. Emmett discovered that the staircase doorway was suddenly clogged with people. He could hear footsteps as she fled down the corridor.

"Would everyone kindly get the hell out of the way so I can get her?" he snarled.

Quinn swung around to stare into the tunnel. "She's getting away."

"It's all right," Lydia said softly. "She won't get far."

"What are you talking about?" Quinn demanded. "You heard what she said. She knows her way around down there."

"It won't do her any good." Lydia caught hold of Emmett's arm. "Trust me."

Another scream echoed off the quartz walls, a cry that came from the heart of a nightmare. It reverberated for a long moment and then went deathly silent. Emmett decided he now understood the true meaning of the word "bloodcurdling." He looked at Lydia.

"I reset one of the little dreamstone traps while you were dealing with the ghost," she said quietly. "I left it in the corridor behind us, just in case. I thought it might give us some cover if we had to retreat."

He looked at her for a long moment. Then he smiled slowly. "Always nice to work with a pro."

Chapter Twenty-Eight

Alice Martinez tossed a file down onto her desk with a tight, angry movement. "You should have filed a missing persons report."

"My nephew was eighteen, and there was no indication of foul play." Emmett lounged against the wall of Martinez's office. "I didn't think the cops would take the case very seriously."

Alice gave him a disgusted look. "With your Guild connections? Give me a break. We'd have been all over the Transverse Wave Youth Shelter."

"That kind of high-profile investigation could easily have convinced Vickers and Matthews to get rid of Quinn. They would have killed him and dumped his body in an unexplored tunnel. As it was, they only kept him alive to use as a hostage in case anyone from the Resonance Guild came looking before they finished excavating the dreamstone."

Martinez was not happy, but Emmett knew there was very little she could do about it. As far as he was concerned, she had no grounds for serious complaint. He and Lydia had, after all, dumped the whole thing in her lap. Thanks to them, the detective had tied up the loose ends of two murders, made several arrests, and exposed the illegal excavation of legendary dreamstone. Talk about a career-making case, Emmett thought. But some people just couldn't look on the bright side.

It was easy enough to dismiss Martinez's irritation, but Lydia's cool withdrawal had him worried. He watched her as she answered Alice's questions with clipped responses. She sat stiffly in the chair, her face angled so that she did not have to meet his eyes. She had retreated behind a veneer of icy reserve. Something was simmering under the surface, but he did not understand it. She had been like this since they had emerged from the catacombs last night. He was starting to wonder if going back underground had triggered some kind of delayed psychic trauma for her after all.

Alice opened the report on her desk. "According to this, your investigator in Resonance City discovered that Helen Vickers was a strong tangler."

"She was also an opportunist," Emmett said. "She went to work for Anderson Ames two years ago and quickly made herself indispensable to him. Read, took advantage of him. He was getting senile, apparently. In any event, she managed to get herself into his will. But when he died—a death, by the way, that probably warrants further investigation—she suddenly discovered that there was no money after all."

Lydia took up the tale. "She went to the shelter to see if there were any assets she could sell off before she closed the place down. Quinn overheard her mention that she found the old illusion trap guarding the hole in the wall. She de-rezzed it and started exploring the catacombs. She discovered the first piece of dreamstone sitting in the tunnel next to the skeleton of the last ruin rat who had tried to excavate. She realized there might be more. She decided to keep the shelter open as a cover, but she called an old lover and offered to make him a partner."

Alice arched one brow. "Bob Matthews."

"Right. The two of them had worked together in the past. But there was a problem," Emmett said. "Not only was the site filled with ghosts and traps but the dreamstone pieces were all individually trapped. Apparently they both had a couple of close calls. They needed cheap, expendable labor."

Alice's face hardened. "Young, untrained hunters and tanglers from the shelter."

Emmett nodded. "Quinn's friend Sylvia heard about the jobs here in Cadence. Quinn got worried after she phoned him, and he went after her. I followed Quinn."

"Straight to Chester Brady's shop in the Old Quarter," Lydia said. "Chester bought the cabinet from Quinn. But he must have gotten curious and followed him around while he asked questions about Sylvia. Vickers got nervous and had Quinn kidnapped. At the time, she probably didn't know he had Guild connections. Afterward it was too late."

"We figure Brady must have witnessed the kidnapping," Emmett said, "and followed Quinn and the kidnappers into the catacombs. That's probably when he stole the piece of dreamstone."

Thanks to Matthews, who had talked freely after his arrest, they all knew the rest of the story, Emmett thought. Matthews had been in favor of killing Quinn out of hand. It was Vickers who reasoned that they might need him for insurance. In the meantime they could use him to help with the excavating.

But then they found the claim check in Quinn's pocket and realized he had sold a valuable object to Chester Brady. That left a trail, and they knew it. Matthews and one of the hunters followed Chester. When he went to Shrimpton's, they assumed he had gone there to steal an artifact. It looked like a golden opportunity to get rid of him, so they seized it.

But while they were about the business of killing Chester, Helen Vickers discovered that one of the pieces of dreamstone was missing. She knew enough about Chester's shady dealings and his tangler abilities to realize that he might be the thief. But it was too late to question him. He was dead. She sent Matthews to search Chester's shop and his apartment, but he found nothing.

Vickers and Matthews had no idea that Chester had left a clue to the cache of dreamstone in Lydia's office.

When they learned that Emmett was in town and that Lydia was asking questions about the cabinet, they panicked. They sent one of the hunters to her apartment to try to scare her off. When that didn't work, they decided to get her tangled up in a murder investigation. Hence the search of Lydia's apartment. It had been made to look like a routine burglary, but the hunter had gone there to find something that could be used to tie her to a crime scene. He had grabbed one of her personalized amber bracelets.

Martinez looked at Lydia. "They assumed that you and probably London too would, if not actually arrested for Greeley's murder, at least be kept very busy trying to talk yourselves out of charges."

"At that point they were just trying to buy enough time to get the rest of the dreamstone and get out of Cadence," Emmett said.

"When their plan bombed, they made one more attempt to find out what we knew by dragging a colleague of mine into the situation," Lydia explained. "And then they tried to murder Emmett."

"They only needed a few more days," Emmett said quietly.

At six o'clock that evening someone pounded forcefully on Lydia's front door. It was not Zane's distinctive knock, so she chose to ignore the summons.

She finished pouring herself a glass of wine and reached for the lid of the pretzel jar.

The knock sounded again. She paid no attention.

"At the rate you're going through these," she said, feeding a pretzel to Fuzz, "I'd better buy stock in the company that makes them."

Fuzz rumbled happily from her shoulder and started to crunch with his usual enthusiasm.

"Help yourself, pal." Lydia reached up to pat him. "You deserve it. Don't know what I'd do without you."

She picked up the wineglass and started toward the balcony. En route she paused to listen. The knocking appeared to have stopped. She told herself she was relieved, but deep inside she knew she was lying.

The evening was warm. She opened the balcony slider and left it that way. She had just settled down onto one of the loungers when she heard someone open the supposedly locked living room door behind her.

Fuzz continued to munch, placidly content. Lydia did not look back over her shoulder. She was pretty sure she knew who had just entered her apartment.

"I don't know what the hell is going on here," Emmett said as he came out onto the balcony. "But if you think I'm going to let you pretend I no longer exist, you can think again."

"Believe me, I know you exist." She took a sip of wine, hoping it would calm her. "You're pretty hard to ignore, London."

"So I've been told." He sat down on the opposite lounger. "You want to tell me what's wrong?"

"Nothing's wrong."

"Was it going back underground? Did it bring back some bad memories? Lydia, if you need to see a shrink, I know a good one in Resonance. A friend of the family."

"A friend of the family." She slammed the glass down so hard that wine splattered on the table. "You mean a shrink with a Guild connection, don't you?"

"Well, yes, he has treated dissonance-energy para-rezes who work for the Resonance Guild, but that doesn't mean he can't handle an ephemeral-energy para-rez. He's very well qualified."

"Oh, I'm sure he is," she said through her teeth. "I'm sure he's first-rate. But as it happens, I don't need a shrink."

"Are you sure? You've been acting very strangely ever since we came out of the catacombs. Maybe going back underground so soon after your bad experience six months ago wasn't good for you."

She leveled a finger at him. "Don't start. If you tell me that you've finally joined the ranks of folks who think I've lost my para-rez pitch, I swear I'll throw you off this balcony."

"I know you haven't lost your pitch," he said calmly. "The way you handled the traps in the tunnels proved that. But there are other things that can go wrong."

"Yes." She picked up her glass. "There certainly are other things that can go wrong."

He was beginning to look wary instead of concerned. "I think I'm missing something here."

"You? Nah." She took another sip of wine. "How could you miss anything? You're a Guild boss—"

"Ex-Guild boss. And I've told you, I prefer the term 'CEO.'"

She sniffed. "Pardon me. You're the *ex-CEO* of the Resonance Guild. How could anything escape your all-knowing gaze?"

"Lydia, I'm here because I'm worried about you. You haven't been acting normal for the past two days."

"There's nothing wrong with me," she said very evenly.

"Is that so? Then why won't you take my calls? Why won't you answer the door when you know I'm standing out there in the damned hall? I'm not leaving until I get an answer."

She looked at him, anger bubbling inside, hot and painful, seeking release. "You want an answer? I'll give you one. The only thing wrong is that I'm mad."

"Mad?" He hesitated. "At me?"

"No. At myself."

He relaxed, but only slightly. "Why?"

"For trusting you."

"What the hell is that supposed to mean? What have I done to make you stop trusting me?"

"Let's start with the way you called in those two guys from the Resonance Guild and posted them as guards outside the shelter."

"Harry and Ray? I know it didn't work out the way I planned because of the trap Vickers left at the door, but it seemed a reasonable move. We didn't know if anyone in the Cadence Guild was involved in the excavation work, so I didn't want to risk using someone local."

"You don't get it, do you? Why didn't you *tell* me that you'd called in two Guild men from out of town?"

He shrugged. "For the same reason I didn't mention it to Detective Martinez. Because I hadn't cleared it with Mercer Wyatt. I didn't want anyone to know I'd imported some extra muscle without getting Wyatt's approval. Guild politics are a little tricky at times."

"Guild politics." She wanted to scream with frustration. "That's what it was all about, wasn't it? Guild politics were more important than keeping your partner informed."

He was suddenly very watchful. "You're pissed just because I didn't mention the fact that I brought in some out-of-town help?"

"I'm pissed because I'm wondering how many other things you didn't bother to tell me because *Guild politics* come first."

"Lydia—"

"We were supposed to be partners, remember? Partners treat each other as equals. Partners keep each other informed."

"I kept you informed, damn it."

"You lied to me right from the start, London. First you tracked me down because you thought I'd stolen your lousy cabinet. Then you hired me to help you find it, but you neglected to mention that you were not only a ghost-hunter but a Guild boss."

"Ex-Guild boss."

"Once a guild man, always a guild man."

Without warning, icy anger enveloped him. "Once a tangler, always a tangler. I wasn't the only one who didn't lay all the cards on the table right at the start."

"What are you talking about?"

"You had two objectives in this affair. You wanted to see Chester Brady's killer caught, and you wanted to prove to yourself and everyone else that you could handle going back into the catacombs. You needed me to help you get the job done. You used me."

She was so outraged, she could hardly catch her breath. "You came to me, remember? You claimed you wanted to hire me, but all along you thought I'd stolen your stupid family heirloom. And then you had the gall to seduce me."

He was on his feet, reaching for her before she realized what was happening. His hands clamped around her arms. He hauled her up off the lounger as though she were weightless. Out of the corner of her eye she glimpsed little bursts of wild ghost energy. Flickers.

Fuzz tumbled discreetly off her shoulder and vanished into the apartment.

"There seems to be a misunderstanding here," Emmett said, his voice dangerously soft. "I could have sworn that you were the one who seduced me."

"How dare you imply that I—"

"That you used sex to manipulate me?"

"That's not true and you know it."

"Yeah? Then why *did* you seduce me?"

"I did *not* seduce you," she stormed.

"What would you call it?"

"We had sex, okay? It happens sometimes between two people *who*—" She broke off, unable to finish.

"Between two people who are attracted to each other?" he suggested. "Is that what you were trying to say?"

She seized on the only face-saving way out of what had become an extremely hazardous quagmire. "Yes. *Yes.* It was just sex."

"Not a deliberate seduction."

"No." She wondered if there was a difference, but decided that this was not the time to go into the issue. "It just happened."

He lowered his mouth until it was only an inch above hers. "It was pretty good sex, though, wasn't it?"

Her mouth went dry. "That is beside the point."

"I don't think this argument has a point. Not one that's worth pursuing, at any rate. Let's get back to the sex."

"Just like a man, to try to use lust to avoid having to discuss a relationship—I mean, to avoid having to talk about a business association."

"Uh-uh." He did not sound particularly interested. His attention seemed to be focused entirely on her mouth. "To be perfectly honest, I don't want to talk about anything right now."

The telltale flickers had disappeared, but she could still feel energy crackling in the air. She was afraid that some of it was emanating from her. She swallowed.

"Emmett?" He was so close she could feel the heat in him. She tried to ignore it. "Sex is not enough."

"You may not trust me completely, but we made a damn good team down there in the catacombs. That counts for something."

He kissed her before she could summon a response. For a moment she hesitated, trying in vain to marshal further arguments. But it was too late. Much too late.

"You're right," she said against his mouth. "That counts for something."

He scooped her up and carried her indoors. She closed her eyes and did not open them until he lowered her onto the bed.

He jerked at the buttons of his shirt, flinging the garment aside. Then his hands went to his belt buckle. She watched him undress, aware of the shimmering excitement coiling deep inside her.

He was big, sleek and fully aroused. The heat in his eyes was hotter than melted amber. When he came down onto the bed and gathered her into his arms, she knew that she was very likely stepping into an illusion trap, possibly the most dangerous one she had ever encountered.

But this was no alien nightmare. This was a dream of another kind. She had made her decision. She would revel in it as long as possible.

And then his hands were on her and she stopped thinking about anything except the sensations that caressed her entire body. Sensual energy swirled through her as his fingers moved on her. She felt herself become hot and damp. She turned her head into his chest and kissed him, inhaling the scent of him.

And then he was on top of her, his weight crushing her into the depths of the bed. He reached down to draw her knees up alongside his thighs, making a place for himself between her legs.

He forged into her slowly, giving her time to adjust to him but allowing no room for retreat. Not that she wanted to pull back, she thought. She had never craved anything in her life the way she craved Emmett tonight.

She sank her nails into the muscles of his back and tightened her knees around him. He made a husky, unintelligible sound and pushed himself deeper inside, filling her completely.

He kissed her again, his mouth at once demanding and desperate. She understood the strange combination because she was experiencing the same driving need. She had to have him, had to find the release that only he could provide. She clutched at him, drawing him closer.

He moved deliberately within her, withdrawing until he was almost free and then sliding heavily back inside. The pressure became more than she could bear. She knew that his control was close to shattering. His back was slick with perspiration.

"Yes," she whispered, clenching him tightly. "Yes, *now*." She lifted herself against him.

"*Lydia.*"

He plunged back into her one more time. Her climax swept through her with shattering intensity. She was vaguely aware of the great, wracking shudders rippling through Emmett. She parted her lips on a small scream, felt his mouth cover hers, and then spun away into a darkness made brilliant with sparkling dreamstone.

*   *   *

He opened his eyes a long time later and looked up at the ceiling. Lydia was curled snugly against him. She felt very good. He was intensely aware of her warmth and softness. She did not speak, but he knew she was awake.

"You were right," he said. "I didn't tell you everything."

"No kidding." But there was no anger left in her voice, only a wry resignation.

"There were reasons," he said slowly. "The Guilds are changing, but it's going to take time. Old habits die hard."

"I know." She groaned and stretched languidly. "I can't blame you for keeping secrets. You had to protect Quinn, and you were right when you said that I had my own agenda in this thing. We used each other."

He felt his jaw tighten. "It was a partnership. Maybe we didn't tell each other everything right up front, but that doesn't mean we weren't partners."

"I vote we don't argue about it anymore, Emmett. I don't think either of us can win. Besides, it's over."

"Not quite," he said.

She went very still. After a moment she raised her head and looked down at him. "What's that supposed to mean?"

He hesitated. This was Guild business, after all. Very serious Guild business. But he knew he had already made the decision. She had a right to be in on the finish.

"There's one other loose end to tie up," he said.

Chapter Twenty-Nine

"This is Guild business." Tamara Wyatt *turned away from the* study window. The movement of her head caused her amber earrings to catch the morning sun. They glowed a dark yellow gold. "Whatever it is you have to say to us, Emmett, it should be kept within the Guild. There is no reason to involve Miss Smith."

During the drive to Mercer Wyatt's mansion in the hills, Lydia had promised herself that she would keep her mouth shut and allow Emmett to handle this. It was his show, after all. But listening to Tamara talk about her as if she weren't in the room was too much. She consigned her vow of silence to the garbage.

"I disagree, Mrs. Wyatt," she said briskly. "In the course of this mess, a friend of mine was murdered, as was a business acquaintance named Bartholomew Greeley. A young boy was ruthlessly terrorized by a rogue ghost-hunter. On top of everything else, my apartment was scorched."

Tamata whirled to face her. "The Cadence Guild is not responsible for any of those things."

Emmett looked at her. "Wrong, Tamara. The Cadence Guild was involved."

"Can you prove it?" Mercer Wyatt demanded coldly.

Emmett held up the folder he had brought with him. "I may not have evidence that will stand up in a court of law, but I think I've got enough to convince you. And when it comes to Guild matters, that's all it takes, isn't it?"

"Yes," Mercer said steadily. "Convincing me is all that is required."

Tamara looked at Emmett. "If you actually have proof that someone in the Cadence Guild was responsible for what was going on at the youth shelter, you should discuss it privately with Mercer. He will deal with it. I still say Miss Smith has no business here."

"Too bad," Lydia said. "Miss Smith is here, and she's not leaving until this is over."

A soft, discreet knock on the door interrupted Tamara before she could argue further.

"Come in," Mercer ordered.

The door opened. Lydia turned to see an earnest-looking man walk into the study.

"Miss Smith," Mercer said quietly, "allow me to introduce Denver Galbraith-Thorndyke. Denver is the administrator of the Guild Foundation. Denver, this is Lydia Smith."

Denver inclined his head in a polite nod. "Miss Smith." He turned back to Mercer with a quizzical expression. "I got a message that you wanted to see me, sir."

"Emmett, here, has some questions for you concerning our Foundation grants." Mercer looked at Emmett.

Denver followed his glance. He pushed his glasses up on his nose and smiled slightly. "Yes, Mr. London?"

Emmett did not move from his position near the bookcase. "You told me you ran a thorough background check on Helen Vickers before you funded the programs at the Transverse Wave Youth Shelter."

"That's right," Denver said. "Why? Is there a problem?"

"Yes." Emmett tossed the file folder down onto the nearest table. "There is a problem. I had my people in Resonance run a check on her, too. They turned up several interesting facts. Ten years ago Helen Vickers was involved in an underground excavation disaster. No charges were brought, but two people died and a valuable artifact went missing. The surviving members of the team blamed Vickers."

"Good Lord." Denver stared at him. "I found no such information on Miss Vickers."

"She was using a different name at the time," Emmett said. "You should have found it. My people did within twenty-four hours."

"I don't understand."

"There's more," Emmett continued. "Two years ago the original founder of the Transverse Wave Youth Shelter, Anderson Ames, died in a mysterious fire. Helen Vickers was his sole heir."

Denver drew himself up. "Are you implying that I failed to do a proper in-depth background investigation on Miss Vickers before I authorized funding for the shelter?"

"No," Emmett said. "I think you did a very good background investigation."

His icy voice sent a shiver through Lydia. This was the shadowy, mysterious Emmett London who had once held the Resonance Guild in an iron grip, the man who had single-handedly transformed it. Ryan had told her that this Emmett London had made enemies along the way. She could well believe it.

"I think you discovered everything that my people turned up and more," Emmett said to Denver. "You had plenty of time to dig deep, and that's just what you did, isn't it?"

"I don't know what you're implying, but I certainly have no intention of listening to these wild accusations," Denver said tightly.

"Yes," Mercer said, "you do."

Tamara looked at him. "I don't understand. What is this all about?"

"All in due time, my dear," Mercer said. "All in due time."

Emmett contemplated Denver. "You realized that Vickers, whatever else she was, was no model of selfless altruism. So you did a little more investigating, didn't you?"

Denver clenched his hands into fists. He was trembling visibly now. "I don't know what you're talking about."

"You learned that she and the man who calls himself Bob Matthews were old lovers. Somehow you uncovered their hole-in-the wall dreamstone excavation project. My guess is that, acting anonymously, you blackmailed them into cutting you in for a piece of the action. In return, you promised to keep funding the shelter and to keep the Guild off their backs."

"This is outrageous! How dare you insinuate such things?"

"You took charge of the entire operation—anonymously, of course," Emmett said. "I'm sure Vickers and Matthews are already trying to tell their lawyers about the mysterious blackmailer, but no one will take them seriously. After all, there's no proof. You kept your own hands very clean."

"You're insane," Denver whispered.

Tamara frowned. "Denver, is any of this true?"

"No, no, of course not, Mrs. Wyatt." Denver swung around to face Mercer. "You can't possibly believe this nonsense, sir."

"I didn't want to believe it," Mercer said wearily. "But this morning after Emmett called to tell me that he suspected you were involved in the illegal excavation at the shelter, I had your house searched."

Denver blanched. "You sent people into my home? But that's illegal. You can't do that."

"We found the London family heirloom," Mercer said. "The cabinet of curiosities, I believe it's called. It was hidden in your basement storage closet. You stole it from Chester Brady's shop after he was killed. And later you posed as the new owner in order to set Greeley up."

Tamara touched Mercer's shoulders. "Are you certain of this?"

"Yes, my dear," Mercer said gently. "Quite certain."

Right then and there Denver seemed to crumple. He sank in on himself as if suddenly too exhausted to stand. For a moment there was absolute silence in the study.

"How dare you?" Tamara's patrician face twisted into a mask of anger and disgust. "You've ruined everything. *Everything!* For a year I've been working on the Guild Foundation. It was the first step toward changing the Guild's image here in Cadence. And now this. If word gets out about the Guild's connection to the illegal excavation at the shelter, we'll be back to square one. The media will have a field day."

"Don't worry, my dear," Mercer said soothingly. "Word won't get out about any of this. It's a Guild matter. It will be handled in the usual fashion."

Lydia snorted softly. "Figures."

Tamara glowered. "What about her? She's not Guild. Who's going to keep her quiet?"

There was a short, brittle silence. Everyone, including Lydia, looked at Emmett.

Emmett shrugged. He said nothing.

Lydia gave Tamara a cool smile. "You want to start changing the Guild's image? Stop trying to police yourselves. Turn Denver over to the authorities. Take the hit in the press."

"Impossible," Tamara said instantly. "We can't risk the bad publicity. The media already classify the Cadence Guild as little more than a very powerful mob. Turning Denver over to the police would only feed that negative image."

Denver removed his glasses and began to polish the lenses with a cloth. "You can't touch me, you know. My family will see to that. I don't care how strong the Guild is, the Galbraith-Thorndykes can and will protect me."

Mercer studied Emmett, who was standing at the window now, hands in his pockets.

"What do you say, Emmett?"

"Turn Denver over to the cops," he said quietly. "His family can afford good lawyers. My guess is he won't do any time. There's very little hard evidence against him."

"Then why go through the motions?" Tamara protested. "And the humiliation?"

"Because," Emmett said, "in the end the big story won't be Denver's involvement in the dreamstone scheme. It will be the fact that the Cadence Guild went to the mainstream justice system about the situation. Lydia's right. It's a major step toward shaking the mob image."

Tamara whirled to confront Mercer. "Listen to me! We can't take the chance of destroying what we've been working for all year."

Mercer looked thoughtfully at Lydia for a long moment. She had the feeling that she was being weighed and judged. Another little shiver went through her. She'd seen that same calculating intelligence in Emmett's gaze from time to time. Perhaps power always revealed itself that way.

Mercer turned his head to smile gently at Tamara. "They're right, my dear. If we truly want to begin the task of reshaping the image of the Cadence Guild, it must start here. I will call the police myself."

Chapter Thirty

The line out in front of Shrimpton's House of Ancient Horrors was three times as long as it had been the day following the news that Chester's body had been discovered in the sarcophagus. The number of people waiting to see the first public exhibition of worked dreamstone was growing by the minute. Lydia had never seen her boss so happy.

"I got a raise," she confided to Melanie.

"You deserve it." Melanie grinned. "I still can't believe you pulled this off. How in the world did you manage to convince the university authorities to allow the dreamstone to be put on display here, of all places?"

Lydia contemplated the crowd filing past the exhibits. "Let's just say I pulled a few strings."

Emmett walked out from behind a nearby display vault, where he had been studying a small dreamstone vase. "She means she convinced Mercer Wyatt to call in a few favors at the university."

Melanie grimaced. "I won't ask what kind of favors."

"I didn't ask either," Lydia said cheerfully.

"Well, one thing is for certain," Melanie said. "Shrimp will never forget this day as long as he lives. He's positively glowing with pride. I wouldn't be surprised if he leaves you the whole bloody museum in his will."

Lydia held up a hand. "Please. Don't even suggest it."

Melanie laughed. "Just joking. My guess is you'll soon be so busy doing private consulting work you'll have to quit your job here at the museum."

"We'll see," Lydia said. "It takes a while to build up a clientele."

"Especially if you're choosy," Emmett murmured dryly.

She glared at him.

"Excuse me. I'd better go give Phil a hand at the front gate," Melanie said smoothly. "I'm sure he's exhausted from selling so many tickets."

She waved as she plunged into the crowd.

Emmett stood quietly beside Lydia for a while. Together they watched the line of people wind through the exhibits.

"Melanie was right," Emmett said eventually. "You probably won't have any trouble attracting private clients."

"We'll see," Lydia said again.

"Think you might need a partner on your next case?" Emmett asked conversationally.

"I doubt it. I mean, what are the odds?"

"Maybe you'll require the services of a good ghost-hunter," he suggested.

"Hard to say."

"Well, then, how about a date tonight? Need one of those?"

"Thought you'd never ask."